BLOOD PROMISE

by
Robert L. Hecker

To my little sister,
Hope you enjoy.
Bob

Blood Promise

A Double Dragon Press Book

Published by
Double Dragon Publishing
PO Box 54016
1-5762 Highway 7 East
Markham, Ontario L3P 7Y4 Canada
http://www.double-dragon-ebooks.com

ISBN: 1-55404-006-X

A DDP First Edition December 5, 2002

Cover Art by Deron Douglas

This book is dedicated to the Gypsies whose lives were lost in the Holocaust of World War II
and
to my darling wife FRANCESKA

Chapter 1

September, 1941

Walking in a driving rain, Ravanna Zorka could almost feel the excitement that permeated New York City. With Europe already firmly locked in the jaws of war, the city appeared to be whirling on the edge of a maelstrom, as though all its activities, all its life forces had been heightened.

Ordinarily, Anna enjoyed the rain. But not today. The telephone call from Mr. Kipchak late the night before regarding her father's illness had filled her with alarm. Could she stop by in the morning—yes, he usually worked on Saturday—and discuss the situation?

Waiting impatiently for the light to change so that she could dash across 5th Avenue, Anna was too preoccupied with thoughts of her father to notice a man walking rapidly with his head down against the rain until he bumped heavily into her. Her thought, as she teetered on the edge of the curb, was not one of fear, although cars and trucks raced past like juggernauts. Rather, it was one of surprise. With so few people walking in the foul weather, how could someone bump into her?

The split second of teetering saved her life. It was just enough time for the driver of a big Mack truck to see her and slewed to a stop at the instant she lost her balance and lurched into the street. The fright in her eyes as she stared at the big radiator of the truck scarcely inches from her face, stilled the angry words of the truck driver who had leaned out of his cab. He contented himself by yelling, "Watch where the hell you're goin', lady."

The grinding of the truck's gears shook Anna out of her shock and she leaped back to the sidewalk just as the truck shot forward, its side panel almost brushing her nose.

Anna's legs were weak as she made her way to the shelter of a building and leaned against the blessedly cold marble. Her breath was coming in short, ragged gasps, and she could feel her heart racing, its beat so strong it thudded against her ribs. Stupid New Yorker. Rushing along with no thought of anyone except himself. My God! She had escaped being killed by a hair's breath.

She huddled against the building's facade and waited for her heart to stop its heavy thudding. The brief respite also gave her time to remember why she was out in the driving rain, and abruptly, one fear was replaced by another.

How ill was her father? He was only 45, too young to be in real danger. But then, her Aunt Sonja had only been 45 when she died last year of cancer.

The thought sent a stab of pain down Anna's spine. At first, news of her father's illness had made her want to rush to the nearest steamship office and purchase a ticket for home. But apprehension made her hesitate. Suppose she had to go back. The Nazis were in de facto control of the government of Hungary. If she went back now, would they allow her to return to America when her father got well? And would her father even want her to come? He had sent her to America in the first place because he was afraid the Nazis would take over Hungary. Would he want her to return now when it was a fact?

The desire to know even the worst drove her from the shelter of the building. She was probably worrying for nothing. Mr. Kipchak would tell her that everything was fine and she could resume her happily uneventful life.

Damn the rain. The cold, wind-whipped downpour maliciously sought out every miniscule opening in her raincoat, determined to drench her to the skin. Thank heavens she was rarely sick. She supposed her immunity to ordinary germs and viruses was because for generations her mother's Gypsy ancestors in Hungary had been forced by their Magyar and Walachia masters to work from daylight to sundown naked in the icy waters of the Borsog and Tisza rivers washing gold from the river bottom. Those who survived had developed an incredible immune system.

Anna made a vow to herself that if she ever had the money, she would have a beautiful plaque—or better yet, a huge statue—erected on the banks of the Tisza as a memorial to the hundreds of Gypsies who had perished so that their masters could live in luxury.

Thoughts of home brought tears that mingled with the rain. She wondered if her father had changed during the past four years. She knew she had. Now, at 22, she was probably as tall as he. And his eyes might be darker, but she thought her face with its high Magyar cheekbones and wide-spaced eyes was more like his than her Gypsy mother's, although she did have her mother's dusky, olive skin, which always made her look as though she had just returned from a vacation in Florida.

Perhaps his hair was now gray. The last few years must have been difficult for him. First, there had been the death of her mother the year before he had sent Anna to New York. Then, there were the Nazis who now occupied Hungary. Her father had certainly been right about that.

Anna could still remember his words as he put her onboard the ship at Fiume on the Adriatic. "This Adolf Hitler and his New Order will pull us all into war. In America you will be safe. You can return when it is over and that madman and all of his kind are dead."

"But, papa," she had said. "Come with me. You must be safe too."

But he had not come with her. Instead, he had elected to stay and manage the Zorka estate with its famous vineyards that had been in their family since the days of King Matthias. And now, . . . She did not want to think about what might be happening now.

At the Bradley Building on East 54th, she took the elevator to the tenth floor and the office of Mr. Kipchak. The elderly lawyer was an old friend of her grandfather. He had immigrated to the United States almost forty years ago, but had kept in touch with her family. So it was natural that he had practically become her guardian after she arrived in New York.

Mrs. Czacnic, his secretary, a matronly woman with an ample figure and thick, gray hair, said good morning to Anna and helped her take off her wet raincoat. When she saw the water-soaked areas on Anna's knit dress, she clucked in display and departed for the restroom to fetch paper towels.

While waiting for her return, Anna tried to pull a comb through her hair, but after a few futile strokes, gave up the task. Moisture had turned her naturally curly hair into an unmanageable mass of ringlets and long, twisting strands. She considered putting on some lipstick and rouge, but decided not to. The brisk walk had brought color enough to her cheeks, and besides, she really did not like to wear lipstick. It drew too much attention to her lips which she thought were a trifle too full. Ever since a boy had once told her that her lips always looked as though she was waiting to be kissed, she had tried to make them as inconspicuous as possible. She did have exceptionally good teeth, thank heavens. Again, courtesy of her mother. Slaves and nomads did not survive if they could not masticate anything that passed for food.

After she had blotted the worst of the moisture from her clothes, Anna went into Mr. Kipchak's office.

Before today, she had always enjoyed visits to Mr. Kipchak. His office, with its large windows, huge old desk and untidy bookcases, had the cluttered look reflective of a man who had trouble getting one task accomplished before he started on another. And there was always the aroma of pipe tobacco, just like the office of her father.

"Ravanna! Late as usual."

Jozsef Kipchak put his pipe in an ashtray and heaved his bulky form from the deep leather chair as though reluctantly leaving the embrace of a lover.

"I'm sorry, Uncle Jozsef. It's the rain."

She did not want to tell him about the near accident. He worried about her anyway as though she were still an adolescent.

He lumbered around the desk and wrapped her in his arms as he always had. She could remember when his hugs had threatened to crush her like a sear autumn leaf in the grip of a giant. Now she could give as well as she took, and he grinned at her through his scraggly beard, his small eyes twinkling behind the thick lenses of rimless glasses.

"I've got to stop that." He spoke in Magyar, the old Hungarian language. "You're beginning to hurt my ribs."

"Not much chance of that," she laughed, lapsing easily into her native tongue. "I can't even get my arms around you."

He patted his stomach with satisfaction. "I'm prepared for a long winter. I'll be alive when you skinny ones are nothing but bones."

"Skinny! You think I'm skinny?"

Kipchak peered at her over the tops of his glasses. "Well, they like them with thin waists and big bosoms today so I guess you're all right. You'll fill out more when you get older."

"Not me. I'll never be fat. My bones are too small."

"Ridiculous. You have bones like a dinosaur. You wait."

"Well, maybe when I'm old—like forty—or real old, like fifty."

Kipchak snorted as she knew he would. He had to be at least eighty and any mention of age threw him into a defensive angst. "Age is relative. If you have the right relatives, you don't get old. Remember that, young lady. Choose your mother and father carefully and you'll live a long time."

She felt her face grow sad at the mention of mothers and fathers and, noticing, he retreated behind his desk to hide his dismay at the faux pas. He allowed himself to be enfolded by the big leather chair and motioned her to a seat on a couch. She was forced to restack some of the papers on the couch before she could make a place to sit and Kipchak growled, "Careful there. Those are important cases."

Anna glanced at the dates on some of the papers. Most were months old. She blew dust from one sheaf that was beginning to turn yellow. "Whose case is this? Abraham Lincoln's?"

"Don't be facetious. I have everything under control. Now let me see. Where did I put that telegram?"

Telegram! Anna hunched her shoulders against a sudden chill. Telegrams were always bad news. "It's my father, isn't it? Is he all right?"

The old man straightened and threw his hands up. "That woman. She's always moving things. But. . . ." He turned to Anna, concern in his eyes. "You're right. It is bad. They want you to come immediately."

A fist closed on Anna's heart. "Why did Uncle Albrecht send it to you instead of directly to me? I could already be on my way."

"I suppose it was because I've been the official guardian of your welfare since you've been here."

That was certainly true. When she had arrived in New York, Mr. Kipchak had already prepared the way. An apartment was waiting and a checking account had been set up in the Chase Manhattan Bank.

"But it was about my father. Uncle Albrecht should have sent it to me."

"There's more to it than that."

The grimness in his voice startled her. "More? What?"

Instead of answering directly, he said, "How well do you know this man Albrecht Grantz?"

"Uncle Albrecht? Well, he's not really my uncle, of course. But he seems like an uncle. I've known him since I was a child. He's been my father's solicitor for years."

"I see. I've been trying to telephone him, but the telephone these days. . ." He shrugged his heavy shoulders as much as the chair would allow. "However, that is now moot. I, uh, received a letter."

"A letter? From Uncle Albrecht?" Her fear at his evasiveness made her voice no more than a breath.

"No. From your father."

"Father? When?"

"A few days ago." He selected a folded sheet of paper from a scattering on top of his desk. "See. I know exactly where everything is."

"A few days ago? Why didn't you tell me?"

"It did not seem important. Until I received the telegram from Herr Grantz. See for yourself."

Her fingers trembled as she opened the letter. It was in Magyar, written in her father's large flowing hand. Except for his occasional letters, she never read Magyar any more and she had to struggle to make out some of the long agglutinative words, many containing thirty letters or more. The gist of it was that her father was suspicious that someone in the government was attempting to usurp the Zorka estate. Thus far there was no concrete evidence, although he was sure that one attempt had been made on his life. At the time it had seemed like an accident, but after he had discovered power-of-attorney papers forged with his name, he was not so sure. If someone was trying to usurp the Zorka estate, an attempt might also be made on Ravanna's life. He did not want to alarm her. So without her knowledge, would Herr Kipchak arrange for her protection?

Anna jerked her eyes away from the paper, her breath caught in her throat. "My God. Maybe it wasn't an accident."

Joseph Kipchak stared at her, his eyes inquisitive. "What wasn't?"

"On the way here. Someone bumped into me. I almost fell in front of a truck."

Kipchak's pudgy hand went to his mouth. "Good heavens! We must call the police."

"It's too late for that. It probably was an accident. But. . . my father. What is his illness? When did it start?"

"Herr Grantz' telegram was not specific. But the timing of his illness does lead to speculation, wouldn't you say?"

Alarm pushed Anna to her feet. "I'm going back. He might need me."

Kipchak held up both his hands, palms out. "I considered that and I agree."

Anna hated the thought of leaving New York. During the past four years, she had made a home in America. She had her B.A. from Columbia University; she had a good job in a brokerage office; she had her own apartment just off 5th Avenue. And she had become an American citizen. Now she felt more American than Hungarian. Her accent had virtually disappeared; she even thought in

English. But her father needed her. "Good," she said. "Would you make the arrangements?"

"But . . . there are considerations," Kipchak continued in Magyar as though he hadn't heard her. "First, we must obtain an entry visa from the Hungarian government."

"Entry visa? For God's stake, I'm a citizen."

"I thought you became an American citizen."

"I did. But I was born in Hungary. That gives me dual citizenship."

"Perhaps. However, the Nazi's have peculiar views about who is and who is not a citizen. They are afraid of spies."

"From the United States? We're not at war."

"Not technically. But it's only a matter of time. We're already delivering lend-lease to the British."

"The United States doesn't want to get involved in another of Europe's wars. Hitler knows that. And I'm sure he wouldn't want anything to happen to an American citizen. Not at this critical time."

"You may be right. There is, of course, the matter of getting there."

Anna was fully aware of the dangers of travel across the North Atlantic: German submarines were sinking American ships even though the United States was not at war. The admonition that "Loose Lips Sink Ships" was displayed everywhere. Perhaps the Germans only sank freighters transporting war material to England and would not sink a passenger ship. But then, maybe they would.

"I can go by way of the South Atlantic. To Brazil and Spain and through the Mediterranean to Fiume. It'll take a little longer, but there won't be much danger."

Jozsef Kipchak made a tight little smile. He knew she was rationalizing away the danger. German submarines were ranging the entire Atlantic from Iceland to the Azores and into the Mediterranean. "And what happens after you get there?"

"Well, if my father is feeling better, we'll have a nice visit."

"I hope you're right." He sounded cheerful, but deepening furrows between his eyes indicated his worry better than words. She understood the reason for his concern. She would be in a country controlled by the Nazis. Although, technically, Hungary was ruled by its Regent, Horthy de Nagybanya, Hitler had forced Hungary to become one more German satellite. Like it or not, Hungary was now part of Hitler's Third Reich. And even though, unlike other countries under German domination, Hungary was not overrun by Gestapo secret police and Sturm Abteilungen terror squads, it was the Nazis and their fascist sympathizers who were running the country. If some Nazi bureaucrat was trying to take the Zorka land, there was no guaranteeing she would be safe. Nor was her father safe. So, she really had no choice. Whatever the danger, she had to return.

Chapter 2

In a verdant meadow on the banks of the Salzach River near Salzburg, Eric Imri patted the neck of the big gelding and considered what price he should ask of the arrogant German officer. He had been leading the stupid Nazi by the nose for half the morning and the dumb Gorgio still did not realize it. Still, he had to be careful. The man might be a fool, but he wore a black uniform and his collar displayed the SS's lightning-flash runes and the four squares and bar of a Lieutenant Colonel, an Obersturmbannführer.

But what made Eric especially cautious was the aluminum skull-and-crossbones on the man's stiffly grommetted hat. The Death's Head insignia of the SS-Totenkopfverbande was not given without reason. The SS-T were the most paranoid and vicious of the SS branches.

However, Eric Imri knew it would take an expert to detect the changes he had made to the horse. The pits in the gelding's teeth had been darkened by an acid so that Eric could pass the fourteen-year-old gelding off as being only nine. In addition, he had severely trimmed the horse's hooves to conceal cracks; then he had inserted thick strips of leather between the new shoes and the hooves to absorb shock so that on soft turf, such as that in this carefully chosen meadow, the animal could trot and gallop without showing evidence of its sore feet. In addition, extra hair had been woven into the horse's mane and tail to give them a luxurious appearance. And Eric had spent an hour currying the animal's rough and matted coat, then brushing it with a mixture of olive oil and water to impart a temporary satiny sheen. In balding areas he had sprayed the skin with a dye that matched the color of the hair so they could not easily be detected, provided it did not rain. Also, the stimulating effect of the Caballo grass he had fed the aging gelding made it feel and behave with the spirit of a two-year-old.

But even the most perfect deception would not last forever. Even now the Obersturmbannführer was looking at the horse with a frown. The stimulating effect of the Caballo grass was wearing off and the gelding's head was beginning to hang and his ears to droop. Would this damn Nazi ever make up his mind?

There was another reason why Eric was anxious to complete the sale. The Nazi had brought two SA-Brownshirt soldiers with him. They were standing smoking cigarettes near the Buick staff car with its Nazi flag on the right fender and SS-T flag on the left. Their relaxed attitude did not mean they were to be taken lightly. One sudden move or a sharp command would bring them quickly with their pistols in their hands. He had to finish the transaction quickly or he could be in real trouble.

Eric's face displayed no hint of his irritation. You never allowed the Gorgio to think you were in a hurry even when discovery of the deception could mean a bad beating. And beating a Gypsy, or killing him for that matter, was not considered much of a crime anywhere in Europe. Twenty years ago, no, ten years ago, a Gypsy might be beaten unmercifully simply for being in some good Burger's district. This was especially true in the Serbic and Balkan areas. Austria might be considered one of the world's most enlightened and civilized countries, especially in this Salzburg area, but when it came to Gypsies, the threads of bigotry were tightly woven into the warp and woof of the nation. And even though today the outright murder of a Gypsy was frowned upon, it did not pay to arouse anyone's anger.

"Take him for another ride," he said with a smile. "You have a good feel for horses. I've been around horses all my life and I know when I meet a natural horseman. You will be able to tell if this fine animal is not all that I have told you."

The Obersturmbannführer rubbed his chin. Obviously, he wanted to believe what he was hearing. In fact, however, he was a poor horseman, one of the worst Eric had ever seen. The first time the German had ridden the drug-spirited horse, he had almost lost his seat several times. Once he had been forced to clutch the horse around the neck with both arms to keep from being thrown.

The two SA troopers had hidden smiles. But Eric had not smiled. If the SS-officer discovered he was being tricked, a beating would be the least of his troubles.

When the Obersturmbannführer pulled himself into the saddle, Eric let his breath out in a soft sigh. The man did not enjoy riding and surely he would not want another test, so this last ride would have to do the trick. It had better be the last. The horse was showing signs of tiring.

At the Nazi's urging, the gelding moved away in a slow walk. The man had to use his spurs to make the tired horse break into a faster head-bobbing walk. Impatiently, the German dug the blunted ends of the spurs viciously into the horse's flanks. Even then, the animal's responding trot was listless and the German looked annoyed. But Eric knew what to do about that.

Making sure the two bodyguard's attention was on the Obersturmbannführer, Eric picked up a bucket he had hidden behind a low bush. Keeping the bucket out of sight of the guards, he held it up where the horse could see it. But the tired animal's eyes were fixed on the ground ahead of him. To catch the animal's attention, Eric dropped a pebble into the bucket. At the soft plink, the horse's eyes rolled and its head jerked up as though pulled by a puppet string. It's drooping ears came forward and it began cantering sideways in short crow hops so that the German had to use considerable force on the reins to bring it around in a tight circle.

Eric allowed himself a moment of satisfaction. Yesterday he had shaken the bucket full of pebbles under the horse's nose for hours until the sound had practically driven it crazy. Now he only had to show it the bucket, and like Pavlov's dog, it reacted, trying to get away from the source of the hated noise. Even so, this had damn well better be the last ride or the sale might fall through. The horse might be too tired to react another time.

Eric replaced the bucket behind the bush and walked to intercept the German. There was no need to hurry. The German was anxious to quit the saddle before the skittish horse made a fool of him. The man had probably just received his promotion to Lt. Colonel and he needed a horse to complete the image of the consummate Prussian officer. What was his name? Von Liebermann. Ludwig von Liebermann. The 'von' was probably a recent purchase designed to enhance the Junker image.

Von Liebermann slid to the ground with all the grace of a sack of grain falling off a wagon. The man wanted to smile because he thought he had done an excellent job at controlling the spirited horse, but the role he had chosen as a stiff Prussian officer would never allow such a display of emotion. Instead, he adjusted his cap and said, "Very well. What is your price?"

Eric kept his eyes from showing his dislike for what the man's black uniform represented.

"The horse is one of a kind," he said, with just the right obsequious tone in his voice. "Its heritage goes back to the legendary Kladruber. Its mother was Shagya Arabian. You are, of course, familiar with both breeds?"

Von Liebermann nodded, but it was evident he was lying. He had no more knowledge of horse breeds than he had of intelligentsia. He had probably been a clerk in a bank before he had volunteered to become a member of the Schutzstaffel. The SA-Brownshirts might be chosen for their penchant for brutality, but SS-T units were given special training in anti-Semitism, sadism and the refinement of brutality.

This one, however, did not fit the image. Von Liebermann was of average height, about 5'10", and slender. His hair, although shaved appropriately close on the back and sides, was brown, not the desired Aryan blond. Only his eyes were SS. They were dark gray and glinted icily as he stared at Eric. The man's thoughts were easy to read. He was thinking that this was no ordinary Gypsy. At more than six feet, Eric was taller than the German. Eric's clothing was the customary Gypsy outfit of baggy pants stuffed into high boots. The customary open vest was worn over a long-sleeved, loose-fitting white shirt. But, unlike most Gypsies, his clothes were clean and without holes or frayed ends. Perhaps his Russian-style leather boots did not have the high gloss of the German's riding boots, but they were well made and polished. His hat, moreover, was not the typical Astrakhan cap of the Transylvanian Gypsy. Instead, Eric wore the wide-brimmed sombrero of a cowboy of Hungary's Hortobagy plain. And his shoulders were draped with a long white Hortobagy overcoat made of thick wool, its wide sleeves and broad shoulders heavily embroidered in red and pink Magyar designs as ancient as time. And while most Gypsy horse-traders were bearded, Eric was clean-shaven, revealing a lean, hard jaw line and lips that were both sensitive and sardonic. His hair was pure Gypsy, curly and a lustrous black. His eyes, however, were not the dark brown of the typical Romani. Rather, they were blue-gray——courtesy of some rich Saxon owner of Gypsy slaves somewhere in the past——even lighter in color than the German's. But they could be just as icy. Their hard gaze, under dark eyebrows that accented his piercing eyes, made the German's gaze waver, then turn away.

To cover his discomfort, von Liebermann pulled a billfold from his jacket pocket and began counting out Reichsmarks. "I have no intention of bargaining with a Gypsy," he said. "I will give you fifty marks. That is final."

Eric stiffened in quick dismay. The offer was absurdly low, although, in this case, Eric knew it was more than the horse was worth. Could he have been mistaken about the German's knowledge of horses? He immediately dismissed the idea. If that were the case, the stupid Schweinhund would have rejected the animal as soon as he spotted its sprung knees and sickle-hocked hind legs.

No. Either the man was too stupid to know the going price or he meant to cheat the Gypsy horse trader. Well, Gypsies had been dealing with men like him for a thousand years.

Eric brought his hands together in a gesture of supplication and tears appeared in his eyes. "My fine Herr von Liebermann, fifty marks would not even pay for the fine horseshoes that I put on with my own hands. And the training. Everyone knows that I am the finest horse trainer in all of Europe, including England where I performed miracles for Lord Chesterfield and the Duke of York. You rode this fine gelding yourself and you are a fine rider. One of the best I ever saw. Did he not perform well?"

Von Liebermann hesitated. "Well, yes, but. . . ."

"There you are. You would not believe it, but before I began working with that horse, it took five men just to get a saddle on him."

Von Liebermann shot a nervous look at the horse and Eric seized the opening. "All that spirit. All that fire. Tamed. At your command, Herr von Liebermann. It would be cruel for a fine horseman such as yourself to have any less, would it not? You certainly would not want to be on parade mounted on an animal that would cause laughter, would you?"

"No. Of course—"

"There. You see. This is the horse for you. You will be the center of attention wherever you go. One hundred marks would not be too much to ask for such a fine animal."

Von Liebermann's eyes narrowed and Eric immediately reversed course, holding up his open palm. "However, for you I will make a real bargain. Only seventy-five marks." He did not wait for a protest, but immediately began the second phase of his attack. "And you would be making money. Consider. In two years, five years. . . should you desire to sell this fine animal, all you have to do is say that it was trained by the famous Eric Imri of Eger and you can easily double your money."

Eric wondered if he had made a mistake in giving his real name. As recently as two years ago a Gypsy's name meant nothing outside of his tribe. Who paid attention to the name of a lying Gypsy? Identity papers were required of all persons in German occupied or German-governed territories. Gypsies, however, were considered non-persons and, therefore, did not require identification.

Even so, it was better that an SS officer did not know your name. In this case, it probably didn't matter since he was going to depart for Eger as soon as the sale was complete. He should be safe in Hungary.

Still, it did not pay to take chances with the arrogant Germans. A German officer, especially an SS officer, was a law unto himself. He had seen SS officers shoot people simply because they did not move aside fast enough.

"I have no desire to double my money," von Liebermann said. "I have made my offer, take it or leave it."

Eric stared at the German, wondering whether he should continue his attempt to bargain. But the German's hand was on his gun holster and the two SA soldiers were walking toward them. Even so, it was not in his nature to give up without a fight. "Ah," he said with a shrug. "People do not know how to bargain any more. Is it not part of your heritage, my good Herr von Liebermann, that a Prussian of such a noble house does not take advantage of some one of less character than yourself?"

"You don't understand, Gypsy." Von Liebermann unbuckled the flap on the holster of his pistol and Eric saw it contained a fine 9mm Walther. "Either you accept my offer, or I will shoot you and take the animal anyway."

Eric had no doubt the German meant what he said. He could murder him here in this open field, and even if someone saw them, they would not dare object, even if they wanted to. Eric had watched the Nazis put their stamp on Europe with dismay. He could see that, whatever the outcome, the old days would be gone forever, even for the Gypsies. And his erosion of the dogmatic faith of all Gypsies—that the world might change, but Romanies would remain the same—had been slow and painful. Faith, even the most strong and traditional, had a way of breaking down quickly under the threat of a bullet in the head. Eric wondered how many people this *Arschloch* SS bastard had already shot with his handsome pistol.

"I prefer the fifty marks." He held out his hand and von Liebermann's lips twisted into a tight smile as he placed the money in Eric's hand.

"A wise choice."

Eric felt an uncharacteristic surge of anger. Like all Gypsies, he had taught himself not to become angry at arrogance and injustice. In the end, the Gypsy always had his revenge. Now he would have to make the best of the situation. He moved toward the horse. "I'll just get my saddle and bridle."

"The saddle and bridle are part of the bargain," von Liebermann said coldly.

Eric stiffened, staring at the German. Then his anger drained away in a familiar sense of resignation. It was a feeling Eric hated. One he had seen in the faces of Gypsies as long as he could remember. It was a subconscious acquiescence to the Gypsy's traditional role: the undesirable, the wanderer, the non-person who could be cheated, beaten, driven away, even murdered with impunity. If someone robbed him, to whom could the Gypsy complain? If someone beat him, raped his women, to whom could he complain? So the Gypsy learned at an early age to accept the inevitable and live to take your revenge on the Gorgio when and where you could.

Except Eric had never been able to placidly accept the traditional role. There was a rebellious streak in him that had often been the despair of his father. "It is a disturbing force you have in you. You must learn to control this force or it will bring harm to you, perhaps to all of us."

So as a boy, Eric had learned to remove his hat and stand with his head bowed and his shoulders slumped like his father when they sold horses to the 'good' people, who usually tried to cheat them.

During those years he had honed his own weapons of retaliation. He had a natural linguistic ability and when his father had discovered how easy it was for Eric to acquire a new language, he had expanded his field of operation so that, with Eric acting as interpreter, they had traded horses throughout Europe.

This suited Eric. The wider their range of operation, the greater were his opportunities to repay the Gorgios for their contempt and subservient treatment with his own brand of retaliation.

He did not realize, however, that the long periods away from his tribe and the close association with other cultures was eroding his Gypsy heritage like drops of water could wear away the hardest stone. The transformation was accelerated when he discovered books. He had spent hours in public libraries throughout Europe teaching himself to read, then absorbing knowledge the way other Gypsies absorbed music.

Slowly, imperceptibly, he had acquired a sophistication, a worldly awareness that made it even more difficult to accept the Gypsy's slavish role with the required fatalistic stoicism.

Added to his smoldering resentment against the Gorgios, was a subconscious resentment at his own people for allowing themselves to be manipulated so easily and for so long. At times, as he watched his father fawning before a fat Burgermeister to clinch a sale, he wondered who he hated the most: the Gorgios or the Gypsies.

So in spite of his resolve—and his father's admonitions—,during a transaction his shoulders gradually straightened and his head came up so that he could stare into the eyes of a Gorgio without wavering. And to his father's surprise, he was able to barter even more effectively and to receive better prices for their horses.

But he had also learned when to accept the inevitable. If the two SA soldiers had not been standing less than ten feet away staring at him, Eric could have taken the German's gun away from him—and his money. Then what? How would he escape? The Nazis were everywhere. He did not mind risking his own life, but if he were caught, it was likely that at least 100 members of the Imri family would also be found and shot.

Besides, he did not wish to be a hunted criminal when he returned to Eger and the Zorka estate. He was only sorry that it had to be for the funeral of Pal Zorka. The rich land baron had been more kind to the Gypsies who worked for him than any of the other wealthy Magyar Hungarians. Zorka had even married a woman of Eric's own tribe. And there was his daughter, Ravanna. Little Anna. She would probably have come back from America for her father's funeral. He wondered what she would look like. He had vivid memories of her extraordinary beauty as a child. She would be in her early twenties now and, if the promise had been fulfilled, she had to be beautiful. Suddenly, he could hardly wait to make the journey home.

The pleasant thought helped Eric bring his anger under control. He felt the lush green grass under his feet and he breathed the sweet clear air. In the distance he could see the sun glistening off the water of the Salzach River. No, the bridle and saddle were not worth even one Gypsy's life, especially his own. He bared his teeth in a friendly smile. "Take them, Herr von Liebermann, as a gift. As you say, a bargain is a bargain."

He turned on his heel and walked away. Ludwig von Liebermann. He repeated the name, locking it in his memory. This war would not last forever and Gypsies had long memories.

Chapter 3

November, 1941

Much to Anna Zorka's relief, the war with Russia had not touched the Eger district in northeast Hungary. Instead, the German Wehrmacht had crossed the eastern border of Poland and was rapidly pushing into the Soviet Union, driving toward the Ukraine and Ostland. Hungary had been forced to become an ally of Germany, but thus far Prime Minister Bardossy had successfully resisted pressure from Hitler to completely mobilize all of Hungary. Anna had been delighted to find that neither the town of Eger nor her father's estate had been devastated by the war.

The estate also seemed singularly unaffected by the death of her father. The big manor house, built more than a hundred years ago in the long-sloping-roof Finnish-style, was located in the foothills of the Bukk Mountains. From the window of her childhood bedroom on the second floor, Anna could see vineyards and wheat fields stretching to the horizon.

A short distance from the manor house were the sheds and cellars where the precious *aszu* grapes were even now fermenting. Soon, they would be ready to produce the world famous Tokay— *Tokaji*, she reminded herself—the rich white wine that at one time was considered the wine of royalty.

Now, all the buildings that throughout the summer had teemed with workers, sat in lonely silence. The bottled wine rested in the cellars while nature turned the marvelous elixirs into the bone-dry *Szamarodni* or the sweet *Eszencia* or *Aszu*. The grain silos were empty, their contents sold to feed the German Wehrmacht. Anna winced at the thought. She did not like the idea of aiding the Nazis even though Hitler had promised to help Hungary regain the territory her country had lost in World War I.

Her country? She seemed to have slipped easily from being an American to being Magyar. All during the long train ride from the Adriatic port of Fiume-Rijeka past Lake Balaton, through Budapest and eastward to Eger, the feeling of coming home had grown stronger. By the time Uncle Albrecht had driven her the many miles from Eger to the Zorka estate, she had shed her four years in America as a snake would shed its outgrown skin.

If it wasn't for the tragedy of her father's death, she would have been excited and happy. Uncle Albrecht had broken the bad news as he drove his new Mercedes car along the dusty roads: Her father had died while she was at sea on the way from New York. Cancer, he said. That had been two weeks ago. The funeral had been held almost immediately in the village Greek Orthodox Church His grave was beside that of her mother in the family plot next to the church.

Anna's vision blurred. Why couldn't she have arrived in time to see him once more? To hold his hand? To feel the warmth of his eyes? Just once more. Why couldn't she have been here for the funeral? She hadn't even been able to see him before he was laid to rest. It was all so unfair.

Through the window, her eyes focused on movement and she saw an approaching wagon drawn by a team of horses. The wagon was loaded with dry alfalfa and sweet grass that had been forked onto it from one of the winter stacks. It was driven by an elderly Gypsy with an unkempt gray beard and even longer gray hair. He wore black trousers stuffed into worn boots and a long-sleeved shirt with a heavy jacket. On his head was a felt Astrakhan cap whose wide brim flopped loosely with each bump of the wagon's steel-rimmed wheels. The clothes looked worn and far from clean, which wasn't too surprising since the Gypsies still washed their clothes at the river with little or no soap, pounding the dirt from the cloth with large stones exactly the way it had been done for hundreds of years.

Anna knew his name. Bela Imri. He was the leader of the Gypsy tribe who worked for her father. The tribe of her mother.

She turned from the window, unable to bear the memories. How unfair was her life. First, her mother had been taken from her and now, her father. She was totally alone. The familiar objects in the room that had seemed so filled with warm memories when she had first walked in, now only added to the pain. The big porcelain stove in the corner, a mate to the larger one down stairs, had been her mother's pride. The flowers decorating the white plaster walls had been hand painted by her mother. The large colorful dishes hanging like pictures on the walls had been collected one by one by her mother. She had been so proud of her selection.

Her mother had always displayed a talent and an appreciation for art and for beauty that was singularly uncharacteristic of a Gypsy. Anna was sure it was only one of the unique qualities her mother possessed that had attracted her father. There was her mother's incredible beauty and her untamed nature. Even Anna had been in awe of her mother. She had seemed like a creature captured in the forest, only tied to her father and her daughter by ribbons of love that were as tenuous as the strands of a spider's web—but just as strong. When her mother danced to the wild music of Gypsy violins, her skirt and her hair flying and her eyes on fire, it had seemed that the binding filaments of love would not be strong enough and her mother would fly away like *Chovihani*, the Gypsy witch goddess. One of Anna's first memories was of her attempts to join her mother in the dance when she had scarcely been old enough to walk. Her mother had laughed and picked her up and they had whirled together in a savage *csàrdàs* while her father sang and clapped his hands. Bela Imri and the other Gypsies sawed away at their violins in a vain attempt to play faster and wilder than her mother's flying feet and tossing hair.

Now, it was over. All of it. Her father lay in the Zorka plot next to the grave of her mother. They were together now, eternally listening to the Gypsy music that had inspired compositions of such men as Bach, Liszt, Kodaly, Brahms and Bartók.

As Anna slowly walked around the room, feeling its history like an invisible aura, her eye was caught by a familiar card laying face down on the inlaid wood of the dresser top. She recognized it instantly: a Tarot card. The remainder of the deck should be in the top right drawer of the dresser where she had put them the day she had left to go to America. Instinctively, she reached for the card to turn it over to see what was on the other side. Then she hesitated. How did this card become separated from the remainder of the deck? Was it significant?

Sight of the card had swept away all her years of sophistication and academic knowledge. Gone in an instant was the skepticism of the blasé American intellectual. Gone was the doubt of the Gorgio. Suddenly she was Gypsy, once more the totally believing pupil as her mother taught her how to work with the Tarot cards: how to shuffle them, how to lay them out in the various diagrams, the order of their turning and how to interpret the symbols. There was no doubting the truth of the cards any more than there were doubts regarding the truth of the stars, nor any of the Gypsy lore that had been bred into her mother through generations of believing.

And the lore was also a part of Anna. Being only half Gypsy had not diminished the power of the superstitions. They were as much a part of her as a pointer dog's inherent ability to hunt, passed on from mother to daughter. The fortune telling, the palm reading, the astrology, all the ancient Gypsy methods of earning money by their wits had been reinforced daily during the first seventeen years of her life. More than four years in a totally different environment could not wipe them out. Like the Oracles of Delphi, all the lore was locked inside her, waiting for a key that would provide release. And the Tarot card was the key.

Her hand trembled as she reached for the card, a hand so automated that she scarcely recognized it as her own. It touched the card and a faint shock radiated up her arm and into her brain. A warning? A scream from some primordial past telling her to stop, to escape back into the present, to leave the card with all the other hauntings of the past.

An impossible task. Already the Gypsy hand was turning the card over and the Gypsy eyes were staring at it in mounting dread. The Tower! Reversed! The symbol of disaster that might have been avoided, but which was now inevitable. Disaster? What? When? Oh God!

She open the drawer and flung the card inside and slammed it shut as though to lock away its mystic power. Damn her mother! Why had she filled her child's mind with such silly superstitions?

She wanted to turn away, but she could not. Her glimpse inside the drawer before she had slammed it shut had seared her mind with the image of all the other Tarot cards laying in tangled profusion. She could not live with that image. Who could have done it? Who would have the nerve? Any Tarot reader would know the cards are extremely personal. That is why new cards are never used. They first had to be touched, held, possessed by the dealer for a long time until, eventually, they took on the dealer's own aura. Only then were they deemed to have mystic abilities. So the violator could not have been Romani. And no Gorgio would have the courage to touch them. Not a Magyar certainly. Her father? Searching for memories of her mother? Not likely. He had dreaded the mystic in her as much as he loved the Gypsy. So who?

What difference did it make? The point was that someone had touched them and had simply thrown them into the drawer after they were finished. Probably a child, the son or daughter of one of the many peasant serving women or the kitchen help. So the card that had accidentally been left out, meant nothing.

The traditional silk handkerchief was in the bottom of the drawer and, working carefully, Anna gathered the cards and folded them into the handkerchief and returned them to their place in the drawer. Thank heavens there were only the twenty-two cards making up the greater arcana instead of the seventy-eight of both the greater and lesser arcana. She probably would never touch them again. They held only painful memories. There was no point in reopening old wounds.

But they should not be left in the drawer. Whoever had been using them might do so again. Her mother would be horrified to think that someone had touched her precious cards.

Feeling both foolish and compelled, Anna took the silk-wrapped cards from the drawer and put them in her coat pocket. Later she would gather the remainder of her mother's possessions and put them somewhere safe. The sooner the better. She was still shaken by the strange coincidence of finding the Tower card.

Her thoughts were interrupted by the sound of a knock on the jamb of the open door and she turned to see Uncle Albrecht standing in the doorway. He saw the whiteness of her face and his dark eyebrows shot upward.

"Are you all right?" His thin, grating voice had always seemed curious to Anna. It did not fit a head that seemed too big for his thin neck. His black hair, peppered with gray, grew low on his forehead. Like many Hungarian men, he had a thick, dropping mustache that, together with his heavy eyebrows and dark, piercing eyes, gave his face a sinister appearance.

But the appearance was deceptive. He had been her father's lawyer since before she was born and she could remember him laughing with delight as he gave her piggyback rides when she was very young. He was such a close member of her family that it was natural for her to call him 'Uncle' Albrecht. It was he who had suggested that her father send her to America to get her away from what he had rightly foreseen as the mounting danger of an unbridled Germany bent on avenging its defeat in World War I.

Now, she smiled. "I'm fine," she said, and felt the color returning to her face. "Just putting away a few memories."

"That is good. Memories are fine, but the sooner you forget the past, the sooner you will forget the pain."

"I know." She suddenly wanted to get away from this room and its ghosts of the past. Most of its images were warm and pleasant. But some were dark and would take a long time to exorcise. She straightened and walked briskly to the door. "You said you had some papers for me to sign."

As Anna preceded Uncle Albrecht down the curving, thickly carpeted stairway with its carved balusters and fine mahogany railing, polished to a luster by generations of Zorka hands, doubts about the future crowded in. How was she going to manage the huge estate? It covered hundreds of hectares. And Zorka wines and Zorka wheat were distributed throughout the world. Of course, her father had not run the entire operation alone. And she was sure she could count on the loyalty of all the employees, except, perhaps, the Gypsies. The nomad was strong in them. They owed an allegiance to no one, and even though they had worked for her father for years, they could just as well be gone tomorrow. She would have a talk with old Bela Imri. He was their chief and could give her some degree of assurance.

In the large corner-room that had served as her father's office, she paused in front of the big desk and stared at the worn leather of the empty chair. Her father had sat in that chair. And her grandfather and great-grandfather. Generations of her family. Each eldest son in the Zorka family had known that someday he would sit behind the big desk, and each had prepared himself for the heavy responsibility. But her father had no son. So now, it was her turn. The responsibility was overwhelming. To be sure, she had always known that someday she would inherit the Zorka estate. But she had given little thought to actually supervising its operation. In the far recesses of her mind, she had assumed her father would always be there, sitting behind the desk in the worn chair, puffing away at his funny long-stemmed pipe, tugging at his drooping mustache and squinting at the account ledgers as though he would rather be doing something else, anything else.

There had also been a vague feeling that when she married, her husband would take over running the estate. Perhaps that was the real reason why she had never had a serious relationship with an American. Only a Hungarian of the ancient Magyars could, or should, be in control of the Zorka estate. Only a Magyar would understand and appreciate its history, its heritage.

She moved around the desk and sat down in the big chair, half expecting to feel the presence of long dead Zorkas. But there was no psychic rejection, no feeling at all except the chill of the cold leather. She looked across the desk at Uncle Albrecht as he sat in an equally worn leather armchair and placed his briefcase on his knees. He opened the briefcase and sorted through its contents, and Anna took the moment to look around the room. When she had been a baby, the room, with its shelves of books and large oil portraits of ancestral Zorkas, had seemed incredibly huge. Now, it appeared to have shrunk until it was almost small. And the staring eyes of the people in the portraits that had seemed so ominous, were now only the brush strokes of long ago artists.

A thought crossed her mind that made her smile: would she have to sit for a portrait that would someday frighten a small child?

Then she caught her breath. There, hanging in a corner shadowed by light from the setting sun, was a portrait of her father. It had to have been painted recently. The painting's surface still had the sheen of new oil. He looked much older than she remembered, his face showing signs of the strain of the last few years.

The artist had been wrong about the eyes. He had caught their strength, his way of looking at the world as though daring it to interfere. But the eyes conveyed no trace of her father's warmth or compassion, no sign of love. Rather, they seemed to be staring straight at her with a piercing intensity. Condemning her? Or warning her.

She tore her gaze away. She already felt guilty about not visiting him for more than four years even though he had repeatedly told her—ordered her, actually—to stay in America where she would be safe until the menace from Hitler had passed. But somehow, she still felt guilty. She should have come anyway. She should have—

"It has been a great deal of trouble to keep these documents in order." Uncle Albrecht's voice interrupted her thoughts. "Your father had a habit of neglecting his bookkeeping."

"I know. I used to watch him. He hated it."

"Ordinarily, legal documents would hardly be necessary, but since you are. . . "—he hesitated, searching for delicacy—"not a male heir, there are formalities."

Anna thrust aside a sharp resentment. This was the old country with old traditions. Well, soon it would not matter whether she was male or female. She would simply be 'The Master of the Zorka Estate. "I understand," she said.

"And this new government demands so many more documents. Social Democrats, you know. The Germans are fanatics regarding documentation."

"Why should they be involved?"

"My dear Anna. This is 1941. The Germans are involved in everything. You will see when you begin dealing with the market place."

"I suppose you're right. I wish that Imredy had never signed that dreadful Tripartite agreement with Germany."

Albrecht looked up sharply. "How can you say that? Without the Germans we would never have recovered the territory stolen from us after the Great War."

He was referring to Hungary's loss of thousands of square miles of territory that had been wrested away in 1918 at the end of World War I as punishment for Hungary's being part of Kaiser Wilhelm's German alliance. Anna, as a Hungarian, also deeply resented the harsh treatment her country had received from the Allies. But she did not approve of handing over her nation to the Nazis in exchange for reacquiring the lost territory.

"That territory isn't worth another war," she said.

Albrecht's face tightened. Only then did Anna notice with a shock of surprise that in the lapel of his dark suit he wore a small emblem that consisted of a cross and an arrow. She had read that it was the symbol of Hungary's Social Democratic party just as the swastika was the symbol of the German Social Democrats. That meant Uncle Albrecht was, in effect, a Nazi!

Still, his politics did not involve her. Albrecht was such a fervent Magyar that he would probably have supported the devil himself if he would turn back the clock to the time when Hungary was one of the largest and most powerful nations in the world. Her father might well have felt the same way.

Her eyes turned to his portrait on the wall. Could her father have worn a cross and arrow? Could he have supported a despot like Hitler with his blatant murder of those who opposed him and his penchant for war? Perhaps it was better that she did not know and would never know.

She turned her attention to the sheaf of papers with an uncapped fountain pen on top that Uncle Albrecht placed before her. She picked up the top paper to scan it and looked up in alarm. "Uncle Albrecht! This is in German."

He made a small shrug. "It is the language of diplomacy. I have made translations in Magyar, naturally."

She began leafing through the papers. "Are the translations here?"

"Well, no. But you understand German. Remember your lessons?" He smiled, his teeth gleaming behind the thick mustache. "Don't tell me that America has stolen your intellect."

She smiled and shook her head. "No, no. I remember. It's just that I'm a little surprised. And rusty."

"Well, don't worry about it. Just sign where I have indicated there on the bottom. I will register them with the government and give you copies for your files. It is all in proper order."

Anna picked up the pen. "Very well. You had better give me a copy of them in Magyar too. Just to keep it official."

"Of course."

There were several pages of documents, all neatly typed in German, and three places for her to sign. She poised the pen at the first blank line that Albrecht had indicated with an X, but she hesitated as the image of Joseph Kipchak flashed across her mind. He would have a conniption fit if she signed anything without reading it first. After all, there was no rush. And reading the papers would give her a chance to practice her German. If what Uncle Albrecht said was true, she might be needing it.

She put the cap back on the pen and handed it to Albrecht. "I think I'll just go over these first."

He made no move to take the pen. "But Anna, we are already past the time when the transfer should have been made. I do not mind telling you that since we have begun dealing with the Germans, such matters have become very important."

"Well, one more day won't make any difference, I'm sure. Just tell them you had a flat tire on the way out here."

"Why? I believe I have everything in order."

The hurt in his voice almost tempted her to keep the pen. But she had made up her mind. She again extended the pen toward him. "I'm sure they are. But tomorrow will be fine."

He stared at her and she thought she saw a hard anger in his eyes. Why should he be angry? The Germans certainly would not hold him responsible. She was about to say that she would take full responsibility when the look disappeared and his eyes resumed their usual merry twinkle as he took the pen. He shook his head sadly. "Ah, my little Anna. I should have remembered how stubborn you are."

She returned his smile, feeling a stab of guilt for her instant of doubt. She spread her hands in a gesture of helplessness. "I'm a Zorka."

"That's right. Headstrong, but beautiful." He stood, and she also stood. He looked at her, his head cocked slightly. "Very, very beautiful. You will be a sensation with the young men. If I were a few years younger, I would be courting you myself."

"Oh, Uncle Albrecht," Anna chided. "What would Aunt Stefi say?"

His eyes grew sad. "I'm sorry, Anna. I thought you knew. She died three years ago."

Her own eyes shared his sadness. She had not known his wife well. But she remembered her as a stout, pleasant woman who always wore the traditional Hungarian long, multi-colored, pleated skirt, long sleeved white blouse, heavily embroidered vest and a small embroidered cap atop a thick coil of hair. Somehow, Aunt Stefi always managed to smell of freshly baked bread. And now, like Anna's father, Aunt Stefi, too, was only a fading memory.

The thought added to her gloom. Another friendly face forever gone. How many others had been taken during the years she had been away?

She took Uncle Albrecht's hands in hers. "I'm so sorry. I didn't know."

He squeezed her hands before he released them and made an attempt to relieve the mood of depression. "So you see, my dear. I am available if you do not find a young man who will suit you."

Anna gave him a hug. "I'll hold you to that. But you've got to promise that you'll wait for me."

"That will be easy," he said with a chuckle. "I've waited for years."

Something in the way he said it made Anna wonder whether he was really joking. Or maybe it was something in the way he returned her hug, holding her just a little longer and a little tighter than was necessary. Then he let her go and went to the door and she laughed at herself. She was beginning to think like a New Yorker: every older man was a 'dirty old man.'

"I will come back tomorrow," he said, as she walked with him toward the front door. "About noon. That way I will get a free lunch."

"Good. I will have the papers ready for you."

"Very good. Until then. . ." Albrecht turned away, then stopped and looked back at her. "You mentioned Bela Imri. Maybe it would be a good idea if you talked to him. He knows as much about your father and the estate as anyone."

"I plan to. I'll go over those papers tonight and see him tomorrow."

"If you're not too tired, you might want to look him up tonight. I understand they're having some sort of a celebration. A wedding, I think. Gypsies have been coming from miles away. You'd enjoy it."

Anna smiled. A Gypsy wedding was always a happy time. And she could use a lift in her spirits. Besides, the Imri tribe was as much a part of her family as were the Zorkas. She was sure she would be welcome. "Thanks for telling me. I'd love to go."

"Well, don't overdo it. Right now I'm sure you need a good night's sleep."

"I suppose you're right. I am tired. I'll just stop by long enough to say hello."

"All right. I'll see you tomorrow afternoon."

After Uncle Albrecht had driven away, Anna went looking for Bela Imri. She noticed that his hay wagon was still outside the barn, but the horses were unhitched. Perhaps he was inside hanging up the harnesses.

When she walked into the old, wooden building and breathed its familiar pungent scents, she realized that the horses were something else she had missed. She stood for a moment, watching swirling motes of dust in shafts of late afternoon sunlight, enjoying memories.

The barn was constructed with a broad central area where the earthen floor had been packed as hard as brick by generations of hooves. On either side there were stalls for horses, their floors covered with a layer of straw. Only a few of the stalls were occupied. Most of the horses remained in the adjoining corral or in fenced pastures.

Anna began walking down the center area, searching the gloom for the old Gypsy, the sound of her boot heels muffled by the earthen floor. It appeared she was alone. Bela Imri must have returned to the Gypsy camp to prepare for the wedding. Did she want to see him enough to make a visit to the camp now? She remembered that the collection of crude huts and tents was near the river, within easy walking distance. She had been there many times, at first with her mother. Later, she had gone alone. She had loved to play with the wild, undisciplined Gypsy children. Her father had disapproved, but had been tolerant. After all, he had married a Gypsy woman.

She heard a sound from one of the stalls and she stopped, trying to peer into the deep shadows. She was able to make out the shadowy figure of a man standing just inside one of the stalls next to a horse that had a bandage around the gaskin of its off hind leg.

"Bela?" she said. "Uncle Bela?"

"Do I look that ancient?" The man spoke in Romani, the language of the Gypsies. His voice was deep and resonant and, somehow, vaguely familiar.

She walked toward him, trying to discern his features. Now, she could see that he was taller than Bela Imri. And where Bela was fat with a heavy belly, this man was slender with broad shoulders and the flat stomach of an athlete. Instead of wearing baggy pants and the dirty, ragged shirt and vest that were as much a part of Bela Imri as his bronze skin, this man wore tailored pants stuffed into expensive boots. His loose-fitting, long-sleeved shirt was clean, as was his thickly brocaded vest. And where Bela Imri's gray hair, like his beard, was long and unkempt, this man was clean shaven and his dark, curly hair, although worn rather longer than Anna liked, was neatly trimmed.

"What's the matter, Ravanna?" His white teeth flashed in a smile. "Don't tell me you've already forgotten the boy you promised to marry."

Anna's step toward him was stopped by a golden memory. There had been a boy she had liked. When was that? When she was eleven or twelve? He had been much older: thirteen, fourteen. A Gypsy boy. The son of Bela Imri.

"Eric? Oh my God. It can't be."

Eric moved out of the shadows. "How many other boys did you promise to marry?"

She could see his face now and she almost gasped. He had changed so much. And yet, he was the same. Beneath dark brows, his wide-set eyes were still cobalt blue. But the loss of childhood fat made his high cheekbones more pronounced and the plains of his cheeks flatter. With his bronze skin, he reminded her of pictures she had seen of American Indians of the Great Plains.

And he was right. She had promised to marry him. "Hundreds," she said with an answering smile. "I was afraid I'd grow up and nobody would want me. I didn't want to take any chances."

He stood in front of her, his hands on his hips and looked her up and down. "I think you did the right thing. If you were a horse I would have to sell you cheap."

"If I were a horse, I'd kick you."

"In that case, I'm glad you're not a horse."

He stood looking at her with an easy insouciance and she shifted uncomfortably, suddenly embarrassed by his gaze. To break the tension, she walked to the horse and examined the bandage on its leg. "What happened here?"

"Cut her leg. She'll be all right."

Anna ran her hand over the bandage. "Nice job. I remember you used to help your father with the horses."

"I still do when I'm here."

"You don't work on the estate?"

"Not very often. I trade horses. All over Europe."

That would explain his good clothes and air of sophistication. "Oh yes. The last time I saw you, you were going off with your father."

"I remember. We didn't come back for two years. When we did, you were gone."

"I've often wondered what happened to you." In a way, her statement was only half true. She had vivid images of crying when he had left with his father. But her disappointment as well as her infatuation had lasted only a few months. Then she had developed other friends, other interests, and the memory of Eric Imri had faded. Adjusting to her new life in America had occupied all her thoughts, and except for brief flashes of nostalgia, she had almost forgotten the dashing Gypsy boy named Eric.

"Did you ever think of me?" To her chagrin, she found herself breathlessly awaiting his answer.

He looked away as though to hide his thoughts. "You have crossed my mind a few times. I wondered what you were doing in America."

"Why didn't you ask my father?"

"I didn't see him that often. And when I did, I couldn't ask."

"Why not?"

"He might have had me shot."

Anna was about to protest his absurd remark when it occurred to her that it might not be so absurd. Her father was Magyar, one of the most powerful of the large estate owners. If he thought that any boy, even a Magyar, was becoming too friendly with his daughter, he could have taken the matter into his own hands and no one would have dared interfere. And if the boy were Gypsy, he could have had him killed and no one would have lifted an eyebrow. It gave Anna a strange feeling to realize that now she probably had the same degree of power.

"Well," she said, "I'm glad you've come back."

"I'm glad you have too." His face suddenly sobered. "I'm very sorry about your father. He was a good man. He treated us well."

"Thank you."

He paused, his level gaze seeming to bore though her. "Are you going to stay?"

She nodded. "Yes. My life is not in America. It is here now."

"That's good. I would hate to think of a stranger taking over."

"Me too."

"You will come to visit us?" His smile returned, but with a mischievous twist. "We can play together like in the old days."

"You're a big boy now. I'm afraid you might have other games in mind."

"Well, don't forget, we're practically engaged."

"Practically. Don't forget that."

He paused. His voice was low and throaty when he answered. "I'll never forget."

Anna turned away to hide a sudden confusion. "I saw your father today, from the house. He looks just the same."

"He hasn't changed much. He'll be at the wedding tonight." His voice held a sudden excitement. "Why don't you come? It's a big wedding. You'll enjoy it."

She had been hesitant about going, afraid of being an outsider. After all, she was no longer simply the child of their patron. Now she was the patron. She might be considered an intruder. But since she was certain she would find at least one friendly face, she nodded. "All right. What time?"

"Time. You know time means little to a Gypsy. Come when you please."

The wedding party would probably start at sundown and go on all night. She hoped she would not be expected to stay. "Have some of the men come to the wine cellar. You'll be needing Tokay."

"Very much so. Wine, even in this district, is expensive."

"How many bottles do you think? Fifty? Seventy-five?"

"There will be many people. Why not a hundred?"

A hundred bottles of Tokay? She was not acquainted with the current market values. But one hundred bottles would have to represent a considerable sum. But, then, it was her homecoming celebration as well as a wedding. "Very well. A hundred bottles."

"*Eszencia*, of course."

She shot him a glance to see if he was joking. Eszencia was a blend of ordinary and honey-sweet Tokay grapes, forming a white wine that was sweeter than the dry standard Tokay. It was also considerably more expensive. But if a few bottles of wine would cement friendly relationships with the Gypsies, they would be worth the price. "It's rather sweet," she reminded. The Gypsies, she knew, preferred the dryer wines. "Wouldn't they rather have the dry?

"You've forgotten. The more sweets there are at the wedding, the sweeter and longer lasting will be the marriage. It's a stupid custom, but there you are."

"I remember," Anna said. The custom of sweets at the wedding was only one of hundreds of Gypsy superstitions. Families would go in debt for years just to have sweetbreads and sweet wine for a wedding. In some tribes, the bride had to be married with a lump of sugar under her armpit. There were hundreds of such superstitions that were kept hidden from outsiders. Unless you were actually raised as a Gypsy, you could never hope to know them all. But to Gypsies, they formed the fabric of their lives. So she was rather amazed at Eric's irreverence. But then, there were lots of things about him that were different from the other Gypsies. He had to be a total puzzle to his father and his people. "Do they still break the jug?" she added with a smile.

"Of course. And will for another thousand years, I'm afraid."

The custom was so old that no one knew its origin. But after the wedding ceremony, the head of the tribe drank wine from an earthenware jug. Then the bride and groom drank and the groom shattered the jug by throwing it behind him. The pieces were then gathered and kept by the newlyweds. The theory was that as long as they kept the pieces of the jug, their marriage would be secure.

Anna shrugged. "Well, whatever works."

"I've been saving a jug for us," Eric said with a smile. "We'll break it at our wedding."

"I'll break it all right," Anna retorted, "over your head." She turned and began walking toward the door.

"Wear your best skirt," Eric said. "When you dance I want everyone to stare."

She looked back over her shoulder. "No dancing for me. I can't remember a single step."

"You don't have to remember. The music will tell you."

His words echoed in Anna's mind as she walked through the gathering darkness toward the house. Perhaps the music would tell her. It was probably a heritage from her mother, but Gypsy music always stirred embers within her that she found singularly disturbing. Tonight she would certainly have to control the impulse. The image of a fiery Gypsy dancer did not reconcile with the image of a conservative, unimaginative Magyar land owner.

But she was confident she could resist the lure of the music just as she could resist the lure of Eric Imri's handsome face and disturbing voice.

As she went into the house, she wondered why that thought had popped into her mind.

Chapter 4

It was the music that drew Anna to the Gypsy camp. The faint sound of violins and strumming guitars carrying across the silent hills called to her with a strangely compelling power. She had convinced herself she should not go. There was no point to it. She was no longer one of the Gypsies, had not been for years. She did not want to go back to that strange world of her mother's. There was no place in her future for such a world.

And yet, the music was like a siren's song, and as though in a trance, she had changed her clothes and allowed the music to draw her to its source like a leaf being sucked inexorably into the center of a vortex.

At the edge of the Gypsy camp, she stopped and tried one last time to resist the compulsion. What strange turn of events had brought her to this place? By rights, she should be in New York enjoying a play or perhaps a concert. Instead, she was standing in the shadows outside a Gypsy camp, wearing a long, embroidered skirt, clocked hose, a long-sleeved white blouse and a waist-nipping black jacket embroidered with intertwining flowers. She wore her dark hair loose, but covered with the traditional Gypsy scarf. It was strange the way a person's clothes had such an influence over the way they felt. When she had shed her sophisticated clothing of the city, she seemed to have also shed the Magyar side of her personality. She felt totally free, acutely alive, just the way she had felt as a child when she had come to the Gypsy village to play.

As near as she could recall, the village looked exactly the same. The haphazard collection of dilapidated plaster-wall houses, the tattered tents and shacks made of discarded pieces of wood, tin and cardboard still looked as though they had been thrown into place with all the foresight of people who lived only for today. The meandering streets were still paved with hard-packed dirt. In open spaces, a few Gypsy *vardos* were parked, their horses standing with heads drooping as though they had given up on life.

In front of the largest house, a makeshift orchestra of violins, flutes, cellos, cimbaloms and big-bellied cobzas guitars was scratching out a sad *lassu*. The dress of the musicians, as well as their instruments reflected each man's personal wealth. The instruments of most of the violinists and cellists, as well as the clothes worn by their owners, were ancient, weathered by sun and rain. The strings of their bows were made of horsehair, strung loosely so they could saw away at two or more strings simultaneously. But two of the violinists were handsomely dressed with polka dotted shirts and polished oxford shoes. These two played beautiful instruments using bows strung with the finest gut and tipped with silver and ivory. They were probably renowned musicians who played in cafes at Eger or Miskolc.

The people looked exactly as Anna had last seen them. The village population of twenty-five or thirty had been swelled by dozens of Gypsies from neighboring camps or villages who had come for the wedding that had taken place earlier. They were now clustered around a dozen fires eating sweetbreads, ears of corn, roasted potatoes and chicken that had been stewed with paprika. And there was hot strudel, chopped walnuts and noodles spiced with grated cheese. In addition to the wine she had contributed as a gift from the Zorka estate, there were bottles of red wine called 'Bull's Blood' from the Eger district as well as fiery *palinka* brandy.

All the Gypsies wore their newest and cleanest clothes. Women who owned petticoats had pulled them up under their long skirts, which they had decorated with colorful ribbons. All of the females except the very young wore scarves over their hair and tied beneath their chin. The men sported their best vests, the ones with the most beautiful embroidery. The children, the dozens of children who always filled any Gypsy encampment like raisins in a pudding, were everywhere, dashing about like swirling neurons. The older children wore the cast-off clothes of the adults. The children below the age of eight or nine were usually naked. They would remain naked as long as the warm weather of the Indian Summer lasted. Anna had even seen naked children when there was snow on the ground. Such privation had made the Gypsies an extremely hearty people—those who survived— virtually inured to living conditions and weather that would have killed most Gorgios.

Anna smiled. Not too many years ago she had been one of those free-spirited urchins whenever she had been able to slip away from her studies—and her father's sight. She had never run naked. But she had wanted to.

She looked for Eric, but did not see him. She was debating about how to make an unobtrusive entrance when she saw Bela Imri standing near one of the fires and drinking from a bottle of Tokay. Good. It was her chance to become reacquainted and he could introduce her to the others.

She took a step, then froze as a strange feeling swept over her. There was Eric. He walked to the fire to stand next to his father. The firelight bathed his form, giving him the appearance of a statue in bronze by Michelangelo. He was half a head taller than all the other Gypsy men and better dressed. He was the center of attention as several came forward to shake his hand and stayed to talk. Like most Gypsies his conversation was easy and natural, spiced with laughter. Much of the laughter, and many remarks, were directed at the bride and groom who were seated in chairs near one of the fires. The groom was dressed in the traditional boots, baggy pants, loose-fitting, long-sleeved shirt and an open, embroidered vest. The bride, who looked to be no more than fourteen or fifteen, was wearing an embroidered dark skirt, a frilly white blouse and an embroidered vest which she wore buttoned tightly. A white scarf had been fashioned into a tiara. In her pierced ears she wore large loop earrings. Each finger had its quota of rings and her arms supported several bracelets that looked as though they were made of gold. On her feet she wore a pair of new, gold-colored shoes. It might have been the first time in her life she had worn shoes. She looked as though they hurt. The groom was smiling and laughing at the jokes and ribald remarks being hurled his way, but the bride sat with her hands clasped and her eyes downcast as though she longed to be back playing with the other children.

When Anna stepped into the light of the fire, all conversation faded into an uneasy silence. As a child Anna had been accepted as one of them, but she was now the ruler of the vast Zorka estate, someone to be respected and feared. So they watched her warily as she moved toward Bela Imri.

"Bela," she said in Romani. "How are you, old friend?"

Bela Imri's face broke into a broad grin and he laughed. "Anna. Eric told me that you had grown into a woman, but I did not expect this much woman."

"It's all me. Nothing has changed. I am still the child of my mother."

"Yes, yes. I can see that you are. Come." Bela Imri spread his arms in a wide gesture that took in the entire gathering. "Welcome to our wedding. Everyone! This is Ravanna, the daughter of Grezelda, who was very wise and the daughter of my friend Magyari Drebric. Many of you know her already. Here, my little Anna. You must share your own wine." He laughed as he handed her his half empty bottle of Tokay.

Anna, keenly aware that Eric was watching her with his sardonic lips curved in a half smile, took the bottle and waved it at everyone before she took a long drink. It had been years since she had tasted the golden elixir, and she had almost forgotten the delight of its smooth sweetness. But even though the wine was sweet, it was also potent, and after the first drink, she handed the bottle back to the old Gypsy.

"Thank you, Bela. Now, enough of this sad music. Will someone play an *esàrdàs?*"

Bela Imri snatched up a fresh bottle of wine in each hand and strode to the musicians. "Here, my friends. Lift your souls with the God of wine. Give us some music we can dance to. Play, you miserable excuses for musicians. Let me hear some good *Tzigan* music!"

As the bottles were passed around, the *primas* violinist struck up a savage Gypsy *esàrdàs* with its heady, leaping rhythms and swooping arabesques while some of the Gypsies beat time with tambourines or their palms.

Immediately, couples began to dance in the dusty street with their hands placed lightly on the other's shoulders. Unlike American and European dancers, the Gypsy danced mostly in one place with their legs and feet performing magic to the driving beat of the Gypsy music, whirling, kicking, intertwining in ancient ritual.

It was impossible to hear the music, to watch the dancers, and not feel compelled by the rhythm. Anna found herself moving her shoulders and hips in time to the urging beat, and she clapped her hands like a flamenco dancer. Eric leaned toward her and said, "We used to dance like that."

His words caused an image to leap into vivid life. She was twelve years old dancing with Eric, her legs flashing, but her eyes locked on those of Eric. She had been madly in love with him. At the thought, she felt her face grow warm. "I remember," she murmured.

"You remember the dance?"

She turned her eyes from the dancers to look at him and her clapping hands lost their coordinated beat. She longed to dance with him. She hungered for the joy of a Gypsy dance, a joy she had never been able to capture in all her years of dancing to the big swing bands in America. "I think so," she said.

He held out his arms and she came to him. When his hands touched her shoulders, his fingers seemed to burn through the cotton material of her blouse while her own hands felt the play of hard muscles in his shoulders.

Then they were among the dancers and, as the music flowed through her, her body responded with a sureness that amazed her. It was all so incredibly familiar, as though she had danced only yesterday. Even the way her eyes locked on those of Eric was the same, as though the years had been sloughed away by some Gypsy magic.

But there was a difference. As a child, her entire concentration had been centered on the intricate dance steps. But now . . . now, as Eric's eyes burned into hers, her body slowly became a thing apart, a strange entity that moved with its own sensations. The music was dragging her soul from her, drawing it inexorably along an invisible path into the compelling eyes of her partner. The sensation was of being drawn into an embrace that stripped her of her will to resist. There were no other people; there was no earth nor sky; there was only Eric, and she let herself meld into him, their auras bonding into one.

Abruptly, the music stopped!

Anna felt Eric's eyes release their hold, and her soul seemed to once more merge with her body. She found that she was perspiring. And her legs were tired. How long had they been dancing? An eternity.

Eric had experienced the same strange sensation and for an instant, he stood with his hands on Anna's shoulders while he tried to determine what had happened. He had danced hundreds of times with many girls, but nothing like this bonding of the spirits had ever happened. Could Anna possess some form of magic that was alien to every other Gypsy woman? The sensation was so powerful that it had made him forget everything. He would have to ask old Manezi for a powerful charm or he could easily become a slave to this girl.

At the thought, he chuckled. While he had not entirely given up on Gypsy superstitions— after all, most were based on truth, however ancient and out of date they may be—he always tried to put the old myths in perspective. The only charm he needed against the spell of Anna was a swift pair of heels. She was too damn beautiful. And those eyes could swallow the soul of a Hindu mystic.

And yet, as they moved back toward the fire with his arm around Anna's supple waist, he had the disquieting feeling that it was not only her eyes that had the power to trap him, it was her entire aura. Even now as they walked, he could feel the wonder of her body. She possessed a warmth, a subtle magnetism that made him want to hold her forever. Perhaps she really was a *gule romni*, a magician.

The jongleurs had caught their breaths with the help of more Tokay and *palinka* and they launched into another frenzied *esàrdàs*.

One of the young Gypsy girls, who had been watching from the sidelines, leaped to her feet and began to dance, her bare feet hardly seeming to touch the ground. Her long skirt, designed for modesty in every day life, swirled and leaped as though it had suddenly been blessed with a life of its own, the carefree, joyous life of a bacchante. Her long hair caught the spirit and swirled and flew with the joy of a bird released from its cage. She danced as the musicians played, straight from the heart. None of them could read a note of music and they played where the spirit took them, embellishing their music with runs, leaps and curlicues. Strangely, even though they seemed to play as uncoordinated individuals with each trying to outdo the others, there was an overall harmony to the wild music, as though each could sense the harmony of the other while they segued without pause from one Gypsy song to another in an unending paean of joy. On and on they played, as though they were caught up by the ghost of Janos Bihari, the greatest of the Gypsy fiddlers.

When one Gypsy girl sank to the ground exhausted, another leaped to take her place, sometimes two or three, while the watchers pounded their tambourines in rhythm and shouted encouragement between drafts of wine or *palinka*.

Anna had been watching in fascination, wondering at the way the music seemed to enter each girl's body, imbuing it with an incredible energy and rhythm. In a sort of wondrous daze, she felt her own body responding to the music. What was there about the sound of music that drove a Gypsy wild? Or a Hungarian, for that matter? It could be a painfully mournful *lassu* or a savagely wild *esàrdàs*, but each note struck sparks from the heart of a Gypsy.

"Why don't you dance?" Eric's voice disrupted her thought.

"No, thanks, I could never dance like that.

Eric's eyes were solemn as he looked at her. "I remember when you were the best dancer in the tribe."

He remembered? The thought somehow gave her pleasure. "We were children. All children can dance."

"They say that all Gypsies can play the fiddle too. But, I can't. You have to be born to it, like dancing."

"I've been away from it too long, I'm afraid. Too many inhibitions."

"You always did have," Eric said with a faint smile. "The other children used to run naked. You never would."

"The other children were naked because they had no clothes. I did."

Eric's expression hardened. "There will be a day when all Gypsy children will have clothes like everyone else. And good houses to live in."

"I hope so. But will they stay in one place long enough?"

"Many are already settled. Every city in Transylvania has its Gypsy ghetto. But jobs, houses? We are still outcasts. We're not even allowed in the schools."

"Gypsy children in school? I'd like to see that."

"It will happen," Eric said grimly. "Times are changing."

"But can the Gypsy change with them?"

"I have. You certainly have."

"I'm not a true Gypsy. I'm only half."

"The Gypsy half is the best. That's why you were such a good dancer."

"Thanks for the compliment, but I don't believe it." She nodded toward the dancers. "Look how they feel the music. I've never seen anyone except a Gypsy have such rapture. Well, maybe with the exception of some Africans."

"I suppose that's because, like the Gypsy, for generations music was all they had, the only thing they could really call their own and couldn't be taken from them. America could not take that from the Africans and it couldn't take the Gypsy from you."

Perhaps, Anna thought, Eric was right about her being mostly Gypsy. The rhythm of music seemed to penetrate every pore of her body and she found it difficult to concentrate. "I have to go," she said. It occurred to her that her abrupt change of subject was so like a Gypsy. Even their music was filled with impetuous leaps and turns.

"So soon? The night has just begun."

"I know. They'll probably be here all night."

"Several nights," Eric said with a laugh. "As long as the wine and food last."

Anna touched her fingers to her forehead. "I guess it's the wine. I'm really not used to it." But it wasn't the wine. It was the music. It was urging her to cast aside the last remnants of Magyar heritage, to give in to its compelling beat. Plus the almost overwhelming presence of the man next to her. She had to get away from both before they forced her into a surrender she might never escape.

"I'll walk with you," Eric said.

Walking back to the house in the shadows of the trees, Anna had a strong sense of danger, more than she had ever experienced walking through the dark streets of Manhattan. Danger from what? Eric? Surely he would not attempt to attack her. Gypsies had a strong moral code, and while a Gypsy man might have no compunctions about making love with any woman who wanted him, she had never heard of a Gypsy forcing his attentions on a woman.

Eric, however, was not an ordinary Gypsy. Perhaps in acquiring a European sophistication, he had also acquired the cavalier attitude most European men had toward women.

The premonition was so strong that she stopped and turned to him. "If you don't mind, Eric, I think I would rather go on alone."

"Ah, you don't trust me."

It was too dark to see his face, but she sensed he was smiling, his fine lips curving into the sardonic grin that had always made her furious. "No," she started to say. "It's just—"

"Perhaps you're right," he interrupted. "You're much too desirable for us to be—"

The heavy blast of a shot sent echoes reverberating off the trees and the low hills. The music ended as though the shot had destroyed the world of sound. Eric whirled, thrusting Anna behind him with such speed and force that she was almost thrown to the ground. He crouched, searching for the unseen enemy.

They came running from the trees on the far side of the Gypsy camp, shadowy forms in the night, carrying rifles, swinging in a practiced formation to surround the startled Gypsies. Eric realized instantly who they were. Hungarian soldiers. He searched for their commander. When he saw him striding past the line of soldiers who had halted with their rifles ready, he was not surprised to see that the leader was a tall German wearing the black uniform of the SS. The oak leaves on his collar tabs indicated that he was a Lieutenant General, an Obergruppenführer.

"What is it?" Anna said. "What's going on?"

"Shhhh," Eric cautioned. "The SS."

"Germans?" Anna whispered. "Here?"

"Hungarian troops. Quiet. Get back. Under the trees."

"No. I'll speak to them."

She started to move forward and Eric grabbed her arm. "Anna. Wait."

"I will not. . ."

She tried to shake off his grip on her arm, but Eric pulled her roughly back against him. "Keep your voice down!" he whispered savagely. "Listen."

The SS general had started to speak to the Gypsies in German and with little choice in the matter, Anna listened. As she did so, her anger mounted.

"You are all very fortunate." The SS officer's voice was high and shrill. He spoke without raising his voice, but in the dead silence, it sliced like shattered glass. "You have been chosen to help in the war against the Russians. You have ten minutes to gather your belongings."

The Gypsies shifted uneasily, and the German officer lifted his wrist so that he could see his watch. "You have nine minutes and thirty seconds."

At that moment Bela Imri stepped from the group of silent Gypsies. He spread his arms and smiled broadly. "My friend," he said in a tone that had elicited pity from the Baltic to the Mediterranean. "We would be happy to serve the people of Hungary and of Germany. You have only to ask."

"Good," the SS officer responded. "Move!"

Bela Imri's smile broadened. Eric watched his father with a mixture of apprehension and confidence. Bela Imri was the best. He could sell a horse to an automobile mechanic. Eric was positive he would convince the Nazi that he had made a mistake. And yet, the man was a Nazi—an SS officer. His arrogance would not allow him to be dissuaded. Would it?

"But, sir," Bela Imri said. "We are only Gypsies. We have no knowledge of how—"

"Stop." The SS officer interrupted by holding up his right hand, palm forward. You are the leader of the tribe?"

Bela Imri nodded vigorously. "Yes. I am Bela Imri. Perhaps you have heard of—"

"Stop." Again the Nazi cut him off. He took a Luger pistol from his holster and pointed it at Bela Imri's head. "Tell your people to do as I tell them."

Bela Imri backed up a step, his face pale. Still, he kept his smile. "But, sir. If you will allow me—"

Bang! The sound of the shot was so sharp, so unexpected that everyone jumped. Bela Imri stood for an instant as though he could not believe the small hole that had appeared in the center of his forehead, and he crumpled disjointedly, his eyes open, staring.

For an instant Eric was rigid with shock. Then a sound was wrenched from his throat and he tensed to charge. But Anna clutched his arm with both her hands. "No! Eric, no! They'll kill you."

Eric growled and wrenched free of Anna's grip. But the instant of delay had given the SS officer time to snap a command and the rifles of the Hungarian police swung into firing position, their muzzles leveled at the group of Gypsies.

It was the Nazi's high-pitched voice that stopped Eric, stabbing through the fire of his rage like a shard of ice. "Stop! All of you! You have eight minutes left." The Nazi turned to one of the Hungarian policeman. "Tell them."

The Hungarian policeman, looking as though he was enjoying the experience, repeated the order in Magyar.

Still, the Gypsies did not move until the Nazi issued another order, and the Hungarians began walking toward the Gypsies with their rifles leveled. The Gypsies held their ground for a moment, then they broke and ran, leaving the body of Bela Imri lying in the dust.

Eric started forward. He had to kill the Nazi—kill him in front of the body of his father.

"Eric, no!" It was Anna's voice. "There's nothing you can do."

The truth of her words drained the strength from him and he almost collapsed. It was his rage that sustained him, that gave him the strength to move farther back into the shadows. There was nothing he could do. Not now.

"You're right. But you are my witness. I make a blood promise: I will find that man and I will kill him."

"Yes. I am your witness. But now, we must stop them from taking the others."

Eric felt his head beginning to clear. As reason returned, so did despair. "How? We have no guns, no weapons of any kind."

"There are people I can call. In Eger, Miskolc, even Budapest. Uncle Albrecht. He is very powerful in politics. I know he can help. Come. We've got to get to the house."

Reluctantly, Eric gave in to her logic and they began walking rapidly toward the house. Behind them the sounds of women's voices, keening in anguish, echoed in the night.

"I don't understand this," Anna said. "I knew that in Germany the Nazis are making Jews work in labor camps, but we're Gypsies."

"Haven't you heard?" Eric said bitterly. "Gypsies are considered non-human. It has always been that way. But even non-humans can work. The Magyars found that out four hundred years ago."

"The Magyars have changed. They don't treat the Gypsies like they used to."

Eric snorted. "Who do you think those men were with the rifles? Hungarians!"

"Renegades, traitors working with the Nazis. Most Hungarians don't think like that."

"Oh? Then why did the Hungarian police issue a decree for the expulsion of thousands of Jews? They were turned over to the German Einsatzgruppen."

Anna stopped walking. "Are you sure? I haven't heard about that."

"They don't broadcast it to the world. Would you?"

"They couldn't keep something like that quiet."

"Couldn't they?" Eric's voice was hard. "You've been too long in America. You don't know what's happening over here: the concentration camps, the massacres."

"Massacres. You mean in a battle?"

"Battle! Only a month ago, thousands of Jews were massacred by Hungarians and Germans at

Kamenetz-Podolsk. That's nowhere near a battle."

"How do you know that?

"Believe me. I know."

A vague feeling of dread crept over Anna. Was all this true? What was happening to her country? There had been no reporting of such atrocities in American newspapers. Also, there had been very little reported about Jews and political dissidents being rounded up and sent to work camps. But a massacre? People murdered? Perhaps Nazis would do such a thing. Not Hungarians. Still, she had just seen a demonstration. Those were Hungarian police troops being lead by the Nazi. If the German officer had given the command, they would have shot every Gypsy. Of that, she was sure.

"I've got to find Uncle Albrecht. He'll tell me the truth."

She resumed walking toward the house, urgency making her almost run. Eric strode beside her, silently sorting out his options. Anna should be all right. After all, she was the daughter of Pal Zorka. But it would be best for him if he got out of the country. In Germany the Nazis had begun interning Gypsies. It looked as though they were now expanding their operation to include all occupied area, which meant he would have to leave mainland Europe. England was the only country that looked as though it could resist the German Wehrmacht. They had successfully weathered the Nazi's air battle, and with Germany now at war with Russia, chances were they would not invade England. That's where he would go.

First, he would learn the name of the SS officer who had shot his father. Now the Nazis had the power. But the war would not last forever, and whether the Nazis won or lost, when it was possible, he would return and find the man. Then he would kill him. He had made a blood promise and it would be kept!

When they arrived at the house, Anna gave an exclamation of joy. "Look. There's Uncle Albrecht's car. He's here."

She started to run, but Eric clamped his hand on her shoulder. "Wait. Why is he here?"

"He must have heard about the raid. Come on."

She pulled free from Eric's grip and darted toward the house. Eric followed more slowly. He had an uneasy feeling, and he had learned a long time ago not to discount the familiar warning. But for now, he had to ignore it. Albrecht Grantz was a powerful man. If anyone could help the people of his tribe, it would be Grantz. But if there was danger, he would have to get Anna away.

The thought made Eric stop. Why was he thinking about her? It was the first time he could remember being concerned about the safety of any woman. Then he realized that since he had first seen Ravanna Zorka, thoughts of her had filled his mind. Warm thoughts. The only explanation was the pleasure of renewing an old friendship. And she was beautiful.

Even so, it was very disconcerting to find that he was concerned for her safety.

But then, somebody had to look after her. Her years in America had made her soft and vulnerable. Too vulnerable. It was best that he forget her. As soon as he made sure she was safe, he would begin his own journey to safety. In a week he would be in England.

He began trotting toward the house.

Chapter 5

When Anna walked into her father's office, Albrecht Grantz was seated at the desk searching its drawers. At the sound of her footsteps, he looked up. and it seemed to her that his face became pale.

"Uncle Albrecht. What are you doing?"

He stood up and walked around the desk. "Anna. I'm so glad to see you. I need some of your father's papers."

She moved into the room, staring at him incredulously. "Now? Tonight?"

"Tomorrow. In the morning. I remember you said you were going to see Bela Imri at the Gypsy camp, so I thought I could find them on my own. They're very important."

"Never mind that now," Anna cried. "You've got to help me. They killed Bela Imri."

"They killed . . ." He stopped and shook his head in disgust. "Those Gypsies. Always fighting. They're like children."

"It wasn't the Gypsies. It was a German. A Nazi SS."

"A German? Why?"

"They're picking them up. They're sending them to a labor camp."

"Oh."

"You've got to do something. They'll kill them if they won't go."

Albrecht tugged at his mustache, his eyes grave. "My dear, it isn't just the Imri tribe. The Germans are picking up all Gypsies in the area. There isn't much anyone can do."

"Why? They can't simply kidnap them."

"They are not being kidnapped. They are being conscripted."

"What's the difference?" It was Eric. He stood just inside the door, and the harsh anger in his voice jerked Albrecht's head around.

"Eric?" Albrecht said the name as though trying to remember what the son of Bela Imri looked like. "I haven't seen you in years. I'm sorry you had to come back to this."

"You haven't answered my question?"

"The difference between kidnapping and conscription? It's one of law, of course. The government has a right to conscript its citizens in time of war."

"Gypsies are not citizens."

Albrecht smiled grimly. "A point, but a meaningless one. The Germans don't care if the people in their labor camps are citizens or not."

Anna said, "As long they're Gypsies or Jews."

Albrecht glanced around as though afraid that someone might be listening. "Don't talk like that."

"Why not? It's the truth, isn't it?"

"You've been away too long. Things have changed." He looked at Eric. "Tell her what it's like now."

"She found out what it's like."

"There's got to be something we can do," Anna protested. "Someone we can talk to."

Instead of answering her, Albrecht said to Eric, "I think it would be a good idea if both of you went into hiding for a few days. Give the Germans time to leave the area."

"Why should I hide?" Anna said. "I'm Magyar."

Uncle Albrecht shifted uncomfortably. "Well, technically, the Germans consider anyone who is half Gypsy as being all Gypsy. You might be in danger if you stay. I'll try to get this straightened out while you're gone."

"This is ridiculous. I have American citizenship too. An American passport. I can go to the American Embassy in Budapest."

"Good. An excellent idea. But first you've got to avoid being picked up. Once you're in the hands of the German SS . . . Tell her, Eric."

Eric put his hand on her shoulder. "He's right about that, Anna. People tend to disappear when the SS or the Gestapo pick them up."

"You have a summer cottage in the mountains," Albrecht said. "Go there. When it's safe, I myself will drive you to Budapest."

Anna struggled against the thought of running. Here, in her own country, she was being forced to act like a fugitive, a criminal. Why should she have to flee when she had done nothing— nothing except be born of a Gypsy woman.

Then she remembered the look on the face of the SS officer as he had shot Bela Imri, and she knew he would not hesitate to do the same to anyone who opposed him. At one time he might have been a kindly man, a family man with a home, children. A man who would not dream of harming anyone. But there must have been a latent brutality in his psyche that had been sensed by the SS. They had given him the authority to unleash his brutality without fear of punishment. She wondered how many other formerly good men—or, perhaps, horrible men—now had the power of life or death over thousands of helpless people. It was a staggeringly dreadful thought.

"All right," she said. "But it's several miles. We'll need transportation."

Albrecht dug his car keys from his pocket. "Here. Take my car."

Anna took the keys and handed them to Eric. "Here. I'm going to need some clothes."

"I'd better pack some food. There might not be any at the lodge."

Albrecht glanced at his watch. "You'd better hurry . . ."

He stopped at the sound of cars approaching. Bright headlights flashed past the window as two cars wheeled to a stop in the yard. Eric leaped to the window and peered between the drapes. "Germans." He turned and tossed the car keys to Albrecht. "They've got your car blocked." To Anna he said, "Quick. Out the back. We'll have to use horses."

But she didn't move. "No. I'll talk to them. They'll listen to me."

"The hell they will. Look at you. You're a Gypsy!"

Albrecht interjected. "He's right, Anna. Go! Now! I'll straighten this out."

The truth of Eric's statement was starkly clear. She was dressed as a Gypsy. Her hair, her face were Gypsy. The SS would surely take her. And once she was in their hands, they could do anything they wanted with her and no one would know.

She grabbed her coat from the chair where she had thrown it a lifetime ago. "All right. We'll be at the lodge." She ran out the door followed by Eric.

He paused at the door. "The SS officer. What's his name?"

Albrecht shook his head. "I don't know. I'll find out."

Eric jerked his head in acknowledgement and hurried to catch Anna. He wished he had time to pick up supplies. He had been taught from childhood to live off the land. But Ravanna Zorka was of another world. She was not toughened by the hard life of a Gypsy. Perhaps there would be some food at the lodge; they should not have to remain there for more than a day or two. By then Grantz should have the situation resolved and Anna could return home. As for him—he smiled grimly as he dashed from the house—if he could not get to England, he would simply lose himself among the Gypsies of Greece or Spain until he learned the identity of the man he must kill. Then if the Nazis came, he would become a Gorgio and meld with the rest of the people like a chameleon.

He caught up with Anna as she pulled open the door of the barn. It was almost pitch black inside and he worked from memory as he quickly slipped bridles on two of the horses. Across their backs, he threw blankets with stirrups attached. These served as saddles in the manner of the *csikos*, the cowboys of the Hortobagy plains. "I hope you remember how to ride." His voice was low as he helped Anna mount.

She hadn't ridden since she was ten years old, but from the instant she felt the horse under her, it was like yesterday. She grasped the reins and pulled the horse around toward the open door. "I remember."

Eric grabbed his horse's mane with his left hand and swung onto its back. "Don't let him run. Follow me."

He led the way out of the barn, taking time to push the door shut. As they entered the woods at an almost soundless canter, he looked back. They had not left a second too soon. German troops, not Hungarians, were surrounding the house. That was odd. They couldn't have known that he would be there. So, they had to be after Anna. Maybe Albrecht Grantz would not be able to help.

Chapter 6

The trauma of shock is designed by nature to protect the body. In effect, the nervous system suspends all functions except those necessary to sustain life at its minimum. The heart beat slows and the blood pressure drops. The breathing becomes slow and shallow. And the senses virtually turn off so the body does not sense pain.

The condition can occur almost instantly if the body receives a traumatizing injury. But if the injury is psychological rather than physical, shock can develop slowly. So it was with Anna.

Sitting on a wide, leather-covered couch in front of a low fire, tightly wrapped in a thick woolen blanket, she stared unseeingly into the flames, unable to stop a series of tremors that racked her body. She tried to focus on what had happened at the Gypsy camp, but her mind refused to respond. It was as though her brain was unable to accept the unremitting flood of negative stimuli that had been bombarding it during the last few hours.

Watching her as he placed more wood on the fire, Eric's brows drew into a worried frown. He recognized the symptoms of shock. It was almost unheard of among the Gypsies since they had long ago developed an immunity to outrages that would have shattered the minds of most Gorgios. He also knew there wasn't much he could do for Anna except keep her warm—and wait. She would either recover or she would gradually weaken until she slipped into a coma-like withdrawal. He hoped it wouldn't be the latter. His knowledge of medicine was limited to treating colds and fevers. Even so, he would do what he could for her. He couldn't let her die. In fact, he suddenly realized he desperately wanted her to live.

They had arrived at the mountain lodge after a grueling two-hour ride along back roads and forest trails. If he had been alone he would have continued on, ridden all night, putting as much distance as possible between himself and the Nazis. But Anna was in no shape to travel. The long ride had given her time to reflect on the events of the last few hours and he had seen the symptoms of shock slowly seeping into her until she was riding like an automaton, allowing the horse to find its own path.

Arriving at the lodge, she had made no move to dismount, and he had been forced to lift her from the horse and carry her inside. Now, he had to get her mind working so she could consciously fight the numbing depression.

The low fire had not thus far taken the chill from the room, and he slipped inside the folds of the blanket so that his own body heat would help her fight the chill. He did not dare build the fire any higher. Except for the evergreens, the trees surrounding the lodge had lost almost all their leaves and did not provide much concealment of escaping sparks. And the odor of smoke would carry for miles.

Albrecht Grantz had said that the Germans were picking up Gypsies all over Bohemia. The SS might have patrols out looking for some of the more nomadic tribes. At this time of the year, only

Gypsies would be in the woods. The soldiers would be sure to track any smoke to its source. Fortunately, the weather, although chilly, was warm for November with little or no wind so he did not have to build a large fire.

"Tell me about America," he said. "Are the streets really paved with gold?"

"Gold?" She considered the question with the seriousness of a child. When she replied, her voice was an unemotional monotone. "No. They're paved with asphalt or cement."

"But everyone is rich, yes?"

She thought for a moment. "Not everyone."

"I understand they all have inside toilets, even the poor."

"That is true. Even the poor."

His next question was carefully considered. "When this matter is straightened out, will you go back?"

"Go back?"

"To America."

"Oh. To America. What matter?"

"After your Uncle Albrecht explains your status to the Nazis?"

"The Nazis?"

"The SS officer who came to the Gypsy camp."

He felt her stiffen and the trembling stopped. Her voice hardened as she said, "He killed Bela Imri."

The image created by her words was like acid in Eric's brain. There was the pain of seeing his father shot. But there had been greater pain in his helplessness. Now, there was the pain of a promise that would continue to eat at his conscience until it was fulfilled. "I know. Do you remember what happened after that?"

She rolled her eyes toward him as though she could not believe he would ask her such a stupid question. "Of course." To his vast relief, she had stopped trembling and there was emotion in her voice as she added. "I'm going to make sure that man is punished. I'll have him in prison the rest of his life."

She actually believed it. Eric could not believe her naiveté. But then, until today she had not witnessed the arrogant power of the Nazis. Punishment for killing a Gypsy? At most, the SS officer might receive a slap on the wrist. More likely, he would receive a medal. But the anger had shaken Anna out of her lethargy.

"Good," he said. There was color in her face and her breathing was normal. Of more importance, she had regained her grip on reality, as bad as it was. He just hoped nothing further would happen to upset the delicate balance. He sat for a moment, his arms around her, letting her absorb the heat from his body. He noticed her eyes were drooping with fatigue and her breathing was steady. "Are you getting warm?"

"Yes."

She snuggled closer to him like a puppy seeking the heat of its mother. Her head was against his shoulder and he could feel her soft breasts against his chest. She was certainly not the mischievous little girl he had played with years ago. At that time she could have run around naked and he would have paid no more attention than he had to any of the other naked, or semi-naked, Gypsy boys and girls. But now . . . He smiled. No wonder she was getting warm. He was generating a temperature hot enough to heat the entire lodge.

He stood up and pulled the blanket around her. She looked up at him accusingly and said in her little girl voice. "Come back, Eric. I'm cold."

"I know. I'm going to get some more wood for the fire."

Outside, the night was clear, the air sweet with the scent of evergreens. A canopy of stars hung just above the trees. The lodge was situated on a foothill of the Carpathian Mountains, and Eric climbed to the top of a nearby ridge where, in daylight, he would have had a panoramic view of the entire valley. The night had the crisp brilliance that only came in late fall and winter, so he should be able to see the lights of approaching automobiles for more than a hundred kilometers.

But there were no lights. None. The entire valley was a bowl of unrelenting darkness.

He found he was breathing easier. The Russian battlefront was hundreds of kilometers away. If the Nazis were in pursuit, there would be no reason for them to drive without lights. Besides, it was unlikely the Nazis would come after them until morning. Ravanna Zorka could not be that important.

Still, it was odd that there were no lights at all. This was all Zorka land and there were no villages, but there should be firelight from at least one Gypsy camp.

Could all the Gypsies have been taken? Maybe his tribe had been the last. The thought filled him with anger. Damn the Nazis. The world was bad enough for the Gypsies without the Nazis. They had little or nothing, but at least, they had each other. And they had survived. Now, Hitler and his SS bastards were trying to put an end to even that precarious existence. And there wasn't a damn thing he could do about it.

That wasn't quite true.

He could do something about one of them. He would surely find the man who had killed his father and make sure he killed no one ever again. In a couple of hours it would be daybreak, and he would take Ravanna into Eger where Albrecht Grantz could take care of her—and give him the name of the Nazi butcher.

He took one last look across the darkened valley. He should get some rest. Tomorrow was going to be a long day.

Filling his arms with wood from a stack of split logs, he carried them to the fireplace. Anna was asleep, lying on her side on the couch with the blanket pulled to her chin. Eric stood looking down at her. She looked young, delicate. Her face, although etched with fatigue, was exotically beautiful.

Moving quietly, Eric put more wood on the low fire, stacking the wood so it would be consumed slowly. The fire helped dispel the cold, but it was still chilly in the room. He checked the three bedrooms of the lodge, searching for additional blankets and food, but there were none. The lodge had been stripped of all valuables for the winter. Probably, he thought wryly, to keep them from being stolen by Gypsies. He had been lucky to find one blanket. He considered sleeping on the bare floor in front of the fire but quickly rejected the idea. Better to share the couch—and the blanket—with Anna. That way they could keep each other warm.

She mewed a protest as he moved her so that she was lying full length, her back against the back of the couch. When he lay down beside her and pulled the blanket over them, he had to hold her in his arms to keep from falling off the narrow couch. He thought she was still asleep, but she said, "Eric."

He was prepared to refuse her demand that he leave as he said, "Yes?"

"I think my father was killed. Murdered."

He moved his head back to look at her. Her eyes were closed, but there was no sign of sleep in her soft voice. "What makes you think so?"

"Somebody tried to kill me too. In New York."

Eric sucked in his breath, anger driving away all thought of sleep. Why should the idea of a Zorka being hurt or killed disturb him so much? "Somebody. You have no idea who? Or why?"

"No. I thought it was just a stupid accident. Now I'm not so sure."

"You'll get it straightened out tomorrow."

"I hope so. Eric, I'm kind of frightened. I don't know what's going to happen."

"Don't worry. I won't let anything happen to you." He said the words to make her feel more secure. But to his amazement, he found he actually meant them.

"Promise?"

He tightened his arms around her. "I promise." He stopped short of making it a blood promise. He had one of those already eating at his conscience. But it was still a promise he meant to keep.

She was silent for a moment. "What's going to happen to you?"

"I'll be all right. There are Gypsies everywhere."

Again she was silent, and he thought he felt her press closer against him. "If anything does happen, find some way to let me know."

"Why?"

"So I can help."

He stared into her face, not sure he had heard her correctly. "Why would you want to help me?"

"That's easy." Her voice was low, a whisper in his ear. "I've fallen in love with you."

He chuckled softly so she would know he saw through her joke. But her words still gave him an unexpected thrill of pleasure. He returned her compliment by kissing her on the tip of her nose. "And I love you," he said lightly.

She tipped her head slightly, and suddenly, her lips were brushing his and he kissed her gently, tentatively, expecting her to pull away from him. It was inconceivable that this aristocratic girl could be in love with him. True, she was half Gypsy. But she was also a Zorka, wealthy, sophisticated, educated. And yet, she was here in his arms and he found he never wanted to lose her.

Anna's confession had also come as a surprise to her. If she had been fully awake, if she had not been drugged by fatigue and by the warmth of the fire, if she had not found such a profound feeling of security in Eric's arms, the words would not have come tumbling out. But they had. And with them came the realization that the reason she had never found a boyfriend, a lover, in New York was because she had been carrying an image of Eric that had turned aside all rivals like an Horatius at the bridge.

Tomorrow she would not allow him to leave. They had found one another and there was no reason for it to end.

She put her hands behind Eric's head and brought his lips once more to hers.

Tomorrow. She did not want to think about it. Now, she wanted only to forget tomorrow and all the tomorrows in the joy of the moment.

Chapter 7

Anna awakened with the feeling that she was locked in a dream with no division between the wonder of the dream and the wonder of reality. She was lying on the couch, warm and comfortable inside the blanket, her nude body feeling the roughness of the wool texture with a sensitivity she had never before experienced. Through half closed eyes she saw that the fire had dwindled to embers and that faint light came from the windows where the edge of dawn struggled through the grimy panes.

Eric? Where was Eric? Why was she alone? He should be here beside her, For an instant, she was gripped by panic. Had he left her? Abandoned her? She rejected the thought. He had promised to stay with her, to take her to Uncle Albrecht. He was probably getting more wood for the fire, perhaps trying to find something for them to eat.

She was beginning to get up when, as though in answer to her questions, the door opened and Eric rushed in, slamming the door behind him. "Quick! They're coming."

She did not ask questions. Instantly, she knew what he meant.

The Germans. What else would fill him with such alarm?

She threw aside the blanket and groped for her clothing that Eric had so tenderly removed last night. He knelt to help her, thrusting articles at her as he found them, his gestures accenting the need to hurry.

She had just pulled on her boots when the door crashed open and two Hungarian policemen entered carrying Mauser rifles. They stopped just inside the door and swung their rifles to cover Eric and Anna, their eyes darting to survey the room. Two more policemen rushed past them and took up positions on either side of the door. When the first two policemen saw that the room was deserted except for the two Gypsies, they moved swiftly to search the other rooms, then they took up positions on each side of the room, their weapons ready to fire.

Anna and Eric had not moved since the door had burst open. Under the leveled guns of the soldiers, Eric stood with his hands at his sides, waiting. When Anna could not stand the silent tableau any longer, she snapped, "You are trespassing. You will leave immediately."

The policemen simply stared at her, their faces devoid of expression. Anna snatched up her coat and strode toward the door, but both policemen swung the barrels of their rifles to block her path. She said, "Out of my way," and put out her hand to push the rifles aside, and one of the policemen swiftly reversed his weapon and struck her in the solar plexus with the rifle butt. The shock was as great as the pain, and she fell back holding her stomach, gagging as she fought to keep from retching.

Eric growled and moved forward and the policemen leveled their rifles at him. He stopped, knowing they would not hesitate to shoot. Trembling with rage, he put his arm around Anna pulling her partially behind him.

Anna had regained her breath and with it, her anger. She said to the policeman, "You will regret that."

A man wearing the uniform and visored-hat of an officer of the Hungarian police strode through the doorway in time to overhear her remark. "Regret what?"

Anna straightened and peered at him. She knew that voice. But the morning light behind him kept his face in shadows. "He struck me. With his rifle."

"Oh. I apologize for that. He was told not to allow you to escape."

Anna gasped, "Uncle Albrecht?"

Albrecht Grantz stepped away from the doorway, and she ran to him and threw her arms around him. "Thank God you're here. Tell these creatures who I am."

Albrecht Grantz stood stiffly erect as he answered, "They know who you are, my dear."

Anna stepped back, a faint alarm building in her stomach. She peered into his face. "Uncle Albrecht. What is it? Are you in charge of these men?"

Albrecht stared back at her stonily and Anna raised a hand to her mouth. Who was this man? He could not be the same person who had been her father's friend, her own friend and guardian.

It was Eric who answered her. "He's in charge, all right. I should have realized you were a Nazi when I saw the arrow-cross you were wearing."

Albrecht began taking off his gloves. "It was something of a shock to see you, Eric. I had no idea you had returned."

"It was you who sent those soldiers to our village."

"I'm sorry about your father. But the SS are very . . . headstrong. I purposely did not bring him this time."

"His name? What is his name?"

Albrecht finished removing his gloves and used them to wave the question aside. "That is of no importance."

Anna put her hands against the sides of her head, unwilling to believe what she was hearing. "But why? Why are you doing this?"

"He wants the Zorka estate," Eric said. "He doesn't give a damn about the rest of us. It was you he was after."

Anna stared at Albrecht. She knew that her eyes were wide and blank, uncomprehending, but she was unable to overcome the awful feeling that this was really all a horrible dream. "Is that true?

"Of course." Albrecht's voice was calm, as though he was explaining an event to a child. "I was very annoyed to see you last night. You had me at a distinct disadvantage. I certainly did not want you to escape a second time, but I had no way to detain you. Fortunately, you accepted my suggestion to come here. I trust you had a pleasant night."

His words were like a dash of ice water. Anna's chin came up. "I still have friends, here and in America. I'll see that you pay for this."

It was Eric who laughed harshly. "You can forget them. I doubt that either of us will leave here alive."

"Nonsense," Albrecht snapped. He took a sheaf of papers from the inside pocket of his jacket and crossed to the table where he spread them out. "I have no intention of harming either of you." He took a pen from his pocket and tendered it to Anna. "You will please sign these, my dear."

Anna saw that they were the same papers he had asked her to sign the night before and she shook her head. "If I do, I'm sure I will never see the estate of my family again."

"It is no longer the estate of your family. It is the property of the State."

"And you are the State," Eric said softly.

"I represent the State." Again Albrecht offered the pen. "Please."

Anna pushed his hand away. "I'll never sign those."

Albrecht 's voice hardened. "Anna, I do not wish to cause you pain. But you will sign before you leave this room. Now, please."

He thrust the pen forward but Anna shook her head. She would show him she could not be coerced. If the Zorkas were known for anything, it was their stubbornness.

"Anna," Eric said. "You'd better sign."

"No," she said. "He'll never take anything of mine."

"What he can take is your life."

Anna stared at Albrecht, fighting to control her anger. "Would you do that, 'Uncle' Albrecht? Would you kill me?"

Albrecht gave a small shrug. "I would prefer not to. Your death so soon after your father's would raise questions."

"That's what I thought." With a gesture of contempt, she swept the papers to the floor and turned toward the door. "Come on, Eric. This place has turned into a pig sty."

She hadn't taken more than a step when Albrecht grabbed her arm and swung her around so violently that she fell, sprawling across the top of the table. Eric snarled in rage and leaped at Grantz. His hands closed on Albrecht 's throat, his eyes blazing into those of the Hungarian. Then one of the guards stepped forward and smashed the butt of his rifle against the side of Eric's head and he collapsed, instantly unconscious.

Anna regained her balance and knelt beside him. Blood was welling from a cut above his ear. "Oh God. Eric!" She felt for a pulse at his carotid artery. It was there. Strong. Thank God.

Albrecht reached down and hauled her to her feet. He had picked up the papers from the floor, and again, he thrust the pen toward her. "I've had enough of this. Sign!"

Anna could hardly believe the coldness of her anger. She was more in control of her emotions than she had ever been. In the past, her anger had taken the form of shouting and explosive violence, like a spoiled child. Now there was no outburst, there was no fear. The intensity of her rage seemed to have burned away every emotion except hate.

"No," she said quietly. "I will not."

Albrecht slowly lowered the pen. "Very well." He turned to one of the guards and pointed at Eric. "If she does not obey in thirty seconds, shoot him."

Anna stiffened. "What?"

"As I told you; you will sign. You have twenty-five seconds more."

Anna was too rigid with anger to find her voice. There was no reason why he should be bluffing. Eric meant less than nothing to him. She was the only one who cared. Only she would suffer.

Albrecht mistook her hesitation for indecision and he added, "Then I shall kill you and sign the papers myself. No one will question the signatures." He glanced at his watch. "You have ten seconds to save his life."

The guard's finger poised on the trigger of the rifle and Anna put up her hand. "All right," she said. "That won't be necessary."

Albrecht gestured to the guard and he moved back. Anna picked up the pen from the table and scrawled her signature on the signature line at the bottom of each paper. When she had finished, she threw the pen on the table. "These won't do you any good. No court will honor a contract made under duress."

Albrecht gathered the papers and placed them back in his pocket. "You're being naive, my dear. Who is going to protest?"

"I will. You can be assured of that."

Albrecht smiled. "You, my dear, won't be here."

Anna stared at him, her anger turning to fear. Now that the papers were signed, there was no reason why he should keep her alive. "You're going to kill me?"

He spread his hands in mock horror. "No, no. I was not lying when I said that your death coming so soon after your father's would raise embarrassing questions. But,"—his smile broadened—"questions will not be asked if you were picked up while consorting with your Gypsy family." He looked at Eric's unconscious form. "And your Gypsy lover."

Anna knelt beside Eric. The bleeding had stopped from the cut in his head and his breathing was regular. "You've got to get him to a doctor."

"A doctor? For a Gypsy?" Albrecht snorted derisively. "You can take care of him. You always were something of the witch." He nodded to the guards. "Take them. Put them with the other dirty *Tzigans*."

As he stalked from the room, Anna felt a powerful compulsion sweep over her. "Yes," she said. Her voice was quiet but filled with the power of anger and conviction. "I am a Gypsy witch. And I put a curse on you, Albrecht Grantz. You will never enjoy the lands of the Zorkas. Never!"

Albrecht continued walking, but for an instant, his step had faltered. Like most people of Transylvania, he despised the Gypsies. But he also feared them. There was something unknown, something mysterious about Gypsies. They were a strange people with strange powers. How else had they managed to survive for hundreds of years? And, while no educated, civilized person put any stock in a Romani curse, one did not wish to take chances either. Anna knew this superstition was strong among the Hungarians. Albrecht Grantz would have many sleepless nights.

The thought failed to lift her spirits when two of the guards lifted Eric and dragged him outside to a waiting truck.

Anna slipped on her coat and, escorted by the other two guards, followed them out and climbed into the bed of the truck. Albrecht had said they were to be placed with the other Gypsies. What then?

As she sat with Eric's head in her lap, she resolved that whatever happened, she would not be separated from Eric, not ever again.

Chapter 8

Eric Imri became aware of a throbbing pain in his head. Pulsing waves of agony, coursing through his skull unchecked, thrust down through his jaw and neck and spread throughout his body. The jouncing did not help. He was lying on his back inside some sort of a vehicle that was traveling over a rough road. With each wrenching jolt, a new shaft of pain penetrated his skull.

He tried to shift to a position that would stop the pounding jolts, and soothing hands were placed on his forehead and a woman's voice said, "No, no, Eric. Don't try to move."

Foolish request. He had to move to stop the pain. But turning to a new position would not help. His right temple continued to hurt like hell even though his head seemed to be cushioned from the worst of the shocks.

He put his hand up and touched a tender lump that had formed above his ear. That schweinhund guard had hit him when he. . . His eyes snapped open. Anna! What happened to Ravanna?

His eyes focused on a face bending over him, and he let his breath out in a sigh. "Anna."

"Thank God," she said. "I didn't know if you would ever wake up."

His head was cradled in her lap. He struggled to sit up, fighting lancing pain. "What happened? Where are we?"

"Eric. Don't move. Not yet."

She tried to hold him down, but he pushed her hands aside and sat up, clinching his teeth against a wave of nausea. When he could focus, he saw that he and Anna were in the bed of an old truck. The floorboards were filthy with dirt and remnants of sugar beets. Two Hungarian policemen were sitting on a bench with their backs against the cab of the truck, rifles across their knees, their fingers already in the trigger guards as though they expected their prisoners to launch an attack. The thought amused Eric despite the pain. The way he felt he could not have successfully attacked a cockroach.

He had to make two attempts before he could say, "Where are we?"

"I'm not sure. We've been taking the back roads. We seem to be headed toward Eger."

"Grantz? Is he here?"

"No. He had his own car."

Eric tried to piece together what had happened and the scene slowly took form. "The paper. Did you sign the paper?"

Anna nodded. "I didn't have a choice. But he'll never use them. I'll see to that."

Eric looked at the grim faces of the guards. "I don't think you're going to get a chance."

"I know he has friends. He might put me in prison. But I have friends too. He can't keep me in prison forever."

Eric could not bring himself to answer. He did not want to shatter her hopes. A man like Albrecht Grantz would not be stupid enough to put the daughter of Pal Zorka in a prison where she could contact friends of her father. More likely he would have the guards stop the truck in some remote place and shoot them both, leaving their bodies for the foxes and wolves. But he would not make it easy for them. When the truck stopped the guards would probably be distracted. He would attack at that instant. His only hope—their only hope—was to get one of the rifles.

With a sigh, he allowed the tension to drain. His strength was slowly returning and if the trip was long enough, he might have a remote chance. But one thing was certain, he would not kneel like a dog so they could put a bullet in the back of his skull. Although, at the moment, the pain was so great that the idea seemed almost welcome.

"Put your head back in my lap," Anna said. "You might have a concussion, but your eyes look all right."

"It feels like a volcano." Gratefully he rested his throbbing head on her thigh, and she gently stroked his forehead and temples. The effect was so wonderfully soothing and he was so tired he could have slept instantly if the jouncing of the truck hadn't kept driving shafts of pain through his body. How interesting, he thought, that a person could think about sleep when he might be shot at any moment. Apparently, there were parts of the body that did not give a damn about what happened to other parts, just as some people had no concern about what happened to others, failing to realize that they were all part of the whole.

His reverie was interrupted by the truck jolting to a stop. His plan! He tried to leap to his feet, but his body felt as though it was moving through deep water. When at last he was able to stand, the guards were already on their feet, their rifle muzzles centered on his chest, and two other guards were out of the cab and coming to let down the tailgate of the truck.

It was just as well. He was swaying on his feet with just the little effort it had taken to stand.

Then Anna breathed, "My God!" and he saw there would be no second chance. They had stopped beside a railroad track that ran through a grassy meadow surrounded by forest. Four wooden cars of the type used to ship cattle were on the track coupled to an idling steam engine. Except for the heavy doors, the few openings the cars had were crisscrossed with strands of barbed wire. Guards carrying carbine rifles stood on the tops of the cars.

But what caused Eric to catch his breath was the sight of hundreds of Gypsies who were being unloaded from trucks and forced into the cattle-cars by Hungarian policemen. Some of the policemen used bayonets fixed to their rifles to jab at those who lagged or resisted. Others wielded truncheons or heavy clubs. Near the panting engine was a black Mercedes touring car with its top down. An SS-Officer stood in the passenger side next to the seated driver, observing the activities, his hands clasped behind his back. With a shock Eric recognized him. It was the Nazi bastard who had shot his father.

Anger washed away all reason and he jumped from the truck, his face contorted with rage. He started toward the man, but one of the policemen smashed him in the side with the butt of his rifle and pain drove him to his knees.

Anna swung to the ground and helped him to his feet. As he watched the Gypsies being herded into a group, shame made Eric's shoulders slump. They were like sheep being guarded by dogs. The Gypsies outnumbered the soldiers three to one. If they all attacked together, some would be killed, but the others could overpower the policemen. He felt like screaming at them to stop behaving like slaves, to turn on the dogs.

Then he looked at the faces of the Gypsies. They were beaten already, conditioned by generations of abuse not to fight back, resigned to whatever fate their masters had in mind. There were signs of hate, even expressions of anger. But, still, they moved stoically toward the railroad cars under the jabs and blows of the guards.

Eric put his hands on the sideboard of the truck to steady himself as the strength went out of his legs, and Anna give him her shoulder for support.

"What are they doing?" Anna's voice reflected her concern. "Where are they taking them?"

"Labor camps. The Germans call them Laborslagers."

"They can't put all those people in four cars."

Eric's laugh was bitter. "Can't they? You'll see."

One of the guards motioned toward the other Gypsies. "Over there, with the rest of the pigs."

Anna whirled to face the man, her eyes blazing. "Mind your tongue, you stupid ass. What kind of a man are you? Doing the dirty work of the Nazis. And you call yourself Magyar. You're nothing but a damned Saxon warme bruder!"

Before Anna's unexpected fury, the guard stepped back and his face reddened at being called a homosexual. "Get over with the others," he snarled. But Anna noted with grim satisfaction that he did not call them pigs nor any other name.

She pulled Eric's arm across her shoulder so she could help support him, and they walked across the rich green grass toward the group of Gypsies with the guards following warily.

Before they reached the group, two Gypsy men rushed to meet them. "Eric," one of them said, his face twisted in anguish. "Talk to these dogs. Tell them they are making a mistake."

Eric said, "I'm sorry, Janos. I've seen this happen before, in Germany and Austria to the Jews. Now it looks like it's the Gypsy's turn."

The man stared at the bloody hair on the side of Eric's head and his shoulders sagged. His eyes shifted to Anna, and when he recognized her, they came alive. "Ravanna. You are a Zorka. They will surely not take you. Tell them we are loyal. We were loyal to your father. We will be loyal to you."

A terrible sadness almost overcame Anna. These people had been loyal to her father. They had been loyal to Hungary. And now their country was deserting them. She was deserting them. But what could she possibly do?

It was Eric who answered for her. "She can do nothing. They are taking her too."

The two Gypsy men looked at her in disbelief. "But you are a Zorka."

"That's true. But I am also Romani."

The fire went out of the men's eyes and without another word they turned away. Now, their last hope was gone.

Looking at the stone-faced Nazi SS officer and at the Hungarian policemen, Anna felt that her last hope might also have vanished. No one here would listen to any form of protest. Whether it was because they were conditioned to treat Gypsies with contempt or because they were being paid not to listen, the result was the same.

The last of the cars was being loaded and more than a hundred men, women and children were brutally pushed and shoved toward the open doorway. The stragglers were beaten with truncheons and rifle butts or jabbed with bayonets as the Gypsies frantically tried to help each other into the cattle car.

"No sitting!" the guards shouted. "Stand. All stand!"

Anna looked desperately for a way to escape, but two Hungarian policemen closed in on them, bayonets poised. One of them shoved Anna into the struggling group so hard she almost fell, and for an instant, she thought she might be trampled. Then Eric pulled her to her feet. "Hold on to me."

She clutched his arm, fighting to retain her grip as she was buffeted by the Gypsies who were trying to avoid being beaten by the guards.

When they reached the door, Anna almost gagged at the foul odor of cattle manure and human sweat. She tried to turn back against the crush of people. "I can't. I can't go in there."

Eric grabbed her by the shoulders. "They'll kill you if you don't."

"Let them! I won't."

"Yes, you will!" He lifted her and shoved her through the doorway into the mass of screaming, cursing Gypsies who were fighting to stay near the little fresh air that came from the open door. Someone pushed her and she fell. Her cry of anguish melded with other groans and cries. She tried to get to her feet, but was crushed back into the filth of the floor by others crawling over her as they fought their way inside and she almost wretched. A hard shoe slammed into her ribs and a boot heel sank into the small of her back. Oh God. She was being crushed and she screamed in rage and fear. She would not die here! She would not!

Gathering all her strength, she fought to get to her feet, clutching for support, her nails breaking on rough cloth. Suddenly, a strong hand slipped under her arm and she was pulled back onto her feet. "Stay with me," Eric's voice said in her ear. "We'll try to get to the side."

Gritting her teeth, she clung to Eric with all her strength as he pushed his way through the increasing mass of Gypsies toward the side. This had to be what it was like in hell: dim light filtered through small openings covered with barbed wire, the stench of excrement, locked inside a box and surrounded by perspiring, writhing bodies, assailed by the nerve-wrenching sound of sobbing, of screaming babies and children. And overlaying all, an awful sense of despair.

The last of the Gypsies were somehow forced into the packed car. The next instant the hell was made infinitely worse as the steel door slid shut, cutting off the light with a clang like a stroke of doom.

With the rough wood of the car's side against her back and Eric shielding her from the worst of the crushing bodies, it was not quite so bad. There was a small, jagged hole in the wall, and by turning her head, she could obtain a breath of outside air. The merest trace of fresh air was like nectar.

There was a jolt and she felt the train begin to move. Taking them where? To what? She peeked through the hole for what could be a last glimpse of her native land. But instead of seeing the green grass and beautiful trees, her eyes were drawn to the German touring car. Standing on the ground next to the car, talking to the Nazi SS officer, was Albrecht Grantz. He was smiling as though the train was ridding him of all his problems. Perhaps it was. But not for long. She would see to that.

"When we get to this work camp," she said to Eric, shouting so she could be heard above the noise of anguished voices and the rumble of the train, "I will see that someone pays for this."

"By the time we get to the work camp, we might not be alive."

Anna's anger was splashed with an icy fear. "What do you mean? Of course, we'll be alive."

"How long do you think we can survive in here? A day? A week?"

"It couldn't be more than an hour or two. We can't stand like this very long."

"Where to you think these work camps are? In Budapest?"

"Well, I assumed it would be somewhere nearby."

"It could be anywhere: a hundred miles or five hundred."

Five hundred! Oh God! She couldn't survive that long! She had a horrible feeling that the direction of her life, like the direction of the train, was unknown and irrevocable. She was being carried against her will on a one way journey into an alien world where her life, her values would be totally different, where her promises of retribution would simply be wishful thinking. Where they were going, they might never have heard of the Zorka name or the Zorka estate. She would be a Gypsy among Gypsies, subject to the abuses they had always endured.

But of one thing she was resolved: She would not accept her fate with the stoic passivity of a

Gypsy. She was half Magyar and thoroughly American and that part of her would never give in.

"What do they do in the work camps?"

"Impossible to say. Farming. Manufacturing. If we go to the battle area we might have to dig tank traps."

"Tank traps? Would they make us work that close to the fighting?"

"Why not? We're more expendable than soldiers."

Anna was silent, trying to visualize what such a camp would be like. But it was impossible for her to comprehend what would be waiting at their destination. There was only one thing of which she was certain: it would not be pleasant.

"What about the babies? The children?"

"They will probably die. So will the old people, anyone who can't work."

The cold matter-of-fact quality in Eric's voice terrified her more than his words. The thought that many people might die was horrifying, but more horrifying was the knowledge that their captors would allow it to happen. Did such monsters really exist? She was on the verge of convincing herself they could not when she remembered the way the Hungarian policemen had beaten the Gypsies and how the Nazi SS officer had shot Eric's father. And now the cattle cars. Only sub-humans would treat other people in this manner.

A new thought struck her and she wondered briefly why each new thought was always of something dreadful. "Do you think we'll be separated? I mean, the men and the women?"

He considered a moment. "I would think so. It's easier to manage people if they're separated."

"It is? You mean because they wouldn't need individual shelters?"

"That's one reason. The other is that it's easier to threaten to kill a member of your family if you don't obey orders."

"Wouldn't it be just as easy if they were together?"

"Not if they were already dead."

Anna's spirit shrank a little more. "I see."

Eric read the growing defeat in her voice. "Look," he said slowly and firmly. "There are always survivors . . . in any tragedy. Our people have survived for generations when others would have died. You've got to find the secret, use what you can. Find a talent for something they can use, something they need. It can be with your mind or your body. But you've got to make it into something they want. Or think they do."

Images flashed through Anna's mind. What skills did she have that would be indispensable to an enemy? Her mind? They certainly would have little use for an accountant. Perhaps an interpreter. She spoke English, Magyar, German and Romani, the language of the Gypsies. But so too, must many others. If only she were a doctor, or an engineer. Anything that would be of use. But there was nothing. If she had to depend upon her skills to survive, she was doomed. She could not even cook very well.

Her body? She was strong, healthy. She could do farm work. Work in a factory. A factory! What would such a life do to her face, her figure? A sharp pang of hope shot through her. Perhaps her looks would save her. Truthfully, she was more beautiful than most women. That should count for something.

She halted this train of thought with a shudder. Did she want to survive because of her beauty? How would she be forced to use it? How would she be used? And how long could beauty alone sustain survival? There had to be hundreds, thousands of women more beautiful than she.

"Maybe we can escape."

Eric nodded. "Yes. But at the right time. If we try and get caught, they'll probably execute us."

"What if we're separated? I could never escape on my own."

"You'd be surprised at what you can do when you have to."

Could he be right? Never had she been called upon to use every ounce of her strength, either mentally or physically. How strong was she? Could she meet the challenge? Or would she cave in when confronted by a desperate situation? She could be strong if Eric was with her, she was certain.

"If we are separated," she said, "we should try to meet somewhere."

"We'll have to find out where we're being taken. Then we can plan something."

The thought of being separated from Eric was suddenly unbearable. "If we are separated," she said fiercely, "I'll find you. I promise."

He smiled at her as though the thought was humorous. "A blood promise?"

"Yes. A blood promise."

At the urgency in her voice, his smile changed into a straight, hard line. He pulled her hard against him and buried his face in her hair. "And I'll find you," he whispered. "That is also a blood promise."

At his words, Anna felt a strange comfort. Despite their surrounding, despite the awful reality of their surroundings and despite the horror of the unknown ahead, she felt secure in Eric's arms. He had given her his promise. There had to be more behind it than just a desire to comfort her. Would he make such a solemn oath unless he really was in love with her? The thought was so pleasant that she was able to give in to her extreme fatigue, and despite being packed so tightly she could scarcely breathe, and despite her fear, she found herself slipping in and out of sleep. In the crush of bodies it was impossible to fall, but when her knees buckled, Eric's arms held her as though he could protect her from the horrors of the world.

Chapter 9

For hours the train rumbled through the night. Eric had no idea about its direction. At first he had tried to analyze the turns and the laboring of the engine as it climbed toward higher ground, then picked up speed on a long slope. He assumed they were not moving south since the Germans did not control Yugoslavia. But were they going northeast toward the Russian front? Or northwest toward Germany? Or perhaps straight north into Poland.

Peering out the small hole in the side of the railroad car was of little help. In the darkness, he could not see far, and of what he could make out, all the trees, all the mountains, all the fields looked alike.

After several hours, he gave up. The train had followed such a twisting, turning course and had made brief stops at so many unrecognizable stations, that he had no idea where they were. Perhaps when they finally left the train, he could observe some terrain feature that would give him a clue. He and his father had traveled most of Europe and he had made it a point to remember all the important landmarks so that in his transactions he could make up an authentic-sounding claim regarding ownership of the horse he was trying to sell. A farmer in Prague could be persuaded that a stallion was from the Carpathian Mountains of Poland, which was famous for its breed of hardy Huçuls, if Eric could accurately describe the area where, supposedly, the horse was bred and raised.

Now, he wished he had paid even more attention. If he could escape, it was important that he know where he was, which way to run. In a way, he hoped their destination was near the Russian front. It would be far easier to escape if there was nearby fighting which would distract the guards. And if they could make it to the Russian lines, they would be safe. Unless the Russians also wanted to exterminate the Gypsies or put them in their own work camps. In these time, it might be better to become a Gorgio until the stupid war was over.

Early in the journey the Gypsies had lapsed into the silence of despair. But as the minutes and hours wore on, the silence was interrupted by increasing moans of pain and the whimpering and crying of children. The stench of fear mixed with the acrid odor of urine and vomit was sickening, and as the air became increasingly rank, those in the middle, in mounting panic, began struggling to get to the smallest crack or hole for a breath of fresh air. But it was impossible. Even the strongest could not fight their way through the crush of humanity. And their struggles only made the situation worse.

Eric used the small hole in the wall as a hand hold to pull himself up as high as he could. "Stop it!" he shouted. "Stop! Or we'll all die!"

It was useless. His voice was a cricket's chirp in a thunderstorm. Even as he shouted, hands clawed at him so that he had to fight hard to hold his place near the small hole.

Eric tried to give Anna some measure of protection by bracing himself against the wall with his hands on either side of her head. It took all his strength to make an inch or two of space and soon his arms were shaking from the strain. Still, he held on, back bowed, teeth clamped tight, holding back the crushing weight of bodies. Then the train rounded a bend and the pressure became overwhelming. It was like the hand of a gigantic beast crushing him and he was smashed forward.

The force was so abrupt and unexpected that Anna's breath exploded. Desperately she fought to breathe while the train sped around the bend, jamming the mass of people against them with crushing force.

Finally, the train straightened, and Eric was able to shove back a fraction of an inch. His face was jammed next to Anna's so she could hear his labored breathing. "Sorry," he gritted. "I couldn't hold it."

She had to fight air into her lungs before she could reply. "We're . . . going to die. Nobody . . . can stand . . . this."

"No!" Eric's voice was an angry command. "Hold on! We've got to live. It can't be much longer."

"Not . . . if they want us . . . alive."

The struggle just to breathe made conversation so painful that they remained silent. The other people gradually realized the futility of struggle and they, too, grew silent, shutting down their senses, enduring, as the Gypsies had done for centuries, simply enduring.

Struggling to breathe, Anna felt a darkness coming into her mind that was deeper than the blackness inside the stifling car and she told herself over and over: Don't pass out. Oh God. Don't pass out. If she fainted she would die, die standing up, unable to fall, unable to find peace even in death.

She forced her mind to Eric's words. She had to live. She had to. She had to find the person responsible for this and punish him. But what punishment could she possibly devise that would be equal to this hell? Thinking about it gave her strength, the strength of anger. Maybe that was the secret to survival: anger. Not courage. Not hope. Surely, not hope. Anger. A deep and burning hatred that made you struggle to live, that made you demand that your body continue to survive so you could seek revenge. Anger for the murder of Bela Imri! Anger for the taking of her lands! Anger for the dead children and all the other Gypsies, and for those who even now were dying in this living hell! That was it! Cling to the anger! Anger was drink. Anger was air to breathe. Anger was life!

Chapter 10

The horrible odor was not that of death; it was the smell of fear mixed with the stench of urine and feces. But it should have been the rankness of death, because when the doors of the railroad car slide open, many of those inside were already dead.

"Out! Out! Schnell! Out!"

The harsh command shouted by a beefy man wearing the gray-green field uniform of a German SS-T staff sergeant was emphasized by blows against the side of the railroad car with the weighted handle of a coiled whip. The command was hardly necessary. Those unfortunate enough to be in the doorway were spilled to the ground by the frantic pushing of those behind as they struggled to escape the horror of the railroad car. Like a human waterfall, bodies spewed from the opening, falling over those already on the ground. The Scharführer, aided by SS guards wearing soft kepi hats and wielding heavy truncheons, shoved and smashed at the people, attempting to control the tide. They were able to succeed when the pressure from inside was reduced. Gypsies still inside waited dumbly while those who had fallen were cleared from the doorway. Those who could walk were herded into a group, many limping or clutching injuries. Those who failed to rise were dragged aside so the others could clamber to the ground where they were prodded or kicked into the group.

The same scenario was taking place in front of the other railroad cars under the watchful gaze of a man wearing the black uniform of an SS-T Lt. Colonel sitting astride a white horse.

The Gypsies were remarkably silent. It was as though the massive horror had driven them into shock. Except for the whimpering of children and the shouts of the soldiers, there were no sounds.

Eric and Anna were among the last to make their way to the door. They had to step over the bodies of those who had not survived the long journey and Anna noticed that most of them were children. She was so exhausted and so sickened she could make no comment to Eric. What was there to say?

In the doorway, she paused for a second to breathe the fresh pine-scented air. The train had stopped in the center in a broad, grassy valley flanked by towering, heavily forested mountains. The dreary morning sunlight, which forced its way through a heavy overcast, added to the sense of desolation. Anna's attention was caught by a complex of new buildings constructed on raw earth. The largest were six shed-like buildings made of slabs of newly sawed pine. Their low, gabled roofs were covered with black tarpaper. The buildings were separated into two groups by an eight-foot high fence made of woven barbed-wire. A similar fence surrounded all six of the barracks, leaving a wide assembly area in front of each group. Heavy gates opened into each of the two compounds. Guard towers were located at the four corners, and in each one Anna could see the muzzle of a machine gun protruding from the side facing the barracks. Several yards beyond the fenced barracks and on the opposite side of a macadam-paved road were other barracks and a small cluster of white-painted buildings fronted by a tall flag pole from which fluttered a Nazi flag. On a knoll beyond the headquarters buildings were a stable and a fenced pasture.

Looking at the setting Anna felt her stomach churning. "This isn't a work camp," she said to Eric. "It's a prison."

"Oh, it's a work camp all right. Laborslager. Run by the Death's Head Schutzstaffel, the SS-Totenkopf.

The stark menace of the raw-looking building was like a desecration of the valley's purity. It was as though man had gouged a raw and ugly wound in the soft breast of nature. The camp itself was not that much different than Anna had imagined a labor camp would be. She had steeled herself to be prepared for primitive conditions. But this was a prison, with barbed wire and machine guns and brutal guards. How could she endure this?

Then it was their turn to leave the railroad car, and Anna was filled with a momentary sense of fear when Eric let go of her arm to jump to the ground. He took her hand to help her down and she experienced a quick pang of relief. Eric would protect her from whatever unknown horrors lay ahead.

Her optimism was short lived. When all the living had left the railroad cars, the Gypsies were herded into a single long line and marched toward a waiting SS technical sergeant who began dividing them into three lines. The men were directed to the right, the women to the left. A third line was formed of children, old people and those who had been injured or were sick.

"Oh God," Anna said . "They're going to separate us."

"Don't worry," Eric reassured her. "It's a work camp. We'll be all right."

"We can't be forced to work. That's slavery. They can't do that."

"They'll be sorry to hear that."

Anna closed her eyes. This could not be happening. This was 1941. The world was civilized. Germany was civilized. People today were not kidnapped, beaten, forced into slavery—not in a civilized country, war or no war. But the reality was that she was here and people were being beaten and killed. Her despair was relieved by the realization that she was an American citizen and they would have to release her. And when she reported this to the authorities, all these barbarians would be put in prison.

Nearing the SS Oberscharführer she heard him saying, "Men right; women left. You." He indicated a man who was tightly clutching a broken arm. "The hospital line." And the man moved into the line with the children and older people. So they weren't such barbarians that they were refusing aid to the wounded.

Ahead of her, a young woman gripping the hand of a child tried to go with the child into the hospital line, and one of the German guards barred her way with his truncheon. "Women's line. Women's line!"

The woman cried out in Romani, "No, no. I stay with my baby. My baby."

The guard did not understand her words but he understood her meaning, and with a snarl, he swung at her arm with his truncheon. The heavy stick struck her on the elbow with a dull crack. The woman screamed and her hand fell away from its grip on the child. The soldier quickly shoved the child toward the hospital line. He tried to push the woman toward the women's line, but she cried out in pain and fear as she fought to follow her child.

"Stop! What is this?" It was the SS officer on the white horse who had spurred forward to find the source of the commotion. The guard sprang to attention and the woman seized the opportunity to run to her child.

"Sorry, Herr Obersturmbannführer. She refused to go in the woman's line."

Beside her, Anna felt Eric stiffen and he whispered, "That officer. His name is von Liebermann. He bought a horse from me."

"I hope you sold him a good one."

"Let's just say, I hope he doesn't recognize me."

Anna scarcely heard him. Her attention was focused on the woman's arm that was clearly broken at the elbow. "Dummkopf!" von Liebermann shrieked. "How can they work if you break their arms? You report to me in one hour. And if you break any more bones, you will take their place."

The guard's face paled and he snapped. "Zu befehl, Herr Obersturmbannführer."

Von Liebermann turned his attention to the woman, "Stay with your child. You will be taken care of in the hospital." He turned and rode away, guiding the white horse in a slow careful walk as though afraid he might make a fool of himself if he tried to go faster.

A few of the Gypsies understood German, and the word quickly spread that the children and the old and sick were to be taken to a hospital. After that, the separation process went smoothly with the Gypsies moving forward stolidly. For generations they had been subjected to the demeaning authority of the Gorgios, so they were not surprised that they had been singled out for forced labor. Even those whose young children were ordered into the hospital line, did not protest. Being in a hospital or a Youth Camp was certainly preferable to what they knew would be the harsh conditions of the work camp.

Just before they reached the SS Oberscharführer, Eric whispered, "The women and the men's barracks are only separated by a wire fence. I will wait for you there every night at ten o'clock. Come when you can."

Before Anna could answer, she was shoved by a guard toward the woman's line. Instead of going, she took a step toward the SS Oberscharführer and said in German, "I am an American citizen. I demand to be released."

All activity ceased as heads turned toward her. The sergeant looked at her coldly. "Demand? You demand?"

"That's right. Your stupid soldiers made a mistake. I demand to be released."

"You are American?"

Anna's gaze was as cold as his. "That's right. Your Führer wouldn't like it if he found out you were holding an American."

The Oberscharführer smiled and looked around at the mountains and the forest. "How would he find out? Who will tell him? You?"

"I'll see that he knows."

"And how will you do that? By telephone, ja?"

The guards laughed and Anna realized the man was toying with her. "He will find out," she said. "I have friends, relatives. They will see that he finds out."

The man's face hardened. "We are not afraid of you Americans. We welcome a war with you. We will smash you."

"That isn't what your Führer wants."

"Here, I am Führer. We will see how good you soft Americans are at work. Get in line."

Anna stared at him in helpless rage. As long as she was held incommunicado, there was nothing she could do except wait and hope that there was enough truth to her lie about friends and relatives that they would indeed report her absence. Then the image of Uncle Albrecht watching her being forced into the railroad car flashed across her memory and her shoulders sagged. By now her trusted 'Uncle' Albrecht probably had taken possession of her land. The thought brought her head up.

She had to live through this if only to see that Albrecht Grantz was punished. She would show this Nazi just how mistaken he was about 'soft' Americans. As she strode purposefully to join the other women, she caught a glimpse of Eric's tall figure in the men's line. He was watching her and she wondered what he would have done if the German had struck her. She was glad it hadn't happened. The guards carried their truncheons as though they would welcome a chance to use them.

When the lines were formed to the guards' satisfaction, the Gypsies walked to the barracks where the gates were opened and they were herded inside the compound, the men on the right and the women on the left. Glancing back over her shoulder, Anna saw that some of the SS guards were picking up bodies from the ground outside the doors of the railroad cars and tossing them back inside. Then, with a belch of black smoke, the engine snorted and began to move, gathering speed as it chuffed across the floor of the valley. Anna wondered how far it was to the hospital. The small children, the old and the sick in the hospital line couldn't walk very far. She was surprised when guards began moving the hospital line toward the nearby woods. The hospital must be located behind the trees, kept apart from the main camp to prevent the spread of disease.

The women were brought to a halt in the cleared area in front of the three women's barracks. A chill breeze was sweeping across the valley and Anna was glad she had her coat. Many of the women, however, had not had time to find jackets or coats and they stood shivering. Anna hoped they would be allowed to go inside the barracks quickly. She assumed there were stoves, although she saw no chimneys.

A big SS sergeant with a round, brutal face and eyes that reminded Anna of a ferret, stood in front of the silent woman. He held a coiled leather whip in his hand. "I am Oberscharführer Wirtz. You will address me as Herr Oberscharführer." He did not shout, but his words were distinct in the clear mountain air. His eyes registered contempt as he stared at the women. In front of the men's barracks, the assembled men were being addressed in a similar manner by another SS sergeant.

"You will obey my orders without question." Wirtz paused as though expecting a challenge. When no one ventured a reply, he continued. "You are very fortunate. You have been selected to work for the Reich and the Führer." As he talked, he emphasized his words by popping the whip's handle against his palm. "The rules are simple. You will be assembled here every morning. You will be assigned to work details. You will perform the work without question. If you do not, you will be shot. Inside the barracks you will find beds and eating utensils. You will be given work clothes. There is to be no fighting, no disturbance. If there is fighting, both people will be shot." He snapped his right arm up stiffly. "Heil Hitler!"

He turned and walked away. The women stood for a moment, not knowing what to do. Then the other guards began shouting instructions and separating the women into three groups, one for each barracks. To her relief Anna was in the group directed into the barracks nearest the fence that separated the men's and the women's barracks.

On the inside, the buildings smelled of newly cut pine. The low ceiling was supported by log beams that still contained their bark. The floor and walls were constructed of rough slabs. There were no windows. Light came from cracks in the wall boards and from widely spaced low-wattage bulbs overhead. A long center corridor was flanked by rough-hewn triple-deck bunk beds. The bunks were jammed so close together there was less than two feet of space separating them. Each bunk contained a thin mattress stuffed with tired straw and a single threadbare army blanket. Hung on nails between each bunk were three small tarnished metal pots, which looked as though at one time they had been used as army canteen containers. On a nail beside each hung a rusting metal spoon. There was no sign of wash basins or lockers to hold personal belongings. There were no stoves, no heaters, and the room was cold.

As Anna stared, appalled that she would be expected to live in such conditions, she was shoved aside by a woman who rushed to capture one of the lower bunks. Anna did not want a lower bunk. In an upper bunk, even with her nose only a couple of feet from the low ceiling, she would not feel as though she were locked in a box.

She chose the last bunk on the right, close to the rear door and pulled herself up onto its worn mattress. It smelled musty as though the straw had been wet when it was stuffed inside the canvas ticking. She considered trying to find a replacement. But they all smelled the same, the foul smell permeating the barracks. Maybe she should be grateful. There were more than fifty women in the room, and with no bathing facilities, it would soon have odors much more unpleasant.

Because of the low ceiling there was no room to sit up and she lay on the pallet with her hands behind her head using the blanket as a pillow. The thought kept beating through her brain like a metronome that she had been betrayed. She had almost been killed in New York. Then the summons to return to Hungary had arrived after her father was already dying. And there were the suspicious papers that Grantz had wanted her to sign. And the timing of the raid at the Gypsy village when Grantz knew she would be there. It must have really upset him when she had escaped. Like a fool Eric and she had taken his suggestion and gone to the mountain cabin.

Now, she was caught in a trap and there was no one to turn to for help. With no way of sending a message to the outside, she was no better off than any of the Gypsy women. Perhaps worse. Now that the SS guards knew she was American, they might single her out for 'special' treatment. She could not suppress a shudder. There was no telling what that 'special' treatment might be.

The other women were speaking in low voices, some crying, but most accepting their fate philosophically. A few had gathered in the narrow corridor, trying to find out what had happened to friends and relatives. Suddenly the door at the front of the barracks opened and Sergeant Wirtz entered. He stopping just inside the doorway. He was carrying the coiled leather whip in his right hand like a symbol of authority. Behind him were four German guards, their arms laden with striped jackets and pants.

"Achtung!" Sergeant Wirtz shouted and the talking ceased. "Line up in front of your beds."

The women began forming lines on each side of the corridor. They were silent, partially through fear and partially through sullen acceptance of mistreatment that had been the lot of the Gypsy for hundreds of years.

Anna clambered down from her bunk and took a place at the end of the line. Apparently, they were to be issued work clothes. She wondered what sort of work they would be expected to perform here in the middle of a mountain range.

"Take off your clothes. Put them on the floor in front of you."

None of the women moved; shock kept them immobilized. Gypsy children might run around in almost total nudity, but adult Gypsy women were highly circumspect. They would never take their clothes off in front of a strange man, so they stood silently, staring at the sergeant as though he were insane.

The face of Sergeant Wirtz became mottled with anger and he screamed, "Off! Take off your clothes. Everything except your shoes."

The women glanced from one to another nervously, looking to see if anyone would obey the insane order. To be the first would be a demonstration of wanton behavior, placing the person on the level of a whore.

In sudden fury, Sergeant Wirtz smashed the nearest woman across the face with the handle of the whip, driving her to her knees, blood spurting from her nose and cheek. "Now!" he screamed, spittle flying from his mouth. "Off! Off!"

Several of the women raised their hands as though to begin the horrible task, but when they saw that others were not complying, they dropped their arms. The big sergeant's face contorted and he raised the whip to strike the next woman.

"Halt!" Anna's voice stopped the sergeant's blow in mid air. His small eyes probed for the source of the command and Anna stepped forward. "Leave the clothes. We will put them on."

Sergeant Wirtz' face smoothed. Here was something he could deal with. He strode down the isle between the rows of women, his boot heels thudding hollowly and Anna had the quivering apprehension a mouse must have at the approach of a snake.

Wirtz stopped in front of her, his ugly face so close she could smell his bad breath. "What did you say?" His voice was no longer shrill. But the low growl held a menace that was even more chilling.

Anna stared into his eyes, controlling a desire to back away. "We cannot disrobe in front of strangers. If you will leave the clothes, we will put them on."

Wirtz' heavy lips pulled back in a snarl, showing tobacco-stained teeth. "You do not give orders here. I do!"

"It's not an order. Only a suggestion."

"A suggestion? I suggest that you do as I say or I will break your dirty neck."

The man's breath was making Anna sick and she swallowed hard. "You can break all of our necks. We will not do it."

The sergeant stared at her white face for a moment and Anna thought he was actually going to attack her. Instead, he grabbed a thin, teenage girl standing next to Anna and swung her around. He crooked a muscular arm around the girl's neck and the other arm behind her head, hooking his fingers under her jaw. He applied a twisting pressure and the girl mewed in agony. "You!" Wirtz said to Anna. "Do it or I break her neck."

Anna's throat, already dry with apprehension, constricted in anger. There could be anonymity in disrobing as part of a group. But to be forced to perform alone in front of the guard's staring eyes would be the ultimate humiliation. She backed a step, her hands reaching for the support of the bunk. She shook her head, unwilling to trust her voice with a simple 'no.'

Wirtz tightened his grip, twisting the girl's head to an impossible angle. "Do it," he snarled. "Now."

My God. Did he really mean it? Would he actually break the girl's neck? Visions of the brutality she had already seen flashed through Anna's mind, removing all doubt. These men were animals. The lives of others meant no more than the lives of pigs or goats. She could tell by the look in Wirtz' eyes that he could break the girl's neck and laugh about it, perhaps reach for another girl and another until Anna was sickened enough to stop the slaughter by complying. She might as well do it now before he killed the girl. A little embarrassment was a small price to pay for the girl's life.

"All right," she whispered harshly. "Let her go."

Sergeant Wirtz smiled. "Do it. Then I let her go."

The girl was having trouble breathing. Her face was changing color and she was almost hanging in the sergeant's powerful grip, and Anna began undressing as rapidly as she could, both to end the girl's agony and to get the hated job over as quickly as possible.

When Anna took off her coat and placed it on her bunk, Wirtz said, "On the floor."

She pulled the coat from the bunk and dropped it to the floor.

As she continued undressing, the other women watched her silently, their faces reflecting scorn and sympathy. Then she was standing naked, her face burning. She wanted to cringe, to cover herself as best she could with her hands and arms, anything to shield herself from the stares of the sergeant and the guards. That was what they expected, what they wanted, for her to feel degraded, humiliated. Slowly, staring into the face of Sergeant Wirtz, she straightened, standing tall.

"Satisfied?" Her voice carried all the hatred that she felt.

Wirtz stared at her flat stomach and her breasts and his smile widened into a grin. "I think we will find special work for you."

Anna's flesh crawled with revulsion, but she held her poise. "Let her go!" she commanded.

Wirtz released the girl and she slumped to the floor, sucking in air in wheezing gasps. Anna quickly bent to help her and the big sergeant wheeled to face the other women. "Now!" he gritted. "No more games." He uncoiled the whip whose braided leather was stained with dark patches. "The clothes: off!"

Slowly the women's hands came up, and avoiding looking at one another, they began to disrobe, stripping off their blouses and thick skirts. Like most Gypsy women, none of them wore a brassiere and some of the younger women did not wear the usual coarse cotton underpants so the disrobing was over quickly. Gypsy women had little embarrassment about their breasts so they used their hands to cover their genitals, their bodies hunched against the stares of the men.

Sergeant Wirtz grunted in satisfaction and walked slowly between the line of naked women, trampling on or kicking aside their discarded clothing. From time to time he paused in front of a girl and surveyed her with interest. Occasionally he would use the handle of his whip to force a girl to lift her chin so he could study her face as though reluctant to touch her with his hands.

At the end of the line he jerked his head toward the guards carrying the work clothes and they dropped them on the floor and began collecting the women's discarded clothing, their eyes darting toward the naked women.

Anna, in her place at the end of the line, felt something solid under her foot and she saw that she was standing on her coat. The Tarot cards. She had forgotten they were in her pocket. Watching for her chance, she slipped the packet of cards from the pocket and slid them under the thin mattress of her bunk. What was it Eric had said? 'Find something they want.' The German guards did not look particularly intelligent or educated. They had probably been recruited more for their penchant for brutality and obedience than for their intellect. Which meant that, like many uneducated peasants, they were probably very superstitious. If so, she might be able to find a use for the cards.

At the door, Wirtz nodded toward the piles of work clothes. "You will put these on. You have fifteen minutes." Before he went out the door, Wirtz paused to stare at the women, his lips lifting in sneering annoyance. "You do not look like you will give us much work. We will see."

He turned and stomped out, followed by the guards carrying the women's discarded clothes.

For a moment the women stared at the closed door as though expecting it to open and the men to reappear. When nothing happened, one of the elderly women near the pile of clothes grabbed a jacket and began pulling it on. As though her move was a signal, the women rushed forward and snatched at the clothing, shouting and shoving. Moving quickly, Anna managed to snatch a jacket and pair of pants. There was no opportunity to check sizes. Some women had appropriated several of the garments, and they, along with those who found that theirs did not fit, attempted to make a trade. The trading was not done quietly. Traditionally, the one asking for the trade was at a disadvantage and wanted to bargain, their voices escalating with the price. With nothing else to trade, some of the women began trading their blankets and eating utensils. Fights began as women attempted to obtain by force what they could not obtain by trade. Anna's own jacket and pants were ill fitting, but she saw that unless the bargaining was stopped, there would be bloodshed. She pushed her way to the center of the room and shouted in Romani, "Stop! Stop this!"

If anyone heard they paid no attention. Grabbing one of the eating pots from the wall she began beating it with a metal spoon. "Stop!" she yelled. "Stop!" The cacophony, aided by her voice, gradually brought silence. When she could be heard, she said, "You are acting like Gorgios! We are all Romanies. If we take each other's blankets and the pots for eating, we will die. If we are to survive, we must help each other."

They stared at her stupidly, as though she were talking in an incomprehensible language. The idea of refusing to bargain was as alien to the women as money. Anna could see they would never voluntarily give up their old way. They were only listening to her now because she was recognized as a Zorka and their subservience to authority was as ingrained as their instinct for bargaining. Seeing a large women wearing a jacket too small for her and a girl across the isle with one too large, Anna pointed at them and ordered, "Give her your jacket. You. Give her yours."

Anna walked through the group, ordering exchanges and, under the lash of her voice, the women sullenly exchanged clothing and returned bartered or stolen spoils. Anna knew that in her rough, ill-fitting work clothes she looked like a clown, but she also knew there was nothing funny about the guards' truncheons, nor their willingness to use them if the fighting continued.

The women were completing their exchanges when the door opened and Sergeant Wirtz shouted, "Out. Out. Schnell."

Silently, the women moved outside, and with kicks and blows, Wirtz and the guards forced them into two ragged lines. Sergeant Wirtz seemed surprised the women all wore clothes that fit them reasonably well. At the other barracks other Oberscharführers were also ordering the women out, and they tumbled into the dull sunlight, many still fighting over mismatched clothing. Farther along, the men were also being turned out. Anna looked for Eric, but the men, too, had been forced to change into striped work clothes and she was unable to pick him out of the groups.

Once the women had been formed into two lines, Sergeant Wirtz conducted a count. From her place near the middle of the line, Anna heard him mumbling the numbers to himself and he ended at forty-six. There were approximately the same number in the other two women's barracks, which meant there were almost a hundred fifty women, and it would seem, about two hundred men. She estimated at least a hundred adults and children had been in the group marched to the hospital. But the camp looked as though it could support three or four times that number, so undoubtedly there would be more slaves arriving.

Slaves? She had thought the word instinctively. But as she reflected, she realized they were slaves. They were being imprisoned against their will; they were being forced to obey orders or be killed, and they would undoubtedly be forced to work.

As if to alleviate any doubt, two squads of German soldiers trotted at double time down the macadam road toward the compound, their Mauser rifles held slanted across their chests, their steel helmets bobbing and their hob-nailed boots thudding in ominous rhythm. The SS Kommandant, Obersturmbannführer von Liebermann, rode beside them on the beautiful white mare. He was not a good rider and he bounced up and down in the saddle causing his head to bob and his hat to slip so that he was forced to hold it on. No one laughed. For, although his horsemanship was comedic, his face retained its expression of imperious disdain, as though to remind everyone that he had the power to inflict brutal punishment or a lingering death.

When the troops arrived at the gates to the compound, their sergeants' shouted commands brought them to a halt. The sergeants snapped other commands and the troops faced each other in two widely spaced lines leading from the gate of each compound toward the road. They stood with their backs rigid, their eyes staring straight ahead, unseeingly. Their robot-like efficiency was terrifying. They acted as though the correct order could make them kill without thought.

Two of the SS guards opened the gate to the men's compound and, at a command from an Oberscharführer, the men began moving forward, with the guards using their truncheons freely to keep the men walking in orderly lines, two abreast. As they approached the gate, one of the Gypsy men shouted angrily at a guard who had smashed him in the back with his truncheon, and the guard attacked him like a mad dog, swinging his truncheon viciously into the man's face. Another guard leaped to help and the two of them smashed at the man's head, aiming for his nose and mouth, which were quickly mashed to a bloody mass of raw flesh, as his cries of pain pierced the bleak morning sunlight. When he fell, they did not stop, but continued to pound at his head and kidneys with all their strength.

At first, the other Gypsy men stared in horror. They were conditioned to expect abuse from Gorgios, even blows and kicks, but now one of their people was being beaten to death in front of them and they leaped to his aid. From his place near the middle of the line, Eric was pressed forward by a surge of shouting Gypsies. Eric cursed silently and threw himself to the side, out of the pack. The fools would accomplish nothing. If they weren't killed outright, they would be injured. And, in this place, an injury was tantamount to death.

The two guards were buried under an avalanche of Gypsy men who swung their fists in an orgy of anger. But, already, other guards had come running, and their truncheons slashed like blunt-edged swords, each stroke drawing blood and grunts of pain.

For a moment it appeared the Gypsies would overwhelm the guards, then von Liebermann barked a command at the German soldiers manning the nearest guard tower and the chatter of a machine gun joined the screams and cries. Geysers of dirt were kicked up within inches of the struggling men, the trail of death walking towards the group. Those who saw the gouts of flying dirt edging toward them, both Gypsy and guard, leaped away, scattering the fighters, leaving only those who were unconscious or unable to move.

Von Liebermann issued another command and the machine gun stopped chattering. In the sudden silence, the Kommandant barked another command and, before the startled Gypsies could respond, the trained guards leaped into action, shoving and pummeling the men back into line. As Eric got to his feet and joined the line, he wondered whether or not von Liebermann would have allowed the machine gun to fire into the melee, which included his own guards. He rather suspected he would have.

With order restored, the Kommandant rode his horse through the gate at a slow walk and stopped at the scene of the battle. Three Gypsy men were lying unconscious, including the man whose beating had started the insurrection. Several others were sitting or laying on the ground groaning. All were spattered with blood as were other men standing in line, some clutching injured limbs or trying to staunch the flow of blood from gaping wounds.

Sitting on his horse silently, Von Liebermann's gaze slowly moved from the men on the ground to those in line. The air was charged with the tension of fear; no one wanting to call attention to himself.

Von Liebermann swung down from his horse and Eric edged farther behind the other men. It would be best to keep out of the SS officer's sight. If he had a long and vengeful memory, he probably would like to get his hands on the Gypsy who, in Salzburg, had sold him the broken-down nag. From the look of the white mare he was now riding, he was making better choices.

Von Liebermann handed the reins to one of the guards who wiped blood from his hands on his shirt before taking them. The SS Kommandant walked almost daintily to the fallen men, taking care to keep clear of the dark patches of moisture that were slowly seeping into the bare ground. He stopped beside the unconscious man whose beating had triggered the battle and studied him for a moment as though deciding whether the man could still be useful. He came to a quick decision, and with one quick motion, drew his pistol and fired a shot into the back of the man's head.

The sharp report caused everyone to start, but the horse panicked. It whirled and reared, pulling the man holding the reins from his feet. One of its pawing front hooves smashed against the shoulder of the guard and the reins were ripped from his hands. The horse's eyes were wide, rolling wildly, and it snorted in fear, its hooves slashing the air as it whirled on its hind legs. Von Liebermann, directly in the horse's path, was frozen in sudden fright.

Thoughts flashed through Eric's mind with blinding speed. This was his chance. If he could save the man's life, he might be grateful. But if he did, von Liebermann would surely recognize him. The chances were just as good that, instead of rewarding him, the man would kill him. But it was worth the chance.

Eric leaped forward and grabbed the horse's bridle. The horse threw her head up violently and Eric was lifted from his feet, but he held on grimly. The horse whirled, tossing her head, trying to rid herself of the weight, her forelegs flailing. The instant the horse's head came down, Eric pulled himself up and fastened his teeth on one of the ears, biting hard through the cartilage. The mare's breath exploded at the sudden pain and she stopped abruptly, her head down. Eric released his grip and stepped back. He gathered the slack reins and tendered them toward the startled SS officer. "You're horse, sir," he said in Magyar.

Von Liebermann recovered his composure quickly. His back stiffened and he took the reins. He jerked his head toward his fallen gloves and Eric picked them up and handed them to him. Von Liebermann holstered his pistol so that he could take the gloves, all the while staring at Eric intently.

"Good work," Von Liebermann said in German "What is your name?" Had von Liebermann recognized him? Eric could not be certain, and not wanting the SS officer to know he spoke German, Eric looked at him, his expression blank.

Von Liebermann's lips curved in a ghost of a sneering smile. "Come, come," he said. "I know you speak German as well as I do. Perhaps better."

Eric contemplated denying his identify. After all, Von Liebermann had only seen him that one time in Salzburg. It might be possible to convince him he had made a mistake, but being caught in a lie would be worse than telling the truth. It would be best if the German thought he was a craven sycophant.

Once he had chosen his role, Eric slipped into the part as easily as slipping on a coat. He let his shoulders slump and he stared at the ground, his expression pained and anxious. "I'm sorry, sir," he said in German. "In the excitement, I forgot."

"Perhaps." The SS Kommandant's hand fell to the butt of his gun.

Without changing his posture, Eric tensed. If von Liebermann drew the gun, he would attack. He could feel the SS officer's eyes measuring him. Then von Liebermann took his hand from the pistol and popped his gloves against his thigh. When Eric looked up, he saw the German was smiling and he had the impression that von Liebermann knew he was playing a part and was willing to overlook it. After all, what difference did it make? He could have Eric shot at any time no matter what role he played. Meanwhile, he was young and strong and could work.

Von Liebermann jerked his head toward the Gypsies and Eric moved back into line. The

Kommandant turned to face the Gypsies and his face hardened as he said in German, "You have cost me time and injured my soldiers. Worse, those of you who are injured will be unable to work. You will be taken to the hospital until you are well enough to do so. The rest of you will have to work twice as hard to make up for their loss."

He moved down the line of men, pausing from time to time to examine a man's wound. If it looked as though the person would be unfit for hard work, he popped his gloves and guards pulled the man from the line. Some of the men who were only slightly injured stepped forward voluntarily, preferring the hospital to work, and the guards shoved them toward the group of injured men.

When he was satisfied he had weeded out all the *nutzlose essers,* von Liebermann climbed back on his horse and rode out through the gate. The Oberscharführer shouted, "All right! Forward! Go!" and the dispirited Gypsies began a straggling march under the close watch of the guards. Eric had the feeling that once the Kommandant was out of sight, the guards would make the Gypsies pay dearly for their attack.

Outside the gate, the Gypsies walked between the two rows of German soldiers who continued to stand at attention, their rifles ready, their eyes focused on nothing. The men were followed by the women who straggled behind in humiliation, not wanting the men to see them in their ugly work clothes. Inside the men's compound, the unconscious Gypsies were placed on stretchers, and the walking injured were made to carry them as the group destined for the hospital moved out through the gate and were herded toward the woods where the previous group had gone. The body of the dead man was left sprawling in the dirt, mute evidence that insurrection was doomed to failure.

When the Gypsies were walking along the macadam road, the Waffen SS soldiers, on command of their sergeants, made a snappy quarter turn and began marching behind them.

The procession followed the road along the floor of the broad valley for about five hundred meters before they were led off on a branching dirt road and into the forest. In another hundred meters the dirt road ended, blocked by a dense stand of timber. Two Army trucks were parked near the trees. The guards shouted for the Gypsies to halt and the Waffen SS soldiers fanned out. Eric wondered at the reason for the move until the guards brought axes and shovels from the trucks and began handing them to the men. If the Gypsies had possessed the axes when they had launched their attack back at the compound, the results would have been frightful. They might have been killed, but they would have taken a number of their slave-masters with them. Now, under the muzzles of the soldiers' rifles, they were thoroughly cowed. When the guards herded them into the woods and indicated which trees they wanted cut, the men began swinging their axes in dejected resignation.

Some of the women were given hatchets and directed to cut and stack branches from the felled trees. Others were put to work dragging the branches to fires where they were burned.

Eric was one of those selected to work on the dirt road and was given a shovel, for which he was grateful. It was much easier to pretend to be working with a shovel than it was to fake swinging an axe. He certainly did not want to develop blisters if he could help it. The blisters themselves might not be dangerous, but with no medical treatment available, anyone who developed an infection was as good as dead. So as he worked, doing only enough to keep the guards satisfied, he altered his grip on the handle of the shovel so blisters would not form. He had forgotten just how much he detested this kind of labor. As a child, before he had begun accompanying his father on his trips, like all the Gypsy children, he had worked in the fields, generally pulling weeds or wielding a hoe. He had disliked the fact that it was forced labor as much as he disliked the work itself. It mattered little that the force was applied by his mother and father who kept his pay. To him, it was no different from the time when Gypsies were slaves of the land owners.

Now he was again a slave. The difference was that this master would probably work him until he could work no more, then shoot him. He would have to find a way to keep that from happening.

Escape? If so, it would be best to do it soon. He was sure the Germans would not feed them adequately, which meant he and the others would grow progressively weaker. It would be best to escape with Anna while they were still strong. He would have to come up with a plan—and quickly.

As he worked, he studied the guards and the surrounding forest. Direct supervision of the Gypsy prisoners was the duty of the SS-T sergeants. If they thought one of the Gypsies was not working hard enough, he was urged into greater activity with lashes from a whip or blows with a truncheon. The Waffen SS troops stayed out of the work area, but they kept their rifles ready.

Watching the women trim the branches and drag them to the fires, Eric thought how much harder such work had to be for Anna than for the others. Gypsy women were used to hard work. But Anna had no such experience. She was an intellectual. Thank God, she was young and strong. If she, or anyone, collapsed, they would most likely be shot. He had told her he would meet her at the fence at ten o'clock. If they were able to do so, he would have to tell her how to give the appearance of working hard. He smiled grimly. There were a lot of Gypsy tricks the Germans would not know. If he and Anna were to survive, they would need every one of them.

Chapter II

The chill sunlight was turning into an even chillier twilight when Anna, holding her tin bowl and spoon, took her place in line with the other women in front of their barracks for the evening meal. There had been no breakfast nor lunch, only a short rest break and the women were ravishingly hungry. Only the threat of the guards' truncheons and the Unterscharführers' ready whips kept order in the line. As the women moved slowly past a field kitchen, a guard ladled thin cabbage soup into each bowl and another dropped in a small slab of coarse black bread. The women who had been served went back into the barracks where they formed into small groups to eat and talk in low voices, each tribe finding its own members.

When she had received her allotment, Anna moved back into the barracks, gulping down the bread. Walking toward her bunk, she searched for other members of Bela Imri's tribe. She found three women whose faces were familiar standing in a group, their voices filled with anger and resentment. When Anna moved to join them, they stopped talking, their eyes hostile. Anna knew why. She was an outsider, not really a Gypsy. A land owner. A Zorka. Someone to be feared almost as much as the Germans. Anna's steps faltered. She could force herself into the group. They might resent her, but they would not reject her. After all, her mother was Romani. And of their tribe.

But which would be more to her advantage? To be Gypsy and blend with the group? Or to be American, and by remaining apart, a constant reminder to the Germans that she did not belong in the labor camp?

Her lips tightened in a bitter smile. Who was she fooling? There could be no individualism in such a place. The Germans could not allow it. To be different was to be a threat. They did not care if she was Eleanor Roosevelt. To them she was simply another body from which they would wring as much work as possible. If she were to survive, it would have to be as a Gypsy.

She nodded to the women as she stopped beside them, trying to recall their names. But she could not. She might remember the names of some of her childhood playmates, but these were older women. Surely, they had to remember her. But they said nothing and Anna began eating her soup. When she brought the first spoonful to her mouth, the smell of rotten cabbage almost made her gag and behind her someone laughed. She turned to see a Gypsy girl near her own age with a tangled mass of deep black hair beneath a blue, polka dotted babushka who was eagerly eating her soup.

"What's the matter, *gadjo?*" the girl said in Romani. "You don't like your soup?"

The girl's use of the derogatory expression for a non-Gypsy irritated Anna, but she suppressed an angry retort. Instead, she smiled and began spooning the soup as rapidly as the girl. To her surprise, after the first mouthful, her hunger drove away any revulsion at the taste. "Well," she said between swallows, "I would prefer a few more worms, but I suppose the stupid men got the good cook."

The girl's dark eyes sparkled under her thick, black eyebrows. "Don't worry. For breakfast we'll probably get fresh eggs and white bread, just like we got from the Zorkas."

Again, Anna had to suppress a surge of anger. Hungarian landlords were not known for their compassion toward Gypsy workers. The landowners provided a bare minimum of potatoes, cabbage and wheat, which the Gypsies themselves ground into flour. The staple diet was augmented by other food they found for themselves, a task at which they were extremely adept, much to the sorrow of many a hen house and pantry.

"If you were a real Gypsy," Anna said, "for breakfast we would have chicken and beer."

The girl laughed ,and despite their hostility, the other women also laughed.

How direct they were, Anna thought. Their thoughts were focused only on the moment. Their discomfort, their misery over the loss of their homes, the forced separation from their men, and perhaps, their parents or children, was thrust aside by the mood of the moment.

"How does it feel to work?" one of the older women said with more than a hint of a sneer in her voice.

Anna stared at the woman until she couldn't meet Anna's gaze any longer and her eyes flickered and turned away. Only then did Anna hold out her hand to show it was red from gripping the handle of an axe. "Terrible. Look. Who ever heard of a Gypsy woman with a blister, unless it was on her tongue."

Again, the women laughed and Anna thought she detected a hint of approval in the eyes of the girl who said, "I am Katalin, queen of the Imri *vistas*. The *kris* elected me." Then she repeated ,as though Anna might not be familiar with the Romani term for the council of tribal elders, "The *kris* elected me."

Katalin's sparkling eyes had turned cold, and her shoulders were hunched forward as though she expected Anna to challenge her authority. But Anna quickly made it clear she was not interested. "Good. I hope you're a good leader. We're going to need one if we're to survive."

At Anna's words, Katalin relaxed into an easy stance, her weight on one leg, balancing with the grace of a dancer. "We are Gypsy. We always survive."

The statement, uttered so matter-of-factly, expressed the blind faith of a people who had survived for hundreds of years despite the worst of man and nature and would, also, survive this latest vicissitude. They always had. But who would be the lucky ones? Was it a matter of luck? Could she do something to tilt the scale in her favor? At the moment, it seemed as though her best chance was to do the work the Nazi's demanded and stay out of trouble.

"Yes," she agreed. "We survive."

As though to countermand the assertion, the barracks door opened and Sergeant Wirtz walked in followed by two guards. "Achtung!" he snapped. "In front of your bunks. Stand!"

Sullenly, the women did as they were told. Anna, at the end of the line, wondered what he could want. Not more work, surely. She estimated it was close to seven P.M. and already dark outside. Maybe some of the women were to be selected to work in the soldier's kitchen. That would really be barbaric. After a long day working on road construction with almost nothing to eat, the women were deathly tired. Still, it might not be so bad. In the kitchen, the quick hands of the Gypsy women would find extra food for everyone. Anna was so hungry that she almost hoped she would be one of those selected.

Sergeant Wirtz waited a moment until they were in place, then he began walking down the isle between the women, moving slowly and staring at each one as he passed. He paused in front of a girl who looked to be about sixteen and jerked his head. "You. Outside."

The girl's face paled and she bit her lips and looked toward an older woman beside her who, Anna thought, was probably her mother. The older woman put her arm out and pulled the girl partially behind her. "No," she said. "Take me. I am stronger. I can work harder."

Without changing expression, Sergeant Wirtz lashed out with the handle of his whip and hit the woman in the face. She cried out and put her hands to her bleeding face and Wirtz jerked the girl from behind her. "For this work," he snarled, "you do not have to be strong. Outside."

The girl hesitated and Wirtz nodded to the guards. One of them grabbed the girl and half led, half dragged her out the door, and the older woman sagged against her bunk, trying to stem the blood that seeped through her fingers. Sergeant Wirtz and the other guard continued walking down the isle, their slow steps sounding a dirge in the deep silence. When they approached Katalin, the guard pointed at her. "That one. I want that one."

His words stabbed through Anna like a hot poker. 'Want?' She tried to shut her mind against the implication, but it was impossible. Sergeant Wirtz had said strength was not required for the 'job' he had in mind. Oh God. The women were so damned helpless. There was absolutely nowhere to turn for help. These men could do anything to them they wanted. Anything. This was what it meant, what it had always meant to be a Gypsy and a woman.

Katalin stared at the guard contemptuously. Then her lips curled in a sneering smile, and without waiting for an order from Sergeant Wirtz, she sauntered to the door, her chin up and her hips swinging.

Wirtz grinned and continued down the corridor. He was moving faster, scarcely glancing at the women he passed, walking directly toward Anna and she searched her mind desperately for a means of escape. God. What was her life that it had come to this? To this moment. To the next awful moments. Had she been born to be a plaything for this beast of a man? The only escape would be in death. But even that was impossible. Why had God made it impossible to die when faced with such a horror? Perhaps if she provoked Wirtz enough, he would kill her. But looking at his face, she knew he would not. People died when Wirtz wanted them to die. He would not allow anyone to escape so easily.

He stopped in front of Anna and she straightened. She could not manifest the disdain Katalin had shown, she was too traumatized for that, but she would not give Wirtz—and the other women—the satisfaction of seeing her cringe. Wirtz lifted his whip and Anna thought he meant to strike her. Instead, he ran the heavy butt down the side of her work shirt, pressing the rough material against her skin. Then he moved the handle to her stomach and moved it up until it stopped at her chest, pushing the material in so he could stare at the swell of her breasts. Anna stood, her hands clinched at her sides, as rigid as rigor mortis, trying to make her mind a total blank.

"You." The voice of Sergeant Wirtz pinioned her like a skewer. "Outside!"

For a second, the darkness she had tried to achieve became real and Anna's knees began to buckle. Then a chill of revulsion tore away the darkness, and her eyes came into focus on Sergeant Wirtz' bestial face. If he were to frown, or sneer, or show anger, she felt that she could endure. But his blank features were like a mask of death; his eyes boring into hers had the dead look of a corpse. With dull resignation she forced her legs to move. After the first steps, she noticed the eyes of the women and her back stiffened. There was no pity in the eyes; only a satisfaction that the daughter of Pal Zorka was going to find out what it was like to be a Gypsy. The eyes also held feelings of relief that it was happening to her and not to them.

Outside, the two guards and their victims were waiting. Night had fallen and stars were beginning to spangle the darkening sky. The air was chilly, filled with the sweet smell of pine. How was it possible that such purity and such evil could occupy the same place at the same time? For the first time that she could remember, Anna wondered at the existence of God. There had been times in her life when tragedy had struck hard at her faith. But nothing like this. Nothing could compare with this awful triumph of evil. All during the walk out the gate and along the road to the guards' quarters, Anna waited for some miracle that would stop the horror. But the night was silent, deathly still, the only sound the crunch of the Germans' heavy boots and the sobs of the young girl as she walked with her head down and her hair falling over her face as though to shut out the world. Katalin strode purposely, with her chin up. Anna had the impression that she felt contempt for any man who was so stupid he had to force a woman into his bed.

Anna's thoughts were in total disarray. She was going to be brutalized, raped and there was no way to escape. If she ran they would only catch her. If she tried to fight, they could easily overcome her. They would not kill her. Not yet.

So, all she could do was try to achieve a mental numbness that would carry her through the horror. But how can you make your mind numb to assault? She had heard that prostitutes could, so perhaps it was possible. But not without long practice. And that would never happen; she would kill herself before she would allow this horror to be repeated over and over.

They entered the guards' barracks through a rear door that opened into the quarters of the Oberscharführer. Wirtz' room reflected the same cold, impersonal blankness as its owner's face. Like the women's barracks, the building was constructed of wooden slabs with the same smell of freshly-cut pine. Also like the women's barracks, the floor was beginning to show cracks and warping as the green wood dried. The furnishings consisted of a single, impeccably made up cot, three straight-back chairs around a table without a tablecloth, a three-drawer bureau, and a wardrobe. Next to the wardrobe was a battered steel filing cabinet. There were two windows, no curtains. On one wall a picture of Hitler was flanked by two Nazi flags. On the top of the bureau were several framed photographs. Light came from a single bulb held in a porcelain-coated shade. An unlit iron stove stood on three curved legs in one corner. Beside it was a scuttle of coal and a box containing chunks of wood.

Sergeant Wirtz grasped Anna's arm. "I take this one." He jerked his head toward the door leading to the guard's quarters. "Take them with you."

"Hans and Dietrick are there," one of the guards said. "We should have brought two more."

"Hans and Dietrick do not deserve women."

"But . . . they will want these."

"Make them wait. Tell them when they do good work, they will have their own. Now, get out!"

The guards pulled the two Gypsy girls to the barracks door and opened it. Katalin stalked through, followed by a guard. The other shoved the young girl through and slammed the door behind him.

Wirtz tossed his whip on the table and went to the stove. "Take off your clothes," he growled as though giving an order to a dog. Without looking at Anna, he bent over the stove and began preparing a fire.

Anna took a breath. Now, it would begin. Could she endure? Was there some weapon she could use to kill Wirtz—or herself? Frantically, she looked around the room. But except for the whip, there was nothing.

Her eyes focused upon the pictures on the bureau, and she saw they were snapshots of Wirtz with members of his family. In the background of some of the pictures, she could see farm buildings and fences. One picture was of a small boy holding a balloon. On the bottom a date was written in ink: April 27, 1917. It was probably Wirtz, and because he was holding a balloon, the date could be his birthday. In another picture Wirtz was standing with his arm around the waist of a plump, blonde girl about his own age. He was smiling so broadly that Anna hardly recognized him. The girl's smile looked forced. Could she be the sergeant's wife?

As she stared at the pictures, an idea began to form. Wirtz had apparently been a farmer. He probably had a limited education. As with many old world peasants, it was likely he had been inculcated with the entire range of Germanic folk superstitions introduced through tales of the Valkyries, of Odin, Thor, Loki, Balder the Beautiful and Hel, the evil serpent surrounding the goddess of death. Did he also possess the age-old superstition, prevalent among many country folk, that some Gypsies women could see into the future and, yes, even invoke Gypsy curses? And if he did, would his superstitious fear be stronger than his sexual desire?

She moved away from the bureau so Wirtz would not suspect she had been looking at the pictures.

With the fire started, Wirtz straightened. He looked at Anna and his eyes narrowed. "I said take off your clothes. I do not want to tear them off." As though to end the discussion, he started to unbutton his tunic.

Anna began to unbutton her shirt as slowly as possible. She focused on Wirtz' blunt fingers as he worked at the buttons of his tunic. She moved toward him so he could not miss seeing her stare at his hands. She backed a step and covered her mouth with one hand while she continued to stare intently at his hands. She was rewarded by seeing Wirtz' fingers freeze and he said, "What is it? What is it?"

Anna backed another step. Without lifting her gaze from Wirtz' motionless hands, she shook her head. "Nothing," she breathed. "Nothing."

Wirtz took a step toward her. His face had lost its blank look as lines of worry wrinkled his forehead. "Nothing? You were looking at something. What? What is it?"

Keeping her look of anguish, wordlessly Anna pointed a trembling finger at Wirtz' hands.

"My hands?" Wirtz turned his hands palm up and stared at them. "What about my hands?"

"No," Anna whispered. "I cannot tell you."

Wirtz' face twisted with the beginning of fright and Anna felt a thrill of joy. She had been right. "You tell me." Wirtz demanded.

Anna again shook her head as though what she had seen was too terrible to tell.

Wirtz put his right hand on the butt of his whip and said again, "You tell me."

Only then did Anna nod. She ran her tongue over her lips as though they were dry with fear and she said, "Let me see your hand." Wirtz always carried the whip in his right hand, so it was undoubtedly his dominant hand. "Your right hand."

He took his hand from the whip and slowly extended it toward Anna. She had him! She blessed her mother for the long hours she had poured Gypsy lore into her head, including the reading of palms. Oh God. She had to remember.

As she took Wirtz' hand, she looked into his face and realized she did not have to be accurate. He was ready to believe. But she had to sound authentic. No telling how many times other Gypsies had read his palm.

She held his right hand supported by her left. "Come. Here, under the light."

She pulled him beneath the light and he came willingly, extending his hand so it was directly beneath the overhead bulb. Anna used the forefinger of her right hand to trace the lines in his palm. It was a broad, flat palm, heavy as lead. Thickly callused. The fingers were blunt and spatulated. The color of the palm was a pronounced red and it was dry to the point of being scaly.

Instead of speaking immediately, Anna stared at the palm intently. She turned it over, looking at the dirt under blunt, cracked nails, touching black hair like wire that covered the back of the hand.

Finally, Wirtz could stand it no longer and he said, "Go on. Tell me."

The worry in his voice gave Anna a sense of satisfaction. The bastard deserved to worry. So what should she tell him? The truth of his innate brutality was easy to read even without looking at his palm. But truth, her mother used to say, would not get you a silver coin. And now she was playing for much more than silver.

She turned his palm back face up. "The right hand," she began, "tells about your past and what you will make of your potential. Let's begin with your health."

"Ja. Good," Wirtz said. "I have good health."

"True. You have excellent health." She paused almost imperceptibly before she added, "For now."

"For now? What do you mean 'for now?'"

"Your palm tells many things and always the truth. You cannot hide the truth from yourself."

Under her finger tip, she could feel the pulse at Wirtz' wrist increase. "Truth? What truth?"

"Let's go to the beginning. I see you are a"—what was the date on the picture? Late April?—
- "a Taurus."

Wirtz' chest swelled. "Ja. That is right. Taurus, the bull."

Anna kept her head bowed to hide her smile. "You are from the country. I see that you have worked on a farm."

"Ja. My family, we are all farmers."

This one was going to be a little tricky. "And you are married."

"Married? Ja. How many children do you see?"

Anna released her held breath. She had been right about the blonde girl in the picture. Married to this brute, no wonder it had been hard for her to smile. And the children? That was easy. She touched just below his little finger. "Five children. I see five children."

"Five? I have only one."

Ah, good. This was the opening she had hoped for. "I see five. You will have four more, if . . ." She let her voice trail off.

"If what?"

"If you watch your health. See how red your palm is? And dry?" She curled his fingers to show the nails. "See how brittle your nails." She ran the tip of her finger along his life line. "You have a nice long life line. But see how it breaks in several places?"

Wirtz bent his blunt head to stare at his palm. "What does that mean?"

"It means you will live to a very old age if you take care of your health."

"There is nothing wrong with my health."

"Your hand tells the truth."

"Truth? What truth? What?"

"The nails, the dryness, the red skin. They do not lie. Let me see your hand of destiny."

"My hand of destiny?"

"Your left hand."

He changed hands and she studied his left palm intently, tracing the lines with her fingers. His palm was no longer dry. It was filmed with sweat. She touched his heart line. "This is your heart line, here. I can see that you are under great strain from people who do not understand you."

"Ja. That is true."

"That means your heart is also under great strain."

"My heart? My heart is good. I am a Taurus, the bull."

"Bulls do not have the problems you have."

Wirtz made a growling sound. "That is very true. I have nothing but problems. Anything goes wrong, it is the fault of the Oberscharführer. Always my fault."

"That is because you are so sensitive. See. Here. On your Mount of Venus. But do not worry. Here, on your Plain of Mars. See this small pattern of lines?"

She pointed to the nonexistent pattern of lines, and as she expected, Wirtz saw what he wanted to see. "Ja. What does it mean?"

"It means great honor will come to you."

"Ahhhh."

". . . If you live."

"My heart?"

"Exactly. You must guard your heart carefully. Avoid strain. Your life will have great rewards . . . see, here, lines at the base of Jupiter . . . if you do not cause your heart to burst. And here. See how deep is your life-line. That shows you try too hard to please others at your own expense."

"At my own expense, ja."

"And here, again, in your fate line. Great success. Great wealth."

"Wealth? Me?

"It's all here in your hand and your hand does not lie. If you do not cut your life short."

"Are you sure about my heart? I feel fine."

"I am not the one to ask. You must ask your palm. What I have seen, you have seen. Have I concealed anything from you?"

"Well, no."

"Have I lied to you?"

"No."

"Has your palm been right about your strength, your power and about how other people use you?"

"Yes. It is right about that."

"Then why would it lie about your heart?"

Wirtz' hand trembled and closed into a fist as though to shut the truth from sight. As he turned away, Anna noticed his forehead was beaded with sweat and there were dark patches on his shirt beneath his armpits. "I don't believe you," he snarled. "You Gypsies are all liars."

Anna was ready with the correct answer. "Even if we are, your own hand does not lie. How could it? It is what you have made it; what you will make it. The hand always speaks the truth."

Wirtz sank to his bed, sitting with his shoulders slumped and his head down. He ran the fingers of both hands through his stubbled hair. "But my hand also held great honor. Even wealth."

"It promised those things, yes."

"If one thing is true, then all must be true."

Anna smiled inwardly. He was thinking exactly as she had hoped. He probably had a heart as strong as any bull, but now it was filled with doubt. He would feel pain where there was no pain, a racing pulse where there was no race. All thoughts of sex had been wiped from his mind by his mounting worry. But now she had to cement her small victory, make sure his cold Teutonic reason did not overcome his superstition.

"I have Tarot cards," she said. "Tomorrow night we can read the cards. They will tell if there is a mistake or a lie."

Wirtz looked up, hope making his dull eyes gleam. "A mistake? Yes. That is possible. Tomorrow you will bring the cards."

Anna went to the door. "Tomorrow. I will bring the cards. But for now, beware of your heart."

She opened the door and walked out, closing the door softly. At every step as she walked away, she expected to hear the sound of the door being wrenched open and Wirtz' harsh command to halt. But the command did not come and she hurried toward the barracks gate. Then she paused. Should she try to escape? She was outside the wire of the compound. The deserted road was before her. If Wirtz did not sound an alarm, she would not be missed until morning.

She looked at the blackness of the mountains silhouetted against the starry night sky. She could hide in the mountains, sustain herself on berries until she could make her way back to Eger. There she could get help. Or could she? Certainly not from Albrecht Grantz. And how many others did he control? He was a power in the community, and there were not many who could—or would—take her side over his. And even they would not lift a finger to help a Gypsy. They might not aid the Nazis in their kidnappings, but they would not stop them either.

So where could she turn? Of course! The American embassy in Budapest. That was her only chance. Her impulse was to run, to leave this hated place as far behind as possible. But which direction? She had no idea where they were. Were they in Germany? Czechoslovakia? Austria? What was the point in running if she had no direction? She might be able to survive indefinitely in the forest, but without any real source of food, she would eventually have to seek out some kind of civilization where she would likely be caught and brought back. What would Sergeant Wirtz do then? The thought had the chill of death. Before she escaped she would need more information. If she used the Tarot cards properly, she could get Wirtz to tell her. As long as she could keep him and the other guards at bay, there was no hurry.

She was approaching the gate to the women's compound when she heard the muffled sound of screaming from the guard's barracks. It was the young girl. God only knew what the guards were doing to her—and Katalin. She put her hands over her ears and ran.

Chapter 12

Eric lay on the thin mattress of his bunk, wondering what time it was. He had told Anna he would meet her at ten. It had to be close to that now. Unlike most Gypsies, he had developed an appreciation for time. Being able to plan and maintain schedules was one of the major reasons why the Gorgios had been able to rise to positions of power over the elements as well as over people who had no respect for time. Although like all Gypsies, he still abhorred watches, he had honed his instinct for time to a fine degree, so that he usually knew the hour within a few minutes of that indicated by a watch.

The other men were asleep, those who could sleep. But after a long, long night in the railroad car followed by hours of hard physical labor, even their worst fears could not keep most of them awake. If anyone did notice when Eric slipped out the door, they would think he was going to the latrine.

Outside, an overcast of low clouds had formed blocking the faint starlight and bringing the smell of winter. The camp's electricity came from a generator that throbbed somewhere in the distance so there was little power available for security lights. Also, the porcelain-shaded bulbs were widely spaced around the periphery fence leaving deep pools of darkness. Eric was confident the tower guards could not see him if he kept out of the direct light. But rather than take a chance, he headed for the men's latrine, which, like the women's, was a deep trench in the earth with a peeled pine log stretched over it to sit on. As he walked, he studied the shadows. There were no lights situated along the barbed-wire fence that separated the women's compound from the men's, so the base of the fence was shrouded in darkness, as he had thought it would be.

From the latrine, Eric walked back toward his barracks. When he reached the shadow of its wall, he edged along the side until he was away from the glow of the periphery lights, then he moved swiftly to the fence and crouched in the darkness to wait.

Would Anna come? He was certain she would if it was at all possible. But she might be late. As with him, she had no way of telling the time and she might not be very good at guessing.

He stretched out on the cold, damp grass wondering how long he could wait without being seen by a sharp-eyed guard. Since this was the first night the camp was occupied, the guards might be more alert than usual. He would give Anna a half-hour. If she did not arrive, he would come back tomorrow night and each night for as long as it took to reach her.

He was struck by wonder at his thought. Why did he have this burning desire to see Ravanna? Why should he risk his life to see a woman he hardly knew and who, he was sure, could never really see anything more in him than a poor, wandering Gypsy? Maybe it was because he felt responsible for her safety. The idea almost made him laugh. Since when did a Gypsy vagabond feel a sense of responsibility for anyone or anything beyond himself? Perhaps for his mother and father. But that was the end of the line.

Memory of his father changed his smile to a grimace of hate. As much as he cared for Anna, he could not allow his feelings to interfere with his quest for the man who had killed his father. The man was out there somewhere and Eric would find him. By the gods, he would find him.

His thoughts were interrupted by a soft sound, and he saw a shadowy figure dash from the darkness of the women's barracks and drop to the ground beside the fence. He got to his feet, and moving rapidly in a crouch, he ran toward her.

When Anna saw him her head jerked up, startled, and he whispered. "Anna. It's me."

He heard her breath released and he flopped down beside her, his face close to hers, only the cruel barbs of the fence separating them. He put his hand through the fence and she held it hard in both of hers.

"Oh God," she whispered. "I was afraid you wouldn't come."

"I'll be here. Every night if it's possible."

"Oh yes. I really need you."

"I looked for you today, but I couldn't find you."

"And I looked for you."

"We've got to be careful about that. They might get suspicious."

"You're right. But if . . . if I'm ever late here, will you wait for me?"

"Yes. As long as I can. Those guards might be stupid, but even they might notice if we have to wait too long."

"I know. I'll try not. But . . . sometimes I might be late."

There was a quality in her voice that alarmed Eric. "What is it? What have they done?"

"Nothing yet. But I don't know how long I can stop him."

"Stop who? What?"

"The Oberscharführer. Wirtz." Anna, her voice trembling in a husky whisper, told him what had happened to herself and the other two girls. Eric ached with impotent anger when she told about being taken to Sergeant Wirtz' quarters, but he felt a swell of pride when she told about how she had fooled Wirtz by reading his palm.

"Tomorrow night I will read the Tarot cards," she concluded. "But if I can't keep his mind off . . . what he wants to do, I don't know what might happen."

Eric clutched her hand fiercely. "You've got to. Tell him anything. Keep hitting at his health. Men who think they're going to have a heart attack don't want women."

"God! Sometimes I wonder. But how long can I keep on reading the cards? I can't do that forever?"

Eric didn't like to think about what would happen if the brutal Wirtz tired of the game. "Maybe he'll find another woman; leave you alone."

"I don't think so. He knows I'm "—she hesitated—"different from the others."

"All right. Keep him thinking that. Make him afraid to touch you."

"How? I can't keep it up forever."

"Maybe you can. What do you know about the stars?"

"The stars? Astrology?"

"Yes. Tell him that you'll cast his chart. That'll take a long time. Once it's cast, you can use it to give him a reading every day."

"Yes. If I can make him depend on me, maybe I can even make him do things to help the others."

"Maybe. But it's yourself you've got to think of first. If he tries to touch you, tell him it'll ruin your concentration. Tell him that Gypsies have to give up even thinking about sex when they're working with the stars or the readings will be wrong."

"Is that true? My mother never told me that."

Eric chuckled. "No, of course not. Or there would never be any Gypsy children. But make him think so."

"All right. I think I can handle Wirtz. I might even be able to make him take me off work on the road. But what about you? Everybody's going to die out there."

Eric tended to agree. But he didn't want to worry her so he said, "Don't worry about me. I've already started working on my way out."

"How? What can you do?"

Eric was saved a lie by the thud of footsteps. Looking toward the periphery fence he saw the beam of a flashlight being carried by a patrolling guard. He also saw that the guard's other hand held the leash of a huge German Shepherd. If the guard did not see them, the dog probably would.

"Go," he whispered. "Quickly."

As she pushed to her feet, Anna whispered. "Tomorrow."

"Yes. Tomorrow."

Then he was running in a crouch through the darkness back to the barracks. When he slipped into his bunk, his brain was whirling with mixed feelings. He was filled with relief that Anna was all right, but he also knew she was treading on thin ice with that big *arschloch* Wirtz. If the bastard found out she was running a flimflam, no telling what he would do.

He drifted into sleep trying to think of a way he could save both of them before it was too late.

The next day he saw something that made him think it could be done. He had been assigned to the wood cutting detail and was wielding an axe against the trunk of a thick pine tree, using as little energy as possible, when he saw the Waffen SS soldiers and the SS-T guards snap to attention. He searched for the cause and saw von Liebermann ride into the area on his white mare. He was followed by an open Kubelwagen being driven by an SS Oberscharführer. Seated beside him was an Obersleutnant of the German Wehrmacht. His collar carried the insignia of an engineer. As he and von Liebermann sat observing the work, two of the sergeants hurried to the vehicle and saluted. Von Liebermann lifted his riding crop in languid return, and the guards turned their attention back to the prisoners. But they did not relax. It was never a good idea to appear inattentive when field grade officers were nearby, especially when one of them was an SS Colonel with a Death's Head on his hat and a pistol on his belt.

The Gypsies also felt the added peril and worked a little harder. The whips and truncheons of the Oberscharführers and the guards were bad, the pistol was infinitely worse.

Eric watched warily as the engineer got out of the Kubelwagen. He walked beside von Liebermann's horse as they moved through the woods toward a party of Wehrmacht surveyors who were staking out the road's route. Von Liebermann slid off his horse, handing the reins to one of the SS guards. When von Liebermann walked away with the engineer, the horse began browsing on grass and bushes. The horse was the key. Von Liebermann already knew that Eric was an expert with horses. He had to find a way to make the Kommandant need that expertise. But how? He must already have someone in charge of his stable. Even the dumbest soldier could shovel manure—as long as there were no problems. So, it was up to him to create a problem. Suppose, for instance, the mare got sick? Would a soldier know what to do? He might if he were a farm boy and the sickness was something ordinary like mange or worms. But suppose the sickness was something unfamiliar? Like poison.

As he worked, Eric studied the plants that grew profusely on the floor of the forest. Judging from the terrain, they were somewhere in southern Germany or western Czechoslovakia. And the weather had not, as yet, turned cold enough to kill much of the summer growth. He should be able to find something: monkshood, foxglove, belladonna, but he could see none of them.

He had almost decided he would have to cause an injury to the animal, a far more dangerous ruse, when he noticed a plant with delicate, fern-like leaves that made him smile. Larkspur. That would do. He'd seen entire herds of cattle become deathly sick after eating the leaves of the tall plant.

But how was he going to get the horse to eat it? The horse was not going to walk over and begin munching. He would have to take it to the horse. If the SS guard suspected anything, he would probably be beaten senseless, or shot. Still, he had to take the chance. There might never be another.

He redoubled his effort with the axe, sending fat chips flying despite its dull edge, until the tree shuddered, cracked and fell with a crash. Eric moved around and began trimming the branches from the fallen tree. When he saw his chance, he reached down and broke off one of the Larkspur bush's feathery branches. Then he gathered an armful of pine boughs he had lopped from the fallen tree. Concealing the Larkspur branch at the bottom of the pile, he began carrying the load toward a group of women who were burning cleared brush and boughs. He altered his course to pass close to the mare where he let several of the pine boughs fall as though they had slipped from his grasp. While the SS guard holding the horse's reins stared at him suspiciously, he quickly knelt and retrieved them, except for the small Larkspur branch which he pushed almost under the horse's nose. "Bedauern," he muttered submissively so the guard.

He was getting to his feet when he was driven to his knees by a hard blow to his ribs. "Get out. Schnell."

Gritting his teeth against the pain, Eric stumbled to his feet. His ribs would be sore for a long time. Still, if his plan worked, it would be worth it.

As he made his way toward the nearest fire, he scanned the faces of the women, hoping to see Anna. But she was nowhere in sight. She was probably working at one of the other fires.

He was dumping his load of branches on the fire when he felt a burning pain across his shoulders and heard the voice of the women's Oberscharführer snarling, "Get back to work, *Schweinhund.* Let the women do that."

Eric ducked his head as he turned so that the next blow of the whip raised a bloody welt on his forehead instead of across his eyes and he saw that an SS sergeant was raising his whip for another blow. "Sorry, Herr Oberscharführer," he said quickly. This was the sergeant Anna had called Wirtz, the son-of-a-pig who had taken her to his quarters, the one she had told had problems with his heart.

Eric sized on the knowledge to clutch his own chest as he quickly added, "Please, Herr Oberscharführer. My heart. I have heart trouble. Swinging the axe is bad for it. You must know. It is like swinging your whip. A terrible strain on the heart."

Wirtz' arm halted in mid swing and the trailing length of the whip fell to the ground behind him. Wirtz grimaced in sudden pain and his peculiar eyes opened wide as though he could not believe what was happening to him. He jerked his head. "Go! Back to work! You cut trees. That's all."

"Jawohl, Herr Oberscharführer," Eric said. Keeping his shoulders bent obsequiously, he sidled past Wirtz. He glanced back to see Wirtz rub a hand across his chest before he began coiling his whip slowly, his mouth creased in a puzzled frown as though he could not believe how such a terrible thing could be happening to him.

As he retrieved his axe, Eric glanced toward the white mare. She was nibbling the Larkspur. She did not have to eat much. Only a few leaves would soon cause inflammation in her mouth and vomiting. It was a sad thing to have to do to such a beautiful animal, but it might save his life. Now, he could only wait and see.

Chapter 13

The overcast sky was losing its light when a Kubelwagen being driven by an SS guard approached at high speed and bounced to a stop near the work crews. The driver, a young SS Oberschutze, shouted at Sergeant Blumdorf, the men's Oberscharführer, and Blumdorf leaped into action. He trotted toward the weary Gypsy men, uncoiling his whip.

"Imri," he shouted. "Which of you is Imri, the horse trader?"

The Gypsies stopped work to stare, and Blumdorf began lashing the nearest man with his whip, driving the man to his knees. "Where is he?" Blumdorf shouted. "Where is Imri?"

Eric dropped his axe and bolted forward to catch Blumdorf's arm before he could deliver another blow. "Here," he said. "I am Imri."

Blumdorf's broad face contorted with fury and he jerked his arm from Eric's grasp. "You *Arschloch!* Don't touch me! Don't ever touch me!" He pulled his whip back to lash at Eric, but the Oberschutze snapped, "Sergeant Blumdorf, the Kommandant wants this man. Mach schnell."

Blumdorf let his arm drop reluctantly, and he jerked the butt of his whip toward the Kubelwagen as he said to Eric. "All right. Go. I will get to you when you come back."

You'll have a long wait, Eric thought as he climbed in the Kubelwagen. He had no intention of returning to the barracks until the stupid Scharführer was asleep. He would not return at all except that he wanted to meet Anna at the fence that night. If he got the job he was after, he would have to think of another place to meet her, a place that would allow them to be alone.

As they drove away, Blumdorf lashed out with his whip at the staring Gypsy men, shouting, "Back to work, you dirty Gypsy pigs. Back to work," and Eric mentally etched the man's name into his memory. Sergeant Blumdorf. One more candidate for revenge.

The SS guard drove the jeep-like vehicle at a fast pace along the rutted dirt road, snaking around trucks hauling pine logs and a tracked bulldozer scraping the surface of the new road. Behind the bulldozer, a work detail of Gypsy men shoveled loose dirt into rough boxes attached to two pine bough handles. When a box was full two Gypsies picked it up like a litter and carried it forward to fill in low areas in the road ahead. At one of the litters, an old man struggled to lift the front end. When he was unable to do so, the SS guard began smashing him with his truncheon. Before the Kubelwagen sped around a curve, Eric saw the old man lying motionless, face down in the mud, his head covered with blood. But the image that stayed with him was the look of pleasure that had been on the face of the guard as he had swung the truncheon. He stared out the windshield trying to put reason on the scene. Where had such men grown up? What values had they been taught? If there had been no war, no despot like Hitler, would that man have been a peaceful farmer? A school teacher? An accountant? Or would he have become a guard in a prison? Or a policeman? Or was it that there had been no such passion for violence until the opportunity was present? Which had come first? Had the lust sought out the opportunity, or had the opportunity brought out the lust?

One thing was certain: the labor camps twisted the souls of everyone, guard and prisoner alike. Anyone who entered hell could not escape being horribly scared by the flames.

There was one more certainty: when one was being beaten, it mattered little how the guard became such a brute. It certainly did not matter to the old man lying face down in the mud. Perhaps his soul now knew the answer.

On the macadam road, the driver drove so fast he had trouble controlling the small vehicle. A little past the headquarters complex, the vehicle almost overturned when the driver clamped on the brakes and skidded onto a gravel road leading to the large stable on the knoll. The stable and a fence surrounding the pasture were painted brilliant white. Around the inside of the fence was a wide bridal path surfaced with tanbark. Von Liebermann, still wearing his riding clothes, was pacing in front of the stable's wide double-door, impatiently slapping his boots with his riding crop. He stopped to watch when the vehicle skidded to a stop, scattering mud and rocks.

Eric released his grip on the edge of the windscreen and climbed to the ground. Von Liebermann gave him a sharp look of recognition, then said, "Kommen Sie," and strode into the building. Hurrying after the Kommandant, Eric felt a grim pleasure. As he had guessed, Von Liebermann and whoever he had chosen to be his groom, were apparently ignorant about horse ailments.

Unlike the Gypsy's barracks, the stable was solidly constructed of cured lumber with no cracks in the walls. The ceiling was high and braced with thick beams. The windows were large and perfectly glazed with no cracks or crevices where wind could enter and cause one of the horses to catch cold. There were stalls for ten horses, but only three were occupied. The mare was in one stall and the others were occupied by a dun-colored gelding and a big blue stallion that looked as though he would be too much for von Liebermann to handle. The floors of the stalls were wood, but the stable's center floor was concrete with a wide isle, depressed in the center for the runoff of water. The rear of the building had been walled off to form a tack room.

The entire area was immaculately clean. Even the straw that had been placed on the floor of the stalls was clean and sweet. Except for that of the white mare. She had been vomiting and was now standing with her head down, breathing heavily, her eyes dull with misery, her sides heaving and saliva drooling from her mouth, which she continuously licked with her dry tongue. A very young Waffen SS soldier was standing beside her with his jacket off and the sleeves of his shirt rolled up. He was using a sponge and water from a bucket to soak her back and sides, looking as miserable as the mare. He was probably the groom, some poor minion who had volunteered for what he had thought would be an easy job and which now might get him shot.

Von Liebermann slapped the side of his boot with his riding crop with a pop that made the other two horses start. The mare did not so much as roll her eyes. "Tell me," he said. "What is wrong with her?"

Eric shrugged. "I will have to made an examination."

"Then do so. Quickly."

"Very well." Eric looked at the other two horses and decided to give the Nazi more concern. "If I were you, I would put those horses somewhere else. This could be contagious."

Von Liebermann's face tightened and he screamed at the soldier with the bucket. "Idiot! Why didn't you do that?"

The soldier bit his lip so hard he almost drew blood. "Sorry, Herr Kommandant. Sorry."

He stood with the bucket in one hand and the sponge in the other, his rolled up sleeves and the front of his shirt and pants soaked with water, his eyes wide with fright.

"Well, do it!" von Liebermann screeched. "Now!"

The soldier dropped the bucket to salute. "Jawohl, Herr Kommandant."

He threw the sponge in the bucket, and glad for the opportunity to escape, leaped to lead the stallion and the gelding outside. Von Liebermann watched anxiously as Eric moved into the mare's stall. Whoever had built the stable had been a fine workman, but he had made the stalls too small. If a horse ever cast, it would not have enough room to throw its head forward and it would have to be dragged out of the stall before it could get up. The small size of the stall also made it difficult to work with a sick horse. When a horse was in pain, it could do a lot of threshing around, and being trapped in a small stall with a desperate horse could be dangerous, even fatal.

The mare, however, was enduring her misery stoically, with little movement, so that Eric was able to move in beside her, confident that she would not grow violent. As von Liebermann watched, he rolled up the sleeves of his jacket and pretended to conduct an examination, peering into the horse's eyes and mouth and feeling her stomach. He knew the amount of Larkspur the horse had consumed was discomforting but not lethal. If he did nothing at all, the animal would recover in a day or two.

But he could not allow that to happen. He had to make the Nazi believe the recovery was due to his ministrations, so he straightened and put on a grave expression. "It isn't worms or colic. I thought it might be a torsion of the bowels, but she'd be in a lot more pain."

"Is it contagious?" Worry made von Liebermann's voice high and tight.

"Not unless it's the Strangles."

"Strangles? What's that?"

"Distemper. But I doubt that. She doesn't have swollen lymph glands under her jaws."

Von Liebermann could not decide whether that was good news or bad. "So, what is it?"

"I think she's been poisoned."

"Poisoned!" Von Liebermann's start was so violent he struck his elbow on a post. "What son-of-a-pig would poison my horse?" His face was contorted in a fury so malevolent that Eric quickly made a new evaluation of the man. Despite his scholarly demeanor when he was calm, fury revealed a hard edge of violence.

"I didn't say somebody did it," Eric said quickly. "It was probably something she ate. Those woods are full of poison plants."

Von Liebermann's face resumed its worried look as he stared at the mare's drooping head and the ropes of saliva drooling from her mouth. "Oh," he said. "Can you save her?"

"Depends on what she ate and now much. If it was Belladonna or Foxglove, probably not. If it was something else, there's a chance."

"Medication. You will need medication. We have medication in the pharmacy."

"Good. I will need iodine, sodium bicarbonate, aspirin." He named as many items as he thought he could justify. He would need none of them, but this might be his only chance to obtain medication that he could smuggle into the barracks for the other Gypsies.

He had no reason to worry about von Liebermann's suspicions. The man knew nothing of horses. Eric could have asked for crutches and he would have agreed.

"All right. We will go to the pharmacy. You can pick out what you need."

As they went out the door, the young German soldier was returning, his face drawn with fear and worry. "Get fresh water," Eric told him. "Bath her mouth."

The inside of the mare's mouth and lips were blistered from the effects of the poison, and there was no reason for her to suffer any more than necessary. The cold water would help relieve her discomfort.

The soldier looked at von Liebermann who nodded and the boy ran into the stable.

As they walked at a fast pace down the knoll to Headquarters, Eric took advantage of the time to implant more ideas. "After the mare is well enough, you should have her hoofs trimmed and shod. The others need it too."

Von Liebermann's long strides faltered. "They need it? Need it?"

"Yes," Eric lied. "I'm sure you noticed that cracking has already started."

"Cracking. I'll have that dummkopf shot."

"It's probably not his fault. You have to know what to look for. If he's not an expert . . ." Eric let the sentence hang.

The Nazi's jaw tightened and he did not answer. Eric smiled to himself. The hook was in the fish.

Inside Headquarters, the Kommandant led the way to a wing of the building that housed a small pharmacy equipped with a doctor's examination table and a weight and height scale. One wall was lined with floor to ceiling cabinets with clear glass windows. The cabinets were well stocked with pharmaceuticals and medical supplies. An open door disclosed an adjacent infirmary room with four empty beds. Von Liebermann moved to the cabinets and flung open their doors.

"Here. Take what you need."

Eric picked up an empty shipping box and rapidly begin filling it with the medication he believed would be most useful to the Gypsies. When the box was full he made a show of looking for the items he really needed.

"What is it?" von Liebermann snapped.

"The most important things: apple cider vinegar and honey."

Von Liebermann's eyes narrowed. "You are joking. That is not medicine."

"These are good," Eric said, indicating the box. "And we will need them. But first we must treat the poison. And for that, we will need what Gypsies always use: honey and apple cider vinegar."

"I don't believe you, nor your Gypsy remedies. You are after food."

Eric took a gamble that von Liebermann's anger was not as strong as his desire to save the horse and he dropped the box of supplies. "All right. You cure him."

The Nazi's mouth opened in shock. Then it snapped shut as fury mottled his face and his hand came up with his riding crop. Eric thought for a moment that he had made a bad mistake. Then the Kommandant's hand dropped and his jaw clinched so hard the muscles bulged in his temples, and his lips thinned until they were edged with white. "Kommen Sie," he gritted. He turned on his heel and walked out the door, his back like a ramrod, his neck red and bowed like a bad-tempered stallion.

Eric picked up the box and followed him. Even with his long legs, he had to move fast to keep up with von Liebermann. As they moved along the building's corridors, the Kommandant's boot heels announced their coming and everyone they passed snapped to attention, holding the pose rigidly until von Liebermann had passed. Walking behind the SS officer, Eric watched the performance carefully. He noted the way von Liebermann made the smallest gesture with his head in acknowledgement of a nod from a field grade officer, but offered not the slightest recognition to the lower grades or to noncoms. And as he moved, he occasionally popped his boot with the riding crop as though to add a further warning to the sound of his distinctive footsteps.

Eric also studied the building and the rooms they passed. Like the stable, the headquarters building was well constructed, as though it had been put together by experienced carpenters. The floors were parquet hardwood and the walls had a wainscot of wood that looked like maple. Weather stripping had been placed around every window and door, and the walls looked thick, as though they were designed to keep out the cold in winter and the heat in summer. It was obvious that most of the money designated for the camp had gone into the headquarters complex and, probably, the officers' quarters, not to mention the stable. When they had built the prisoner's barracks, either they had used up all their construction funds or they had deliberately built them so the inmates would suffer from exposure, perhaps die if the winter was severe.

In the kitchen, through which von Liebermann led Eric, three huge coal-burning, cast-iron stoves radiated welcome heat and the smell of baking bread. Eric walked slowly so he could absorb as much heat as possible. His eyes feasted on huge kettles of simmering stew where he saw carrots and onions and pieces of meat. They had interrupted the cooks' preparation of the evening officer's meal, and in an oven whose door had just been opened by one of the cooks, who was now standing at rigid attention, Eric saw freshly baked potatoes, and he had to force himself to pass without lunging for the incredible feast.

He was almost relieved when von Liebermann went through a door into the kitchen's supply room. But the temptation returned with greater intensity when he saw dozens of loaves of hard-crusted white bread stacked on a table in the center of the room. Their aroma was like a powerful stimulant. Eric fought back an insane desire to touch one of the loaves, simply to touch it, to feel the crust under his fingers, to dig into the soft center, to wrench loose a chunk and stuff it into his mouth before von Liebermann could turn and catch him.

He did none of these. He stood impassively as von Liebermann said to a cook who had been taking onions from a bin, "Give him what he needs. Honey. And . . ." Von Liebermann looked at Eric.

"Apple cider vinegar," Eric prompted.

"Apple cider vinegar, yes," von Liebermann echoed.

It did not seem physically possible, but, somehow, the cook cringed while at the same time remaining as rigid as a steel post. "Jawohl, Herr Kommandant."

"Well, do it!"

The cook leaped as though kicked by a horse and flung open a bottom cabinet. He pulled out a large five-liter can of clover honey and put it on the table. He looked at the Kommandant. "More, Herr Kommandant?"

The Nazi again glanced at Eric and caught him staring at the bread. "Enough, Gypsy?" he snapped.

Eric jerked his head around. "Yes, yes. You have apple cider vinegar?"

The man's fear of authority was so great that he almost shouted, "Jawohl, Herr Gypsy," and sprang to another cabinet and yanked open the door. He peered at an array of bottles, trying to sort out the vinegar. He turned his head to look at the Gypsy, on the verge of panic. "I have white vinegar and red wine vinegar."

"No," Eric said. "It must be apple cider vinegar."

The cook began sorting through the bottles, his hands trembling and sweat running down his cheeks. Eric was surprised and puzzled by the man's fear. If the man had been a prisoner, he might be severely beaten or killed merely for hesitating. But this was a soldier. He had nothing to fear except perhaps a dressing down or, at worst, a few days in a guard house. But the man's fear went beyond reason. It was as though he looked upon the SS officer was some kind of demon who could condemn his soul to hell. And the fear was not unusual. Eric had seen it in the face of the young groom. Even the SS sergeants. Was it solely for von Liebermann, or did it apply to any SS-T officer? Maybe the silver Death's Head on their visored caps had something to do with it. He would have to find out.

While the cook rooted among the bottles in the cupboard, Eric said to von Liebermann, "The vinegar will help counter the alkaline in the poison. The honey will sooth the lining of the stomach and help absorb the vinegar. The fructose in the honey will also give the animal energy, which it badly needs."

Von Liebermann's chin lifted as he stared at Eric. "Why didn't you tell me this before?"

"I wanted you to trust me."

"You wanted to make a fool of me."

Eric felt a lump begin to form in his stomach. The man was a total egomaniac. In the future, he would have to be very careful about how he was approached. "No, no, Herr Kommandant," he corrected. "It is only that you have such a mastery of horses, I assumed that you also possessed more than ordinary knowledge of equine medicine. I did not think that an explanation was necessary."

The SS officer's lower lip pushed forward in a thoughtful pout as he studied the Gypsy. Eric knew that if the man were to detect even a hint of derision, he would probably be dead within the hour.

But von Liebermann wanted to believe. He made a tight smile and picked up one of the loaves of bread and tossed it to Eric. "Here, Gypsy. You must remain strong if you are to work for me."

The cook's smothered grunt of triumph as he emerged from the cabinet clutching a large bottle of apple cider vinegar was lost to Eric. He was savoring von Liebermann's words. The first part of his gamble had paid off.

As they went out the door, von Liebermann made him remember who he was. "If the horse dies," he said matter-of-factly, "I will have you thrown in the latrine pit."

"It will not die, Herr Kommandant."

"Good. You will still be whipped. Five lashes."

"Whipped? Why?"

For the first time, Eric heard Von Liebermann chuckle. "For the horse you sold me in Salzburg. Three days after I bought it, it died."

Five lashes. Eric almost thought it was worth it. Almost.

Chapter 14

Anna lay in her bunk waiting for the summons she knew would come. She pulled the single thin blanket around her in a vain attempt to keep out a gathering chill. This time she would take the blanket with her. Last night when she had returned from her visit with Oberscharführer Wirtz, she had to fight the Gypsy women in the bunk below who had appropriated it. She did not blame the woman for taking the blanket. For generations the Gypsies had lived with the credo that appropriation of unattended articles was not a crime, but rather, a right. It was one of the customs that had grown out of a desperate struggle to survive, just as Anna was now engaged in a struggle to survive.

For the hundredth time, she touched the deck of Tarot cards in her pocket to make sure they were there. They were to be the key that would not only save her life, but which she hoped would save her from being raped. It all depended upon the story told by the cards and her wits.

"Will they come again tonight?"

Anna turned on her side and saw the young girl who had been chosen the night before clutching the edge of the bunk with hands stained with pine tar and ground-in dirt. She was so small that her huge eyes were scarcely level with the top bunk. She still bore the marks of abduction in the form of dark bruises on her face and her eyes were worn and bloodshot from hours of crying.

"Yes," Anna said, and at the girl's look of fright, she quickly added. "I don't think they'll chose you again."

"Why not? She gave them a good time last night."

Katalin sauntered toward them, a cigarette trailing smoke, her lips curled in a smile. The girl stared at her like a startled fawn, then her face contorted in shame. She buried her face in her hands and flung herself onto her bunk, sobs racking her body.

Anna glared at Katalin. "Why did you have to make such a stupid remark?"

"Stupid? When is the truth stupid?"

"When it's used to hurt somebody."

"She's too soft. She'll never get out of this place."

Anna knew she was right. The girl did not possess the necessary toughness, the will to survive. Her only hope was if, somehow, she could be goaded into reaching down into herself and finding a tough knot of hate that would make it a personal affront not to survive. But Anna could not believe Katalin was trying to do that for the girl. Such psychology was not part of her knowledge, and certainly, not of her instinct. But being malicious was.

Anna indicated the cigarette in Katalin's hand. "I see you've found a way to survive very well."

Katalin laughed and blew smoke at Anna. "And you. I don't see any bruises on you."

Anna felt her face tighten. Is that what these women thought, that she had been the plaything of Sergeant Wirtz? But why should she care what they thought? Except that telling herself she did not care, failed to make it true. There was something in everyone—except psychopaths—that made them care what other people thought of them, no matter how much they denied it. But how could she make them realize the truth without giving away her secret? If she did that, anyone of them could do the same—or attempt to. And that would ruin it all.

No. She had to find another explanation that was plausible.

"I got him drunk," she said with a superior smile. "You all know how great men are as lovers when they're drunk."

Some of the women laughed and one said, "My husband, the lover. One drink and he couldn't get his pants off."

Katalin studied Anna, blowing smoke toward the ceiling. "Maybe he'll want to finish it tonight."

Anna smiled archly. "If he does, we'll see who gets finished."

Katalin laughed. "Well, I hope they choose me again. I need cigarettes. I bet I can even get some schnapps."

"I hope you give them something for it." Anna could not resist the dig. "Something they don't want."

The Gypsy girl's face darkened, then her smile flashed. "I'll give them something all right. It's called 'the Gypsy Curse.'" She made the sign of horns with her right hand.

The women's laughter was cut short by the opening of the door. A chill wind swept through the barracks as Sergeant Wirtz and three SS guards walked in. Two of the guards were those from the previous night. As he stood just inside the door, Wirtz pounded the handle of his whip into his palm so that it made the familiar popping sound. "Achtung!" he snarled. "Line up in front of your bunks. Schnell! Schnell!"

While slowly forming two lines, each woman's face reflected her emotion. For some it was contempt. For some it was apprehension. For most it was fear and loathing. Only a few were able to keep their faces impassive, a difficult feat for Gypsy women who were used to displaying their emotions like a banner. Anna stood staring straight ahead, but she sensed the girl beside her trembling, and she could hear her shuddering breaths of fear.

Wirtz led the way down the line, pausing from time to time to peer at one of the women. He made two women open their shirts so he could see the size of their breasts. But Anna knew he was not going to choose any of them. She was the one he wanted. He was putting on a show as he moved toward her.

But the SS guards were making their selections. One of those from the previous night whispered something to Wirtz and the sergeant laughed and pointed out Katalin. "You. Come. You have made a conquest."

Katalin stepped forward and took hold of the guard's arm. "Koman Sie, mein little knockwurst," she said in a mixture of bad German and Romani. "I hope you got plenty cigarettes."

The new guard selected a buxom women whose face paled as he shoved her toward the door. The other guard ignored all the women until he saw the girl trembling next to Anna. He pointed to her and grinned. "There you are. Come."

Anna thought the girl was going to faint. She began to sway and her eyes closed and the guard grabbed her by both arms. He was a big, powerful man, more than six feet tall, His round, moon-like face, with eyebrows so pale they were almost invisible, made his slightly bulbous eyes seem to stare fixedly. He moved behind the girl and half carried, half pushed her toward the door. She was like a doll in his hands, her head lolling limply, her breath coming in whimpering gasps, and Anna wondered how a man could possibly find sexual satisfaction in such abject fear. Was it really her body the animal wanted? Or was it her mind? Perhaps his satisfaction was not in the act, not even in the inflicting of pain, but rather, in the degradation and the fear. Could he find any satisfaction at all in a woman like Katalin? Or would he always seek out those he could torture into a counterpoint of his own insanity? Were there many like him? She knew the answer. When there was no war, when there were no helpless prisoners upon whom to prey, they were the wife beaters, the child molesters, the sadistic criminals or vicious officials. They were all out there—waiting.

Anna put her hand up to wipe at her eyes and a hand knocked it down. "No moving!" Wirtz said. "I did not give permission to move."

Anna straightened and lifted her chin. Wirtz was as much a brute as the other guards, but at least his desires did not run to frightened young girls. Perhaps she had made him so apprehensive last night that tonight he would steer clear of her.

She was wrong. Without a word, Wirtz grabbed her arm, jerked her around and shoved her toward the door. She caught her balance and stalked down the isle between the eyes of the women with her head up. She had no idea if Wirtz had selected her because he remembered her promise to read the Tarot cards, or because he had rejected her ideas and simply wanted to consummate what he had been cheated out of the night before. But whatever the reason, she would not give him—or the other women—the satisfaction of showing fear. If he insisted on using her body, that was all he would possess. He would be using a living corpse.

The walk to the guards' barracks seemed to take forever and, yet, was over too soon. There was too much time to think, too much time for the mind to dwell on the horrors to come, but not enough time to delay the onset of those horrors.

Inside the Oberscharführer's quarters, the fire was already making the top of the stove glow, and after the chill outside, it was stifling in the small room. Wirtz shoved Anna to the center of the room where she stood watching him warily, volunteering nothing, her breathing fast and shallow. Her breath caught in her throat when Wirtz stared at her with his pale, dead eyes and began unbuttoning his blouse. Then he said, "The cards. You brought the cards?" and she began breathing again in a rush of joy. She was in charge now. She was the one in control.

She took the Tarot cards from her pocket and without waiting for permission she went to the table and placed the silk-wrapped deck of cards on its top. "I must wash my hands."

Wirtz nodded toward the basin and the pitcher. Anna poured the cold water into the basin. She found a sliver of yellow soap that looked as though it had been made from wood-ash lye and rendered lard, and washed her hands and face. She dried her hands on Wirtz' towel but could not bring herself to touch it to her face.

She moved back to the table and looked up at the bare light which was almost directly over her head. "Do you have candles?"

Wirtz tossed his jacket on the cot and opened the door of the cabinet. "How many?"

Anna's sense of triumph increased. He was practically asking her permission. "Three," she said.

He brought out three short, thick candles, and at her direction, placed them about the room, setting them in their own wax. When he turned out the light, the effect was exactly as she had hoped, the flickering candles creating an eerie, supernatural atmosphere. She saw Wirtz glance toward the bottle of schnapps and she said, "You wish to drink. Go ahead. It will have no effect on the cards. Your fate is already ordained."

The sergeant moved to the table carrying the bottle and a glass. Before he could sit, Anna stopped him by holding up her hand. "Which way is north?"

Wirtz jerked his head. "That way."

Anna pointed to the chair facing the direction he had indicated. "You will sit there."

Wirtz stared at her for a moment.

Anna wondered if she should have made the directive in the form of a request instead of a demand. She quickly gave him back his sense of command by saying, "The magnetic currents of the earth flow from south to north. They will flow through you into the cards."

Wirtz grunted in understanding and sat in the indicated chair, and Anna reminded herself not to push this man too hard or too far. With his combination of arrogance and low intelligence, she was playing on the edge of disaster. When he lifted his arm to take a long drink of the powerful liquor, she saw that sweat already stained the underarms of his shirt.

Moving slowly and deliberately, partially because she was struggling to remember the ritual her mother had taught her and partially to heighten the mystic, she spread the large silk handkerchief on the table and smoothed it flat. She lifted the deck of Tarot cards and stroked them hypnotically as Wirtz watched. Then she shuffled them carefully, three times, pausing between shuffles to turn some of the cards so they would be reversed when placed on the table.

When she finished, she handed the cards to Wirtz. "Now you must shuffle. Three times. Keep them on the silk. Do not let them touch the table. Between shuffles, turn some of the cards as I did."

The sergeant's big hands were trembling so that he had difficulty shuffling and turning the cards. When he had finished, Anna took the cards and placed them in front of her on the handkerchief. She hesitated. Which spread should she use? There were several variations. The nine card spread was the most effective, but she couldn't remember the order in which the cards were to be read. The same was true of the circular spread, although it really would not matter if she made a mistake. The stupid sergeant wouldn't know. Besides, she planned to interpret the cards to suit her own purpose no matter what they told.

At the same time, despite her sophistication, she retained a strong respect for the cards. There was something mysterious about them, and while she might bend their message, she would rather not disregard it totally. The cards might then bring her bad luck, and she had enough of that already. She was glad she only had to deal with the twenty-two major cards. If she also had to deal with the forty small cards, she could never bring off the deception.

She decided on the horseshoe spread since it was the most simple, and telling Wirtz to concentrate on each card, she slowly and deliberately took seven cards from the top of the deck and placed them face down on the table. When they were arranged, she stared at them for a full minute, knowing Wirtz was also staring intently, allowing the apprehension of their portent to seep into his mind. To her surprise, she found that when she reached for the first card, her fingers were trembling. No wonder the cards carried so much hope and fear for those who believed. Here, in the light of the flickering candles and with the subject almost shaking with apprehension, she found it was virtually impossible not to be drawn into the web of their power. She resisted by racking her memory for the meaning of the various cards. Could she remember anything? Or would she have to make it all up? What was the meaning of the first card?

Slowly, she turned the card over. "This card is your past influence." The words came without hesitation, as though the card itself had told her its purpose. The instant she saw that the card pictured a reversed devil, it was as though her mother was suddenly inside her head and the voice that came out was not really hers. She knew without looking that the subject's eyes were locked on the personification of evil as her mother's voice said, "The devil. Reversed. That is bad. Very bad. You have been influenced in the past by a powerful person, a very powerful person, who is not good for you. He has entered into your inner self. He is seeking your soul. The way he does this is to inflict a lust for power. Another way is to suppress your basic intelligence so that you act, not with your own mind, but with the basic instincts of an animal. You must be very strong to resist. But the messenger of God will help you. The Devil will fight hard to defeat the Message of God, but in the end, only your own power to resist can save your soul from the eternal tortures of hell."

When her voice trailed off, Wirtz' breath was coming in harsh gasps and sweat was running down his face and neck, staining the collar of his shirt, which he unbuttoned and pulled loose. His glass was empty and he poured it full and took a quick gulp before he gestured impatiently for her to continue.

Slowly Anna reached for the next card. "This card is your present circumstances." She turned over The Sun. Upright. Wirtz sighed with relief. So, he knew a little about the cards. She would have to be careful.

As the sergeant listened intently, twining and untwining his sweating hands and refilling his empty glass, Anna used the card to pull him back from despair by saying the sun was a very fortunate sign. He was a man of great courage, great strength of character, daring to have original ideas so that he could never be truly subservient to any master however powerful. With his strength, he could resist, even triumph over his old nemesis, the Devil.

As she worked her way around the horseshoe spread, she continued to weave the picture of a man caught in the clutches of circumstances that were trying to drag him to his doom, but he would receive unexpected help in saving his soul.

When the fourth card turned up The Star, she instantly saw its potential, referring to the kneeling girl as someone who could help him, someone who might even be the promised Messenger of God.

The sixth card proved to be The Hanged Man, reversed, and Wirtz gasped and clutched at his chest as thought someone had driven a knife into his heart. He only lost his look of pain when Anna pointed out that being reversed made it a good card and that, while he must pass through a trial of courage and faith, the halo around the head meant he could, with help from the Messenger of God, persevere to defeat the evil of the hangman.

When the final card she turned was Justice, she went weak with wonder. Was she really playing a role? Or had the power of the cards taken over and what she was seeing, what the strange voice was saying, was the truth, that justice was waiting; It was up to the subject whether it would lead him to fame and fortune and a place in the celestial heaven, or to false power and an eternity in hell?

When she completed her interpretation, Wirtz sat staring at the cards, unable to tear himself away from the power of the message: his soul was in the grasp of the Devil and only his own strength, with help from the unknown Messenger of God, would be able to save him.

Wirtz shoved both hands toward the cards as though to push away the message, to deny its import, and for an instant, Anna thought he was going to sweep the cards to the floor. But his fear of the cards was stronger than his rejection and he stood abruptly, toppling his chair with a crash.

He had consumed almost the entire bottle of schnapps, but except for his eyes being half closed, the liquor did not appear to have an effect on him. "I don't believe it," he snarled. "It's all lies. Gypsy lies. I should have you shot."

Anna stood her ground. She must not ruin the message by now seeming to deny it. She pointed to the cards as though they were the embodiment of commands from a higher power. "Lies? See for yourself. I did not make the cards. You made the cards. That is your life, not mine."

Wirtz wiped the back of his hand across his mouth and his eyes wavered. "I still don't believe them."

Anna sized his indecision to lead him into the next part of her plan. "Very well. There is a way we can find out if they were right."

Wirtz paused in emptying the bottle of schnapps into his glass. "Ja? How?"

"The stars. Your fate is written in the stars. No one touches the stars. Not my hands. Not yours. They cannot lie."

Wirtz slowly nodded. "Ja. The stars. The Führer himself listens to the stars."

"As does your Reichsführer Himmler. Also Reischsmarschall Goring."

Wirtz drained the glass before he replied. "Ja. You can do this, work with the stars?"

Again Anna felt a surge of triumph. He was moving like a lamb down the path she had carved for him—no, she corrected—like a pig, a pig going to slaughter. "Yes. I can make your astrologic chart."

"How long? How long will it take?"

Anna chose her words carefully. These next few seconds might well be the key to her own survival. "That depends. I am on the brush clearing detail. I have little time. . . .."

Wirtz waved the thought aside. "I take you off that detail. You will only work for me."

"Good. I will, of course, need paper, pencils, books."

"I will get what you need."

"I will have to work in the barracks. The other women. They will be suspicious, jealous. They might destroy my work."

"They do and I will have them all shot."

"The Kommandant might not like that."

"The Kommandant?" Wirtz voice and his thinking were being slowed by the liquor.

"If you shoot the women, who will do the work?"

"Oh. Ja. The Kommandant would not like that."

"So what can we do?" Anna prompted. "If there was somewhere else I could work. . ."

Wirtz' face cleared. "We have places. I will see to it. You go there now. Start now."

"Now?" Anna was suddenly filled with alarm. She had to return to the barracks tonight so she could tell Eric.

"Ja. The sooner you start the sooner we get rid of the lies."

Desperately Anna sought for an excuse to return to the barracks for one more night. "No. This is not a good night. The cards are too powerful. I must give them one night to rest."

"The cards?" Wirtz' eyes opened wide as they were drawn to the damning cards. "Oh. Then tomorrow. Early."

"Yes. Tomorrow. I will begin tomorrow."

As she said the words, Anna was shaping her plan. She would be out of the barracks. That had been her first goal. Now, the question was: how long could she stay out?

Chapter 15

Anna lay shivering on the ground next to the barbed wire fence where she was to meet Eric, wishing she had gone back into the barracks after leaving Sgt. Wirtz. But that would have meant evading the questioning and accusing stares of the women. The fewer questions she had to answer the less chance there was that she might be betrayed by someone seeking to curry favor with Wirtz or one of the guards. Still, she could have picked up her blanket. The wool material, although threadbare, would have provided a little protection from the cold that seeped from the ground and invaded every fiber of her body. Lying in a slight depression where the dampness tended to accumulate, did not help. But it was the only place where a guard passing outside the compound perimeter fence could not see her.

Unlike the previous night, the sky was clear and she was able to see deep into an infinite heaven of stars. But she could not see deep enough to find answers to the questions that were buffeting her concepts of good and evil. How was it possible that God in his wisdom and compassion could create beasts who wore the guise of men? And if He did not create them, how could He allow them to inflict their horrors on good people, people who believed in God, who relied on the protection of faith? Why was it necessary for so many good people to sacrifice their lives to stop such monsters when a powerful God could stop it in an instant if he so chose.

Ah, there was the rub: if he so chose. Obviously, he did not choose to do so. So the question then was, why not? There was no answer to that in ten billion stars.

To take her mind from the disconcerting conundrum, she sought comfort by thinking of her father and her mother being together somewhere in that heaven of light. Thank God they were beyond this time of terror. How long would it last? How long would she have to continue her desperate deception? How long could she do so? A month? A year? Then what? If America came into the war, it would be over quickly and they could all go home. Home? The idea filled her with bitterness. Albrecht Grantz would be found and punished. Of that she was certain. He had many deaths on his soul. When he died, there would not be a place for him up there among those clear, clean stars.

She heard a small sound and sensed rather than saw Eric sink to the ground beside her on the other side of the fence. As he lay down she heard his sharp intake of breath. "What is it? Are you hurt?"

Eric's chuckle was grim. "Mostly my pride. Von Liebermann had me given five lashes for the horse I sold him in Salzburg."

Anna could feel the pain in her own back. "Oh, Eric. Will you be all right?"

"From five lashes? I've had worse from my father. He could have had me killed."

Anna gently eased her hand through one of the small barb-bordered squares, and Eric took it in his and touched it to his lips. She felt the rough stubble of his beard, and she wished there was enough light so she could see him as more than a dark shadow.

"Your hand is freezing," he whispered. "How long have you been here?"

"Quite a while." Speaking in a whisper, she told him how her plan had worked, was in fact working even better than she could have hoped. "He's going to find a place for me to work, somewhere in the headquarters area. I won't have to go back to the barracks at all."

"Can you keep him away from you?"

"I think so. I've got him thinking I'm the Messenger of God. He needs me to keep his soul from burning in hell."

Eric chuckled. "He's going to need more than that." His voice dropped to a worried whisper. "How long can you keep it going?"

"I'm not sure. I can take my time working up his chart."

"And after that?"

Anna was silent for a moment. They both knew the day would come when she would run out of tricks. "It won't have to be too long. I'm sure that America will come into the war. Then it'll be over in a month or two."

"I think you're right about them coming in. But it won't be over in a month. The Germans have been preparing for years. They've got more men and tanks and planes than you'd believe."

"Not more than America."

"More than God. I've seen them."

"You have? Where?"

"All over Europe. The German's wouldn't let anybody see what they were up to, but they don't think of Gypsies as people. They've got concentration camps all over Germany. They've been picking up people they want to get rid of for years: politicals, Jews, Jehovah's Witnesses. I was too stupid to believe they would kill Gypsies."

"Do you know where they have factories? Airfields? Things like that?"

"Of course. I sell horses to people who make airplanes, tanks, cannons. They're the ones with the money. They and the officers."

"Too bad you can't tell the British."

"What do you mean?"

"If they knew where the factories were, they could drop bombs on them."

"I'd like that. Anything to end this war before. . ." He was about to say before they were all dead, but he held back. To destroy hope was to destroy will and right now it was only Anna's will to survive that was saving her from that SS brute of a sergeant.

But Anna was not fooled. She knew the Gypsies' chances of surviving a long war were practically nil. The Nazis intended to work them until they dropped. And even though she might have escaped the work detail, it was unlikely she could keep Wirtz—or other brutes like him—at bay for long. "I won't let them use me like those other women," she told Eric. "I'll kill myself first."

Eric squeezed her hand in understanding. "If you have to do it, take some of the animals with you."

They lay in silence, holding hands through the barbed wire, each trying to give courage to the other. Eric felt a helpless anger. As much as he wanted to help, there was nothing he could do. Or was there? With Anna out of the prisoner's compound, perhaps—just perhaps—they could escape.

"How will we see each other?" Anna said. "I won't be able to meet you here."

"Maybe I won't be here."

Anna gasped in alarm and he quickly told her about his work with the Kommandant's horse. "He wants me to look after all his horses," he concluded. "I'll try to get him to move me out of the barracks. If I can do that, I'll get word to you somehow."

"And if we're both out, we can get away."

"Maybe."

"Maybe? We can do it. They won't have guards on us."

"It isn't just getting away," he explained. "We've got to do it in such a way that they won't find us. If they do. . . well, we'll have to make sure they don't take us alive."

"We'll do it. We've got to. And soon."

Eric was all too aware of the urgency. He was reasonably certain he could make his job as the Kommandant's groom last indefinitely. He might be able to maneuver von Liebermann into taking him out of the barracks and obtaining better food. But how long could Anna hold off that bastard Wirtz? And what would happen if one of the officers decided he wanted her? Her hold over Wirtz would not save her then. She wanted him to escape so he could help England win the war. The hell with the war. He wanted to escape so they could live.

They lay holding hands as long as they felt they could do so without getting caught, ignoring the increasing cold, silently drawing strength from each other, the limits of their world a barbed wire fence and machine guns waiting in the darkness.

How strange, Eric found himself thinking, that of all the girls, all the women whose hands he'd held, of all the times he'd lain in safe, warm beds next to soft, smooth women and had accepted their kisses and enjoyed their caresses, none of them had given him the pleasure he now felt lying on the cold ground, his cheek almost touching Anna's through the barbed wire, holding hands with fingers numb from the cold, their minds numb with the nearness of death. And how often had he sought excuses to end a liaison, any excuse to cut short the time, time he would gladly give anything to have now.

This was what it was like to be so much a part of someone that you hated to leave their side. This was what it was like to ache to put your arms around someone and never let them go. This was what it was like to want to protect someone so desperately that you were willing to sacrifice your own freedom, you own life. How could such joy hurt so much?

A faint cry jarred through Eric's thoughts and at the distant guards' barracks exterior lights flashed on. Two guards with German Shepherds appeared out of the darkness and ran toward the building, the dogs straining at their leashes. The door to the soldiers' barracks opened, spilling light into the darkness and Katalin ran outside. Her flight towards the women's barracks was barred by the two guards with their dogs and for a moment Eric thought they would attack the girl.

"Go," he whispered harshly. "In a minute this whole place will be swarming with guards."

Anna pulled her hand back through the fence and got to her knees. "When will I see you again?"

"I'll let you know. Now run."

Eric rolled away from the fence and dashed to the side of the men's barracks. Anna ran to the women's barracks. But instead of going inside, she paused to watch Katalin. The girl snarled something at the two guards and they stood aside to let her pass, then they resumed running toward the guards' barracks. Katalin walked swiftly to the compound gate and one of the perimeter guards opened it for her. As she moved into the shadow at the entrance, Anna stepped forward.

"Katalin."

Katalin stopped, searching for the source of the voice. When she saw Anna, she peered to see who it was. Then her chin came up and she said, "Oh. It's you. Back already?"

"What happened over there? Where is the other girl?"

"She's still there."

"Wouldn't that bastard let her come back?"

"She won't be back—ever."

Anna knew instantly what she meant. And instead of feeling shock or even anger, she was flooded by a sense of relief. The humiliation, the pain, the horror was over for the girl.

"How did she do it?"

"One of the pigs was in such a hurry he didn't bother to take off his pants, or his belt. She grabbed his dagger." She made a sweeping gesture across her throat with her hand and Anna turned her head away. It was a horrible way to die. If the time ever came, could she bring herself to do the same?

Chapter 16

It appeared to Anna that the small room in a wing of the German headquarters section had been constructed as a maintenance tool shop. There were pegs and hooks on the walls where tools had been hung and the wooden floor was scored from the blades of shovels and hoes as well as by workman's hobnailed boots. All the tools had been removed except for two shovels, a hoe and an axe, all with broken handles, that were stacked in a corner. There was one small window at almost ceiling level. A bare light bulb was situated precisely in the center of the ceiling and shaded with the standard porcelain hood. The de rigueur four-drawer metal file cabinet was in one corner. Against one wall was a battered wooden desk that was so small Anna suspected it had been pilfered from some child's bedroom. In the center of the room was a wooden table with a round top. There were three mismatched chairs. Two were straight-back chairs, one at the table and the other in front of the desk. They had a plain functional look as though they had been turned out in a Gothic factory. But the third was a lovely Queen Anne piece, with delicate hand carved cabriole legs, back and armrests. It was upholstered in a thick tapestry depicting trees and flowers, its braiding intertwined with silver thread. Whoever had carried it into the room had displayed a total lack of grace since it had been placed at the battered table next to one of the cumbersome Gothic chairs where it looked like a princess forced to endure the presence of a disreputable peasant.

But what made Anna cringe was that everything except the file cabinet had been given a thick coat of white paint and the air was heavy with the smell of turpentine. Even the graceful lines of the Queen Anne chair had been slapped with a coat of paint. An attempt had been made to keep the paint off the beautiful upholstery with only partial success.

The item of furniture that provided Anna with a deep satisfaction was a metal cot that had been placed in one corner of the room. On its metal springs was a rolled mattress, a set of sheets and two blankets. The cot meant she would not have to go back to the barracks, nor, it appeared, would she have to work with the other women in the forest where the chance of survival was practically nil.

Sgt. Wirtz gazed around the room with a smile. "Good, Ja?" He caught sight of the tools in the corner and frowned. "I send somebody for those."

Anna remained in the doorway, which opened to the outdoors, reluctant to be alone with Wirtz. She was not entirely certain he had given up his carnal desire for her, and she wanted to keep to a minimum the opportunities for him to change his mind. "Yes. Very good."

Since it was only shortly after sunrise, she knew Wirtz would have to hurry to take charge of the Gypsy women's work details. Only a short time before, as the women had lined up outside their barracks to receive their breakfast, consisting of a small chunk of black bread and watery cabbage soup—the same food they had received for supper—,one of the German guards had singled her out and escorted her to the headquarters building. There she had been met by Wirtz who had brought her to this room. It would have taken a detail most of the night to get the room cleared and Anna smiled. She must have generated a terrible fear in Wirtz to make him move so fast. It was a fear that she would have to keep current. If he lost it, she would lose what little control over him she possessed.

Anna could only guess at what the room might have cost Wirtz. While he could order any of the underlings to do his bidding, the other sergeants, and particularly, the officers, would have to be either convinced he had orders from a superior to confiscate the room or he was able to bribe them. Either way, it must have cost him dearly and was, therefore, a palpable indication of the strength of his desire to have his chart cast.

The thought also struck her that if Wirtz had not received permission from his superiors and was operating on his own, he could be in some peril if they found out, which was additional leverage she might be able to use.

She took a step into the room, leaving the door open despite the morning chill. "There are several other things I will need." She made it a point to keep her voice hard, trying to imitate the tone that was in the voices of the officers when they addressed noncoms.

Sgt. Wirtz went to the small desk and pulled out a drawer. "You have papers and pencils and a straight edge for drawing. Ink will be provided if you need it."

"I will need a compass and several—"

"Compass?" Wirtz' head snapped up and his eyes narrowed. His thoughts were as easy to read as those of a child: He thought she wanted the compass to use during an escape.

"No, no," she quickly corrected. "Not a magnetic compass. A . . ."—she searched her vocabulary for the word— "Zirkel. For drawing circles."

Sgt. Wirtz' face resumed its hard mask. "Ja. For the chart. I will get it for you."

"And books. There are several books I will need."

"Books? What kind of books?"

"An Ephemeris, for one thing. So I can look up the positions of the sun, moon and planets when you were born and where they are now."

Wirtz took a note pad from his shirt pocket and, using a pencil from the desk, began making a list. "Ephemeris. Ja."

"Try to get an Ephemeris that was published after 1930."

"1930? Why 1930?"

"The planet Pluto was discovered in 1930. It won't be in an early addition."

Wirtz looked at her for a second before he glanced down to write the date, but in that second Anna saw a look of respect in his eyes that hadn't been there before. Knowledge. He was afraid of people with knowledge. Maybe not actually afraid, but he certainly held them in respect. In order to increase his respect, she dragged other erudite-sounding phrases from her subconscious. "I'll also need to calculate terrestrial the latitude and longitude of your birthplace. And I'll have to convert your local time to Greenwich Mean Time and that to Sidereal Time, so I'll need a Gazetteer, preferably one with acceleration tables so I can calculate the acceleration on the interval."

Wirtz' pencil was moving rapidly as he attempted to keep up with Anna's rapid delivery. She wasn't certain what some of the terms meant, but she did remember they were all connected with the casting of astrological charts. Wirtz had probably heard them too, so their use would strengthen her credibility.

She ended her list by saying, "And a lock."

Wirtz wrote the word before its meaning sank in. When it did, he looked up. "A lock?"

"For the door."

Wirtz looked from Anna to the open door while he decided whether her request was justified. Anna put additional snap in her voice as she added, "Yes, a lock. I will not be able to concentrate if I have to worry about some person coming in at any hour of the day or night." She lowered her voice conspiratorially as she added, "Maybe an officer."

Wirtz nodded so quickly that Anna was sure he had not obtained permission to use the room. "Ja," he said. "A bolt." Then he looked at her, his eyes suspicious. "You will not try to keep me out?"

"Of course not. I will need your cooperation." As though the subject was already accomplished, she began pacing the floor as she had seen her father do, her hands clasped behind her. "We will first do your general chart. Then we will do a daily chart so that you will know day by day what is the best action for you. We will know which are your good days and which are your bad days. We will know which days are best for your health and which are bad for your health. We will know which days are best to approach your superiors and which are the bad days."

"Ja. That is important."

As so often happened when she was under the greatest stress, Anna had a flash of inspiration. "Can you get me the birth day of the Kommandant?"

"The Kommandant? Why would you need that?"

"I don't need it exactly. But suppose you knew his good days and his bad days? You would know when to approach him and when to stay away."

A slight gleam appeared in Wirtz dead eyes as he realized the opportunity. "Ja. I will find it."

"Good." Anna sat at the desk and pulled a piece of paper in position to write. "Now, to start I need some facts from you."

A line of worry creased Wirtz' forehead. "Now? I have no time."

"Just one thing then. I know your birthday. What time were you born?"

"Time? I don't know."

"Very well. We can back track and get that. Just bring me any personnel information you have with dates."

"Personnel information?"

"Pictures, letters, papers—military papers."

"Ja. I will do that."

"And anything like that you can get about the Kommandant."

The lines in Wirtz' face deepened. "Why? He could have me shot."

"If our information is not accurate, you can't blame me if I make a mistake."

The consequences of Anna making a mistake about the Kommandant's good and bad days made Wirtz rub his hand across his mouth. His new found advantage could become a deadly liability. "I will try," he said. "Now I must go." He took a step toward the door, then stopped as he remembered. He dug a broad black elasticized band from a pocket and handed it to Anna. "Put this on your arm. You can go to the kitchen for food."

Anna slipped the armband over the sleeve of her jacket. It meant her association with the barracks was officially severed. With the black band, she could move around the facility at will, as long as she stayed out of trouble. But one false or suspicious move and she would be punished as quickly and severely as any other prisoner.

Wirtz paused in the doorway and stared at her. He was clearly having second thoughts about what he had done. It was one thing to bring one of the Gypsy women to his room for any purpose he chose, but setting one of them up in a room of her own and giving her the armband of a Kapo was pushing his luck.

But his ambition and his curiosity were greater than his fear and he commanded, "You start working." He slapped his palm with the handle of his whip to emphasize the point he was still in charge. "Start working," he repeated.

As he stepped out the door Anna said, "And a stove. I can't work if I'm freezing."

Wirtz did not bother to answer, but she saw his shoulders hunch as though one more stone had been added to an already heavy load. She closed the door and leaned her back against it and stared at the small room, her eyes fixed, her mind on the edge of shock. What was happening to her life? Only three short days ago she had been secure in her position as owner of the vast Zorka estate, a person of stature, with her future laid out as though carved in tablets of stone. Now, she was here in this dungeon of a room, forced to use her wits to save her life, her future as fragile as blown glass, her body, even her life, subject to the whims of a company of beasts; the only thing standing between her and them was her mental agility and a frail door without a lock.

There was one thing she could do to give herself some measure of protection. She went to the broken tools in the corner and picked up the axe. The handle was broken off about a foot from the heavy, ugly blade making it more like a hatchet than an axe. But it would make a formidable weapon. She put it next to the bed where it would be within easy reach if anyone came in during the night. Against one of the strong, brutal guards she would likely get only one chance to use it, but surprise might give her the edge she would need. And if she failed . . .?

In order to take her mind off the fearsome thought, she sat down at the desk and began the task of preparing Wirtz' chart. Until she received the booklets she had requested, she had only her memory to guide her, but she was sure she could remember enough to make a credible showing. Her mother had made forecasts for Anna every day of her life, and she had often watched, intrigued that the figures and lines could give meaning and direction to her daily existence. She was not sure when it happened, but at some point, she had begun to doubt. In New York, she had studiously adhered to the advice her mother had dispensed, based upon a chart plotted weeks in advanced and mailed to her. But as the mail from Hungary became more desultory and her daily charts often arrived days too late, she had survived her initial panic and found to her surprise that she could live just as well without the charts. Gradually, her natural skepticism changed to outright disbelief, and she had begun discarding the forecasts without bothering to read them.

Now, she racked her mind to try to remember the procedures of charting. She started by noting Wirtz' birthday. But her knowledge about him ended there. She did not know where he was born so she could not determine his time zone. And she did not know the time of his birth. There was not much she could do until she had more information.

She could, however, start on the basics of the chart. Using a pencil and a piece of paper, she drew a large circle. Then, using the straight edge, she divided the circle into twelve pie-shaped spaces and began labeling them with the signs of the zodiac. Fortunately, she had good visual memory and she retained an accurate mental picture of the positions of the houses.

When the houses were positioned, she drew a small circle in the center to represent the earth. She then used the straight edge to mark the twelve spaces of the house cusps. These slices would later be filled in with the planet signs and the Ascendant and Midheaven angles. As she worked, she wondered where her mother had learned the mathematics used to calculate the planets' longitudes and the other angles. She had no formal education. And if anyone had asked her to sum a column of numbers or do simple multiplication or division, she would have thought they were crazy. But she could do the mathematics of a chart swiftly and accurately. It was something her own mother had taught her and, to her way of thinking, had no relationship to mathematics. It was merely something you did to make a chart. Now it was something Anna had to do to save her life.

The white mare was standing with its head up and its ears cocked. She had stopped vomiting and there was no drool from her mouth. The effects of the poison had run its course and the medication had helped settle her stomach.

As von Liebermann watched, Eric made a show of examining the mare. He peered intently into each of her eyes as though they were mirrors of her condition, as in a way, they were. Like humans, an animal's eyes reflected its health, and a Gypsy could tell a lot about a horse by the brilliance, color and condition of its eyes.

Now, however, it was all show for the benefit of the SS officer who was standing anxiously slapping his boots with his riding crop.

Eric finished his examination and turned to the Obersturmbannführer. "By tomorrow, you can ride her."

Von Liebermann's thin lips lost some of their grim tightness. "Good. You have done excellent work. You will be rewarded."

This was the time, Eric thought, to solicit the job, although he would have to approach the subject obliquely. If the Nazi thought for one moment that he desperately wanted the job, his ingrained perversity would probably make him refuse. If he was anything like the other SS pigs that Eric had seen, he would take delight in creating misery. Misery on a mass scale gave them pleasure, but there was more pleasure in inflicting pain on an individual. Group torture was too generalized to create real emotion. Murdering hundreds of people did not provide the intense thrill of watching the slow death of one person. And he certainly did not want to be that one.

"Thank you, Herr Obersturmbannführer." He stood with his shoulders slumped and his eyes downcast in the proper suppliant posture. "But I did not do it for a reward. My only thought was for the animal."

"You can stop lying," von Liebermann said with a twisted smile. "I know that you Gypsies don't give a damn about animals."

"Generally, that is true, Herr Kommandant. But I have worked with horses all my life. I have grown to understand and appreciate them."

"I'll bet." Von Liebermann studied Eric intently. "But I do not doubt that you know horses."

"That's true, sir. I have noticed, for instance, that your other animals need some looking after."

Von Liebermann turned his head to look at a sorrel mare and a dun gelding that were in nearby stalls. "Looking after?"

"Their shoes, for one thing."

"Shoes? They've been shod recently."

"The work is poor."

"Poor?"

"It should be done over before they go lame."

The thought of lame horses made the SS Obersturmbannführer clinch his jaw in sudden alarm. He strode to the door and pushed it partially open and shouted. "Helmut!"

He was striding back toward Eric when the young German groom leaped through the doorway and trotted toward them. "Jawohl, Herr Obersturmbannführer," fear making his voice tremble.

Von Liebermann stood in front of the sorrel mare. He pointed at the mare's forefeet with his riding crop. "Look at those shoes. The work is poor."

Eric almost felt sorry for the groom who was staring at the mare's hooves. He was totally bewildered, as well he should be. The work was first rate. But von Liebermann did not know that. "She will go lame," he shouted. "They will all go lame. I will look like a fool. Four horses and not a one I can ride!" He turned to Eric. "And what was that other thing? About their teeth?"

"It's called 'floating teeth.' The sharp points need to be filed down."

"There! You see." Von Liebermann raised his riding crop and Eric thought he was going to strike the boy. But the boy did not flinch, remaining at rigid attention and the SS officer lowered his arm. "How long will it take you to do the job?" he said to Eric.

"If I have proper equipment, only a few days."

Von Liebermann snapped at the groom, "Do we have the equipment?"

"Some, Herr Obersturmbannführer. Not all."

"Then get it. Go to Arnschwang. Regensburg if you have to. Do it today."

Arnschwang. Eric knew the place. It was a small village in the Bayrischer Wald, north and east of Regensburg. If the village was nearby then they had to be in Germany, somewhere near the Czech border. One more piece of knowledge to salt away.

"Jawohl, Herr Obersturmbannführer," the groom said.

"Dismissed."

The boy snapped his arm out in a quick salute. "Heil Hitler." He spun on his heel and ran out the door as though he was afraid von Liebermann might shoot him in the back.

But the Kommandant had already turned to Eric. "You will not return to your barracks. You will live here. From now on you are the chief groom."

Eric was so sure it would happen that he felt no sense of elation, only the pleasure that he had successfully manipulated this arrogant Gorgio. "Yes, sir," he said. He looked around the stable. "Where should I sleep?"

Von Liebermann smiled. "You Gypsies are used to sleeping with the cows and the pigs. This should be like heaven to you."

"Yes, sir," Eric said. "It will do nicely."

"I will have someone bring you a Kapo arm band. It will admit you to the kitchen for food.

"Yes, sir."

Von Liebermann patted the nose of the white mare and nodded, which Eric took to mean he was pleased. "You are now responsible. If you keep my horses in good shape, you will be rewarded. But if you do not . . ." He let his cold eyes and grim mouth finish the thought as he went out the door.

Eric stood in the semi-darkness of the stable and took a deep breath. The air was heavy with the pungent odor of manure and alfalfa, but to him it held the sweetness of freedom. Or at least, a semblance of freedom. He was still a prisoner and any attempt to change that status would result in a painful death. Also, he was saddled with the responsibility of the horses. Fortunately, they appeared to be in good health. He would have to go through the motions of taking off their shoes and reshoeing them, but that was an easy task and one he could string out for days.

Picking up a brush with stiff fiber bristles, he began brushing the mare vigorously. He would have to make sure the horses stayed healthy. What he had to worry about was a random disease or sickness striking them, like the deadly equine fever that could kill a horse in a day. And there was always the possibility that one of the stupid animals might eat a poisoned plant such as the Larkspur.

He shrugged and murmured, "*Cest' le vive.*" He had no control over either eventuality so there was no point in dwelling upon them. He would do as well as he could. The objective he had to keep in mind was surviving until he and Anna could escape. He wondered where she was. The thought of Anna made him picture that gorilla, Wirtz, and his stomach churned. He hated to think she was in the hands of that animal, even though she had assured him she was the one in control. Wirtz had taken her out of the barracks. So where would she be? In the same room with Wirtz? If she had to do that, it would be impossible for her to keep him at arm's length indefinitely.

Eric was beginning to feel sick. He would have to find Anna before he worried himself into an emotional cripple. Once he had that Kapo arm band he could move around the area with relative freedom. Then he would get some answers. He had the nagging feeling he had better do it soon or it would be too late.

Chapter 17

Sgt. Wirtz sat at the white-painted table in one of the white-painted chairs and stared as though hypnotized at the wheel-like Zodiac chart Anna had drawn. To him, it was his entire life, his immutable fate, spelled out in precise lines and mysterious symbols.

Anna also stared at the chart. But her reaction was one of pride. Despite her rather hazy recollection of her mother's instructions, she had been able to construct a chart that looked highly professional. The Zodiacal signs were in the right places—she was sure of that—and the ten planet signs looked authentic, although she was not as certain of their form as she was of the Zodiacal signs. Her use of the Ephemeris had been as much a matter of hard study as it was memory.

Wirtz, she had learned, had been born in a small town in the Swabian area of Southern Germany. She had carefully plotted its latitude and longitude from a map Wirtz had supplied. Wirtz was not certain of the exact time of his birth, but Anna had said that for her preliminary work it was not necessary. She had made a great show of extrapolating the time difference between the local time of his area and Greenwich Mean Time.

Remembering how to use the Ephemeris had been difficult, not only because she could not remember exactly how to determine each planet's position at the time of birth, but also, because the few Ephemeris pages Wirtz had given her were hand drawn and hard to read. He explained unhappily that he had only been able to borrow an Ephemeris long enough to copy part of its data.

"I can't do a perfect job unless I have the complete book," Anna had explained, glad for any excuse to explain inaccuracies.

She would not have thought it possible, but Wirtz actually looked uncomfortable. "That might not be possible," he said.

"Why not? You copied these pages."

"You don't need more. Those pages include my birthday."

"I need to plot the location of every planet at the time you were born. And for a daily guide, I have to plot them every day."

Wirtz shifted his weight from side to side like a bear trying to decide which way to charge. "I will try to get them. It is going to take a little time."

Anna smiled at him with her mouth, but her eyes remained hard. "I have plenty of time," she said. "I am not so sure about you."

Wirtz glanced down at his left hand and edged it behind his leg as though to shield his fate from her eyes. His lips were paper dry when he spoke. "I cannot borrow it again. I was almost caught this time."

Caught? A tingle of anticipation shot through Anna. She sensed she was on the edge of knowledge that might be of use. "You are an Oberscharführer," she prodded. "Who could refuse you?

"The Kommandant," Wirtz blurted, as though the words would make her stop asking him. "The book belongs to the Kommandant."

Anna bent her head over the chart so he could not see the triumph in her face. So the Kommandant was interested in astrology. If she had to be casting someone's horoscope, she would prefer it be for Lt. Colonel von Liebermann than for Technical Sergeant Wirtz. Somehow she would have to trick Wirtz into disclosing her talent to von Liebermann. If the man really was a believer, could he resist having his own personal astrologer?

"I see. That could put you in a dangerous position."

"I managed to get the book for a few hours. But for longer . . . Impossible."

"Well, there might be a way." She put a finger to her mouth and tapped her lips gently as though she was thinking hard. "If the mountain will not go to Mohammed, then perhaps Mohammed can go to the mountain."

"Huh?" Wirtz' face wore a look of bewildered hope.

"Where does the Kommandant keep the Ephemeris? In his quarters or his office?"

"His quarters."

"Good. I would only need to look at the Ephemeris for a few minutes each day. If you could arrange for me to do so while he is in his office, he need never know."

"How can I do that? He allows no one in his quarters."

"Who cleans for him?"

Wirtz' mouth formed into an O. "Cleans? Of course. One of the troopers. But it could be a prisoner." His eyelids came down, giving him a look of cunning. "The Kommandant might appreciate a handsome woman cleaning his quarters."

Anna had not thought of that aspect, and the thought of the arrogant Death's Head-SS bastard touching her, chilled her resolve.

But she could not turn back now. What she had done to Wirtz she could probably do to von Liebermann. It depended upon how much of a fanatic he was. The fact that he possessed the Ephemeris gave her reassurance. "That would be perfect. Can you arrange it?"

Wirtz smiled and slapped his palm with the butt of his whip. "I think so. I know his orderly, Hauptsturmfuhrer Brock. He is always looking at the Gypsy women. I will get that nymphomaniac girl for him. He will owe me a big favor for that."

He had to be referring to Katalin. But she was no nymphomaniac. Was she? More likely she was playing a role more difficult than Anna's, although a role with fewer dangers.

"Good," she said. "Tell me when you have arranged it."

"Soon. It will be soon." He gestured toward the chart on the table. "Now, tell me about tomorrow. Will it be good or bad?"

Anna bent to the chart, her pencil in her hand. Making it up as she went along, she began pointing out the current positions of the planets and what this could mean to Wirtz' fortunes. But all the time her mind was churning as she tried to think of a way to ask the pig about Eric. If Eric had been successful in getting the job of von Liebermann's equerry, the news would spread throughout the camp. Wirtz surely would have heard.

When they completed the reading, with Wirtz smiling happily, knowing his immediate future looked bright, Anna led the way along the conversational path. "I was thinking, it might take a day or two for you to get the Hauptsturmfuhrer's approval for me to work for the Kommandant. I hate to waste so much time."

"Waste? You can do like you did today. You told me tomorrow was going to be a good day."

"But without the book, I could be wrong." She watched Wirtz' happiness fade and she quickly added. "If I could just get a look at it for a minute or two, I could not possibly make a mistake."

"That cannot be done. The Kommandant is in and out. Too dangerous."

"Doesn't he ride his horses a lot? Perhaps when he is going for a ride . . ."

"Ah, yes. He would be gone for at least an hour."

"If only there was some way for you to tell exactly when. Perhaps if you knew his groom."

"His groom?" Wirtz snorted. "The man is an idiot. A stupid clod from the city. He only said he knew horses to get a soft job."

"There is talk among the Gypsies of a famous horse trader who was going to be his groom."

"Oh, yes, yes. A Gypsy horse trader. That is true. Just today he started."

Anna gripped the edge of the table so hard it hurt, but she managed to keep her voice even as she said, "Maybe you could get him to tell you when the Kommandant plans to ride."

"He will tell me." Wirtz gripped the handle of his whip with both hands as though it was someone's neck. He stood, anxious to begin his intrigue. "I will arrange it. And that other matter too: the Gypsy girl, for Hauptsturmfuhrer Brock."

He was chuckling as he went out the door into the night. "Tomorrow will be a very good day," she heard him say to himself.

"Not as good as mine was today," she murmured.

Eric was safe. Unknowingly Wirtz had given her a greater sense of joy than he would ever experience. As groom for the Kommandant, Eric would be away from the murderous work details where his life could be taken by a brutal guard or by slow starvation. But suppose he had not been allowed to move out of the barracks as had she. The guards might single him out for mistreatment. The Kommandant would be angry if they mutilated or killed his Gypsy groom, but their punishment would come too late for Eric. And even if he had been allowed to leave, where would he stay? In the stable? Or would the Kommandant's groom have special quarters?

Her speculation suddenly exploded with a surprising thought. Why was she thinking like this? She knew, even as she denied the thought: she wanted to go to him.

She tried to put the dangerous idea out of her mind. But why had she put herself in jeopardy with Sergeant Wirtz by asking all those questions if she had no intention of using the knowledge? And she desperately wanted to see Eric. She needed him. She needed his strength, his ability to survive. She needed him to teach her how to be a Gypsy, how to stay alive when everyone wanted you to die.

He could not come to her. He had no way of knowing where she was. She would have to take a chance at finding him. But not in the daylight. If someone saw her, she would lose the little freedom she had managed to acquire.

At night? If caught wandering around the complex in the daylight she might be able to concoct a plausible excuse. But at night? There could be no excuse if she were caught at night.

And suppose she was able to reach the stable and the person she found there, the groom, was not Eric. A German would surely turn her in. Or brutalize her. She could hardly complain without risking the chance of being shot.

Was it fear that made her mouth dry while the rest of her body was bathed in an unnatural perspiration? How could she be so desperately afraid when here in her room there was no danger? All she had to do was stay where she was and the chances were good she could survive the war in safety. Was finding Eric worth the risk?

There was another thought that gnawed at her mind. How would she react in a real crisis, in a moment of great physical danger? It was a thought that every person harbored. Were you a coward or a hero? If you were lucky, you could go through your entire life wondering, never confronted by the truth. And for her, what was the truth? Her manipulation of Sergeant Wirtz was not really an act of courage. After all, her life had not been in danger. And if it had been, fighting him would only prove she had the animal instinct of survival. People often reacted courageously to a sudden crisis when they had no time to think of the possible consequences. But could those same people deliberately put their head in a lion's mouth?

Better not to think about it. Better to be like soldiers who have to believe that awful things might happen to everyone else, but not to them. The failure to believe you were one of the lucky was to allow fear to take over.

But she could not stop thinking about Eric; she could not stop reminding herself of all the terrible things that could happen to her if she was caught, even as she was putting out the light and slipping out the door.

In the chill air, the scent of pines tried to overpower the miasma of hopelessness that filled the valley like a fog. Anna could almost feel death oozing from the silent prison barracks, which were caught in a web of barbed wire like doomed flies. It was as though everyone knew they would soon be dead, if not from starvation, then from the brutal treatment of the guards.

Whoever had designed the camp had decided there was no need for barbed wire barricades around the other structures, so Anna was able to make her way toward the stables without encountering any obstacles.

Keeping to the shadows of trees as much as possible, she moved slowly and cautiously, crouching close to the ground, pausing after a few steps to listen. For once she was grateful her uniform bore the hated stripes. They offered perfect camouflage in the shadow-splashed darkness. Her greatest danger was from the dogs used by the guards patrolling the prison barracks. She did not think they would be able to hear or scent her from this distance, but she took no chances, and when she saw one of the dogs stop and look in her direction, she dropped to the ground where she lay as flat as possible until the dog looked away.

Near the stable, she moved into the shadows and paused to listen. Was the only entrance the large double doors? And if Eric were there, where would he be? It would be pitch dark inside and she could not afford to stumble about in the darkness. However, unless she decided to abandon the quest, she would have to take a chance.

She edged to the double doors and felt for a lock. There was none. Finding a handle, she pulled one of the doors open enough to squeeze through into a thick darkness that was heavy with the dank odor of manure and horses. There was no sound, no movement.

Thank God, the door hinges were well oiled. She was able to close the door soundlessly, and she stood peering into the blackness, wondering what to do. How would a stable be laid out? The few she had seen had a wide central isle and stalls on each side, which meant if she walked straight ahead she should be moving down the center isle.

But moving to where? If Eric was here, where would he be? The only way to find out was to do some exploring.

Gingerly, she began moving forward, her hands out to keep her from running into anything, her steps a slow shuffle, her heartbeat unbelievably loud.

She stopped. Had she heard something? A soft rustling? Of course. Horses. In the stalls. Horses slept standing up, didn't they? Which meant they probably moved as they slept.

This was foolish. She couldn't very well search the stable stall by stall. She might succeed only in panicking the horses which would bring guards on the run. She would have to take a chance and call out, but softly.

Her soft cry was suddenly throttled as a hand was clamped over her mouth and a strong arm snaked around her waist. In a frenzy of panic, she writhed desperately, fighting to break free. She was able to get her fingers around the hand over her mouth and she pried it free. But she was afraid to scream. Whatever happened to her here could not be as bad as what would happen to her if the guards came. Her only hope was to break free, to escape into the night.

She struggled desperately, tearing with her hands, kicking with her feet, trying to bite the clutching fingers.

"Anna."

The voice in her ear froze her instantly. "Eric." Her fear was released as she breathed his name and almost collapsed.

Turning her so she was facing him, his face buried in her hair, his breath against her cheek, he clasped her so fiercely she thought he was going to crush her ribs.

"What are you doing here?" he whispered. "How did you find me?"

She clung to him with the strength of joy, reveling in the wonder of his arms, unable, unwilling to break the spell by answering. She turned her head and with the instincts of a baby finding its mother's breast, her lips found his. Then he lifted her and carried her through the darkness to a bed of straw. She again searched for his lips, and when she found them, she allowed their tender warmth to invade her mind, stripping away all fear, all memory, leaving only the wonder of being here at the end of longing.

Then Eric's hands were on the bare flesh of her back and his lips on her breasts and she gave herself to the incredible sensations that swept her body, heightening the sweet anguish by giving in to her body's demands for ever greater pleasures, riding the incredible sensations up and up until she was swept to a peak that left her floating among the stars.

She was at last conscious of warmth and the heady pleasure of Eric's body on hers, the sound of his breath in the dark silence as he held her in his arms while he, too, struggled back to reality. Anna lay with her eyes closed, enjoying the feel of the muscles of his bare back under her fingers. How strange that love could be so wonderful, contentment so full, in this place of danger. Would making love with Eric be as sweet if they were in another place, another time? She knew it would. And there was exquisite pleasure in knowing there would be other places, other times. The place might be worlds away, and the time measured in eons, but the wonder would always remain. They had found something that could never be taken from them.

Under her hands she felt Eric shiver and she realized the chill of night had crept into the stable. "You'd better put on your clothes," she whispered. "You'll catch pneumonia."

He turned his head and kissed her gently on the cheek. "I don't care. I'm going to stay just like this until I die."

She laughed, surprised at the huskiness of her voice. "No, you're not. If you die, we can't do this a million times more."

"God, I don't think I could stand it. I almost died this time."

"Me too."

She found his lips, and this time his kiss was warm and tender instead of a searing flame. But the flames were there, lingering on the edge of eruption, and she felt a rush of chill air as he moved away from her with a groan. "We've got to be careful. Guards come around here all the time."

"Guards? I didn't see any."

"Sweet Mother of God. You were lucky. They're all over the place." He found her clothes and handed them to her. "Where are you staying? Not in the barracks?"

"I told Sergeant Wirtz I couldn't do his horoscope until I had a place to work. He fixed up a storeroom in one of the headquarters buildings."

Eric shrugged into his jacket as he said, "How did you know where to find me?"

"I didn't, really. I found out from Wirtz that you had been made the new groom. I thought you'd probably be close to the horses."

Eric let his breath out. "I'm glad I was. If it had been that kid in here, no telling what could have happened."

"I know. I thought of that."

"But you came anyway."

"I had to find you."

They were both dressed now in the rough prisoner's clothing, but it still felt wonderful as Eric pulled her close. "I'm glad you did. But we can't do this again. It's too damn dangerous for you."

"I don't care." She put her hands behind his head and kissed him hard before she said, "I don't care how dangerous it is."

"I know. But if anything happened to you. . ." He let the thought die. "If you have a room of your own, I'll come there."

"It'll be just as dangerous for you."

He chuckled. "No, it won't. I've been hiding from the *Gorgios* most of my life. They won't find me. Now, tell me exactly where you are."

After Anna explained in detail, Eric said, "I'll come there every night if it's at all possible. If there's some reason I should not come, put some kind of rock against the corner of the building. And if I find out I can't be there for some reason, I'll. . . let me see. . .. We need a signal you can see without coming here. I'll hang a saddle blanket over the top bar of the corral. You should be able to see that before it gets dark."

"All right. But I hope it never happens."

"So do I." She could hear the strain in his voice as he added, "That stupid Wirtz worries me. Most of these SS bastards are real psychopaths, and from what I've seen of him, he's worse that the others. He could come apart at the least provocation."

"I can handle him. He's afraid of me."

"For now, yes. That could change if he thinks you might be the cause of his bad luck. We've got to get you away from him."

"Then it would be back to the work detail."

"No! That can't happen. We've got to get away from here."

"We can't just run. They'd find us in a day."

"I know. We'll have to work out a way that they won't miss us or they can't find us."

"And that'll take time."

"Yes." He stood up. "We've got to find a way to protect you until I can work that out. We've got to get you away from Wirtz."

Anna knew he was right. Wirtz was as unstable as nitroglycerin. But her connection with the occult was her only means of remaining free. If not Wirtz, then who?

Then she remembered something Eric had said: most SS guards were psychopaths, often former criminals themselves. Most were poorly educated. Superstitious. Even their leader, Himmler, was a disciple of the occult. As was Hitler himself. Was the same feeling pervasive among the officers? Were they selected because they had a penchant for the occult? And if they did not, would it be in their interest to pretend they did? Thinking aloud, she murmured, "Maybe one of the officers."

Eric grasped the implication immediately. "That might work. Wirtz wouldn't be able to make trouble if you worked for an officer. But not just any officer. He should be in a position where he could be of use."

"The Kommandant. Why not him?"

Eric was slow replying. "Hummm. Image means a lot to him. You should see him ride. I think he only does it because all the old Prussian officers ride. Have you ever seen a scar some of them have on their face?"

"Yes. What are they?"

"Saber scars. A lot of officers have them. Kind of a badge of courage."

"More like a badge of incompetence."

"Some let themselves be cut deliberately. Shows they're real men."

"Von Liebermann doesn't have one."

"Right. So he might be interested in finding another way to be like the elite. What better way than to be like Hitler himself? He might be anxious to get involved in the occult."

"He already is. When I told Wirtz I had to have an Ephemeris, he copied pages from one that belonged to Liebermann."

"Good. You'd be safe if you could work for him."

"But how can we let him know? Wirtz can't tell him."

"No, but I can. I'll see him every day. I can make it sound like a rumor; a Gypsy girl who does horoscopes. He won't be able to let that go."

Anna pictured the Kommandant's thin, pinched face, his wide brow and pale eyes. He might be a difficult man to fool. With Wirtz, she was able to play upon his peasant superstitions. But von Liebermann was educated. Perhaps his only connection with the occult was a desire to emulate Himmler and some of the other SS officers. Then she smiled. Pretend or not. He could not afford to be branded a skeptic. Still, she would have to evince a strong sense of authenticity. If he suspected for a second she was actually a fraud, would she be in greater danger than she ever would with Wirtz?

Her smile widened. "I had better tell Wirtz that soon he's going to have a bad day. A very, very bad day."

Chapter 18

Sergeant Wirtz escorted Anna into the living quarters of the Kommandant. They stopped inside the door where Wirtz whipped his hat under his arm and snapped to attention, his body as rigid as a cannon's barrel.

Anna had thought the quarters of the Kommandant would be sumptuous as befitting the ruler of a serfdom, small though it was. But his quarters were as Spartan as those of Sergeant Wirtz, with a bare overhead light. The white-painted walls were stained where pine tar from the uncured wood was beginning to seep through. Unlike Wirtz' room, however, the floor was covered with a thin, hand-woven rug. A coat rack next to the door held the Kommandant's long leather coat and his visored cap.

Floor to ceiling shelves between two windows contained a sparse collection of books. With the exception of Hitler's 'Mein Kampf,' all were either military or occult. Interestingly, they were almost all by Germans. Of the military she recognized Clausewitz, Ludendorff and Kluck. Works on the occult included Bruno, Schelling, Bohme and Otto.

In the center of the room was a heavy table with four massive chairs that looked as though they had once occupied the Keep of a medieval castle. The desk, by contrast, was a delicate Louis XIV, beautifully decorated with inlaid wood and mother-of-pearl. She wondered how any person could stand living in the presence of such a graphic contrast of ugly practicality versus functional beauty. Perhaps von Liebermann was not capable of making such a connection; he probably saw only articles of furniture that fulfilled his requirements.

There were two other doors, both closed. One probably led to a bedroom and the other to a bathroom, unless von Liebermann carried his spartanism to the extreme of using a latrine in common with the other officers.

As Sergeant Wirtz stood at attention, Anna could smell his fear. He had started sweating long before they reached the Kommandant's quarters. She could hardly blame him for being worried. She knew why they had been ordered to report to the Kommandant, although she had not thought the summons would come the first night after she had seen Eric. Wirtz, however, had no idea why he had been summoned. The fact that he had been directed to bring Anna indicated it was going to be bad for him.

Now, von Liebermann stood on the far side of the table with his hands clasped behind his back and stared at the sergeant. His thin lips were compressed in a tight line and through his glasses his eyes were pale gray marbles. Not once had his eyes moved a fraction of an inch toward Anna. She might have been as invisible as a spirit as von Liebermann walked slowly around the table and stopped in front of Wirtz so they were almost touching.

"Tell me," he said softly.

A slight tremor shook Wirtz as though the words had pierced him like blades and rivulets of sweat coursed from his temples. Wirtz started to answer but the words would not come and he was forced to clear his throat and start again. "Zu befehl, Herr Obersturmbannführer. It was a test. Only a test. To see if she qualified."

"Qualified?"

"Jawohl, Herr Kommandant. The woman is Gypsy."

"I know that." Von Liebermann did not raise his voice, but the contempt in his tone left no doubt of what he thought of the sergeant's intellect.

"She reads palms, Tarot cards, astrology. I was testing to see if she was qualified to be your personal astrologer, Herr Kommandant."

"And is she?"

"Jawohl, Herr Kommandant. She has the gift."

"And you are qualified to judge?"

Wirtz hesitated. "I was doing my best, Kommandant."

"The Führer has forbidden mingling of the races." Von Liebermann's voice took on a harsh snap. "Tell me, sergeant, was there mingling of the races?"

"No, Herr Kommandant. No mingling."

"Then why did you provide her with a room of her own?"

"She needed a place to work, Herr Kommandant."

"And all this without my permission? Or knowledge?"

Wirtz lips were bone dry, but he was afraid to lick them. "It. . . it was to be a surprise."

"A surprise?"

"Jawohl, Herr Kommandant."

Von Liebermann put his face within inches of Wirtz'. "I do not like surprises, sergeant."

"No, Herr Kommandant. It was a mistake. I see that now."

"A mistake, yes." Von Liebermann turned away and Anna could sense the sergeant's relief. But his relief was shattered when von Liebermann added, "And since you enjoy surprises, Oberscharführer, I have one for you."

He walked slowly to the far side of the table and Wirtz felt compelled to fill in the unbearable silence. "Jawohl, Herr Kommandant."

"From now on you are no longer an Oberscharführer. You are a corporal, a Rottenführer."

Wirtz' jaws bunched but he managed to grunt. "Jawohl, Herr Kommandant."

"And not here, Rottenführer Wirtz. You have been transferred to a panzer division on the Eastern front. Perhaps you can find some surprises for the Russians."

Casualties on the Eastern front were heavy, and with winter approaching, they would only become worse. As a corporal, Wirtz would have no privileges, only the privilege of being shot by the Russians or freezing. His voice was strained as he said, "Jawohl, Herr Kommandant."

Von Liebermann gestured with the back of his hand. "Dismissed."

"Jawohl, Herr Kommandant." Wirtz snapped his right arm out in a quivering salute. "Heil, Hitler."

Von Liebermann did not bother to return the salute and Wirtz wheeled and went out into the night, closing the door behind him.

At last von Liebermann turned his gaze toward Anna. He stood staring at her with the same look of contemptuous arrogance he had used with Wirtz. But Anna refused to be intimidated. She was almost certain she had been summoned along with Wirtz because the man wanted her 'gift,' as Wirtz had put it. If she were wrong, he would no doubt have her shot. Either way, she was prepared.

"Was that dummkopf right? Are you an astrologer?"

Anna felt a familiar sense of victory. Again she had bet her life and won. The sensation was so exhilarating that she felt she could become addicted to it—if the stakes were not so high.

His question, she knew, was two edged: he wanted to know if Wirtz was lying and he wanted to know if Anna spoke German. "Yes," she said in German. "I made his chart for him."

"You speak German very well."

"Yes."

"You know how to read?"

"Yes."

The expression in the German's eyes changed subtly, and he looked at her as though he was surprised to see she was actually human. "You are educated. Where?"

"Columbia University. In New York."

"New York." Von Liebermann almost betrayed admiration. Then he caught himself, and she thought for a moment he was going to smile. "Ah, yes. You are the one who claims to be American."

"I am an American citizen. You have no right to keep me here."

"If you are American, how is it that you are with the undesirables?"

"The Gypsies? My mother was Gypsy."

"So. You are half Gypsy. And the other half?"

"My father was Pál Zorka."

"Zorka. Ah, yes. He told me about that."

"He?"

"Obergruppenführer Heydrich."

"Heydrich? Why would he be interested in my father?"

"Not your father. You."

"Me?"

"But you know him. He took a personal interest in you."

"I don't know him. I've never seen him."

"Of course you have. At the Zorka estate. They say I look a great deal like him."

"I don't know . . ." Anna stopped as she was struck by a horrible realization. That was why von Liebermann had looked vaguely familiar. He had the same narrow forehead, the same plastered-down brown hair, the same rimless glasses. "The man who was talking to Albrecht Grantz. The man on the horse."

"You see. You do know him."

There was also a cruel image of Bela Imri bleeding in the dust and Reinhard Heydrich standing over him with a gun in his hand. But she had better keep that image to herself. "Yes," she admitted. "We've met. The next time I see him I'll tell him about my treatment here."

This time von Liebermann did chuckle. "You are very quick witted. No wonder you fooled poor Sergeant Wirtz. Now, we will see if you can fool me." He pulled one of the chairs away from the table. "Sit down."

She did as she was told and von Liebermann sat in a chair opposite her.

"What did you use for an Ephemeris?" His voice was a sneer as though he expected a lie.

"Wirtz copied part of yours."

Von Liebermann's head snapped back. "Mine!" Then he smiled. "He is more clever than I thought. I had no idea. You know that Obergruppenführer Heydrich and Reichsfuhrer Himmler have their horoscope cast daily."

"I've heard that." She had heard no such thing, but if the suggestion reinforced von Liebermann's faith, she was willing to help.

He got up and went to the bookcase and brought back a copy of Raphael's Ephemeris and placed it on the table. "I have been carrying this with me for months. Now I am rewarded. You will make my general chart."

"Very well."

"Then you will prepare a daily chart."

"Very well."

"And if you ever do see Obergruppenführer Heydrich again, that <u>is</u> something you can tell him."

Anna smiled to hide her true feeling. If I ever see the bastard again, she thought, I'll kill him, if Eric doesn't do it first. "I'll have to know all about you," she said.

Von Liebermann's eyebrows shot up. "You need only the date of my birth."

"I need to know the exact time and the exact place. And to be truly accurate, I should know your family background and the signs of your parents."

Von Liebermann was about to answer when the door to the bedroom opened and Katalin stood in the doorway, her head back, blowing cigarette smoke toward the ceiling. She was wearing her stripped jacket, but her legs were bare. Through the doorway Anna could see a bed with brass-tube head and foot boards as well as a large armoire and a dresser with a mirror.

"I thought it was you," Katalin said angrily in Romani. "Why are you here? You think you can take my place? I will kill you first."

The sudden opening of the door had startled Anna and sight of the Gypsy girl added to her confusion. She put her hand to her throat defensively while she caught her breath. "I'm not here to take your place—" she began.

"You!" Von Liebermann pointed to Katalin. "I did not give you permission to come out! Get back there."

Von Liebermann was obviously embarrassed at being caught with the Gypsy girl. It was one thing for the lower ranks to give in to their baser instincts and use the female prisoners, but field-grade officers were expected to abstain from engaging in such fraternization. Adolph Hitler did not wish to have his officers contaminated by the flesh of Untermenschens. Even so, sexual relations with female captives, either willingly or unwillingly, was a relatively common practice in the work camps and among the troops on the Eastern front. On the Western front the people of France, Holland, Belgium and Denmark were considered closely related to the Aryans, more civilized and, therefore, given better treatment by their conquerors.

But for a camp Kommandant to take one of the prisoners as a mistress would not be a good mark on his record. So, when Katalin looked at him blankly, he turned to Anna. "Tell her to go back and close the door. Tell her that if she comes out again without my permission, she will be shot."

"Yes, Herr Kommandant." She turned to Katalin who was staring at her darkly with her hands on her hips. Speaking Romani, she said, "I am not here to take your place. I am to make an astrologic chart."

"You? A fortune teller? I don't believe it."

"Well, I am. So go back in and close the door. You have nothing to fear from me."

Katalin gave her a heavy-lidded look that shouted skepticism, but she reached for the door. "All right. But if I find out you're lying, I'll cut your heart out."

"You won't get a chance. He said if you come out one more time without his permission, he'll have you shot."

The Gypsy girl lifted her chin and sniffed. "After tonight, he won't have me shot no matter what I do."

She closed the door and Anna heard the bed creak.

Von Liebermann went to the door and made sure that it was closed tightly. "You will forget this."

"It is no concern of mine," Anna assured him. To get him away from the dangerous subject, she said, "I will start on your chart tomorrow. From you, I will need the information I told you." She stood and picked up the Ephemeris. "I will take this with me." She knew she was taking a chance by being assertive, but it was best she begin exerting as much domination over him as he would allow. She had to maintain control to keep him from realizing the truth about her limited abilities and because she instinctively knew that von Liebermann respected power. To be weak was to relinquish control. And to lose control was to lose everything.

"I assume I will stay in the room Sergeant Wirtz acquired for me?"

Von Liebermann's eyes shifted for an instant toward the closed bedroom door before he nodded. "Yes. That will be satisfactory."

As Anna turned from the bookcases, she noticed that two of the books were on chess. This might be another avenue she could use to cement her role. She had played chess as long as she could remember. One of her earliest memories was looking up at her father over a chessboard as he patiently outlined the moves. Later she had learned the standard gambits and the gambits that had won championships. She could still remember her father saying, "The rules are all there, waiting to be broken."

"You play chess?" She already knew the answer.

"Yes. When I can find someone suitable." He eyes took on a hopeful gleam. "You play, of course."

"Of course." She couldn't resist adding, "When I can find someone suitable."

Without waiting for von Liebermann's reply or his permission, she walked out into the night, half expecting his sharp command to stop her before she could pull the door shut. But the command did not come and she smiled as she walk away. She may not have beaten the SS officer—her life remained delicately poised on the knife-edge of his whim—but she felt that, for now, she was in command. And if she was clever with his daily astrologic forecast, she could make herself indispensable.

If only there was something she could do for the women and men still trapped in a daily work routine on a diet without enough calories to sustain life let alone work ten to twelve hours. They were all doomed. It was unlikely any of them would survive. Even Katalin, despite her talents, would not survive unless she could sustain Von Liebermann's interest in her. No. That was wrong. If Von Liebermann lost interest, there were plenty of other men. Always there would be other men for Katalin. In the end, her ages-old method of survival might allow her to survive longer than any of them.

She had to see Eric and tell him what had happened. She thought about going to the stable, but realized Eric was right about the danger. If she were caught, it would be the end for both of them. There was far less danger in him coming to see her. But would he? Would he come tonight when she wanted him so desperately?

In her room she was reaching up to find the overhead light when she stiffened in alarm. That awful smell. Familiar. Oh, my God. Wirtz!

She whirled toward the door and a powerful hand clamped over her face, yanking her violently backward, slamming her hard against Wirtz' chest as his other hand fastened on her throat, lifting her, cutting off her breathing. She fought for air, her body writhing, her legs flailing helplessly. Oh Jesus. He meant to kill her. Strangely, her thoughts where not on the agony of dying, they were on Eric. She was conscious that her body was going limp, her movements diminishing, but rather than a sense of alarm at the nearness of death, she felt a deep sorrow. She would never see Eric again. And he was her only reason for wanting to live.

She tried to open her eyes, but the effort was too much for her. She wanted to swallow, but her throat hurt too much. She coughed as she sucked in air. Air. She sucked it in greedily. It was sweet. Suddenly, it registered on her fogged mind that she was breathing. She could not be dead.

Then she remembered! Oh God! Wirtz!

Her eyes snapped open in alarm and she found herself looking at the overhead light. She was laying on a bed. Her bed!

The light hurt her eyes and she raised a hand to shield them, trying to sit up.

"Ah, good. You are awake."

She turned her head. Sergeant Wirtz had pulled a chair close to the bed and was sitting facing her. As usual he was sweating and she wondered idly if he would perspire the same way in the middle of winter.

"Stand up."

She lifted her head, then let it fall back. "I can't."

"You need some help. I will help you."

He stood and grabbed her by both shoulders with his powerful hands and hauled her from the bed. When he let her go she thought her legs would collapse, but she managed to lock her knees until she was standing unsteadily.

With each passing second, she felt a little of her strength returning, and with it, a wonder of why he hadn't killed her. She knew why when she saw his whip lying on the table and next to it was a length of coarse hemp rope.

"You told the Kommandant about our—arrangement," Wirtz said. "You made it very bad for me."

She slowly shook her head. "No." Her voice was a croak, but it was there if she forced it. "I said nothing."

"I knew it was a mistake to believe you. You are a Gypsy whore. So I will do what I should have done in the first place—after you are punished." He picked his whip up from the table. "Take off your clothes."

Anna's legs were steady now and the shock of his words drove her back a step, her eyes locked on the whip. Jesus! Jesus, no. It would flay the skin from her body. She had to escape! But there was only the door and she could never get past Wirtz. She thought of screaming, but instantly realized this was a place of screams. Her only escape was to kill him or force him to kill her. Frantically, her eyes searched for an escape. In the corner! The axe!

She lunged toward the corner, her hands reaching for the broken haft. And it was there. Her hands locked around it. She turned, swinging the blade up—

Bam! Her head exploded in a blaze of agony as Wirtz smashed the heavy butt of the whip against her temple and the axe fell from her nerveless hands. She had lost! Now, her death would be a horror. Numbly she felt Wirtz wrench her around and hold her hands together in front of her. The rope was wound around her wrists and tightened until she winced with pain. He left her for an instant and she stood swaying, trying to comprehend what was happening. The blow to her temple had given her a throbbing headache and she was having trouble focusing her thoughts. Then it ceased to matter because her hands were yanked upward by the rope until she hung suspended from a ceiling beam. The pain in her wrists increased to a flaming agony and she stood on her toes to relieve some of the awful pressure.

Wirtz laughed. "Too bad you can't read the cards. You would find a hanging man. But not the death card. Not yet."

He walked toward her and Anna felt as though her blood had stopped flowing. What was he going to do? Oh God! What was he going to do?

As though she were having a nightmare, Anna watched as Wirtz slowly and carefully unbuttoned her striped blouse. "Wouldn't want to damage such nice clothes," he said. "Someone is going to need them."

"The Kommandant," she said desperately. "He'll find out. He'll have you killed."

"I'm not going to wait for that. By the time he finds out, I will be miles from here. A new place, a new identity. It will be better than the Eastern front."

He had unbuttoned her jacket and he pulled it up around her shoulders, then he was forced to stop. With her arms stretched over her head, he could not get the jacket off and he stared at it in bewildered consternation while he tried to decide what to do. He solved the problem by pulling the back up and draping it forward over her head so that she hung half naked, with her head covered, unable to see. Oh no, no. To see what was coming was bad. But not knowing was a horror.

She felt his fingers working on the knot of the cord holding her pants and she twisted violently, trying to stop him. He cursed and smashed his fist into her groin so hard she groaned in pain. "Hold still! You don't hold still, it will be worse."

Worse? My God! What could be worse? By looking down she could just see the top of Wirtz' head as he bent over the knot at her waist and, without thinking, she brought her right knee up, smashing it into his face.

His scream was muffled by blood that spurted from his shattered nose and he fell back against the chair with a crash.

Then the scream turned to a guttural snarl of rage and she closed her eyes, knowing he was picking up the whip. Now all she could do was try to block out the pain that she knew was coming.

Instead of the crack of the whip, there was a rush of cold air on her nude body as the door was yanked open, and she heard an animal-like sound that was pure hate. It was followed by the meaty sound of a fist striking flesh and she saw Wirtz fall to the floor.

He was up instantly, raging. And she heard the thud of bodies colliding with the awful power of rams in the rutting season. The room shuddered as the two men, locked together in a violent dance, smashed into the furniture. Oh God! Who was it? Eric? It had to be Eric. Dear God! Wirtz would kill him! She had to see!

She jerked her head violently forward and back and succeeded in flipping the jacket from her eyes.

It was Eric! And Wirtz had him by the throat, shaking him like a mad dog. Suddenly Eric raised his hands and smashed his palms against Wirtz' ears. Wirtz bellowed in pain and Eric twisted from his grip. Before Wirtz could straighten, Eric brought his knee up into Wirtz' already broken nose and followed it by smashing his elbow into the side of Wirtz' neck. Wirtz' head was driven sideways and he fell, rolling away. Eric snatched up one of the chairs and went after Wirtz, the chair raised to strike.

The chair never fell. Wirtz lashed out with his heavy boot, catching Eric in the thigh, driving him back against the table with a jarring crash.

Then the big sergeant was on Eric again. He wrenched him around and slipped his arms under

Eric's armpits and locked his fingers behind Eric's neck and as he applied pressure, the muscles across his back and on his arms bulged until they threatened to split his shirt. The cords on Eric's neck stood out like wires as he fought to counter the terrible pressure. Wirtz' teeth gleamed in his bloody face as his lips pulled back in a rictus grin.

Anna heard her voice screaming, again and again in useless agony and only the horror of the scene kept her from fainting.

Incredibly, Eric lifted his legs so that for an instant his full weight hung from his tortured neck. The sudden move caused Wirtz to stumble forward and Eric was able to brace his feet against the wall and shove, sending them both back into the table that collapsed with a crash. Then Eric twisted out of Wirtz' grip and he rose to his hands and knees, breathing in harsh gasps, struggling to get to his feet.

But Wirtz was already up, blood staining his uniform, the axe in his hand. Oh God. The axe! He staggered drunkenly, searching for Eric through blood-blinded eyes. Then he saw Eric and steadied, his back to Anna, the axe swinging up.

Anna mewed with agony and swung her legs up and wrapped them around Wirtz' thick neck. The move caught Wirtz by surprise and he reeled back. Anna tightened her grip, groaning as she put every ounce of her strength into her legs. Wirtz dropped the axe and clawed at her ankles, prying them apart despite her desperate effort to hold on.

Then he twisted around and his bloody horror of a face thrust into hers, his eyes wide and staring, his huge hands reaching for her face like claws. She closed her eyes. Now, he would surely kill her. It was better this way.

His hands never reached her face. She heard an awful thud and his hands slipped down her naked body, nerveless, dying even as they fell away. She opened her eyes and saw Eric standing with the axe in his hand. Its flat head was covered with blood and hair and the side of Wirtz' head was a misshapen crater.

Eric used the blade of the axe to cut her free of the suspending ropes and she collapsed in his arms sobbing.

He carried her to the bed and lay beside her, cradling her in his arms, stroking her hair and whispering over and over, "It's all right, my darling; it's all right now," until her sobs gradually subsided into shuddering gasps.

"I thought he was going to kill you," she murmured. "Oh my God, Eric. I thought he would kill you."

"He would have if it wasn't for you. You were a tiger." He suddenly chuckled. "He didn't know he had to fight two Gypsies. He didn't have a chance."

"I couldn't let him kill you. I couldn't let him."

Eric's chuckle turned into a laugh. "You should have seen his eyes. He couldn't believe what was happening. You were like a leach."

The picture that flashed through Anna's mind of her legs twined around Wirtz' neck suddenly seemed incredibly ludicrous and she, too, chuckled. "A leach. Yes. I was a leach." And she laughed hysterically until Eric once again kissed her tear-stained cheeks.

She was laying quietly, her face against Eric's chest, when he said, "It isn't over, you know."

She glanced toward Wirtz' body, alarm jerking her head up. "Not over?"

"Wirtz'll be missed. When they don't find him, they'll make a search."

Anna shook her head. "Maybe not." She told Eric about her meeting with the Kommandant. "Von Liebermann broke Wirtz to a corporal. He was reassigning him to the Eastern front. If they can't find him, they'll think he ran away, deserted. He was going to anyway after . . . after . . ."

Eric's arms tightened around her. "I know. But they won't find Wirtz. I'll get rid of him, bury him in the stable, under the manure. They won't look there."

"A good place for him."

"We'll clean this place up. They'll never know what happened."

"I found out something else, Eric. The man who killed your father."

Eric pulled back and his eyes went bleak so quickly it was as though a switch had been pulled deep in his mind. "Who?"

"Heydrich. General Reinhard Heydrich."

"Heydrich. I've heard of him. He's up there at the top with Himmler."

"That's right. You'll never be able to get to him."

Eric was silent and she knew he was thinking of his father. She pulled him close as though to hold him from harm. "Let it go, Eric," she whispered. "It's over."

"Not much else I can do, is there?" He was smiling at her, but his eyes remained bleak. They both knew it would never be over until they were both free of this horror of a place. Their lives were as fragile as bubbles and the Nazis held the pins.

Chapter 19

Eric spurred the white mare into a brisk gallop across the meadow. Lately, von Liebermann had been so busy trying to handle the influx of prisoners that he had little time for riding, so one of Eric's new chores was to exercise the horses. He was pleased with the arrangement. It meant his contact with the Kommandant was kept to a minimum, and it also meant he had more opportunities to ride. And as he rode, he continually expanded his range until now he was riding for a kilometer or more, either along the road that led to Arnschwang or deep into the surrounding forest.

When riding in the woods he watched for avenues of escape. How easy it would be to climb upward under concealment of the trees into the trackless reaches of the Bohmer Wald. The soldiers would be unable to follow him with their vehicles, and he did not think von Liebermann had enough influence to request assistance from the Luftwaffe. They were certainly not going to burn up precious aircraft fuel looking for one Gypsy. And therein was the problem.

There would be no escape without Anna, and while the Kommandant might not call out the Luftwaffe to catch a Gypsy groom, he would certainly use every resource at his command to bring back Anna. He had come to rely upon her daily forecasts for his every move. There were duties he could not delay, orders he could not ignore, but when possible his actions were based upon Anna's interpretations of the figures of his horoscope. Trusting to the stars relieved him of the necessity to make decisions. And since his fate was directed by the stars, they also relieved him of responsibility. If he made mistakes, it was not his fault. The fault was there—in the stars.

Chess was also taking much of von Liebermann's free time. He had confided to Anna that he did not like to play chess with his subordinates. He always won, so he never knew whether it was because of his skill or because they were simply sycophants who allowed him to win. But Anna had seen the peril early and had used all her skill to give him a match. At first, he had beaten her handily, but as her memory of the game came back, she found she was able to match his skill and then to beat him. Von Liebermann was chagrin, but at the same time elated. Here was a person who was not afraid of him; a person he could trust.

However, by gaining the Kommandant's confidence, Anna had also tightened her bonds. How could he allow her to escape when he could not function without her? The only solution for both of them was to remain in von Liebermann's good graces and wait for the war to end.

As Eric dismounted and began unsaddling the mare, he looked down into the valley where another trainload of prisoners had arrived. This was the fourth train to bring in slave labor since he have arrived. At first von Liebermann had ridden the white mare to meet each train just as he had when Eric and Anna had arrived, but lately he had remained in his quarters, leaving the disagreeable tasks of segregating the prisoners to his subalterns. The atavistic SS men did not find the job disagreeable. Eric watched in morbid fascination as the guards used their whips and cudgels on the helpless prisoners. And more than once a shot rang out as one of the prisoners either refused or was unable to rise after being beaten to the ground. As he watched, the ritual of forming the prisoners into lines was conducted: the women and men into two lines, the old, the sick, and those too young to work, into a third.

There were so many. Seven cars. And, unlike the previous trains, none of these were Gypsies. These were Jews with yellow six-pointed stars pinned on their clothes. Judging by the way they were dressed, they were from the city, which meant they would not last long at the hard, physical work. Only the strongest of that first group of Gypsies were still alive, and not many from the later groups. Eric had thought they would have to build additional barracks to house new prisoners. But with the rapid attrition and callous overcrowding, the original barracks were able to accommodate the surplus.

When he had witnessed the arrival of the other trains, Eric's anger and disgust at the carnage had made him so ill he had been forced to retreat into the stable, unable to watch any longer without getting sick. It suddenly struck him as he now watched the brutality that, while he still felt a bitter, frustrating anger, he did not have the same nausea that had always before forced him to turn away. Now, it was as though he was watching a scene from a movie. He heard the shots; he saw the blood; he almost felt the blows. But there was an unreality about it that made it bearable.

Watching the line of old people and children walking into the woods on their way to the hospital, he felt a mounting suspicion. Was there really a hospital? And if so, how far away was it? How far did those people have to walk?

He had not as yet removed the saddle blanket from the mare and he left it in place. He lifted the saddle from its rack and replaced it on the mare. After fitting the bridle, he mounted and road at an easy canter toward the forest, taking a course that led him obliquely away from the pitiful column of prisoners and their guards.

Hidden by the trees, he swung in a long loop around the mountain. He was confident he would not be missed. There were still three hours or more of daylight, and it was not unusual for him to take each of the horses in turn for a long exercise ride. He was not worried about becoming lost, even though he had never been in this part of the forest. No Gypsy ever used a map, and despite wondering willy-nilly through often unfamiliar areas, a Gypsy never got lost. And Eric's years of wondering through the back roads of Europe had also given him an unerring eye for landmarks. An instinct for direction was also there somewhere in the ancient memory of his mind, an instinct as sure as the needle of a compass.

He had to ride for most of an hour before he was able to make his way through a canyon with a rushing stream and over a ridge that lead him around the far side of the mountain and to a valley where the column had appeared to be headed. He reined in and studied the wooded floor of the valley. The group could be anywhere among the trees. But there was no evidence of a hospital. Could they have taken a different route? Not likely. This valley, which branched off from the wide, shallow valley where the camp was located, was flanked by mountains that would be difficult for even a young, healthy man to climb.

There was the possibility they had stopped. But where? And why?

As though in answer to his questions, he saw a flash of light among the trees on the floor of the valley and he heard the sound of a motor. A truck? Could they have loaded the people into trucks? But why do that here? Why not save them the long walk and bring the trucks to the camp?

The sound of the motor died, but he had located its source and he guided the mare down the slope, threading in and out among the trees. He had almost reached the floor of the valley when he heard the staccato burp of a machine gun and he pulled up abruptly, half expecting to feel bullets smashing into his chest. But there were no bullets, no whine of ricochets, nor smashing of nearby tree limbs that would indicate a miss. They were not shooting at him. Who then?

He had a hollow feeling in his chest that made it hard to breathe as he urged the mare forward. He knew! He knew what he would find.

The sound of the machine gun was so loud he had to be almost on top of it. He dismounted, and after tying the reins to a tree, crept forward, keeping to the cover of trees and boulders.

And there—what he suspected was there in front of him, and he forgot everything except the horror. In a small clearing, the prisoners had been lined up in front of a long pit whose raw earth was piled on the far side. A truck was stopped with its tail facing them, and a machine gun mounted in the truck bed fired burst after burst into the defenseless men, women and children. They had been forced to remove their clothes and they stood naked in a bitter wind with their heads down, holding hands, their eyes closed, waiting for the terrible jolt of the bullets. Except for the whimpering of some children and the soothing voices of their mothers, they awaited death with the silence of terrible despair. When the bullets slammed into them, they fell backward into the pit. Those who were dead fell like rag dolls and lay still. But others were only wounded and they cried out in pain and fear. Some tried to rise and were cut down by SS-guards with rifles and pistols who stood at the ends of the pit.

What could he do to stop the horrible slaughter? Charge the truck? Wrest the machine gun away and turn it on the guards? He would never make it. He would be seen running across the clearing long before he reached the truck. Then he, too, would join the bodies in the pit. Besides, he was already too late. The machine gun stopped firing because it had run out of targets. The rifles and pistols fired a few more desultory shots, then they, too, were silent. It was over.

But before he turned away, Eric saw four other raw patches of earth in the valley. This was where the people from the other trains had ended their journey. This was the 'hospital!' Many of his own people lay in a jumble of bodies beneath one of those ugly mounds.

He stumbled back to the mare on stiff legs, his eyes blinded by tears. What could he do? Who could he go to for help? He had seen prisoners on work details beaten and shot so often he had come to accept it. But this! This was mass murder. The slaughter of old people, sick people, women and babies.

Some day! Some day the power would be in his hands and he would be an object of vengeance that would never end.

It was the one thought that pounded through his mind as he made the long ride back to the stable.

Anna noticed that for some reason von Liebermann was finding it difficult to concentrate on the astrologic chart she had spent the day preparing. Usually he sat across from her, staring at the symbols as she interpreted each one.

But this time he hardly glanced at them, pacing gloomily, lighting cigarette after cigarette, then quickly snubbing them out in an overflowing ashtray. Since the night Anna had encountered Katalin in his quarters, Von Liebermann had changed their conferences to his office, and now, he paced between the center table and his desk as though searching for a means of escape.

As would any Gypsy fortuneteller, Anna watched her subject carefully, incorporating the telltale evidence of his actions into her interpretations. And like Gypsy fortunetellers throughout the ages, she was struck by how easy it was to delude the subject into believing whatever she said. There were two logical reasons for that: the subject wanted to believe, and the Gypsy was careful not to say anything that could not be believed. For this reason, their words often took the form of questions instead of direct statements. If the subject replied, he provided a clue to the next question. If the subject did not reply, his body language often provided the necessary clue.

Now, Anna watched her subject's pacing, the compulsive smoking, the way his forehead was knitted with worry and on his chart she pointed to the sign for Mars. "Mars is going to be in your house for a few days. You have probably experienced the beginning of turmoil entering your life."

"Yes. That is true."

She waited for him to continue, but the SS officer had retreated into his own thoughts. She indicated the sign of Mercury. "This is the sign of the messenger. You have recently received disquieting news."

"Disquieting? Yes, it is disquieting. They are asking too much. I don't know if I can discharge the responsibility."

Anna pushed the chart aside. Von Liebermann was not paying attention anyway. "You have been given new duties? Greater responsibilities?"

"Yes, yes. Much greater."

"I see for you a promotion."

"I am to be a full Colonel, a Standartenführer."

"I also see a change in your habitant. Perhaps new quarters, larger, more modern."

"I would assume so, yes. Yes, of course they would be more modern. The place has been renovated dozens of times."

The place? Not here? Her protector was going to be leaving? Alarm made Anna forget her role and she stood up. "When? When are you to leave?"

"Soon. Very soon." Von Liebermann took a linen napkin from a drawer and wiped sweat from his forehead. "I will have to leave it all, everything I have worked for."

Anna felt another shock of fear. "Your horses? You will have to leave your horses?"

"Yes. My horses. Everything." His eyes swiveled toward her. "Except you. I cannot leave you."

The fear settled in her stomach, burning like acid. If he left the horses, he would also leave Eric. She ran her tongue over her dry lips. "If it is a larger responsibility, you will command many more people. They might not appreciate our—relationship."

"They will have to." He took a quick stride to the table and she could see the panic in his eyes.

Anna seized upon his desperation like a drowning person grasping at anything that promised rescue. She had to find words that would make him refuse the assignment. But carefully. She must lead him carefully. "This could be a great opportunity for you. The one I have been predicting."

Von Liebermann did not hear. He was locked into his own fears. "Did you know I was a school master before I took the oath? Yes, I told you that. But a school master. I did not have to deal with such matters as over crowding and prisoners and shortages of food and medicine and building roads and graveyards. Now they want more. More for God's sake."

Desperately Anna pointed to one of the signs on the chart, any sign. "You may not have to go. See. Here is an inconjunction in the aspect of Mars and Venus. You should offer your services. But only if they are absolutely necessary."

The Kommandant stopped pacing and hope blossomed in his eyes. "Does that mean I can refuse the assignment?"

She wanted to shout 'yes,' that he <u>must</u> refuse. But in reality, she knew such a thing was impossible. When an SS officer received an order, he had to obey. "Refuse? No. I do not see refusal. But delay. The time is not right for you to make such a move. It is not right for a major increase in responsibility."

"I knew it. I felt it." Von Liebermann resumed his nervous pacing. "But it is too late. They care nothing for my feelings. The orders are specific. We must leave tomorrow."

Tomorrow! The strength drained out of Anna so abruptly she sank into the chair. Her mind was reeling, but she needed her wits now more than any time in her life. She could not leave Eric. She had to convince von Liebermann that he did not need her. She would take her chances with the new Kommandant, but she could not leave.

"You are forgetting," she said. "Yours is the sign of Cancer. You are self-contained. Strong. Purposeful. You have the strength to discharge this great responsibility without help." She tapped the chart. "It is here, in the stars."

"Yes. Everything is in the stars. But I need your help to see it. I will need to know what they say. You will come with me. I will see to it." He went to the door and opened it for her. "You must work carefully. There is danger in so much responsibility. Great danger. If I should fail . . ." He straightened and attempted a weak smile. "But I will not fail, will I? You have seen my strength. They have seen my strength. They have been witness to my capabilities or they would not have called me for this great mission. Wouldn't you say that?"

Anna gathered her papers with numb fingers. Tomorrow. He would force her to leave with him tomorrow. She had only hours to think of a way to change his mind. "Yes, Herr Kommandant," she whispered. "They have seen your capabilities."

"I will need my chart early tomorrow. I must be aware of the future. There must be no surprises. Do you understand? No surprises."

"Yes, Herr Kommandant. No surprises." She walked past him into the night and he closed the door. No surprises. How was she going to live with the one he had dropped on her? She had to tell Eric. Oh, God. She had to see Eric as soon as possible. She looked toward the setting sun. Brilliant shades of red, pink and gold spread across the sky. Shafts of sunlight blazed through holes in the surreal clouds like pathways to heaven, promising a glorious tomorrow. But not for her. Not for her.

Chapter 20

It was dusk when Eric stopped outside the stable and unsaddled the mare. He should rub her down and give her a good brushing, but he was in no mood for the chore. He would allow her to graze for a while before he brought her into the stable. Then he might feel more like working.

He carried the saddle and bridle into the darkness of the tack room which he had converted into a room for himself. There was no heat and he did not have a bed, but he had been able to appropriate two thin, straw-filled mattresses which he piled one atop the other. With an extra blanket he had obtained and, if necessary, a layer of horse blankets, he was able to keep warm. There were no closets, but except for his striped prisoner's uniform, he had no clothing.

He did not need a light to place the saddle on its rack and to hang up the bridle. He was reaching for the switch to the overhead light when he heard the rustle of straw, and with the instincts of a cat, he dropped to the floor and rolled away from the expected attack. The attack did not come. He lay on his stomach, listening.

The rustling sounded again. Coming from his bed. Anna? Impossible. She would have called to him the instant he entered.

"Where have you been? I've been waiting for hours."

The words were spoken in Romani. A woman's voice. One he recognized. A woman of his tribe. Of course, Katalin. He had known her since they were children and had never much liked her. Even as a child she lacked a quality he had searched for in all his friends. Gypsies did not have a word for it. The Gorgios called it 'class,' What the hell was she doing here?

He got to his feet and turned on the light. She lay on top of the blankets on his bed. She no longer wore the hated prison uniform. Von Liebermann had given her a small wardrobe of civilian clothes, and now she was dressed in a peasant's skirt and a white blouse with a wide neckline she liked to wear pulled down off one shoulder. Her skirt was pulled up to display her legs. She had taken off the men's boots she had taken to wearing, so that her feet were bare.

Eric stood under the light, staring down at her. "What the hell are you doing here? You'll get us both killed."

"No, I won't. He's with Anna, like he is every night. Getting his fortune told,— he says."

"That's right. Why else would he keep her alive?"

Katalin's smile was lazy insolence. "Why does he keep me alive?"

"Are you so bad in bed that he needs her too?"

As he knew it would, the remark stung her and she stood up. "He doesn't need anybody. I am the only one."

Eric let a sharp retort die. She was no better nor worse than he, using whatever talents she had to stay alive. "Sorry. I know that."

She walked toward him, her hips swinging, her bare feet moving silently on the earthen floor. "I'm here to be with you."

There was no mistaking the invitation in her hips and in her eyes and he felt the impact in his groin. She stopped in front of him and reached up to touch his face. "I like your beard. It makes you look like a banker."

Eric smiled. Gypsy men often wore mustaches, but seldom closely trimmed beards. So any man with a beard probably looked like a banker to her. "Maybe when this war is over, I'll be a banker."

"Bankers have nice houses. You will need a woman to go with it." She pulled her shoulders back, knowing that the swell of her breasts above the top of the blouse would be impossible to ignore.

Eric recognized the trick and refused its invitation. "Why are you here? You know what will happen if even one guard sees you."

She tilted her head and looked at him out of the corners of her eyes. "To see you."

"Thanks for the compliment. But I think I'd rather have my life."

Katalin's smile turned into a pout. "You don't mind risking your life to see her."

Eric felt a chill of apprehension. "I don't see her. You think I'm crazy?"

"I don't believe you."

Eric turned away in sudden relief. She was guessing. If she had been able to prove he saw Anna almost every night, then someone else might be able to prove it also. The Kommandant might not want to, but he would have to act. Anna's punishment might be light—Von Liebermann thought he needed her—but Eric would probably be hung by his wrists with his hands tied behind him so the weight of his body would slowly pull his arms from their sockets. It was a particularly agonizing form of punishment he had seen used on prisoners in the work details at the whim of their SS guards.

So it was stupid of Katalin to come here. If they were caught, they would both dangle from a rope. "That doesn't matter. You've got to get out of here. Somebody could come by any minute."

"Why? The Kommandant won't let anybody but you touch his precious horses."

"There's that other groom—the boy. He comes by some times."

"They've got women in their barracks. New ones from the train today. He won't come by." She moved close and put her hands on his shoulders, looking up into his face. "I get lonesome. I don't have anybody to talk to. Nobody. I think sometimes I'm going to go crazy."

It had to be difficult for her. Unlike Anna who could be self contained within her mind, Katalin lived outside herself. She spoke little German and von Liebermann did not speak Romani so there could be no real conversation between them. And, like most Gypsies, she did not read, so that form of companionship was also denied. She truly must be desperate, desperate enough to risk both their lives by coming to the stable. And ignorant enough to think she would have to offer him her body to keep from being sent away.

"All right," he said softly. "As long as you're here, you can stay for a few minutes."

"Oh, Eric. I knew you liked me."

She reached down to pull her blouse up over her head and Eric took hold of her wrists. "No, Katalin. We talk. That's all."

She had no understanding of his rejection. There was hurt in her voice when she said, "You don't want me?"

"It isn't that I don't want you, but . . ." How could he make her understand he was in love with Anna? Men took her all the time who were in love with other women. Her concept of love was distorted by a lifetime of reality. "But not now." There was something he could tell her that she would understand. "I've just seen dozens of people murdered. I can't get it out of my mind."

Blood Promise

"Murdered? Where?"

He held her hands tightly, emphasizing his words with the pressure of his fingers. "You've got to keep this to yourself. If von Liebermann, if any of them, suspect you know, they'll kill you."

"What? What is it?" She was standing on her toes, her face close to Eric's when the door opened. Eric and Katalin jerked their heads toward the sound in startled alarm. Anna stood in the doorway, her eyes wide.

"Anna!" Something had to be terribly wrong. She would never place both their lives in jeopardy by coming to the stable unless it was an emergency. "What is it? What's wrong?"

Anna did not move. She stood frozen in the doorway, her eyes locked on Eric and Katalin. Eric took a quick stride and pulled her inside the room and closed the door. Katalin went to a small bag she had left on the floor and took out a cigarette that she lit with a wooden match.

Eric's sharp tug had pulled Anna against the rack of saddles and she leaned against it, her legs weak, her eyes closed.

"Why?" she whispered. "Why Eric?"

"It isn't like that," he answered. "She wanted someone to talk to. That's all."

Katalin laughed. "That's right. I was lonesome."

The tone of Katalin's voice implied she was not telling the truth and Eric felt like throttling her. "Shut up, Katalin," he snapped. "Anna, believe me. This is the only time she's been here. You know it couldn't be anything else."

But the pain in her eyes told him she did not believe him.

"I came to tell you that von Liebermann has been transferred. He's going to be Kommandant of a bigger camp." She took a deep, shuddering breath. "He's taking me with him."

Eric felt as though someone had driven a fist into his stomach. "When?"

"Tomorrow."

Tomorrow! Mother of Christ! That did not give him any time to think. But maybe he would not need time. There was desperation in his voice as he said, "Did he say anything about taking his horses?"

Anna shook her head. "He can't. It's forbidden."

Eric glanced at Katalin who was sitting on his bed, her knees pulled to her chest, her arms around her legs. He wanted to tell Anna that somehow they would have to escape before they could be separated, but he did not want to say anything in front of Katalin. She would probably demand to be taken with them.

"What about me?" Katalin's face was pale, her voice small with anxiety. "Will he take me?"

Anna swung to face the Gypsy girl, her eyes blazing through the tears. "What do you care? You'll have each other."

Katalin's face cleared and she smiled. "That's true. You can think of us while you're telling him those lies about his future. You might even take my place."

"And I'll be better than you ever were!"

Anna reached for the door and Eric took hold of her arm. "Anna. We've got to talk. We've got to decide. . ."

She yanked her arm free. "She wants to talk. Talk to her!"

She snatched the door open and was gone into the night. Eric pulled the door shut to close off the light that could betray her, then stood with his forehead pressed against the door. Damn! Damn! Damn! Tomorrow. He would have to find some way to see Anna before she left and get this misunderstanding straightened out.

Katalin came up behind him and rubbed both hands across his back and shoulders. "She's right," she whispered. "We'll have each other."

Eric lifted his head and a rage shot through him that was so strong it burned like fire. He yanked the door open and shoved her out into the night. "Keep away from me!" he gritted. He was so angry he did not care if the guards did see them. "I hope the hell I never see you again."

Katalin had stumbled to her knees and she stared up at him, her lips pulled back from her teeth. "You'll see me," she snarled. "You'll beg to see me."

"Like hell," Eric slammed the door as much to shut out the sight of the hate in her eyes as to shut out the spill of light. He fought to control his anger, to think. And his rage took a new course. It wasn't just Katalin. It was them again. The Nazis. They had all their lives in their hands, twisting them to suit their own ends with no thought that they were dealing with real people, people with feelings, people who could be hurt, their emotions shattered as easily as their limbs. God damn such men. What the hell was he going to do?

Chapter 21

Anna sat in a compartment inside the rushing train with her face set in stony resolve. The time for tears was over. The reality was that she had lost. Every turn of the wheels was taking her farther from the days of joy with Eric, farther from the moment of betrayal. Now, she must look forward. But forward to what? To nothing; nothing but survival. Survival culminating in a dreadful revenge against Albrecht Grantz for shattering her life. With Eric only a bitter memory, regaining her family's estate was the one reason—the only reason—she had for living.

But as she sat in the comfortable seat in the first class compartment of the train, wearing a new dress and coat, looking out the window at the mountains and forests, she would have traded all the comfort, all the security to be again in that horrible cattle car, surrounded by the dead and dying, breathing air fouled by excrement and death, but sheltered in Eric's arms, feeling his body pressed against hers, knowing he cared for her.

Cared for her! A bitter smile twisted her lips. Had he ever cared for her, or had he simply used her? She had looked for him an hour ago when two smirking SS guards had escorted her aboard the train, but he was nowhere to be seen. Had he even tried to see her? Probably not. He had probably been busy hiding Katalin so that, with von Liebermann's protection gone, she would not be put back on a work detail. The thought made her smile grimly. Risking his life to save Katalin was like trying to save a fish from drowning. Katalin, with her talents, was perfectly capable of saving herself. And when she was finished with Eric, she would toss him to the wolves just as Katherine the Great disposed of her burned out lovers.

To take her mind off the painful memory, she focused on the passing scenery. It was startlingly beautiful. The train was winding through a narrow mountain pass next to a rushing stream. The weak sunlight of late December filtered between the high mountains and played with the ripples of the stream. She thought the train was moving in a northern direction, but she could not be sure. Her sense of direction was not as keenly honed as that of the nomadic Gypsies. Even so, she was quite sure they were not in Germany. She had read the names on the village stations they had passed since leaving the camp: Furth-im-Wald, Domazlice, Stankov. They sounded Czech, but she couldn't be sure.

And what did it matter anyway? Wherever the destination, she would endure.

The compartment door opened and Hauptsturmführer Brock, von Liebermann's orderly, stood in the doorway holding the door open. "Come," he said. "The Standartenführer wants you." When she stood up, he added, "Bring your charts."

Anna had been expecting the summons. Von Liebermann had been on the edge of a nervous breakdown all morning. As the time approached to leave the camp and Sturmbannführer Muller, the new Kommandant, had not arrived, he had become increasingly agitated. Unable to delay any longer, he had been forced to break protocol by turning over command of the work camp to one of his officers who would be in temporary command until the arrival of Muller. In addition, there had been the demanding task of supervising the loading of his personal effects on the train. Now, with his first chance to reflect on the uncertain responsibilities of his new command, his nerves would be unraveling. Carrying the Ephemeris and her manila file-folder, Anna followed Hauptsturmfuhrer Brock down the corridor to the large stateroom that von Liebermann's new rank of Colonel warranted. Brock rapped exactly two times and at von Liebermann's "Kommen," he opened the door and stepped back so Anna could enter.

Just inside the door Anna stopped. This was her first look at an SS officer's train compartment. She had expected to see the best in first class compartments, but she was dumbfounded to see it was furnished like the living room of a baronial estate with ornate French Rococo chairs and couches, upholstered in deep plush of a dark purple hue. The floor was cushioned with a thick carpet whose pile had been sculpted and dyed with a large SS rune symbol. The walls and ceiling were paneled in sections of black walnut in which arbors of grapes had been carved. A beautiful desk made of rosewood inlaid with ebony and ivory was situated so that light from the windows illuminated the writing surface.

The elegance of the room was stunning, but Anna's eyes were locked on the figure of a woman seated on one of the couches with her legs crossed, smoking a cigarette. Katalin.

Anna felt an ambivalent confusion. She despised the idea of the Gypsy girl's presence. She would prefer to have her out of her life forever. At the same time, she felt a keen sense of joy that she was not with Eric. Katalin had caused her to lose Eric, but there was some comfort in knowing the *arschloch* would not be able to benefit by her betrayal.

Von Liebermann motioned Anna to the desk. "We will arrive in Prague in a few hours."
Prague? So they were in Czechoslovakia.

"It is only an hour from there to our destination," Von Liebermann continued. "I must know what to expect."

Anna opened the file-folder and removed her work papers. "I have the chart for today. I know you haven't had time to look at it—"

"Forget it. I know about today. It is terrible. One of my worst. It is the future that I must know. What to expect. Will it be good or bad."

Anna wondered how far into the future she could safely extrapolate. If she only knew something about his new assignment, it might give her some insight. "It would help," she said as she opened her notebook, "if I knew the location of your assignment, the circumstances."

Von Liebermann nervously ran his hand up the shaved back of his head and drew on his cigarette. "Location. Sixty some kilometers north of Prague. A place called Terezin."

At the sound of the name, a memory from her history classes flashed through Anna's mind. "Terezin? The famous fortresses?"

"That's right. The Small Fortress and the Great Fortress. The Czechs have been using the Great Fortress as an army garrison. The small one is a prison and a penitentiary."

"I don't understand. Why are we going there?"

"Because Obergruppenführer Heydrich has transformed Terezin into a Konzentrationslager for Jews. It is now to be known as Theresienstadt."

A concentration camp? Anna did not understand the fine line that separated a work camp from a concentration camp, but it sounded horrible. "And you will be the Kommandant?"

Von Liebermann nodded. "It will be a terrible responsibility. That is why they gave me the promotion."

Anna studied the deep lines in von Liebermann's face. She could understand why he was desperately afraid of this new assignment. If he failed in the task of operating a small, out-of-the-way work camp, it would hardly be noticed. But failure as Kommandant of a large concentration camp could be catastrophic. It would not only end his career, it could get him shot. There was no way his future was going to be pleasant. Von Liebermann was not a man who took changes in stride. Once he had established a routine, every disruption produced an agony of unknowns.

"Remember," she said, "I told you that the next few days would be bad."

Von Liebermann raised both hands as though to ward off the impending evil. "I knew it; I knew it. But you must work. If tomorrow is unfavorable, I will have to do something. I cannot take over a new post on a very bad day."

"What can you do? Aren't they expecting you?"

"Yes, but . . ." Von Liebermann put his hands over his face. "I can be sick. In Prague. They cannot force a person to take over a new command if he is sick."

"That's true. The delay of a day or two would change the unfavorable aspect. It might be changed already."

"Yes, yes." He took a monogrammed handkerchief from his pocket and wiped at his face. "I must know before we reach Prague."

"You will know," Anna promised. "I guarantee it."

She did not have to prepare his chart to know what his next few days would be like. He would not have the courage to pretend illness when they reached Prague. He might be afraid of the fate told him by the stars, but he was more afraid of the fate that could be commanded by General Reinhard Heydrich. And whatever the conditions of his new post, he would face them with trepidation, concealed by an icy aloofness, as though he were immune to fear. In the end, because of his penchant for efficiency and driven by his fear of failure, he would produce the demanded results. But all the while he would be trembling with apprehension. Which meant he would need her and her counseling more than ever.

Yes, she could see von Liebermann's future quite clearly; she was glad she could not see her own.

From outside the doorway of the stable Eric straightened from the task of pitching straw and narrowly watched the approach of three black-uniformed SS officers and their contingent of security guards. This had to be the new Kommandant. He was coming to inspect the stable he had inherited with his new command. It was ironic and, somehow, typical of the SS that he had chosen to inspect the horses before inspecting the prisoners. There was no doubt about his priorities. Unless he took a violent dislike to Eric, it appeared that his job would be intact.

But much more depended upon this initial meeting than simply his job. He was determined to escape. When he learned von Liebermann had departed unceremoniously that morning and had taken Ravanna with him, he had been disconsolate. He'd had no chance to explain, no chance to tell her why that bitch Katalin had been in his room. What must she think of him? He could still picture the tragic look in her eyes as she had stormed into the night. He could not live with that broken, despairing look haunting his dreams. He had to find her. Had to tell her the truth. Now, he had another promise to keep.

But where was Anna? If she knew her destination, she had not told him. And he was in no position to ask about von Liebermann's new posting. But he would find out. And he would go to her and together they would leave this rotten war to the savages. That was also part of his promise.

Watching the approach of the three officers, he tried to determine which was the new Kommandant. Not the one on the right. The symbol of his rank on his tunic collar indicated he was only a Hauptsturmführer, a captain. And he was young. No more than early twenties, with round, ruddy cheeks and strands of fine blonde hair escaping from beneath his visored hat which bore the dreaded Tote of the Death's Head Schutzstaffel.

The man next to him, the one in the middle had to be the captain's commanding officer. He was a full Standartenführer, as tall as Eric, with the broad shoulders and narrow hips of an athlete. He walked with long easy strides. Relaxed. But with his back perfectly straight, his hand holding a baton swinging easily. A prominent jaw with muscles bunched along his jawbone made his face appear almost square. His eyes were dark brown, slightly sunken under a wide forehead. His hair, cut very short on the sides and back, was such a dark brown it appeared to be black. Eric judged him to be in his early thirties. On his left breast was pinned a red, white and blue ribbon from which dangled an Iron Cross, First Class. Next to it was a silver wound badge. On his left sleeve was the black and silver cuff badge of the elite Leiberstandarte Adolph Hitler.

That one would not be the new Kommandant. He was a soldier. A man who would be more comfortable looking down the barrel of a gun than herding prisoners like swine. The man on the colonel's right: he was the one.

He was several pounds overweight and he had stuffed himself into his black SS uniform so that it fit him poorly. He looked as though he would be more comfortable wearing a double-breasted business suit. His insignia indicated he was a major, a Sturmbannführer. His face was almost perfectly round and his dark blue eyes were small and set close together behind thick glasses. His lips were heavy, with a mean, cruel twist. Before the war he might have been a shopkeeper, or a town's mayor. God help the horses if this man decided that, like von Liebermann, the perfect image of a Prussian officer was astride a horse.

Eric carefully leaned the pitchfork against the wall of the stable and straightened respectfully. When the group halted in front of Eric, he expected the Standartenführer to do the talking, but after a brief glance at Eric he stood studying the stable and the surrounding corral and pastures.

The fat Sturmbannführer took a step forward, keeping an eye on the pitchfork. "What is your name?"

"Eric, Herr Sturmbannführer."

Eric noticed that at the sound of his voice, the eyes of the Standartenführer had flicked toward him like a camera taking a revealing picture. "You speak German."

Damn. Eric did not like such attention. The way to survive was to be invisible. Perhaps he had put too much strength into his voice. He would have to watch that. "A little, Herr Standartenführer."

The Standartenführer eyes seemed to take another picture before they left him and went back to studying the building.

The Kommandant however, heard only the words not the tone and he grunted with satisfaction. "You are the groom?"

"Jawohl, Herr Sturmbannführer."

"I am Sturmbannführer Ernst Muller, the new Kommandant. You will take orders from me."

This man, Eric sensed, would be impressed more by military precision than by sniveling subservience and he snapped, "Zu befehl, Sturmbannführer."

Muller glanced toward the Standartenführer as though to make sure the colonel caught the obedience that his presence produced, but the colonel was looking out across the fields with a faint smile playing at his lips.

"Show us the stable," Muller commanded. "The horses. We wish to see the horses."

"Jawohl, Herr Sturmbannführer."

Eric was turning away when Muller suddenly stopped him. "Wait! Are you a Jew?"

"A Jew? No, Herr Kommandant. I am *Romani*, a Gypsy."

"Oh," Muller said.

The young captain laughed. "Not much difference, if you ask me."

Eric felt his muscles tense with sudden anger and he turned his face away. During the last few years he had found it increasingly difficult to keep a blank expression when insulting remarks were made about Gypsies. He had usually been able to make the insulter pay by raising the price of his merchandise. But now he had nothing to sell. So this was no time to be sensitive. These men were killers. All he could do was file away the remark—and wait.

When he looked back at the Germans, he saw the tall Standartenführer watching him. Now, the man jerked his head toward the door. "Show us your horses."

"Jawohl, Herr Standartenführer." The colonel motioned to the two guards to wait outside and Eric led the way into the stable. Thank God he kept it clean. A few weeks ago he might not have been so particular, but the constant threat of severe punishment at the whim of a displeased SS officer had made him as meticulous about cleanliness as any German housfrau. Scrubbing and sweeping were a hell of a lot easier to endure than hanging by your wrists or being beaten by a whip.

The officers nodded in approval as they looked at the clean stalls and the glowing coats of the three horses that were in their stalls.

"Who helps you here?" Muller adjusted his glasses, looking for Eric's helpers. "How many?"

"No one, Herr SturmbannFührer. There was another groom, a soldier, but he was given other duties."

"Good," Muller said. "Very good."

"Who is your veterinary?" The Standartenführer did not look at Eric as though simply looking at an inferior would be degrading.

"I am, Herr Standartenführer."

The tall SS officer ran his hand over the flank of the dun colored mare. "Commendable. Do you ride?"

"Only when they need exercising." The German turned his head to stare at Eric coldly. He raised an eyebrow a fraction of an inch. Eric got the message and quickly added, "Herr, Standartenführer."

"That will not be necessary," Muller said. "I will be riding a great deal."

Eric's heart sank as he said, "Jawohl, Herr Sturmbannführer." Exercising the horses was his only excuse for getting away from the camp, for reconnoitering the area. But this fat pig would probably be like von Liebermann and ride a great deal at first, then tire of it until he hardly rode at all. All he had to do was wait.

"You must love horses?" the captain said. "I could never keep such a place so clean."

Eric couldn't believe that anyone, even a young SS fanatic who looked as though he should be in a Hitler Youth uniform, could make such a stupid remark. They all knew what would happen to him if he did not keep the place immaculate. Perhaps they wanted to believe that people worked for them because working for the Nazis was such a privilege. But he knew how to play that game.

"I do, Herr Hauptsturmführer. I love horses." He was laying it on a bit thick, but that was what they wanted to hear. Actually, he liked horses more than most Romanies. Gypsy horses were given the care and food they required to do their job. No more. They were not pets. There was no personal attachment.

But Eric had begun to feel a certain kinship with the horses of von Liebermann. Like him, they were slaves to the whim of their master. They could be beaten, starved, or killed and no one would notice or care. And while he felt no love for the horses, he treated them with more deference than he would have a few weeks ago.

"Which one?" The Standartenführer lifted his sculptured lips in a thin smile as he looked at the three horses. "Which one do you love the most?"

Eric did not like the tone of the Nazi's voice nor the question itself, which seemed pointless from a man who looked as though he did nothing without a point. Eric nodded toward the white mare, which to anyone who knew horses, was clearly the best of the three. "The white mare, Herr Standartenführer."

The SS Colonel unbuckled the flap on his holster and pulled out a Luger P-08 automatic pistol. He grasped it by the barrel and extended the butt toward Eric. "Here," he said. "Kill her."

Muller gasped and stared at the colonel to see if he was serious. Eric knew he was. The man's words had been casually conversational, but there was nothing casual about the way his eyes were measuring Eric. Eric knew why. This was his punishment for being insolent. The Nazi had heard something in his voice that had told him his true feelings. Eric was lucky the man had not said, 'kill yourself', which he was sure he would have done with the same casual tones.

Slowly Eric reached out and took the pistol, holding it awkwardly. "I know nothing about weapons, Herr Standartenführer."

"Let me show you." The Standartenführer took the pistol and pulled back the slide to jack a cartridge into the firing chamber. "There. All you have to do is put it against her head and pull the trigger." He handed the pistol back to Eric with a smile. "Be careful where you point it. We wouldn't want anyone hurt."

"Herr Standartenführer," Muller said nervously. "Are you sure . . ." His voice trailed off as the SS Colonel turned his eyes to look at him. Muller remained silent, but his gaze locked on the pistol and he fell back a step.

Eric stood holding the pistol. This was more than a punishment. This was a test. It would be just as easy to shoot the SS officers as the horse. There were the two guards outside, but the pistol held several bullets. He could shoot them too. Then what? Then he would be hunted with dogs, troops and airplanes. And when he was found . . . No, he would not be taken alive. If he killed them, he would be killing himself.

Holding the pistol gingerly, Eric took a step toward the mare. Would the Standartenführer actually allow him to kill the horse? Horses were not so plentiful that they could be wantonly destroyed. Most likely, the Nazi would order him to stop at the last second. He merely wanted to see if Eric would obey orders no matter how absurd they were.

But suppose he was wrong and the man did not stop him. Could he do it? Could he put the muzzle of the gun against the temple of the beautiful mare and send a bullet into her brain?

What choice did he have? It was more likely the gun was loaded with blanks and the officer was simply seeing if he would obey orders without question. He surely would not be foolish enough to put a fully loaded pistol in the hands of a prisoner.

As though he had read Eric's mind, the Standartenführer took the pistol from Eric's hand and pointed it toward one of the pine posts supporting the roof and pulled the trigger. The sound of the shot was deafening and splinters flew from the post. Muller almost fell backward, and Eric flinched while the horses surged back and reared in fright. Only the young captain had not moved. Apparently, he was used to the unexpected from his commander.

Light from the open door was momentarily blocked as the two SS guards ran in, their rifles held for firing. They stopped when they saw the tableau and the Standartenführer waved them back outside.

"Out," he said. "It is all right. Stay outside."

The Standartenführer went to the post and delicately traced the white wound with his fingers. The bullet had gouged a chunk of wood from the post and it hung loosely like a piece of flesh. "You see. They are not blanks."

He came back and put the pistol in Eric's hand. "It is automatic, ready to fire." He nodded toward the horse. His lips were smiling, but there was a whip in his voice as he added, "Go on. Kill it."

Eric stared at the German. He had only a fraction of a second to decide whether the man actually would kill him if he refused. He did not take his eyes from the German's as he took the gun by the barrel and extended it. "No. I don't kill perfectly good horses."

Muller sucked in his breath and the captain stiffened. The colonel's eyes changed, losing their glint of humor. He made no move to take the pistol. "Suppose I told you to use it on yourself?"

"I would do it, Herr Standartenführer. But first I would kill you."

It was a calculated gamble based upon years of evaluating human nature as he traded horses. He was betting his life he had read this man correctly and that the test was over.

For an instant, Eric thought he had made a mistake when the German took the pistol and pointed it at his chest. Then the Nazi turned and in one fluid motion put the pistol to the mare's temple and fired: bam! bam! bam!

The mare's head exploded and, with a grunt of surprise, a great gust of breath come from her lungs. She stood, held up by nerve endings that had not yet received the message that the brain was dead. Then her legs buckled and she crashed to the floor. Her legs threshed and the muscles of her sides quivered briefly. Blood and gray matter oozed from the side of her head.

As the SS Standartenführer calmly holstered the pistol, he glanced at the dead mare indifferently. "Give her to the cooks." He turned and walked out the door followed by a shaken Muller and his aide. Eric watched them go with mixed feelings. What a cold, heartless bastard. Thank God all Germans were not like him. If they were, nobody could stand against the German war machine.

Then he reconsidered. How would such a man match up against a devil-may-care, laughing Irishman—or as was more likely, a British Tommy? Which would be the first to crack? In the last war it had been the Germans. He would put his money on the man with the best outlook on life, the man with the sense of humor but who, if necessary, could be tough as sun-dried goat meat. That had to be the British, especially the Scots. In the long run, they were too proud, too stubborn to be beaten.

He went to the stable door and stood watching the officers and the guards walk toward the distant headquarters. The Standartenführer had to be an inspector who was checking the camp's condition before it was turned over to Muller, the new Kommandant. With the German's usual Teutonic penchant for keeping records, he would write a comprehensive report for Einsatzgruppe Commander, Reinhard Heydrich. At the thought of Heydrich, Eric clutched the door frame hard. Another cold blooded bastard. Anna had said Heydrich was the man who had killed his father, the man whose death would fulfill his blood promise.

Thoughts of Anna produced a gloomy depression. How was he ever going to find her? There were thousands of Gypsy prisoners. Even if he could somehow escape without being caught, he would never be able to track her down.

Then he brightened as he realized he did not have to find Anna. He had only to find von Liebermann. There would be records somewhere that would tell where the man had been transferred.

Such records, however, probably would not be kept here. They would be kept in Berlin or at Einsatzgruppe headquarters in Prague.

His depression surged back. There was no way a Gypsy could get a look at those records. Now if he were that SS Standartenführer bastard, he would walk in anywhere and . . .

Eric straightened slowly while hope surged through him so powerfully that his hands began to shake. Why not? Why couldn't he be an SS officer? If he wore the uniform of an SS Colonel, who would dare question him?

He shook his head in disgust. To get the uniform he would have to kill the son-of-a-pig—and his guards. And how could he possibly do that without getting caught?

Then an idea began to form as Eric stood watching the SS Colonel and his entourage climb into the big Horch touring car for the ride to review the work sections. The colonel, his aide and the two SS-guards had arrived in the touring car that had its canvas top lowered. They would most likely leave in it, taking the road west toward Regensburg or east toward Prague. He would have to intercept them at an isolated place on the road. It would be his only chance.

Intercept them with what? The two guards carried rifles. And both officers carried pistols. He would need a weapon himself. Damn. He wished he knew more about firearms. But in Europe, a Gypsy with a gun was asking for instant death. So Gypsies stayed far away from firearms. But with a machine gun, one did not have to be a marksman. All one had to do was point and fire. He would have to get a machine gun. And he knew where.

Checking to make sure he had his black armband in place, Eric walked purposefully down the path to the headquarters building. Muller and his aide were away on the inspection tour with the Standartenführer. So the Kommandant's office should be deserted. And while he had never been in the office, Eric was sure there would be weapons there.

The SS soldiers guarding the headquarters building were used to seeing Eric and they paid no attention as he headed for the kitchen. It was early for the evening meal, but today because of the inspection, the schedules were in disarray.

Entering the building Eric turned away from the kitchen area and walked down a corridor that should take him to the offices. If he was stopped, his story would be that Sturmbannführer Muller had asked him for information about the horses.

But he saw no one. In the office area, he paused. Which was the Kommandant's? A door near the front of the building bore the hooked-cross of a Nazi swastika and the twin lightning SS rune. It seemed like the logical choice.

He knocked, standing slouched with his head down and his shoulders hunched.

There was no answer, no sound. He took a chance and turned the knob and pushed the door open, standing to the side so he could make a swift retreat. But there was no cry, no challenge.

He peered around the jamb of the door and saw an anti-room. Deserted. There were several steel filing cabinets and a desk holding papers in orderly stacks. This would be the office of the Kommandant's aide-de-camp. He was tempted to try a quick search to see if he could locate copies of the orders that had transferred von Liebermann, but quickly realized it would be like looking for a snake in a forest. It could take hours.

He shut the door behind him and crossed to an open door on the far side of the room. A quick glance told him this was the office of the Kommandant. There was a carpet on the floor and the furniture was of good quality. A large desk occupied one side of the room. But what interested Eric was a tall wooden cabinet against the far wall. If the Kommandant had a rifle, it would either be in that cabinet or in his living quarters.

The cabinet was not locked and he swung the doors open and grunted with satisfaction. There were two rifles standing upright in a rack. On the bottom of the cabinet was a machine gun of the type many of the guards carried. It had a stock attached for shoulder firing and a long clip for ammunition. It was called a Schmeisser MP40. He had seen it used often enough so he was sure he could handle it. He took it from the cabinet along with two extra clips loaded with bullets. There was a knapsack hanging from a clothes rack and, by folding the gun's collapsible stock, he was able to fit it into the knapsack.

He closed the cabinet door and left the room, carrying the knapsack and almost bumped into an SS corporal. The corporal had a mail packet in his hand and he looked at Eric in surprise. His mouth opened to shout an alarm and Eric said quickly, "Is that the mail, Herr Rottenführer?"

The corporal hesitated. "Ja."

Eric relied on the soldier's instincts to obey orders without question and he said firmly, "The Kommandant, Sturmbannführer Muller, sent me for it."

The corporal stared at Eric's striped clothes and his eyes grew round. "The Kommandant?"

Eric pointed to his black armband. "You know me. I am his groom. I am to take his horse to him at the work site. He wants me to also bring the mail." He held out his hand and the bewildered corporal handed him the mail packet, which Eric put in the knapsack before he snapped a stiff-armed salute. "Heil Hitler," he said and walked away. Behind him he heard a weak, "Heil Hitler."

Outside, Eric hurried toward the stable where he hid the Schmeisser and the clips of ammunition. Flies were already buzzing around the head of the dead mare and the smell of the blood was making the other two horses nervous so he led them out into the corral. He carried a saddle and bridle from the tack room and placed them where they would be readily available. He would prefer to ride out now so he could prepare the best ambush for the SS inspector, but he had no way of knowing whether they would be heading over the Bayrischer Wald toward Regensburg or across the border into Czechoslovakia.

He brought a brush from the stable and began brushing the gelding, standing where he could keep an eye on the headquarters buildings. They would most likely bring that fat pig Muller back before they went on their way. Unless they chose to spend the night. He hoped they would not. Unlike many people who tended to postpone facing the unknown as long as possible, Eric preferred to act quickly. Until a problem was resolved, he was restless, expending energy uselessly in mentally pursuing a million possibilities. And with this situation, he would prefer not to dwell on the possibilities since most of them appeared to end with his death.

The sun was beginning its slide toward the horizon when the Horch returned. The officers went into the headquarters building while the two SS guards remained in the car. That was encouraging. If the Standartenführer did not intend to leave immediately, the guards would have gone in with him. Eric hoped Muller did not encounter the corporal who had brought the mail. The man might ask if the Kommandant had been given his mail and a negative reply would quickly bring a search party and he would have to make a run for it.

But there was no evidence of disturbance when a few minutes later the Standartenführer and his aide left the building and climbed into the Horch which made a half turn and headed northeast toward Czechoslovakia. They had left the car's canvas top lowered. Good. That would make it easier for him.

Eric hurriedly saddled the gelding and slipped on the bridle. He retrieved the knapsack from its hiding place and, slinging the bag across his back by its leather strap, he mounted and trotted into the trees in the direction he usually rode when exercising a horse. Once concealed by the trees he swung in an arc that took him toward the northeast. Unlike the road, which followed the easiest path through the canyons, he headed in as straight a path as possible across the mountains. It was difficult going for the horse as he picked his way through forest-choked valleys and over boulder-strewn slopes. Eric did not drive him too hard. Time was important, but he would lose more time if the beast went lame.

When at last he came over a ridge of granite and saw the road below, the gelding was breathing hard and foam flecked its flanks and nostrils. There was no sign of the big Horch and he could only hope he had been able to get ahead of it.

There was no concealment on the rocky slope and he pushed the horse hard until he reached the floor of the valley and rode into the forest that bordered the road.

He remained under the trees riding parallel to the road, looking for a suitable place for an ambush. He found a place where the valley narrowed and the road forded a small stream. He could hide behind a tree or a large boulder close to the road. When the driver of the Horch slowed to cross the stream, he would make his attack. Provided he was not too late and they had already passed.

Tying the horse out of sight in the trees and carrying the knapsack, Eric ran to check the mud at the edge of the stream. No sign of a recent vehicle crossing. He was ahead of them. Unless—the thought chilled him—they had taken a different route. He knew these mountains fairly well, but he certainly did not know every byway. It was possible his journey had been made for nothing.

Then a sound made him smile grimly. The car. It was approaching, the driver was using a low gear to assist in the braking as he headed down toward the stream crossing. Eric quickly waded the stream to the far side and concealed himself behind a boulder and took the Schmeisser from the bag. He secured the two spare clips of ammunition under his rope belt and made sure the one in the gun was seated properly by smacking it on the bottom the way he had seen the guards do. He unfolded the gun's stock easily enough, but it took him anxious moments to work the bolt handle on the side of the gun. He was finally rewarded by the familiar click of a cartridge sliding into the firing chamber. Now, all he had to do was point it and pull the trigger. The trick was going to be in taking the Standartenführer's uniform with no blood on it. To do that, he would have to take out the two SS guards and the captain and force the colonel to get out of the car. He would make him disrobe before he killed him. He did not like to think about that part. Cold-bloodedly shooting the guards was going to be difficult enough. If they weren't all SS-Totenkopfverbande bastards he might not be able to do it.

His misgivings were interrupted by the sight of the Horch approaching through the trees, still with its top folded down. As he had anticipated, the driver slowed almost to a stop before he shifted into low gear and moved into the stream. Now!

Eric moved from behind the tree to the center of the road and pointed the Schmeisser at the startled men in the touring car. "Halt!" he shouted. "Halt!"

But instead of stopping, the driver stepped on the accelerator and the car bucked as its rear wheels spun on the slippery rocks of the stream, sending up a spray of water and gravel. The SS guard in the front seat swung his Schmeisser into line quicker than Eric thought possible and loosed a burst at him just as one of the spinning wheels gained traction and the car slewed sideways sending the guard's shots high into the trees. But he was already leaning out of the teetering car, correcting his aim for another shot. The thought that flashed through Eric's mind as he pressed the trigger on his own Schmeisser was that the stupid guard had made it impossible for him to prevent getting blood on the Standartenführer's shiny black uniform.

Then his machine gun was spewing fire and, to Eric's total surprise, it bucked in his hands like a living thing, hurling itself up and completely over his shoulder so that he was standing empty handed, his mouth open in dismay. His eyes focused hypnotically on the flashes from the muzzle of the guard's

Schmeisser and something hit him in the stomach so hard that he was staggered backward just as his head exploded in a burst of white pain that instantly changed to brilliant red. Then the red vanished and all that remained was inky blackness.

Chapter 22

It was dusk under overcast skies when the train slowed and eased to a stop. Anna pressed her face to the window and tried to see where they were. This had to be Terezin, their destination. Hauptsturmführer Brock had told her to gather her things because they would soon be leaving the train.

It was a ludicrous command. Except for the Ephemeris and her work papers, her only possessions were a coat, the clothes she was wearing, her Tarot cards, a small comb and a toothbrush with no toothpaste. She had only to put them in her bag, slip on her coat, and she was ready.

She tried to estimate the elapsed time since their car had been switched to another train in the marshalling yards of Prague. Watching from the car window, she had been dismayed at the number of men in the familiar striped clothing of slave laborers performing maintenance on rails and locomotives, and at the number of German Wehrmacht soldiers guarding them. If this was an example of the way the war was progressing, it appeared the Germans were in complete control. She wished there was some way she could obtain news of the war. Von Liebermann had a radio, but it was never on when she was in the room. Her only source of news was in glimpses of German newspapers on von Liebermann's desk. And their headlines always blazed with German victories. Could they be true? What was going on in the United States? Was Germany going to conquer the world? It was a thought of horror.

During the ride from Prague, she had tried to remember as much as she could about the famous old fortress of Terezin. It had been constructed by the Austrian Emperor Joseph during the eighteenth century and named for his mother: Empress Maria Theresa. Now it was a concentration camp. For Jews?

Like most Americans, she was dimly aware that for years the Nazis had been harassing the Jews. In 1938, there had been some news about the infamous Crystal Night when the shops of Jews had been ruthlessly attacked and ransacked. Since Hitler had become Reichschancellor there had only been sporadic reporting of the way hundreds of German Jews had been rounded up and interred in work camps throughout Germany, supposedly to wait for deportation. Perhaps Theresienstadt—nee Terezin—was to be a deportation center. But deportation to where? At one time the Nazis planned to establish a Jewish homeland on the African island of Madagascar. But that idea had been abandoned. What about Argentina? Palestine? The U.S.? At least the Jews had places to go, places where they were wanted. But the Gypsies—for them there was no place. No nation in the world would welcome a Gypsy. Once a Gypsy was in a concentration camp, his only way out was by dying.

But like the Jews, Gypsies were survivors. The difference was that the Jew had his religion to sustain him. The Gypsy had only his will.

When Hauptsturmführer Brock opened the door, she followed him down the corridor. He went back into the train as she stepped out onto a concrete platform that was level with the car's exit.

The air was heavy with impending rain and she pulled the collar of her coat close around her neck. She did not have a hat, but her hair had grown long and thick and it protected her neck and ears from a biting cold.

The station seemed to be on the edge of a town. Terezin? The streets she could see were devoid of trees but well paved. They were lined with large apartment buildings that crowded the sidewalks. There were no lights, no movement of any kind. Except for the panting of the train's engine, there were no sounds. It was as though it was a deserted city, and Anna had a moment of panic when it occurred to her that perhaps she was to be abandoned here.

Then she heard footsteps and two SS soldiers with rifles stepped out onto the platform and took up positions where they could watch the street. Colonel von Liebermann came down the steps followed by Katalin and Brock. Two more SS soldiers, with their rifles slung and carrying the Kommandant's bags, followed them onto the platform. They set the bags down, unslung their rifles and took up guard positions.

"What is this place?" Katalin wore a new cloth coat and she pulled it close against her throat so that Anna would be sure to notice.

"He called it Theresienstadt. We're in Czechoslovakia."

"Oh."

Anna realized that Katalin's reaction would have been the same if she had said they were in Tasmania. Czechoslovakia was only a name she might have heard in a casual conversation. Was ignorance the same as being uneducated? And was there really bliss in ignorance? Not when the unknown was filled with terror. Katalin was uneducated, but she was far from stupid. The look in her eyes as she stared at the dark and silent buildings, betrayed her fear.

Von Liebermann, wearing his long leather great-coat, also must have felt the town's miasma. Pulling on gloves, he glanced nervously at the dark, deserted street. "There's supposed to be a car," he snapped. "Where the devil is the car?"

Brock's eyelid began to twitch and he looked at his watch. "We are five minutes early. They will be here."

Before von Liebermann could reply, there was the sound of approaching vehicles and Brock smiled. "This should be them, Standartenführer."

A convoy of three military trucks led by a long Mercedes sedan with small Nazi pennants fluttering on the front fenders, swept around a corner and roared up to the platform. When they stopped, a squad of German soldiers leaped from the canvas-covered truck beds and, at the barked direction of a sergeant, formed two ranks in the street facing the platform. The rear door of the Mercedes opened and an SS Captain sprang to the ground and snapped to attention. He was tall, more than six feet, with broad shoulders. His black uniform, which he wore without a coat, fit him so well it appeared to be custom tailored. His hair was reddish blonde and curly and worn uncharacteristically long on the sides and back; SS officers usually chose to emulate the Prussian military style in which the sides and the back were clipped very short and high. His features were chiseled, but with the healthy smoothness of youth while his eyes were of such startling blue that the dim light could not hide their pale brilliance. He was, Anna concluded, the living prototype of SS Reichsführer Heinrich Himmler's perfect 'Nordic' Aryan. Himmler was such a fanatic about preserving the Nordic stock that when his SS officers wished to marry, they had to submit photographs of their bride for his approval. If the shape of the girl's skull, the distance between her eyes, or the shape of her nose did not meet his standards, he declared her to be 'not suitable' and the marriage forbidden. Conversely, SS officers who were truly Nordic types were requested to mate with select young Lebensborn women in biological if not actual marriages to produce genetically acceptable German children. Looking at this Hauptsturmführer's handsome features, Anna wondered whether he was one of Himmler's favorite breeding studs. And would being both classically Nordic and an SS officer produce the ultimate in arrogance.

He brought his arm up in a rigid salute. "Heil, Hitler," he said in a crisp, clear voice. "Welcome, Herr Standartenführer. Hauptsturmführer Deiter Voss - at - your - service." He separated the final words in a staccato flourish like an accomplished musician emphasizing a particularly telling cadenza.

Von Liebermann returned Voss' salute with a languid touch of his riding crop to the peak of his cap. "You have kept me waiting, Hauptsturmführer Voss." His voice was calm but edged with the icy menace that seemed to be ingrained in every SS officer.

The Hauptsturmführer was not dismayed. He sprang forward with a smile. "You are right, Herr von Liebermann. Things are in terrible shape here. You can see, we need your leadership."

Von Liebermann's head came back and he looked down his nose at the young captain. "One of my first duties should be to have you shot."

"And you would be right, Herr Standartenführer. Being late was inexcusable. Never mind that your train was several minutes early. And never mind that the stupid car would not start. And never mind that we received a large shipment today that had mixed Jews and political prisoners together. And never mind that—"

"Stop!" Von Liebermann raised his hand in resignation. "I will not have you shot if you get us to our quarters before we freeze."

"Jawohl, Herr Kommandant." Voss jerked his head at the sergeant who quickly directed two of his men to break ranks and load the new Kommandant's bags in the boot of the Mercedes while the others piled into the trucks.

Hauptsturmführer Brock directed von Liebermann's SS guards to join the others in the trucks. He was reaching for the door of the Mercedes when Voss said, "Allow me."

He reached in front of Brock and opened the door and held it while von Liebermann and the two women climbed into the back seat.

Anna noticed that as he held the door for them, Voss surreptitiously studied Katalin and her; When he was sure that neither von Liebermann nor Brock would notice, his gaze lingering on their legs and breasts. She also noticed that Katalin gave Voss an equal appraisal and an invisible smile tugged at her lips as she settled back in the seat. Von Liebermann did not notice, but Brock did and his lips tightened.

A strange reaction. Was Brock's disapproval because of his loyalty to von Liebermann? Or did he have designs on Katalin himself? There was also the possibility he had taken an instant dislike to the young captain, seeing in him a threat to his position as von Liebermann's aide-de-camp.

Anna dismissed the subject. Either way, it had nothing to do with her. It was, however, another bit of information to store in her memory to be retrieved in preparing some future horoscope as though the news had come from the stars.

Voss pulled down a jump seat for Brock. Then he climbed in front next to the driver and motioned him forward.

As they made their way through the deserted streets, Anna turned her attention to the buildings they passed. Unlike most European cities whose streets meandered as though they had first been animal paths, the streets of this town were laid out in a perfect grid with all corners at right angles. The streets were narrow with room for only two cars. Most were surfaced with brick or stones, but a few glistened with recently poured macadam. There were few trees and those struggled through holes in the narrow sidewalks.

Each side of the street was lined with two and three story houses and apartments with no break between them. For the most part, they were constructed of brick or stone with slate roofs. The sound of the truck motors swept through the canyon of buildings like the thunder of a summer storm.

The car's heater was blasting hot air and Anna began to be uncomfortably warm. She was sandwiched between the left side of the car and von Liebermann who sat in the middle of the seat staring straight ahead, both gloved hands gripping his riding crop. At one point Voss twisted around in the front seat and said, "You would not guess it, sir, but these buildings we are passing are all quarters for Jews."

Von Liebermann was silent as though the information was of no interest, but Brock said, "These? They live like royalty?"

Voss laughed. "Not quite. Actually, the interiors are being modified. Each one of those buildings will soon be able to house three or four hundred."

Von Liebermann leaned forward for a better look out the window. "Three or four hundred? Are you sure?"

"Yes, sir. It will be necessary. We estimate there are more than eighty thousand Jews in Prague alone."

Von Liebermann appeared stunned by the figures and Anna stared at the façade of the buildings in amazement. "What happened to the people who lived here?"

Voss' pale eyes flicked to her as though weighting whether to answer. When von Liebermann did not give him any signal he could interpret as disapproval, he said, "Many remain. However, should the need arise, they have volunteered to resettle elsewhere."

"What is the native population?"

Again the captain's eyes flicked toward von Liebermann before he answered. "Approximately four thousand."

"And you plan to house eighty thousand here?"

This time Voss did not hesitate. "Oh, no, no," he laughed. "This is to be a model ghetto, more in the order of a spa. Everyone will be comfortable."

He turned back, ending the discussion, leaving Anna with the feeling that, like Alice, she was about to go through the looking glass into a world populated with strange and terrifying people.

In less than a minute, the procession came to a stop in front of an old three-story building made of stone with steeply-sloping slate roofs. Across a narrow sidewalk, three wide marble steps led to a revolving glass door. A bronze plaque imbedded in the stone next to the door indicated that this was the Hotel Theresa.

Captain Voss led the way into the small lobby, leaving the soldiers to bring the luggage. The small lobby had the forlorn elegance of a dowager whose perfume had deteriorated until all that remained was the musk. A wainscot of very dark mahogany, hand carved with coats of arms, protected the lower part of the walls. On the floor, the parquet squares had been meticulously crafted so the wood grains formed perfectly matched patterns. But the exquisite parquet was almost completely covered with a large faded-green carpet. Two large couches and three over-stuffed chairs, upholstered in worn green tapestry, looked as though the hotel had been built around them. The plaster walls and the high ceiling were painted in a pale green that had been designed to compliment the furnishings, but over the decades, had faded to a dingy white. The light sconces and the wrought-iron chandelier could have been installed after the invention of electricity. An oaken reception desk was built into the wall opposite the door. A metal-grilled door to a lift was in a small alcove near the desk.

The concierge behind the desk was an SS-sergeant, and as they entered, he snapped to attention with a sharp click of his heels. Captain Voss held out his hand and the sergeant swept four keys from the marble top of the desk and slapped them in Voss' palm. Voss smiled and made a courtly sweeping gesture toward the lift. "This way, *si'l vous plait.*"

As they walked to the lift, he raced ahead of them and pulled aside the grilled door. The elevator was too small for more than four. Someone would have to wait in the lobby. It could not be von Liebermann; as Kommandant he waited for no one. Lieutenant Brock was expected to accompany him. And Captain Voss had to work the controls. So either Anna or Katalin would have to wait. Von Liebermann would have to choose.

Anna found the situation amusing. Von Liebermann was unexpectedly placed in a position where he had to declare his priority. Would it be Katalin or Anna?

Katalin also recognized the implications and she quickly stepped forward. Von Liebermann stopped her by raising his gloved hand. Then he jerked his head a fraction of an inch toward Anna and she stepped into the car. Voss slid the grilled door shut and worked the controls. As the elevator began to rise, Anna looked through the grill into Katalin's eyes. They were burning with such intense hatred that Anna felt as though she had been attacked. Why should Katalin hate her? She had nothing to do with the selection. Maybe that's what happened when you had a good mind and nothing to fill it except selfish thoughts of yourself. She would make it a point to stay away from the Gypsy girl.

"I have personally selected the best suites, Herr Standartenführer," Voss said. "They are on the top floor where you can overlook the entire area."

Von Liebermann was not impressed. "Don't you have a proper headquarters?"

"No, sir," Voss said cheerfully. "Obergruppenführer Heydrich himself selected the hotel. He felt that its central location and good construction would be appropriate."

Von Liebermann's melancholy deepened. "It seems that most of my job has been taken out of my hands."

"Not true, Kommandant. We have only begun here. Carrying out the plans of Obergruppenführer Heydrich will require a keen mind and total dedication."

"Are you implying that I do not have total dedication?"

Again Voss was not intimidated by the edge in von Liebermann's voice. "Naturally not, sir. You were selected because of your excellent record. Everyone here will carry out your orders to fulfil your destiny."

His use of the word 'destiny' seemed odd to Anna and she looked at Voss sharply, but his face had the guileless innocence of a child.

Von Liebermann snapped his riding crop against his boot waspishly. "As yet I have no clear idea what those orders are."

"I have the papers, sir. They are very detailed. With your permission, I will brief you in the morning."

Here was a place where von Liebermann could exert his authority and he snarled, "Tonight. We will go over them tonight."

Voss grinned as though he were the one who had won a point. "Tonight. Yes, sir. I am - at — your - service."

The corridor to the third floor had come into view as they spoke. The elevator was moving so slowly it was difficult to tell if it had actually stopped until Voss swept back the grilled door.

The corridor smelled of fresh paint and the walls and woodwork gleamed in dim light from wall sconces. Voss led the way to a freshly painted door in the middle of the corridor. If there had been a number on it, it was now painted over. "This is your suite, Herr Standartenführer," he said as he inserted a key in the lock. "I have placed your secretaries in suites on either side."

He did not hesitate at the word 'secretaries' and Anna wondered whether it was usual for a high-ranking officer to travel with such an entourage. Voss might believe one of them could be a legitimate secretary, but he would have to be extremely naive to believe that both were secretaries.

After opening von Liebermann's door, Voss snapped on the light and stepped back into the hall. "With your permission, sir, I'll show the ladies to their rooms, then return."

"Yes, yes," von Liebermann said. "That will be satisfactory."

He and Hauptsturmführer Brock went into the room and Brock dismissed them by closing the door. Captain Voss strode down the hall to the right and opened the door adjacent to that of von Liebermann's and snapped on the light." He smiled at Anna. "This is your room, madam. I hope you find it suitable."

Anna caught her breath. The room was large and newly decorated, its textured plaster walls painted eggshell white. The ceiling was high, with rounded cornices, centered with a beautiful crystal chandelier. Heavy brocade drapes were pulled across floor-to-ceiling windows that occupied the entire wall opposite the door except for pairs of tall French doors that opened onto small balconies overlooking the street. On the floor was a soft blue, wall-to-wall carpet with a sculptured nap. The furniture, including chairs, a sofa and a table, were of Boulle design, heavily gilded in gold and inlaid with mother-of-pearl and upholstered in blue plush. Leaded-glass windows in the arched-top doors of a huge sideboard revealed a collection of exquisite blown-glass and cut-crystal vases.

Anna assumed that a door on her right led to the bedroom and she pointed to a similar door on the left next to the sideboard. "Where does that lead?"

"It opens to the center suite."

"The Kommandant's?"

Voss inclined his head without answering.

"What part of his suite?"

She detected a trace of a smile as he said, "The study."

Which meant that if Katalin had a similar suite on the opposite side, her door would open into von Liebermann's bedroom. So Deiter Voss had made his evaluation. She wondered what his reaction would be if he had been proven wrong. She was certain he would have laughed and pretended that it was all good fun.

"I have arranged for dinner to be served in the Kommandant's suite," he said. "I assume you will join him."

"If it isn't too soon. I would like to take a bath. I assume there is a bath."

"Oh, yes indeed." He strode toward the bedroom door. "Allow me to show you."

"No," Anna said quickly. For an inexplicable reason she did not want him in her bedroom. His manners were impeccable, but there was something about his ready smile and light banter that bothered her. Maybe it was his eyes. They seemed to be constantly analyzing the effects of his words. "I'm sure it will be satisfactory."

His smile flashed as he said, "Yes. Of course." Before she could stop him he reached out and took her bag from her hands. "Here. Allow me to. . ." The bag slipped from his hand and spilled its meager contents on the floor. "Oh, I am sorry." Voss quickly dropped to one knee and replaced her comb and toothbrush in the bag. He was reaching for the scarf-wrapped deck of Tarot cards, but she swiftly knelt and picked them up. Voss did not look up. He gathered her notes and papers and put them back in the bag as she held it open.

Anna felt sure he had deliberately dropped the bag so he could see the papers. Was he a spy for Himmler or Heydrich? Was von Liebermann right in believing he had been placed in a sensitive position as some sort of test?

A dozen possibilities raced through her mind, all of them ominous. She reached for the Ephemeris but Voss beat her to it. Holding the booklet he looked at her quizzically. "Astrology? Is this part of your secretarial duties?"

"Why don't you ask the Kommandant?"

Anna held out her hand, but instead of giving her the booklet, he stood and began leafing through its pages.

"I, too, am a student of the occult." He reached to help her to her feet, but she chose to ignore his hand.

"I would hardly call astrology the occult."

"And the Tarot cards?"

So he did know what was wrapped in the scarf. "I'm a Romani. Many of us read the cards."

Before he answered, Voss handed her the Ephemeris. He took a package of French Gauloise cigarettes from his inside jacket pocket and lit one with a gold lighter embossed with the SS Death's Head. He extended the pack toward Anna and she shook her head. Voss' voice was softly insolent as he said, "Perhaps you would read them for me some time."

She stared at him, wondering if he was serious. He did not seem to be a man who would put stock in anything beyond his senses. "Again," she said, "you should talk to the Kommandant."

"Of course. I'm certain he will give his permission. You know, of course, that Reichsfüher Himmler is a devotee of the occult."

Which, Anna was sure, accounted for Voss' interest. "And Reichsprotector Heydrich," she said.

Voss shrugged. "I believe he is part of the Ahnenerbe."

"The Ahnenerbe?"

"The Führer's Occult Bureau. You're aware, of course, that the Führer is also a devotee of the occult. Especially where it involves the Spear of Longinus."

"What spear is that?"

As though her question had given him permission to remain, Voss crossed to stand with his back to the drapes, as far from the door as possible, Anna noted.

"The spear used by the Roman Centurion who thrust it into the side of Christ when he was on the cross."

"I remember the story." Why was he telling her this?

"The head of the spear is still in existence. It was kept in the Hofburg Museum in Vienna. I personally believe it to be one of the primary reasons that the Führer was so interested in taking control of Austria."

"What is so important about an ancient spear?"

"Ah. You have a very perceptive mind. The point is not the spear itself; it is the legend. Whoever claims it and solves its secrets, holds the destiny of the world in his hands for good or evil. That's why it's sometimes called 'the spear of destiny.'"

"And Hitler believes this?"

"And Reichsführer Himmler. He had a replica of the spear made in 1935, for himself. He keeps it in his room at Wewelsburg."

Anna had read about Wewelsburg. It was a castle in Germany that Himmler had constructed at a cost of millions of Reichsmarks. It was supposed to be an overwrought reproduction of the great castles built by the Saxon Kings. She would well imagine such monsters as Himmler and Hitler believing in the fairy tale of a magic spear.

"And the real spear? Is it still in Vienna?"

"God no. One of the first things Hitler did when he entered Vienna was to pay a visit to the Hofburg Museum. Then he had Major Buch take the spear and a lot of other symbols of the German Empire, to a special Museum in Nuremberg."

Anna looked down at the Ephemeris booklet. "What is the point of all this?"

"The point is that we can help each other."

Anna had thought that was what he was leading up to. However, she had not expected him to be so blunt. "I see. Since so many of your superiors are involved in the supernatural, you feel that it would be in your best interests to also be involved."

"Precisely."

"I assume that you have already done some studying on the subject."

"Everything I could get my hands on."

"So you know about Standartenführer von Liebermann and my relationship with him."

Dieter Voss smiled and gestured with his hands, palms upward. "I felt it was in my best interest to learn as much as possible about my new commanding officer."

"And if I agree to give you astrological readings—with the Kommandant's permission . . ."

"Of course."

". . . what will I get in return?"

"Freedom. The good life. As much as I can arrange. I am not without resources."

"I gathered that," Anna said dryly.

She was going to accept his offer. Not to do so would be foolish. Why make him an enemy when she did not need enemies? Better that he should be an ally. Then too, she might be able to use the charts to her advantage, as she did with von Liebermann.

"All right," she said. "I will help you if I can."

Voss grinned and walked to the door. "Good. You will see. This place will not be so bad." He opened the door and before he stepped out, he added. "Not so bad for either of us."

After he closed the door, Anna walked to the drapes and parted them to look out the window. Moonlight filtered through the overcast and highlighted the somber buildings of the small town. It looked very peaceful. But she knew the stones and bricks concealed misery and fear. Voss was wrong. Whatever happened, it would not be a good life. When the town was called Terezin, there might have been joy and hope. But as Theresienstadt, it held only pain and death.

Chapter 23

March, 1942

The knife was known as the Fairbairn-Sykes Fighting Knife, or simply the S-K Knife. Its two inventors had designed it for one purpose and one purpose only: killing. The stiletto blade was six and seven-eighths inches long and sharp enough to use as a razor; its grip was heavy and roughened to provide a firm grip in wet weather.

Eric held it in his hand the way he had been taught: low, firmly but delicately, to give full use of the wrist, which was where a real knife fighter gained his advantage. He stared at the man facing him who was armed with a similar knife; not at the man's eyes, but rather, at his knife. Only a fool—and a dead one at that—watched his opponent's eyes. Even if they gave away his move, by the time you switched your concentration from his eyes to the movement of his knife, it was too late. No. You watched the hand with the knife. And when it moved, you moved faster. And you did not go for your opponent's body with your own knife, you went for his knife hand, his wrist, his arm. Speed! That was what won fights. In hand-to-hand combat and in knife fights, the man with the greatest speed and muscular coordination was invariably the winner.

Twice the instructor had been able to slip past Eric's guard and slash him across the padded wrist. The edges of the training knives were dull, but even with the padding, it hurt like bloody hell to be whacked on the wrist or forearm with the heavy blade. The hurt was compounded when you were told your hand had been cut off and that you were as good as dead.

He had tried the same maneuver on the instructor, but Sergeant Tim MacCready, formerly of the Scots Horse Guards, was too experienced and he had blocked Eric's move neatly and countered with a quick, hard slash to the wrist.

Eric knew if he tried any kind of thrust, the results would be the same. The Scotsman was waiting.

Instead, Eric flicked the knife toward MacCready's chest and let it go. MacCready had already begun his counterstroke at Eric's exposed wrist, but the flying knife took him by surprise and his move was milliseconds slow and he missed just as Eric's left elbow smashed him behind the ear with an audible crack. MacCready's eyes rolled back and he crumpled to the ground.

Eric straightened and looked down at the burly instructor. "Sorry about that, sir. But you're dead."

There were murmurs from the men who had been watching. Like Eric, all were dressed in the baggy, camouflage-painted coveralls of British commandos. "I say, old man," one of them said. "That's not really cricket, you know."

Eric stared at the man. "We're not playing cricket."

The man saw the smoldering fire in Eric's hooded eyes and he shifted uneasily. Eric no longer had the beard and in the weeks since Czech and Greek patriots had smuggled him out of Europe, the smooth contours of his face had grown lean and hard, and his eyes always seemed to hold a burning anger that made the other men talk softly when they spoke to him.

"He's right." MacCready climbed to his feet, slipping his knife into its sheath. "This is na' a bludy game. I know a lot a' ya think that killin' a mon wi' a knife is na' the ruddy thing ta do. Especially if ya do it when he isn't lookin'. Auld school and all that. But they sure as hell would'na mind doin' it ta ya. So come off it. Imri did wha' 'e had ta do to take me oot. Ya'd damn well better learn ta do the same. Now pair uff an' git ya crackin'."

Eric picked up his knife and was turning to search for a partner when a corporal trotted up to him. "Sir," he said. He looked for a badge of rank on the collar of Eric's coveralls, but there was none so he repeated, "Sir. You're wanted in the captain's office."

"It's about time," Eric muttered. He'd already been in the commando training school longer than he thought was necessary, even though almost from the first day, he had requested to cut the training program short. He wanted to get back to Germany, to begin his search for Ravanna. But, until now, his requests had gone unanswered.

He reported to MacCready then followed the corporal across the green field used as a training ground.

Aston House, the ancient manor located near Stevenage in Hertfordshire, was one of many large estates voluntarily surrendered by its owner to British forces as quarters for troops. M.I.6, when it had begun dispatching agents into Europe, had originally set up a school near Highgate in north London to train intelligence agents. While the school proved to be adequate for training in the use of codes and operation of wireless sets and enemy methods of operation, it could not accommodate the type of physical combat which an agent might require for evasion and escape. In 1941, M.I.6's Experimental Station 6 of the SOE's Small Scale Raiding Force commandos had appropriated Aston House as one of their training centers. Under the urging of the Twenty Committee, they had reluctantly agreed to extend their training to include M.I.6 agents such as Eric Imri.

Inside the manor house, the corporal led the way to what had been the house's library and was now the office of Captain James Drury, Station 6 training officer. Eric hoped his heavy combat boots were not leaving a trail of mud on the highly polished tile floor of the vestibule and the morning room where he waited outside the library door while the corporal went inside.

As he waited, Eric became aware of the sound of music. The faint sound was coming from the living quarters upstairs. The song was unfamiliar, but it was being played by one of the big American bands: Glenn Miller, or one of the Dorsey brothers he supposed. For the past few weeks he had heard them enough to gain a grudging acceptance of their brand of music if not a fondness. He had not realized how much he missed Gypsy music until he had heard a Bartòk symphony on the BBC. As with most Gypsies, music was imbued in him. Even journeying throughout Europe, there had never been a time he could remember when the sound of a Gypsy violin had not been part of his life. The image of his father sawing away at his violin brought an inner smile. He had been such a God-awful player. But his father loved music, and every night he had taken his weather-beaten violin from his bag. Its bow, as often as not, was strung with frayed horse hair, and sometimes, a string was missing on the violin, but what his music lacked in finesse it made up in intensity. When other Gypsy musicians were in the area, his father had joined them, filling the night air with fiery Gypsy *esárdás* and plaintive *lassus*.

Strange the way the music had opened doors. In the most hostile of communities, when Bela

Imri drew his violin from its tattered bag and launched into a frenzied *esárdás*, the rough farmers and laborers would gather around and sing and dance and, eventually, buy horses.

Now, all of that was gone. One more score to settle with the Nazis and the butcher, Reinhard Heydrich. The bastard probably did not realize the loss of their music would do more to break the spirit of the Gypsies in the work camps than anything else the Germans could do to them.

Eric sighed, a disgusted growl. As long as he was kept playing at war here in England, Heydrich's days of terror were not going to end.

He hated to wait. He had always been impatient, unwilling even to engage in long bargaining harangues when selling a horse, much to the disgust of his father. The measured ticking of a nearby grandfather clock reminded him that every second was precious. While he was undergoing endless days of training in this cozy little oasis, Anna could be dying in some Nazi concentration camp.

He caught a glimpse of himself in a mirrored panel and shook his head. Nobody would recognize him as Romani. The mirror reflected a lean, tough British commando who could make a parachute jump, scale the shear face of a cliff, shoot a variety of guns with precision, or kill a man with his bare hands. But none of these skills would help him find Anna. He had his own plan and if these fools would not provide him with the resources he needed, he would find a way to get back to the continent on his own. It was already three months into 1942 and time was running out.

The corporal opened the door and held it for Eric to enter. Captain Drury was standing near a bay window at the far end of the room talking to an older man in army uniform who wore the rank of a full colonel. On his chest he displayed two rows of ribbons. Eric recognized those for the George Cross and the Conspicuous Gallantry Medal. And he thought the red one edged with blue was for the Distinguished Service Order.

Captain Drury, commander of the Center, was slender and of medium height. His eyes were brown, sunk deep under brows that were beginning to whiten, although his hair remained a dark brown. With a pronounced widows peak and parted on the right, his hair lay so smoothly against his skull and was so precisely cut and combed it gave the impression that nothing short of dynamite could dislodge a single hair. His lips were well shaped, but circumstances usually kept them compressed into a thin line. His trim mustache and level gaze gave him a decided military look. The flashes on his uniform indicated he had been a member of the Suffolk Regiment. Rumor had it that before the war he had been a prosecuting barrister, which gave him an understanding of government bureaucracy, although he had never been able to understand its inherent obfuscation.

Eric came to attention with such a de rigueur British stomp on the polished and ancient wood floor, it made Captain Drury wince. "Corporal Imri reporting as ordered, sir!"

"Stand easy, corporal."

Eric spread his feet and clasped his hands behind him in the military version of being at ease.

"Corporal," Drury continued, "I'd like you to meet Sir Malcolm Justin, Director of M.I.6."

Eric's eyes flicked toward the older man. M.I.6? They were responsible for counter-espionage. Of more importance, they controlled British secret agents abroad. Spies. Did this mean his request was being considered? Whatever mission they had in mind, it must be big to involve the M.I.6 director in person.

"Sir Malcolm," the captain continued. "This is Corporal Eric Imri, the man I was telling you about."

To Eric's surprise, the colonel stepped forward and held out his hand. "Imri. Pleasure to meet you."

Eric silently shook the man's hand, feeling a strong grip. He found himself looking into pale gray eyes that probed him with the quick penetrating flash of an X-ray. Sir Malcolm motioned to a large chair whose leather upholstery had the sheen of long use. "Sit down, corporal. This might take a few minutes."

If they had questions, Eric did not want to be in a position where they would be towering over him. He shook his head. "Thank you, sir. I'd prefer to stand."

"As you wish."

Sir Malcolm took out his pipe and began a slow ritual of scraping out the dottle and refilling it, unaware he was filling the room with the noxious odor of stale tobacco.

Eric watched him, his face impassive. He wondered if his many requests for a mission on the continent was the reason why he had been singled out for this meeting. What other reason could there be? Almost all the other men had months more training than he. Several had engaged in raids along the German occupied coasts or islands.

Or perhaps—Eric's lips tightened in sudden anger—perhaps they intended to discharge him as being unsuitable.

He dismissed the thought. He had been training a shorter time than the other men, but he could hold his own with the best of them in any of the commando skills. And none had his command of European languages, nor his burning desire to get back on the continent.

Sir Malcolm spoke without looking up, "How's the training going?"

"As well as can be expected, I suppose."

Captain Drury's nostrils pinched and Sir Malcolm stopped working with his pipe to look up at Eric. "Problems?"

"No, sir. I'm making progress."

Sir Malcolm eyes warmed. "How's the shooting?"

Eric understood the man's amusement. The story was all over camp about his attempt to escape by killing the SS-colonel. What a fool he had been. He had no idea a machine gun would kick the way it did, spinning itself completely out of his hands.

If it hadn't been for the intervention of Czech partisans, he would be dead. That, and his luck. One of the German guard's bullets had impacted on the extra ammunition clips he had carried in his belt. Another had struck him a glancing blow in the temple, knocking him unconscious. It was then that Czech partisans, who also had been waiting to ambush the SS-colonel, had opened fire. They had carried Eric to a village and given him medical treatment. The death of the SS-officer had resulted in severe reparations. The Germans conducted an intensive search of the area and killed anyone who they thought might be remotely connected with the partisans. Dozens of innocent Czechs had been shot or hanged. So Eric had been quickly smuggled out of the area. When he was well enough to walk, he had been turned over to British agents who had put him in their evasion and escape pipeline. He had been passed down the line through Yugoslavia and Greece and eventually to a Greek *caique* that had transferred him to a British ship.

In England, his request to be sent back to the continent had caused him to end up in the British SOE with Danes, Poles, Norwegians and other Nazi haters. But he was the only Gypsy. Maybe that had something to do with this meeting.

Sir Malcolm had his pipe drawing to his satisfaction and he clinched the stem with his teeth and talked around it, his hands clasped behind his back. "Tell us about the German labor camp?"

The question irritated Eric. When they had first brought him to England he had told Military Intelligence about the Arnschwang camp so many times that he had refused to discuss it further. "I've already told that to your people. I'm sure you've read my file."

If Sir Malcolm was put off by this minor insubordination, he did not show it. Calmly, he took the pipe from his mouth. "So you have. We've concluded it's one of their class three labor camps."

Captain Drury raised an eyebrow. "Class three, sir? They have classes?"

"As near as we can tell. They've had work camps and concentration camps, as they're called by Himmler, since 1934."

Eric's back stiffened. Concentration camps? Anna was supposed to have been going to one of those. "How many concentration camps are there?"

"We're not sure. In Germany proper, Dachau and Emsland, we believe, are the oldest. Now there are several more. Buchenwald, Sachsenhausen, Ravensbruck and Mauthausen, that we know of. We think they might be building more in Poland. A nasty business."

"You mentioned categories."

"Oh, right. They are all supposed to be labor camps. Class One is for short term prisoners. Class Two is tougher, for longer term prisoners. And Class Three, well, we don't believe prisoners are meant to survive in a Class Three environment."

Eric wondered what class the forest camp was. Probably a class three, since it was obvious that none of the Gypsies were expected to survive. If there were worse camps, they had to be places of pure hell.

Captain Drury shook his head as though he couldn't believe what he was hearing. "Why so many? Do they have that many political prisoners."

Sir Malcolm's chuckle was as dry as autumn leaves. "To Hitler, the enemy is anyone who does not agree with him. And there are thousands of Germans who see him as the mad man he is. Then too, he has other people he considers undesirables: Jews, homosexuals, Jehovah's Witnesses."

"And Gypsies."

Sir Malcolm's eyes flicked toward Eric. "Gypsies, yes, of course."

"Jehovah's Witnesses?" Captain Drury said. "Why them?"

"They refuse to be inducted into the German military. At one camp, the SS said if they didn't get the necessary volunteers they would kill ten Witnesses. They killed forty before they gave up."

"Who? The Witnesses?"

"No. The Nazis."

Sir Malcolm paused as though the death of the forty men required a moment of silence. The idea brought a momentary pique to Eric. They were horrified by the deaths of a few religious fanatics, but hundreds of Gypsies had died—were dying—and nobody gave a damn.

He controlled his anger the way he had always controlled it when someone dismissed his people as inconsequential, by storing it deep inside where he could use it when it would count. Anna, he told himself. Remember Anna. Finding her is the most important thing in your life right now.

"There must be hundreds of work camps," he said. "How do they keep track of everybody? Or do they bother?"

"Oh, they bother, all right. The Germans have a penchant for orderliness. They keep records on everything. The camps are administered by the SS's WVHA, the Main Office for Economics."

"Where is that?"

"Gestapo Headquarters."

"Berlin?"

Sir Malcolm nodded. "Number eight Prinz AlbrechtStrasse."

Eric made a mental note of the address. That was where he could find the file on von Liebermann. And von Liebermann would lead him to Anna.

Drury said, "The officer in charge is SS Lieutenant-General Pohl."

Eric turned his head to look at the man. "Are you sure, sir? I thought it was Heydrich."

"We're both right. Reinhard Heydrich is Pohl's superior officer. Pohl runs the Berlin office of Management."

Eric's voice held more eagerness than he wanted when he asked, "What can you tell me about Heydrich?"

At the question, a strange expression crossed the face of Sir Malcolm and he gave Captain Drury a quick look. Was it surprise? Or dismay?

Instead of answering, Sir Malcolm said, "What do _you_ know about Heydrich?"

Eric cursed himself for asking. But the question had slipped out as though his mind had been commanded by some outside force. He would have to watch himself. He did not want anyone to know he was interested in the SS butcher. If they knew what he had in mind, they would never help him return to the continent.

"Only that I heard he's the man responsible for putting my people in work camps."

"I can assure you that he is." Sir Malcolm took a long pull on his pipe. "What are your feelings about that?"

"My feelings?" What sort of an answer did the man expect? That he had no feelings? Why should he ask such a question? Perhaps he thought Gypsies had no loyalties to their people, only to themselves. Or was it that he had guessed why he was interested in Heydrich? Eric's reply was guarded. "I hope that some day he will be punished."

"If you had it in your power to insure that punishment, would you do it?"

They had to know! Why else would they be asking such questions? But if they expected him to admit he had made a blood promise to kill the man who had murdered his father, they were mistaken. No Gypsy, and certainly, no horse trader ever admitted anything incriminating.

Still, it was impossible for these men to know about the oath, so he gave them the same answer that any rational person would give. "Of course I would."

Captain Drury brushed at his moustache and Sir Malcolm moved to look out the window. Eric had the impression they were poised on the edge of telling him why they had asked him here. But why were they hesitating? In the seconds before Sir Malcolm turned back to face him several possibilities tumbled through his mind, but one thought kept sorting itself out: whatever they were going to tell him they expected it to be bad.

"If you had succeeded in killing those Germans," Sir Malcolm said slowly, "how did you plan on escaping?"

More questions? They were still reluctant to get to the point. He realized suddenly that this man, who seemed so coolly assured, was at a total loss about how to deal with him. The man undoubtedly understood other Englishmen. There was even a thread of commonalty with such alien species as Cockneys, Welshmen and Scots. And he could relate somewhat to the people of the continent, except perhaps the French, who no one understood. But how did one relate to a Gypsy? How did they think? What did they feel? Where were their loyalties?

Eric decided to make it easy for the man by putting on his English mask. If there was nothing here for him, he could quickly revert to his role of being a stupid Gypsy. "I was going to dress in the SS officer's clothes," he said. "Assume his identity."

"Why not one of the guards?" Captain Drury said. "Wouldn't it have been safer?"

"No authority. No one questions an SS colonel."

"Could you have brought it off?"

"Yes."

Silence hung heavy for an instant. Smoke from Sir Malcolm's pipe swirled in a shaft of sunlight from the window like the thoughts in Eric's mind.

"Would you like another try?"

Sir Malcolm's voice was low and quiet, but it pierced Eric like a knife. His first impulse was to say yes before they changed their mind. Isn't that what he had been hoping for? But suspicion made him hesitate. Why were they granting his request now? And why did it come from the head of M.I.6? There had to be some very heavy strings attached. "I want to go back, yes," he said cautiously.

"So you can kill Heydrich?"

"Yes." He said it quickly. To have hesitated would have made them suspect there was another reason, perhaps a stronger one. And they would have wanted to know what it was. They might understand, perhaps condone, revenge, but if he told them about Anna, they would never understand. They were centered on fighting a war, not rescuing a girl from some concentration camp.

"We might be able to help you."

Eric had to clinch his jaw to conceal his elation. But he remained silent, waiting for the string.

"We have an operation underway to eliminate Heydrich." Sir Malcolm paused to observe the effect of his words. Eric gave him a brief nod of acknowledgement. "Since he replaced von Neurath as ReichsObergruppenführer, Protector of Bohemia and Moravia, Heydrich has acquired the sobriquet 'Butcher of Prague.' The Czech government in exile, here in London, believes that it will hearten the people and help the resistance if Heydrich is eliminated."

"You mean assassinated?"

Sir Malcolm made a face as though he had bitten into a lemon. "If you must call a spade a ruddy shovel."

"In essence," Captain Drury commented dryly, "we must become monsters to destroy monsters."

"Be that as it may," Sir Malcolm continued. "Operation 'Anthropoid,' as it has been named for some unknown reason, is already underway. Two Czech partisans are in training at an SOE station at this moment to do the job."

For some reason Eric experienced a sadness, a sense of loss. It was as though a driving force was being taken from him. He had wanted to kill Heydrich personally, to tell the man why he was to die before he killed him. Now, that was being taken out of his hands. His voice was quiet as he said, "So why do you need me?"

"What we need is an SS colonel."

So that was it. Eric blessed the gods who had made him tell the truth.

"Let me show you." Sir Malcolm spread a map of the Prague area of Czechoslovakia on the desk and bent over it. He pointed to a place just north of the ancient city. "Heydrich's H.Q. is here in an old mansion. The nearby village is called Panensk, Brezany. It's on the route to Dresden. Now, if Heydrich received a message to meet someone at the"—he moved his finger—"Prague-Tesnov railway station, he would almost certainly take this route. Our men could be waiting at a suitable place." He straightened painfully and put a hand on his lower back. "So we know his probable route. All we have to do is set the time so our men could be in position and waiting."

"Going to be dicey," Drury said. "Heydrich moves around a good deal. We've got to make sure he's in the right place at the right time." He looked at Eric. "To do that, we need someone on the inside of his organization."

Eric's chin came up. Maybe . . . just maybe he could yet confront the man. What had they called him: The Butcher of Prague? He almost blurted, "An SS colonel?"

"Precisely. We would provide you with the uniform and the necessary ID papers. That would give you access to Heydrich's headquarters in Prague."

Prague? No. That wouldn't help. That would not give him access to the records he needed to find Anna. He had to first get to Berlin. "No," he said. "Don't you think that an SS officer showing up in Prague unannounced and giving orders would be very suspicious? It would be more logical if the orders came down from higher headquarters."

Captain Drury crossed his arms across his chest. His voice was heavy with skepticism when he said, "Munich?"

Eric shook his head. Without asking permission, he crossed to the map of Europe and put his finger on the German city. "Berlin."

Sir Malcolm took the pipe from his mouth and stared at the map as though it was an invading enemy. "Berlin? I think you're getting rather far afield here."

"I don't think so, sir." Eric had the strange feeling he was back on an English landlord's estate trying to sell him a lame horse. "The SS colonel I was going to kill was an inspector of labor and concentration camps. That gave him the authority to travel anywhere. And the power. When he arrived, everybody looked like they were going to mess their pants."

"But that's Heydrich's department," Drury said. "He won't be impressed."

"Agreed," Sir Malcolm answered. "An invitation to meet a work camp inspector wouldn't carry much weight with Heydrich."

"That's right," Drury added. "It would be ideal if orders to be in a certain place at a certain time came directly from Himmler himself. Heydrich wouldn't dare question them."

"But headquarters in Berlin would," Eric pointed out. "They would know Himmler's whereabouts. They might even check with him and that would give the whole thing away."

"Then from whom?" Drury pulled his arms tighter across his chest. "A fictitious officer?"

"Not fictitious. They should come from someone Heydrich knows."

Sir Malcolm rubbed the back of his neck and looked toward the ceiling. Eric was silent. Once the *Gorgio* decided he wanted the horse, it was best to let him work out the details.

Sir Malcolm broke the silence. "Some time ago I was discussing what might be a chink in Hitler's armor with Shelly Wigganham. It might be the chink we're looking for."

Drury unfolded his arms and put his hands in his pockets. "I hope it's a big one."

"It might well be. Have either of you ever heard of Colonel Wolfram von Sievers?" Both men shook their heads. "Von Sievers is head of Hitler's Ahnenerbe."

"Ahnenerbe?" Drury's hands came out of his pockets. "What's that?"

"Hitler's Occult Bureau."

Eric wondered whether he had misunderstood Sir Malcolm's words. "Did you say 'occult bureau?'"

"That's right. As you may know, Hitler has been involved in various occult societies since he was a teenager. Some of his closest associates are known practitioners of the occult: Haushofer, Walter Stein, a world cult leader named Heilscher. And von Sievers himself. This von Sievers is rather a mysterious character. There are no pictures of him—at least, none that we know of. He's reclusive. Staying most of the time at Himmler's Wewelsburg castle."

"Wewelsburg?" Drury glanced at the map. "Where is that?"

"Westphalia. In Germany." Eric said. "A terrible place."

Sir Malcolm's jaw went slack. "You've been there?"

"They were rebuilding the old castle for years. Some of the SS officers wanted horses."

"Did you ever get inside?"

"No. But we heard a lot about it."

"We?"

"The Gypsies. Most of them wouldn't go near the place."

"What did you hear?"

"That Himmler had a huge round table built in the banquet room. It has thirteen places. And there's a 'Hall Of The Dead' in the basement. He keeps urns there with the ashes of his apostles when they die."

"That coincides with our information. That's where von Sievers stays most of the time."

"It sounds," Drury said, "as thought Himmler is as involved in the occult as Hitler."

"Perhaps more," Sir Malcolm replied. "The point is that Heydrich is also a member of The Occult Bureau. He might disregard an order from even Himmler, but I doubt that he would have the courage to ignore an order from The Bureau."

"From von Sievers," Eric said.

"Right. From von Sievers."

"So I'm to impersonate this von Sievers."

"It makes sense," Drury cut in. "It wouldn't even have to be an order. A request. For Heydrich to meet him at the railway station."

"Precisely. And if von Sievers said he would be with Heilscher, Heydrich would move heaven and earth to comply."

"Suppose the real von Sievers got wind of an impostor? That would throw a ruddy spanner in the machinery."

"Not likely," Sir Malcolm said. "Von Sievers is in Japan with Haushofer."

"Japan?" Drury lifted both eyebrows. "Are you sure? Why would they go there?"

"Perhaps to confer with Matsuoko."

"The Prime Minister? Is he involved in the occult?"

"We're not sure. But we are pretty sure that it was Karl Haushofer who suggested the Japanese attack on Pearl Harbor."

Eric was growing impatient with the diversion from the subject and he said, "This von Sievers. How long do you expect he'll be away?"

"For some time. Matsuoko could be introducing him into the Green Dragon Society. That would take considerable time." He bent over the map. "Enough for us, in any case."

Eric recognized the advantage over his own plan. As a camp inspector, he could easily be exposed by even a cursory search of personnel files. But as a member of Hitler's occult bureau, people would treat him as though he had the plague. Every Gypsy had learned to exploit the fear most people had for the mystic. Impersonating von Sievers would not only be the ultimate exploitation, it would also provide him access to virtually any department.

"Which department would you say has the records for the labor camps?"

"Labor camps?" Sir Malcolm said. "They have no bearing on this."

Eric searched for a plausible excuse that would explain his—or rather, von Siever's—interest in the work camp records. "Heydrich is in charge of recruiting workers for the camps. Logically, he would communicate his itinerary to SS headquarters in Berlin. If I could get a look at his schedule, I would know the best time to set up the—incident."

"True," Sir Malcolm said slowly. "That would be the WVHA. Their Manpower Utilization Office should have all such records."

"And we could select the date, the time and the place for a supposed meeting with von Sievers." There was excitement in Drury's voice. "We could anticipate the route he would take to get to such a meeting. Where is that map of Prague?"

Drury went to the desk and bent over the map. Sir Malcolm joined him, his pipe lying in an ashtray forgotten.

Eric watched both men with faint amusement. He felt as though a great rock had been removed from his stomach. He would help them in their Operation Anthropoid. The death of Reinhard Heydrich would end his blood promise. But the assassination of Heydrich was only half his mission. Sir Malcolm did not know it, but he had provided Eric with the connection that would lead him to Anna. All he had to do was stay alive. He wondered if he should give his own mission a code name. The only name that came to his mind was 'Operation Ravanna.'

Chapter 24

April 1942

Anna stood at the window of her room and looked out at a scene that was becoming increasingly familiar. Another large group of Jews had been unloaded from a train and were being herded down the brick-paved street toward the small square in the center of Theresienstadt where they would be forced to stand for hours for role call. Each had a yellow Star of David cut from paper pinned to his clothing above his heart. In addition, on a cord around his neck, each had a tag containing a transportation number. Most carried suitcases and bags as though they were going on holiday, which Anna knew, was what they had been told.

The illusion was quickly dispelled the moment they left the station. A squad of SS guards, under control of a hulking Block Leader who reminded Anna of Sergeant Wirtz, pushed and shoved them into movement, their truncheons swinging freely against cowering women and children as much as against the men. As Anna watched, a woman dropped behind the group to grasp the hand of a trotting child and one of the guards pounded her repeatedly across the back and buttocks.

With the glass of the window cutting off sound, it was like watching a scene in a horror movie. But it was not a chimera; it was real and she should be shaking with the same intense rage she had felt the first time she had witness the brutality. But somehow, the rage was not there. Where had it gone? What she felt now was sorrow, sorrow and helpless impotence. The change had taken place so slowly that she had failed to note its diminishing. How easy it was to grow accustomed to brutality when it occurred day after day. Was it because intense rage was so difficult to sustain? It could almost be plotted as a graph, with the peaks gradually becoming lower until there was no longer any rage at all, only a flat line of despair. Was it the same for the victims? Could they sustain a resolve to resist indefinitely? Could she?

She turned away, unable to watch any longer. Let this be a warming. She must not allow herself to fall into the trap of becoming indifferent. She must not allow herself to become so inured to these people's suffering that she could witness such atrocities and feel nothing.

But how could she prevent it? She looked around the room at the beautiful furnishings, at the paintings on the wall, at the rich drapes and tapestries, and felt the warmth of central heating that held back the April chill. She lived in an ivory tower, a tower that insulated her from the reality beyond the window. Where would those poor people live? What would they eat? How would they keep warm? Day after day she saw them arriving, hundreds of Jews. And somehow they were swallowed up in the maw of the city like water in a sponge. What happened to them?

She had to find out.

Oh God. If only Eric was here to help her hold to her sanity.

The thought had sprung unbidden from some dark corner of her mind and she quickly pushed it back. Eric. His betrayal had done as much to plunge her into this black despair as her witness of the maltreatment of the poor Jews. She would never be able to climb out of that dark pit until she accepted Eric as part of her past and nothing more. The lesson had been bitter, but it was still a lesson. Once again she reminded herself as she had so often during the last few weeks that if she was ever to escape, she could depend on no one to help.

Escape? It had become an obsession. She could not keep up this charade forever. Either she would begin making mistakes or von Liebermann would find someone who was more adept at salving his ego.

But she had no chance of escape as long as she was a virtual prisoner inside the hotel. She was still a U.S. citizen and if only she could get to the United States legation in Prague, they could help her. Once inside the legation, the Nazis could not touch her. So she had begun a campaign designed to get her out of the old hotel.

It had taken her weeks of preparation, of subtle manipulation of von Liebermann's horoscope before she could make him believe that to provide accurate day by day predictions, she had to expand her horizons. At last, he had moved in the direction that the stars, her stars, had indicated and ordered her to assume a more active interest in camp activities.

Captain Voss had helped pave the way. He preferred the Tarot cards to astrology, watching her with cynical detachment as she poured over the cards. She could never quite tell if he actually believed the cards or was pretending so he could use his demonstrated acceptance of the occult as a lever to gain entrance to the Nazi hierarchy. Fortunately, it mattered little what he thought. He was forced to obey the cards or be branded an occult atheist. And as with von Liebermann, Anna made sure that the cards told him what he wanted to hear—and what she wanted him to hear.

Then came the devastating news that had plunged her into an even deeper despair.

It had been an unusually warm sunny day for February and she had felt even more trapped by the four walls when she had brought up the idea that the hotel was so confining it was difficult for her to concentrate. Captain Voss, smoking one of his Gauloise cigarettes as usual, had looked at her with his eyes twinkling and his lips twisted into the typical cynically smile that he knew infuriated her.

"Would you like a vacation? Perhaps a visit to the south of France or a Greek Isle? I have some friends in Panzer Divisions who would make us welcome."

His subtle reference about accompanying her was not lost on Anna. She suspected his attempts to seduce her would become serious if he was not afraid that she would tell von Liebermann. "Not a vacation," she countered. "Only a chance to walk outside. To feel the sun. A chance to clear my mind."

"It's February. The sun has no strength. And the wind could take your nose off."

"That's not the point. I need to—well, to use a phrase—to clear my palette."

"Walking in the village is verboten."

"Then a ride. In the car. It wouldn't have to be far."

"That sounds dangerous. If you were to . . ." He paused and pursed his lips as though thinking, ". . . disappear, the Kommandant would have me walking on air."

"You think I might escape? Where would I go?"

His eyes danced over her fashionable clothes. Her whole new wardrobe, courtesy of the SS, was in such marked contrast to the clothes worn by the women of the surrounding villages that she would be as distinctive as though she were still wearing her striped prison garb. "Where indeed?"

"You could come along. That way you could keep an eye on me."

"Now that is tempting."

Anna winced. She hadn't wanted to give him any erotic ideas. Although she was certain he had no trouble finding female companionship, she was keenly aware that one of the major reasons he tolerated her readings with the Tarot cards was because he harbored an image, faint though it may be, that she really did posses some psychic powers that could well cause him trouble. If she gave in to his charms even a little, it would begin to erode the illusion. And right now, her image was the only thing keeping her alive.

"Perhaps we should forget it," she said. "I wouldn't want you to overstep your authority."

She had played to his ego and he responded as she had thought he would. His face flushed a little and his back stiffened. He drew on his cigarette before he said, "We are making arrangements to have visitors from the foreign press. I might be able to arrange for you to join them. As, say, a representative of the United States."

"You mean write a story?"

"Of course. We would see that it reached your American press."

Anna didn't know what to say. If they were bringing in foreign reporters, they would have to show them the entire complex. It was her chance to find out how the Jews were being treated. And if they actually would allow her to write a story, she would include information about the Gypsies and how they were being worked to death in the labor camps.

Stupid idea. They would never permit such a story. Joseph Goebbels, the German Minister of Popular Enlightenment and Propaganda, would never allow the truth to be published. The tour of press representatives would probably be rigged. But still, it would give her a chance to visit areas she had no hope of seeing on her own. She could draw her own conclusions.

There was one more reason why she felt she should accept. Identity papers. It was impossible to go anywhere in Nazi occupied territory without identity papers. If she ever did escape, she would have to have them. "Very well," she said. "But I'll need some kind of press credentials."

"We can arrange that."

"And identity papers. They should indicate that I'm a journalist."

She could tell by the way he threw back his head and laughed that he had seen through her trick. "Identity papers? Gypsies have no identities. They are like the wind and the rain. Or should I say like the locusts and the plague."

Anna's forced smile was bitter. "And the Germans are like milk and honey?"

Voss did not lose his smile, but his eyes changed so that, for an instant, she caught a glimpse of sadness. Then he wagged his head and threw up his hands. "You Gypsies have no sense of humor. Very well. I will see that your papers make you an official journalist. But I think we had better make you Hungarian. An American journalist might not be appreciated in light of the present circumstances."

"Circumstances?"

Voss' look was puzzled. "America is our enemy."

"Enemy? We're neutral."

Voss paused before answering as though to analyze the truth of her conversation. "You don't know," he finally said. "I thought you were making a joke."

"Don't know what?"

"Your President Roosevelt has put America in the war."

Anna felt an almost overwhelming sensation of pride and relief. If what he said was true, the war would soon be over and she could go home. Then her mood changed as she remembered that at home she would have to deal with Albrecht Grantz to get her property returned. But with the protection of the Germans removed, that should not be difficult.

"When?" she said. "When did it happen?"

"Eleven December. Shortly after Pearl Harbor."

"Pearl Harbor?"

"On the seventh of December the Japanese made a preemptive strike on your Pearl Harbor in Hawaii. Roosevelt declared war on Japan the next day. We had no choice but to support our ally."

Anna scarcely heard him. She was lost in a euphoria of hope. "No," she murmured. "I suppose not."

"Your Roosevelt made a mistake. This is not 1918. This time we are strong—and we are ready. This time America will not win."

His words snapped Anna out of her reverie. "Oh yes," she said. "I'll look forward to riding down Broadway in a German tank."

Voss was too intent on his dream to notice the irony in her voice. He nodded. "It will happen. Just as soon as we eliminate Russia and the English."

"I still think it would be better if I was considered American."

Voss pulled at his lower lip. "You may be right. Many Americans do not agree with Roosevelt's war. A favorable article by an American could be useful."

"I'm sure it could."

Voss stood up and looked at the Tarot cards still spread across the table in a circular spread. He tapped the center card which was the Magician. "This will be a year of success for those willing to take risks. Isn't that what you told me?"

Anna had made the interpretation as a prelude to asking for more freedom. Now, looking out the window, she couldn't help but think how right the cards had been. It had been weeks since that reading and from what she had been able to learn from Voss and von Liebermann, the Nazis were winning on all fronts. If America were going to win the war, it would not be soon. She had better keep looking for a way to escape.

This tour today might show her a way.

An hour later she was in the hotel lobby where Captain Voss introduced her to three men. Herr Matsu Kobi was from Japan. He wore steel rimmed glasses and a severe black suit. Señor Reynoldo Hobart was a tall blonde man who, to Anna's surprise, was from Argentina. Then she remembered that a great many people from Northern Europe had settled in Argentina. The country was probably full of blondes.

The third man, Herr Kurt Obler, was from Switzerland. He was short and heavy and wore his hair parted on the left with the hair fanned across his forehead just as Hitler wore his.

Captain Voss introduced her as an American journalist from New York. Anna clutched her new identity papers in her coat pocket with her left hand as she prepared to shake hands. But instead of shaking hands, each man greeted her with a smile and a suggestion of a bow. She had the impression they were not particularly fond of Americans. Studying them, she had doubts about their objectivity in reporting anything they saw.

When von Liebermann stepped out of the elevator, Anna had to admit he looked like a man in total control. Wearing his black SS uniform with its silver braid, a black Sam Brown belt, and with metals gleaming on his breast, he was almost handsome. But when he put on his cap after greeting the journalists and she saw the silver Death's Head, the ensemble turned ugly. It was the uniform of executioners; the uniform of men whose sole role in life was to brutalize other people.

Captain Voss introduced her to von Liebermann as Miss Zorka, a journalist from New York and the Kommandant pretended to be meeting her for the first time. Anna, playing her part, allowed him to brush her hand with his lips as he said, "Charmed. I trust you will help us dissuade the false stories that are circulating in the American press."

"I'm sure I can," she replied. "The world should know the truth."

He glanced at her sharply, then led the way outside where a big Mercedes with pennants on the front fenders was waiting. The driver held the rear door open and they climbed inside. Anna sat in the center of the rear seat with Herr Matsu on one side and Señor Hobart on the other. Von Liebermann took one of the jump seats facing them and Herr Obler gingerly lowered his bulk onto the other. Captain Voss climbed in front beside the driver and put the glass partition down.

As they drove along the brick-paved street, Captain Voss turned and said, "Notice that we do not have an escort. The people are very friendly, sympathetic to our Führer's goals."

Looking out the windows, Anna saw why they did not require an escort: German troops were standing discreetly out of sight inside doorways and on rooftops. If the journalists noticed them, they gave no indication. Their attention was fixed upon a few well-dressed people walking along the sidewalks. All wore the required yellow Star of David pinned to their chests. Some were couples and others were families with children. A few nodded toward the passing limousine and smiled.

"Notice that the people are all well fed," von Liebermann said. "They are quite happy here."

"They should be," Herr Obler said. "For them the war is only a rumor."

"That is true," Señor Hobart added. "They do not have to worry about bombs or artillery like the heroic German soldiers."

Anna was puzzled. Could she be wrong? Was this ghetto actually the haven for Jews she had been told it was?

She was trying to equate the image of prosperity with the brutality she had seen from her hotel window when the limousine stopped in front of a bakery shop. As they stepped from the car, the proprietor, a portly, smiling man wearing a Star of David pinned to his white apron, rushed out to meet them.

"Ah, Herr Kommandant. Welcome. Welcome to my shop."

He led them inside where Anna breathed in the wonderful odor of freshly baked bread. There were two customers inside the shop: a smiling woman and a child who appeared to be ten or twelve. They also wore the Star of David. The baker pointed out his well-stocked display cabinets and shelves to his visitors, who scribbled notes on secretarial tablets. Instead of writing, Anna turned to the woman, "How long have you been here?"

"Three months, madam. We were among the first to arrive." The woman's German was touched with a Serbian accent. She was probably one of the Jews brought from Prague or one of the nearby cities.

"It must have been difficult to leave your home."

"Yes. But we are safe here. And when the Russians are no longer a threat, we will go back."

She seemed to believe what she was saying. Anna searched for words that would give her encouragement. "Perhaps next year you can celebrate Passover in your own home."

"Oh, we had a wonderful celebration here. Everyone exchanged gifts. We didn't miss home at all."

Anna tousled the hair of the boy. "I guess it won't be long before you'll be having your, uh, Bat Mitzvah."

The boy looked toward his mother, his eyes huge and frightened. "Oh yes," his mother answered for him. "His brother has already had his. We have a wonderful Rabbi."

The woman's eyes shifted, suddenly as frightened as those of her son. Anna turned to see what had caused the reaction. Von Liebermann was standing beside her looking at the woman. He smiled as he said, "Good evening, Frau. If there is anything bothering you in any way, please feel free to tell us."

"No, no, Herr Kommandant," the woman cried. "Everything is perfect. Perfect."

Von Liebermann held his smile as he looked down at the boy. "You are a handsome young man. I'm sure you are looking forward to the day when you will be allowed to serve the Führer."

"Y-Y-Yes, sir," the boy stuttered.

Von Liebermann was not listening. "Come. I want you to meet the Jewish Council."

He took hold of Anna's elbow and led her out the door with Captain Voss and the three journalists trailing behind them.

As the limousine traversed the narrow streets between tall beige-colored stone and brick apartment buildings, Captain Voss gave them a brief history. "The fortress was actually built by the Austrian Emperor Joseph the Second in 1780. He named it Terezin as a tribute to his mother, the Empress Maria Theresa. Its purpose was to protect the surrounding territory. It was considered impregnable. Notice that all the streets intersect at right angles, creating a perfect grid. Most of the buildings you see were barracks for the soldiers."

"How many Jews are here?" Señor Hobart wanted to know.

"Perhaps two thousand. There is ample room for everyone who wishes to come."

"You don't force Jews to come here?" Anna said.

"Not at all. We have long waiting lists. Many actually try to pay for the privilege."

"Are there other ghettos such as this?" The question came from Herr Obler.

"They are being established. This is a model. Even now similar ghettos are being constructed in Poland, Germany and Austria. The Jews can hardly wait for them to be completed."

Could he be speaking the truth? Were the Jews happy to leave their ancestral homes where for generations they had endured the wax and wane of anti-Semitism and come to havens such as this? Perhaps it was a form of Hobson's choice: if they did not leave they would have to endure the latest and most brutal of the anti-Semitic cycles. At least here the conditions might be relatively primitive, but there was some degree of safety.

On the northern edge of the city, they passed a stone bridge that spanned a dry, moat-like gully. On the other side of the bridge was a turreted structure made of huge gray stones that looked rather like a medieval castle.

Herr Obler voiced the question that Anna was about the ask: "What is that place?"

"The Small Fortress. The city actually consists of two fortresses: the large one, where we are, and that small one."

"Is it inhabited?" Herr Matsu paused in his scribbling.

"Not now, no. Until Czechoslovakia was liberated by the Führer, it was used as a penitentiary for dangerous criminals. But, as you can imagine, it was not up to German standards and its inhabitants were transferred to more humane surroundings."

Anna looked at the narrow, dark windows in the grim structure and shivered. She would not like to spend a night inside its massive walls. One would not have to be a spiritualist to conjure up an entire army of tormented souls.

By contrast, a short distance beyond the small fortress they passed Brunnenpark where children were playing in a large ornamental pavilion. The journalists faithfully made notes as Captain Voss pointed out the happy faces of the children and how well fed they were.

In a moment the limousine stopped in front of a grim three-storied stone building, and the journalists trouped after Voss as he led them up a flight of stairs and into a room on the top floor. It was a large room with a high ceiling and walls paneled with dark oak. Light came from tall windows in two walls. A long conference table occupied the center of the room. On the table were several Torah scrolls. Seated at the table were fourteen elderly men, each wearing a yellow Star of David. All were bearded and several wore yarmulkes. They had been in a heated discussion that broke off abruptly when the visitors arrived. They stood and a man who had been at the head of the table came forward. He was tall, bearded. His worn, black suit looked as though it had been made for a much heavier man. Or the man had lost a great deal of weight.

"Gentlemen and lady," von Liebermann said. "I would like you to meet the people who control the ghetto: the Council of Elders. Their leader is Doctor Steiner. Doctor, gentlemen, these are members of the press. Herr Matsu, from Japan; Herr Obler from Switzerland; Señor Hobart from Argentina. And Fräulein Zorka is American."

There had been no reaction from the council members when the men were introduced, but when they heard that Anna was American, they looked up and their eyes came alive with the same look Anna had seen in the eyes of émigrés when they looked at the Statue of Liberty or the American flag. There was magic in the name, the magic of hope, the magic of liberty.

But she could bring them none of those things. She could offer them nothing but the knowledge that she might be able to tell their story to the world.

"You may speak freely to the press," von Liebermann said. He turned to the reporters. "Gentlemen, if you have questions, do not hesitate."

"Is it true," Señor Hobart poised his pencil over his notepad, "that you control the camp?"

"Yes," Dr. Steiner answered. "That is our privilege."

Anna looked at the set faces of the elderly men. Was she mistaken or did she sense a bitterness in Dr. Steiner's words. And something else. Fear?

"In what capacity?" She stared into his eyes, searching for evidence of truth. "How much authority do you have?"

"Authority? We have complete authority. For housing, food, supplies, sanitation. We have our own legal and financial departments."

"They even have their own currency," Voss said. "Show them, Doctor."

"Of course." Dr. Steiner took a bill from his pocket and handed it to Anna. The bill was for ten crowns. It looked much like official Czech currency except that it was imprinted with a picture of Moses holding the Tablets of the Law. She passed the bill to the other reporters who studied it with interest.

"How many of your people are here now?" Anna made notes as she asked, hoping she looked like a real journalist. "How many do you expect?"

For the first time Dr. Steiner hesitated before he answered, his eyes flicking toward the Kommandant. "We are at maximum capacity." He was looking at Anna, but she had the feeling he was talking to von Liebermann. "In truth, we do not have the facilities for more."

"Do not worry," von Liebermann said. "The situation will be remedied very shortly."

"I hope so." Dr. Steiner's voice betrayed his worry and fatigue. But at the words, von Liebermann stiffened and popped his gloves against the palm of his hand, a gesture he made when he was irritated.

Captain Voss quickly smiled and said, "Hope is how we all live, Herr Doctor. I'm sure that your God will look after you."

"Our God," Steiner corrected. "There is only one."

"Of course," Voss agreed. "If there is one at all."

Dr. Steiner turned to von Liebermann. "How do you answer such cynicism?"

"With results," the Kommandant said. "The Führer is our God. You would do well to make him yours."

The lines in Dr. Steiner's face deepened. "Has five thousand years of civilization come down to this?"

"Today," Anna said, "even a year is too long. People today want results today. God is too patient for them."

Dr. Steiner's weary eyes turned to stare at her as though he had to study this person who thought like a Jew. "Patience, yes. One thing the Jews have is patience."

"You see," von Liebermann said. "We have only to be patient. In a few weeks, a few months at most, we can all return to our homes."

"And," Anna added, "since Hitler said that the Reich will last a thousand years, we can look forward to nine hundred and ninety-one more years of paradise."

Von Liebermann smiled. "Exactly." He turned to the three reporters. "Do you have additional questions for the Council?"

"I have," Anna said and von Liebermann's lips stiffened. To Dr. Steiner, Anna said, "When is your Passover?"

Dr. Steiner's shaggy eyebrows lifted. "The 10th of April."

"Next month. That's what I thought. And . . . oh yes. Do boys here celebrate Bat Mitzvahs?"

"No. For a boy it is a Bar Mitzvah."

So, Anna thought, the woman in the bakery had not been Jewish. She wondered how many other happy, smiling people they had seen wearing the Star of David were actually Czechs or Germans. Probably all of them. Or, like the Council, they were Jews, afraid to depart from the roles they had been assigned. Could this entire affair be a well-orchestrated charade for the sake of the press? If it was, perhaps the reporters were Nazis themselves, or Nazi sympathizers. Either way, there would be no truth coming from this tour.

Von Liebermann again asked if there were more questions and he glared at Anna as though to dare a response. When no one did, he clicked his heels and made the gesture of a bow toward Dr. Steiner. "Herr Doctor. If there is anything I can do to help, please do not hesitate to inform me."

Von Liebermann walked out the door followed by the three reporters and Captain Voss. Anna hesitated. Was there some way she could let these people know she was not sympathetic to the Nazis? Just as quickly she rejected the thought. What good would it do? There was nothing she could do to help them even if they wanted—or needed—her help.

She was walking out the door when Dr. Steiner bumped her arm causing her to drop her notebook and pencil. "Oh. I'm so sorry," he said and bent quickly to retrieve them for her.

"That's all right," she said. For an instant, as Dr. Steiner fumbled with the notebook and pencil, she thought it might be an opportunity to say something to the elderly man, but Voss had turned to see what was wrong and the moment was gone.

She took the notebook from Dr. Steiner who again apologized, "I'm sorry, Fräulein. Terribly sorry."

"That's quite all right," she repeated. Clutching the notebook, she hurried past Voss who stood for a moment staring at Dr. Steiner before he turned and followed Anna.

The next hour was spent touring the ghetto. They inspected a huge kitchen with vast kettles and immaculate, coal-burning stoves. Anna was gratified to see its storerooms were stocked with cheese, cereal grains, vegetables and several kinds of sausages. "It isn't kosher," Captain Voss said, "but in war, we all have to make sacrifices."

When Anna opened her notebook to inscribe a note, she was startled to see that a ragged piece of paper had been inserted between the pages. Two words in English were scrawled across the page as though they had been written in haste. She held the notebook so the note could not be seen by the others and pretended to write as she deciphered the scrawl. It read: Hotel basement. 10.

Her hands trembled as she palmed the note and slipped it into her pocket. If Dr. Steiner had felt it necessary to be secretive, then there was terrible danger in the words—for both of them. She had seen what brutal forms of punishment the German SS men could inflict. And no one dared question their right. The Führer himself had given the SS carte blanche to discipline prisoners in any way they saw fit. The SS had extended the privilege to include any person, not just prisoners. Von Liebermann, with a snap of his fingers, could have Dr. Steiner, or her, or anyone, killed. They would simply disappear.

So it would be the worst kind of folly to try to meet Dr. Steiner that night. But she knew she would.

A few minutes before ten Anna put on a pair of slacks and a sweater. She slipped her feet into soft-soled walking shoes. After pulling on a knit hat, she turned off the lights. At the door she pressed her ear against the panel. There was no sound. It occurred to her as she cautiously turned the doorknob, the door might be locked. She had never tried to open it in the evening. Always her dinner was brought to her, and she ate in her room while she worked on von Liebermann's astrologic forecast for the next day, then on a long range forecast. He liked to be briefed early in the morning after he had read his copy of Das Schwarze Korps, the SS newspaper, and when it was available from Nuremberg, Der Sturmer, the official publication of the Nazi party.

But the knob turned easily and she slowly edged the door open a crack. She put her eye to the crack and studied as much of the hall as she could see. The hall was dimly lighted, since most of the lights had been turned off to save electricity. She half expected to see a guard but none was within the range of her vision. If she was discovered, she had her story ready. She was taking a paper to the Kommandant that he had asked her to prepare.

Slowly she opened the door wider, providing a view of the entire hall. Still no guard. Apparently, they believed there was little danger within the walls of Theresienstadt and that the many guards patrolling outside were adequate. She wondered how Dr. Steiner planned to get to the basement of the hotel without being seen.

But at the moment, her concern was how to get to the basement herself. She could not use the noisy lift. But there had to be a stairway in case of fire. In older hotels the stairs were often next to the lift, and easing her door shut, she drifted silently down the hall. She had been right. Next to the lift's grilled door was an open doorway. There was no light inside, but she could make out stairs.

Quietly, she began descending the stairs. In the blackness she could see little, and she clutched the brass railing as she cautiously moved downward. The slow movement gave her time to think. What was she doing here? Even if she did talk to Dr. Steiner, what could come of it? And if she were caught, it would probably mean her death, or at best, severe punishment. Stupid, stupid, stupid.

At the lobby there was a closed door. Dim light entered the stairwell through small stained glass windows in the door. There was no sound. Apparently the lobby was deserted. The stairway was narrower leading to the basement, and despite her soft-soled shoes, her steps seemed incredibly loud as her feet searched and found each raiser. With each downward step the blackness closed in like a descending hood. She stumbled. She had reached a landing. Shuffling her feet forward, her outstretched hand touched painted wood. A door. It had to lead to the basement. Was it locked? Feeling along the side of the door she found a round knob. It turned. She pushed the door, but it would not open. She leaned her shoulder against it and it began to open with a faint squeak. She winced at the sound. When she inched the door open, she felt a wash of warm air and smelled burning coal.

Standing in the partially open door, ready to retreat, she saw a large room eerily illuminated by the glow from the iron-grilled door of a large coal-burning furnace. The ceiling was festooned with a network of ducts and pipes. Dripping water made puddles on the concrete floor that glistened in the flickering light. It was oppressively warm in the room. She tried the door's inner knob. It would not turn. If she allowed the door to close she would lock herself in. Holding the door open, she was able to rake in a piece of coal from the floor and she used it to wedge the door open a crack.

She put her back against the door and listened. There was no sound, no one in sight. This had to be a wild goose chase. The only way into the basement was through the door, unless there were service doors where the coal or other supplies were delivered. Even so, it would be impossible for anyone to enter the building after curfew.

She was turning to go back when from the corner of her eye, she saw a dark figure detached itself from the shadows behind the furnace. The figure made a slight hissing sound and she turned to stare. Dr. Steiner? How could he possibly have made his way here without being seen?

The figure moved forward and she saw that the man was too short and slender to be the doctor. And crossing the concrete floor, he moved with the quickness and grace of an athlete. Anna felt a momentary panic. Had she been betrayed? Was this man one of the SS guards? She felt for the knob of the door, knowing as she did so that it was already too late.

"Don't be afraid," the man whispered. "Dr. Steiner sent me."

Anna's breath came out in a rush. "Where is he?" Her voice was so low she was scarcely aware she had spoken.

The man put his face close to hers and she saw that his face and his clothing were blackened like those of a chimney sweep. He was carrying a grimy knapsack and he reeked with a foul odor that made her gag. "He's a little old for this kind of work. My name is Chaim Weisner. I have his message." He noticed the way she turned her face away and his teeth flashed in a smile. "Forgive the smell. I got here through the sewer."

"The sewer?"

"It's our highway. I'm on the sewer work detail. I know every turn." He was speaking German but with an accent Anna could not place.

"Is Dr. Steiner coming here—through the sewer?"

"No. We are going there."

"Through the sewer?!"

"Well, if you want to use the front door, I'll meet you there."

Through the sewers! She could never bring herself to do that.

Anna backed away and the man stood watching her. It was not too late to turn back. What could she learn anyway? She had seen the ghetto. She had seen the people. To be sure, there were some questions she could not answer. Some mysteries. Such as how such a small ghetto could house so many people. But it was not her concern. Her curiosity could not hope to accomplish anything except to get her into trouble.

But the questions would not go away. Even so, could she stand the stench of the sewer long enough to reach Dr. Steiner?

"I don't know," she said. "I don't think it's a good idea."

Chaim stared at her. "You say you're American."

The way he accentuated the word 'say' made Anna realize he was not convinced. So Dr. Steiner probably was not convinced either. "Actually, I'm Hungarian." She heard his intake of breath. He knew that if this was a trap, he would probably be severely punished, then probably sent to a work camp. "Half Hungarian," she corrected quickly. "Half Gypsy. But I am an American citizen. I lived in New York the last seven years."

"Then you won't mind if we use English," he said in English.

Anna shook her head. "No, of course not."

"I lived in New Jersey for eight years. Newport News. You know where it is?"

"Somewhere down south."

"Close enough."

They stood looking at each other like two fighters, each wondering how much they could trust the other.

"Why does Dr. Steiner want to see me?"

"To tell you the truth about Theresienstadt."

"The truth? We saw the workshops, the kitchen, the bakery. You have everything here."

"Lies. A charade for their benefit. You come alone and we will show you the real Theresienstadt: people dying, starving, living like animals."

"I can't believe that."

"Lady, there are more than ten thousand people here. You don't see any of them. Where the hell do you think they are?"

It had to be true. Day after day she had seen groups of people walk into the ghetto carrying their pitiful bags and suitcases and vanish into the maze of buildings. She had never seen any leave.

"All right. But I can't be away too long."

"We understand." He reached into his knapsack and took out a pair of rubber boots. "You'd better put these on."

After she had changed into the boots, Anna followed Chaim to a grating in the basement floor, all the while telling herself she was a fool. Excuses spun through her head, all the reasons why she should not put her own life in jeopardy. She should be looking after her own interests, her own survival. The plight of the Jews was not her concern.

But also spinning through her mind, was a quotation by Dante: *'The hottest places in Hell are reserved for those who, in time of great moral crisis, maintain their neutrality.'* She might have been willing to take her chances in Hell, but she could not ignore a deep anger that burned though all her trepidations, all her excuses. Injustice. It was injustice, she realized, that had always been the source of her deepest anger. And the treatment of the Gypsies and the Jews was the epitome of injustice. No man, no group of men had the right to inflict such pain and suffering on innocent people. It-was-not-right! So in the end, it was not compassion; It was not curiosity; It was a smoldering rage at injustice that drove her to follow the strange little man into the sewers beneath the streets of Theresienstadt.

When they emerged twenty minutes later, she was shuddering as much with revulsion as from the cold. The sewer system beneath the city had been constructed when the conduits were tunnels of concrete and stone. Many had a raised walkway, but some did not and she had been forced to slosh through inches of running water. At first the darkness, relieved only by the dim glow of Chaim's flashlight, had been oppressive. But slogging through the water, she was glad there was not more light. After the first few minutes she had been able to adjust to the stench, but she could not close her mind to the revulsion when some unknown object touched her rubber boots.

When at last they climbed concrete steps and passed through a doorway that opened into a small room, she tried not to remember that she would have to make the return trip.

Using his flashlight, Chaim found a pair of women's slippers on a shelf and handed them to Anna. She slipped out of the boots, trying not to touch them with her hands any more than necessary and put on the slippers. Chaim then led her through another doorway into a small room where dim candlelight flickered on brick walls. It was a toilet room with a single filthy commode and an equally filthy washbasin. In the room were Dr. Steiner and two members of the council. Anna hoped they had not been forced to wait long.

"Ah," Dr. Steiner said as he took Anna's hand. "I was afraid you would not come."

She had to look terrible and smell worse. Her hair was a mess. Her sweater was streaked with grime and the hem of her skirt was wet. "I'm not sure why I did."

Dr. Steiner smiled. "I know why. I saw it in your face today. That's why I gave you the message."

"You took a big chance."

"I know. I'm glad I was not wrong."

"Maybe you were. Why did you do it?"

"What is happening here must be made known to the world. We cannot—"

He stopped when Anna held up her hand. "You should know, I'm not a reporter. I am American, but I'm not a reporter."

Dr. Steiner's face drew into lines of despair. "I am sorry to hear that. We had hoped . . ." He broke off and his sad eyes turned to her. "I should have known that they would not allow a real reporter into Theresienstadt."

"Why not? I know that life here must be difficult for you, but from what I saw—"

"You saw what they wanted you to see." She had been interrupted by one of the council members, a thin man with a gray beard and deep-sunken eyes.

"Are you telling me it was all staged?"

"That's right. All of it. We wanted you to know the truth."

"I'm sorry. I really can't help."

"But if you're not a reporter," Chaim said, suspicion in his voice. "Why were you with them?"

"Because it was the only way I could leave the hotel."

Suspicion was still in Chaim's eyes as he added, "You live in the hotel. If you're not a reporter, what are you?"

"A prisoner." She told them what had happened to her and how she had survived by becoming the Kommandant's astrologer. She concluded with, "I just wanted to get out of that place for a while. It was Captain Voss' idea to put me with those reporters."

"Then you do have a certain amount of freedom," Dr. Steiner said.

"Only within the limits of the hotel. Until today."

"But perhaps those limits could be extended."

"Extended? What do you mean?"

"Perhaps von Liebermann will not allow you the freedom of Theresienstadt, he might allow you to makes trips outside, perhaps into Prague."

"Perhaps he would, but . . . How would that help?"

"There are people in Prague, Jews and non-Jews, who should be told what is happening here. They could tell the world."

"You want me to be a messenger?"

"Someone must."

"But not I. Why should I? You know what would happen if I got caught."

"There is no one else. None of us can leave. Not alive."

"And what is there to tell anyway? How do I know what I saw wasn't the truth."

Dr. Steiner stared at her for a second in utter disbelief. Then his face clouded and he took two quick steps to a door and flung it open. "Here! Here is the truth."

Through the open door Anna could see a large room with a timbered ceiling that looked as though it might have been a barracks for soldiers. It was dimly lit by two naked bulbs. But what caused her to catch her breath in anguished surprise were the faces of dozens of people. Rows of four-tiered bunks took up all but inches of the vast floor space and people were stacked in the bunks, two and three to a bunk. Men, women and children jammed into the bunks like sardines, huddling together for warmth.

"This room used to shelter twenty soldiers. It now has two hundred Jews. This is their toilet. One toilet. And these are the lucky ones. They at least have a bed. Hundreds don't have this much."

Anna moved to the doorway, drawn by disbelief. This could not be staged. It was not possible to create such degradation, such misery on demand. She had thought the Gypsy work camp was bad, but this was infinitely worse. "Nobody can live like this," she whispered.

"You're right. We're dying. Hundreds every day."

"But the Kommandant. He must not know."

Chaim snorted. "He knows. Who do you think set up that farce for the reporters."

Anna felt a hollowness building inside her. During the last few weeks, she had begun to feel almost sorry for von Liebermann. He seemed to be a nondescript, ineffectual man who had been thrust into a situation beyond his capabilities. How easy it was to believe what one wanted to believe. She realized now that his concerns were not for the welfare of these people. His concerns were because his superiors might not believe he was doing a good job. Beneath his nervous anxiety, he was as much a cold-blooded SS butcher as the worst of them. She owed him nothing. He had no more concern for her welfare than he did for any of these people. She was of use to him. And the moment that ended, she would be abandoned. God. How could she have forgotten that?

"All right," she said to Dr. Steiner. "I'll do what I can."

Dr. Steiner closed the door. "Thank you." There was a deep weariness in his movements and in his voice and Anna could not help comparing him to von Liebermann. Each felt a responsibility for these people. But what a horrible difference in that responsibility.

"Captain Voss," she said. "I think I can get him to take me to Prague. I'll try to deliver any messages you have."

"Good. It will be in a day or two. Chaim will leave it in the basement of your hotel. He'll show you where."

"All right."

"And now, we must leave here." He nodded toward the commode. "People are waiting."

On the way back to the hotel through the sewer Anna ask Chaim for the answer to a question that had been bothering her. "Chaim, the Small Fortress. They would not show it to us today. Why?"

Chaim did not answer immediately and Anna was about to repeat the question when he said, "It's where they torture and murder people. That's one more thing the world should know."

Anna followed the small man silently. Torture and murder. What was she getting involved in? Could von Liebermann know about the Small Fortress? How could he not? It was part of his domain. Did he go there during the day when he made his 'inspections?' And Deiter Voss? Did he also know? Again, how could he not? Apparently, his charming banter and friendly smile concealed a soul as black as the worst of them.

She was thinking of ways she could use the new insight in her readings when they entered the basement furnace room of the hotel.

As she changed back into her own shoes, Chaim pointed out a concealed area behind an overhead duct. "Tomorrow night. I'll leave a message here and instructions where you're to take it."

"All right. But remember, I can't promise anything. I've first got to get permission to go into Prague. And I may not be able to deliver it the first time."

"That's okay. I'll check here every day. You can leave any messages for us in the same place."

He moved into the shadows and vanished like a wraith. If it hadn't been for the faint sound of the cover to the sewer's entrance being slid into place, Anna could easily have believed he never existed.

Actually, she wished he hadn't. Now, she had to put her life in peril. Still, helping the Jews would give purpose to her life, give meaning to her capture and imprisonment. Had her entire life been directed toward this mission?

She was pondering the question when she opened the door leading to the stairs and someone touched her arm. She turned, fright tearing away her breath. Then she saw a face, a smiling face. Katalin.

Chapter 25

May 1942

In the 1930's, Berlin was considered one of the most beautiful cities in the world. But by May of 1942, the city had endured more than a year of bombing by the British Royal Air Force. The blast of 4,000-pound, high-capacity bombs and fires from incendiaries had devastated large tracts of the city. And while the German's year-long aerial blitz of London (which virtually ended in mid-1940) had killed or wounded 46,000 Londoners, in slightly more than a year Berlin had experienced almost 100,000 casualties. And with the United States now in the war, the raids promised to become even more intense. Already the streets were lined with rubble scraped into huge piles by the compulsively neat Germans. The destruction was egalitarian. Stately mansions and huge three-storied apartments alike were shattered hulks, with empty windows, crazily leaning walls seemingly supported only by a base of tumbled brick and blocks of stone, some with magnificent, fire-blackened chandeliers dangling precariously over charred ruins of oaken floors and wall panels. The air, which should have been sweet with spring rhododendrons, was tainted with the pungent smell of smoke and an unidentifiable sourness that brought bile into Eric's throat.

Looking out the window of the big Humber staff car that had picked him up at the Potsdam Railway Station, Eric was saddened by the destruction. At the same time there was the bitter satisfaction of knowing that those who had made his people suffer were themselves being made to suffer. And yet, why did such beauty have to be destroyed? And where would it end? Would Hitler force the Allies to reduce all of Germany to rubble? He almost hoped he would.

Eric had been carefully noting their route since they had left the station. He had never been in Berlin's inner city, but at SOE headquarters in London he had been briefed on the topography and had memorized the location of all important buildings and streets. They were now proceeding north on WilhelmStrasse and he leaned forward and said to the driver, "Turn left on Prinz-Albrecht."

The driver, a young Oberschutze, blinked nervously as he quickly said, "Jawohl, Herr Standartenführer."

Eric leaned back against the cushions and smiled. He knew why the man was nervous. No one enjoyed being anywhere near Gestapo headquarters. Especially when they had an SS officer in their car.

When they turned the corner, Eric saw the old stone building with its jutting portico at number 8 Prinz-AlbrechtStrasse just where British intelligence had said it would be.

"Do you want me to stop, Herr Standartenführer?"

Eric shook his head. "No. I'll check into the hotel first."

"Yes, sir." The driver stepped on the accelerator as though the building might reach out and sweep him into its grasp.

Eric was pleased at the man's reaction. He hoped every person in Germany had developed such fear of the SS. Kindness and consideration might win hearts and minds, but when one needed information, such an approach was too slow. Fear was quicker. Fear produced action. And time was definitely not on his side. Sir Malcolm and his M.I.6 intelligence staff had been 99% certain the real Colonel von Sievers would not return unexpectedly from Japan. But there was always that 1% possibility that they were mistaken. And every day the percentage increased. The sooner he accomplished his mission and left the city, the better were his chances of survival.

He chuckled as he pictured the expressions of Sir Malcolm and Captain Drury when they would discover he had disobeyed their orders. He was supposed to leave Berlin and go north to the city of Bergen as soon as he had sent the Judas-Goat Teletype to Heydrich. In Bergen he was to be picked up and taken to Sweden where he could wait out the war. But he had no intention of leaving Germany; not until he had found Anna. When M.I.6 learned their Gypsy colonel was still on the loose inside Germany, the entire SOE would be in a bloody tizzy.

The staff car turned the corner at Pariser Platz and skirted the Brandenburg Tor. Atop the huge gateway the goddess of victory lashed at her stone horses as though determination alone would carry her to glory.

The car passed the former British Embassy, crossed WilhelmStrasse and came to a stop in front of the Hotel Adlon. When the elderly doorman caught a glimpse of the pennants on the car's front fenders, he rushed to open the door and held it stiffly while Eric stepped out. Eric paused to adjust his hat with its polished silver Death's Head and to take off his gloves, making each movement as deliberately arrogant as possible. The hotel doorman was holding the door open and Eric said to his driver, "Wait here."

"Jawohl, Herr Standartenführer."

Picking up his briefcase, Eric strode to the hotel entrance. To the doorman he said, "Have my bags brought in."

As he crossed the hotel lobby toward the reception desk, he passed other SS and Wehrmacht officers who sprang to attention. Eric keep his face stony, but there was a knot of anxiety in his stomach. This was the first test. His black SS uniform had been provided by the British. Would it pass inspection? Was he correctly wearing the Knights Cross, Order of the Iron Cross on his left breast pocket? Was his swastika Kampfbinde worn properly on his left arm? Were his collar patches correct? He saw the puzzled expressions of those who noticed the inverted cross under the National Emblem's eagle on his left sleeve instead of the usual swastika. No wonder. They had probably never seen the insignia of the Ahnenerbe. But they all knew the Reichsführer SS cuff band that marked him a member of Himmler's staff and he heard the whispers after he had passed.

At the desk, the waiting clerk was hastily pulled aside by the hotel concierge who greeted him with a broad smile and a stiff Nazi salute which Eric acknowledged with a wave of his gloves as he'd seen von Liebermann do so often. "Wolfram von Sievers," he said loud enough for the nearest officers to hear. Within minutes the word would spread that one of Hitler's chosen was staying at the hotel.

"Yes, yes, Herr von Sievers," the concierge stuttered. "We have your reservation."

Eric was pleasantly surprised. When Sir Malcolm had assured him their contacts in Berlin would arrange transportation and hotel reservations, Eric had been skeptical. But the staff car had been waiting outside Potsdam station, and now, it appeared his reservation was in order. He hoped M.I.6 had been equally efficient in the preparation of his forged identity papers and orders. Not that he expected to have to use them until he reported to the SS offices in the Gestapo building. Few people had the temerity to demand the papers of an SS colonel.

The concierge dipped the registration pen in ink and handed it to Eric and he scrawled von Sievers' name on the register. He hoped he was doing it right. He had only stayed in a hotel two or three times in his life, and they had been small hostelries that were surprised if their guests even bothered to sign the registry.

When he had finished, the concierge snatched up a key and hurried around the counter. "This way, Herr Standartenführer."

Eric followed him into the elevator where they rode upward in silence. He saw that sweat had formed on the back of the concierge's neck and was staining his shirt collar. Good. Let the bastard sweat. Many were the times that men such as this obsequious pig had made him sweat. As a boy, both he and his father had often been humiliated by some bureaucratic burgermeister or *arschloch* policeman who had made their necks run with the sweat of fear. Now it was his turn.

The suite where the concierge led was situated on the west side of the hotel fronting WilhelmStrasse. The large room was cluttered with heavy 18th century overstuffed and crochet-covered furniture. Several sideboards displayed antique plates hand-painted with pastoral scenes. The bedroom was dominated by a huge four-poster bed canopied in thick plum-colored velveteen. In his wildest dreams Eric had never envisioned such elegance.

The concierge swept the drapes aside from the wide windows, bathing the room with spring sunlight. "Observe the view," he chortled. "You can see the magnificent Brandenburg Tor and the Tiergarten."

The view was breathtaking, but Eric had no intention of accepting it. "What is that building?" He pointed to the British Embassy.

"It was the British Embassy, your Excellency. It is now—"

"And that?" Eric indicated a huge marble-facaded structure on the opposite side of the bustling Pariser Platz.

"The French Embassy, Excellency. But—"

Eric wrenched the drapes from the man's startled hands and swept them across the window. "Not acceptable! I am not British! I am not French. I am German. I want to look at things German. I want a front room with a view of Unter Den Linden."

"Yes, yes. I understand." The concierge used his handkerchief to blot at his cheeks. "I do not have another suite immediately, Herr Standartenführer. But later this afternoon—"

"Later! What do you mean 'later?'"

The menace in his voice drove the concierge back a step. "I only mean, Excellency, that all suites are occupied. It will take a little time to vacate one."

"Very well. I am not unreasonable," Eric said and the concierge put the handkerchief back in his breast pocket. "I will give you ten minutes."

Alarm gripped the concierge making his voice shrill. "Ten minutes? But, surely, sir—"

Eric raised his hand and the man's voice stopped abruptly. "Ten minutes. Then I will take charge personally. And you will be living at number eight Prinz-AlbrechtStrasse."

The concierge blinked and his face paled so quickly that Eric thought he was going to faint. "Yes, Herr Standartenführer. Immediately." He ran for the door.

Left alone, Eric smiled. The mention of the Gestapo's address had put the fear of God into the man. He must remember that. To these people, fear of the Gestapo was probably greater than the fear of being shot. Compared with the rumors of what went on in the basement of the grim Prinz-

AlbrechtStrasse building, a quick bullet would be preferable.

But if he were not careful, he might find out if the rumors were true.

Minutes later he was ushered into another suite whose French windows opened to a balcony overlooking the beautiful lime trees of the Unter Den Linden. Several nervous maids were busily clearing the room of its previous occupants personal belongs, remaking the bed and vacuuming the deep carpeting.

Eric favored the concierge with a smile. "Excellent."

The concierge blotted sweat from his forehead. "If I may ask, Herr Standartenführer, will you be staying long?"

Eric fixed him with a cold stare. "I will stay until I leave." Without waiting for a reply, he picked up his briefcase and stalked to the door. "If I have any messages, I will be at Gestapo headquarters."

As he walked to the elevator he carried a satisfying picture of the concierge's white face.

The driver of the big staff car had a similar look when Eric told him where he wanted to go. "Take WilhelmStrasse," Eric commanded. As they made their way down the broad, straight thoroughfare, Eric stared at the monolithic government buildings: the Ministry of Propaganda where Goebbels had his headquarters, the Foreign Ministry and the Reichschancellery. The structures were all of the same neo-Grecian design, with tall columns and massive stone facades surrounded by sweeping lawns and towering trees. Only nearby bomb craters and a few shattered windows detracted from their aura of solid, everlasting strength.

Traffic on the main thoroughfare was light, consisting primarily of people on bicycles, rumbling army trucks, charcoal-burning buses and red post-office vans.

When the car stopped in front of Gestapo headquarters, the Scharführer leaped out to hold the door.

"Shall I wait, Herr Standartenführer?"

"Of course."

As the driver ran to open the large door, Eric studied the infamous structure. For its headquarters, the Gestapo had chosen an old, five story building constructed of gray stone blocks. The building was situated flush against the sidewalk with four curved steps leading to a glass-paneled front door. The portico consisted of two slender columns supporting a spandrel, which served as a base for a rococo sculpture of figures wearing generations of coal dust.

The doors opened into a huge vestibule paved with blocks of Carrara marble and lighted by a massive chandelier that was suspended from the vaulted ceiling by a long chain. A charwoman was on her knees using soapy water from a bucket and a brush to scrub dark spots from the pristine marble.

Eric's boot heels echoed like shots as he walked toward a lone desk situated in the precise center of the room, directly beneath the chandelier. Guards wearing gray Waffen-SS uniforms and steel helmets stood at attention on each side of double doors at the rear of the vestibule, while two others guarded the front entrance. A sergeant wearing a black SS uniform was seated behind the desk. When he saw Eric he leaped to his feet and held his right arm out in a rigid salute. "Heil Hitler," he shouted.

Eric waved his gloves in return. "General Pohl. He is expecting me."

"Jawohl, Herr Standartenführer. Your papers, please."

Eric took a tooled leather folder from his breast pocket and slapped it on the desk. The sergeant flipped open the folder and extracted identity papers and orders. He gave a perfunctory look at the name and the SS seal on the identity papers then slipped them all back in the folder and handed it to Eric.

During the procedure Eric had been watching the guards, deciding what he would do if the sergeant shouted an alarm. He estimated he could make it half way to the door before one of them shot him in the back. His face.did not reflect his relief as he took the folder and returned it to his pocket as though this was an every day occurrence.

"Obergruppenführer Pohl," he said.

"Jawohl, Herr Standartenführer. The General is expecting you." He snapped his fingers at one of the guards near the inner door. "Oberschutze, escort the colonel to the office of General Pohl."

Eric silently cursed. The last thing he wanted was to meet General Pohl who probably knew von Sievers by sight. British SOE had assured him that the general would be away for several days. If they were wrong, he was in real trouble.

As the sergeant wrote the name of Colonel von Sievers in his log book and recorded the time, the Waffen-SS private first-class opened the door and held it for Eric to enter. Beyond the door was a long corridor with several branches. At one side was a wide curving stairway of white marble that led downward. On the opposite side a similar stairway angled upward. The guard led the way to an elevator and pushed a button.

Waiting for the lift gave Eric time to look around. Several prisoners wearing familiar striped uniforms were working under the watchful eyes of SS guards. They were using two-wheeled dollies or carrying boxes and crates from a rear freight elevator through wide doors to a rear courtyard where trucks were being loaded. Eric was reminded of ants whose nest was under siege. But he asked no questions. It would not do for a colonel to request information from a corporal.

When the lift arrived, they rode to the top floor where the doors opened onto a wide, carpeted hallway. Across from the elevator, the guard pulled open a pair of floor-to-ceiling oaken doors and held them for Eric to enter. Eric shifted the briefcase to his left hand and rested his right on the holster of his pistol. If Pohl saw through his deception, he would take as many of the Nazis with him as possible before he was killed. He certainly would not be taken alive.

As Eric entered, his escort saluted and said "Heil Hitler" and walked away, closing the doors behind him.

Eric was in a mahogany-paneled outer office with a carpeted floor and a high ceiling. An SS Obersturmführer was seated behind a large desk that guarded another pair of oaken doors. He sprang to his feet and snapped a hasty "Heil Hitler" before he came around the desk. "Colonel von Sievers. Welcome, sir. May I take your briefcase?"

"No," Eric answered. "Not yet."

"Very well. Let me tell Sturmbannführer Krischer you've arrived." He went to the door and knocked.

"Krischer?" Eric said. "I am to meet with General Pohl."

"The major will explain, sir."

Eric took his hand from the pistol holster. Apparently the SIS had been right and Pohl was away.

The door was opened from the inside by a husky SS major. He had a wide forehead and slightly bulging eyes and his hair was shaved so high on the sides and back there was only a small thatch on top. His eyes were pale blue and his lashes so white they appeared bleached. On his left cheek was a saber wound that was only partially healed. Holding the door he snapped a quick salute with a, "Heil Hitler," then held out his hand with a smile that displayed large square teeth.

"Major Max Krischer, Excellency. At your service."

Eric took the man's hand intending to give it a quick squeeze, but Krischer wanted to demonstrate his strength and applied a crushing grip. Instead of attempting to countered the grip with his own strength, Eric let his hand go limp, but he stared into Krischer's eyes so coldly that Krischer stopped smiling and quickly released his hand. Eric continued to express his displeasure in an icy stare with his lips compressed grimly and Krischer blinked nervously.

"Ah, welcome, sir. I hope you had an uneventful trip."

"Where is General Pohl?"

"At Oranienburg, sir. We are in the process of moving."

"Oranienburg?"

"Just outside the Sachsenhausen Konzentrationslager, sir. It provides us with more space."

Eric's lips curled. "And it is safer from the air raids."

Krischer flushed and touched the saber scar on his cheek as though to draw Eric's attention to this evidence of his courage. "Not at all, sir. We have outgrown our quarters here. That is all."

"I understand."

Eric brushed by Krischer and walked into the office of Lieutenant-General Pohl. It was decorated with the Nazi version of sumptuousness as befitted the head of the SS Main Economic and Administration Office, with a huge desk made of dark walnut and flanked by Nazi flags on staves. Behind the high-backed leather chair was a large portrait of Hitler. Dormer windows overlooked the street.

Eric walked around the desk to a window and took his time staring at the traffic on Prinz-AlbrechtStrasse before he turned to the major. "When do you expect him to return?"

"Not until Saturday, sir. But his office is at your disposal, of course."

"Thank you. It will have to do."

Krischer walked to the desk and picked up a Teletype flimsy. "I'm not exactly sure of your mission, sir. The Teletype is somewhat, ah, confusing."

Eric raised an eyebrow. "Confusing?"

"It indicates that you are to be given the utmost cooperation—which we will, of course—during your, ah, inspection."

"So?"

"Ah, inspection of what, sir?"

"Whatever I say."

"Oh. Of course."

Eric walked to the desk and sat in General Pohl's huge chair. "Perhaps it would help if I explained the purpose of this inspection, which, I may say, I do not appreciate having to make."

"Yes, sir. I'm sure it would, sir."

"I am here at the personal request of Reichsführer Himmler and Obergruppenführer Heydrich. They are concerned about negative reports regarding your operations."

"Negative, sir?"

"Negative. I am to make an inspection of your efforts to carry out the orders of the Führer, then report personally to Obergruppenführer Heydrich. I assume you are capable of sending a Teletype to Einsatzgruppe-D in Prague."

"Yes, sir." Krischer was having a difficult time controlling his dismay while maintaining the deference that was due an SS colonel.

"Excellent." Eric glanced at the gold Le Coultre on his wrist. His primary mission for the British was to get that Teletype sent to Heydrich. But to maintain his cover story, he first had to go through the motions of conducting an inspection. British Intelligence had suggested that he begin with a mysterious facility on the Tiergarten. It would not only provide a good test of his acceptability, but he could pick up information they would welcome when he made his report to M.I.6.

"It's a full two hours before lunch. We will begin at number 4-Tiergarden. Then we will return here and you will explain this move you are making."

Krischer's chin came up. He did not welcome the ordered schedule. "Jawohl, Herr Standartenführer. If you will allow me."

Krischer held the door and Eric got up and walked out. He could appreciate the man's chagrin and anger. He had been in the same subservient position many times and it had always made him angry. He much preferred being on the other end of the orders.

The National Coordinating Agency for Therapeutic and Medical Establishment, code named T-4, was housed in an old building that had once been a prison in the Tiergarten district of Berlin. Eric was not certain why British Intelligence thought the medical facility warranted an inspection, but he was willing to accept their evaluation, although he did not relish the idea of touring a hospital.

But it was not a hospital. Their escort, Dr. Prosner, was an elderly man with fine white hair and a bushy mustache who wore a white smock. Eric and Major Krischer followed the Doctor to a large shed that had been constructed in the old prison yard behind the main building. There, with a great deal of hammering and sawing, a number of prisoners wearing typical striped pants and jackets were building vans on the beds of old trucks. Completed vans were painted red like German mail trucks and ambulances.

Keeping clear of flying sparks generated by a man using a cutting torch on a truck chassis, Dr. Prosner said, "I am sorry that Dr. Becker could not be here to tell you about his work in person, but he is currently conducting experiments at Limburg."

Eric had been studying the vans on the trucks which were in various stages of construction. "They look like ambulances. Is that their purpose?"

Dr. Prosner chuckled. "Not exactly. Although we hope the 'patients' think as you do. Actually, they are being sent to the Einsatzgruppen for their cleansing operations. Come let me show you."

Dr. Prosner led them to the rear of a van and opened the double doors. "Notice that the cabin is reinforced for strength and faced with metal."

With the doors open, Eric could see there were long benches on either side and no windows or openings of any kind. The vans had to be designed for the transport of high security prisoners.

"How many prisoners can you carry?"

"Prisoners? Oh, yes, of course. The patients. Well, that is one of the major drawbacks. The most we have been able to carry is forty-five."

"Forty-five people. In there?"

"Too many actually. It makes extraction difficult. Although the gas does take effect at a faster rate due to the reduction of available oxygen."

Eric stared at the interior of the van with a slow horror building. "Gas? What kind of gas?"

"Carbon monoxide. From the truck's exhaust." Dr. Prosner squatted to point out a pipe welded to the truck's exhaust duct. "You see. The driver has control of a valve inside his cab. On the way to the burial site, he opens the valve slowly. The patients simply go to sleep. It is very humane."

"What patients are these?" Out of the corners of his eyes Eric saw Major Krischer staring at him. He should not have asked the question. The real von Sievers would, of course, know the answer. He was quite sure that he did too.

His suspicions were confirmed by Dr. Prosner who said, "Jews primarily. A few Jehovah's Witnesses and politicals."

Eric could not keep the bitter irony out of his voice as he added, "And Gypsies, I trust."

"A few. Most are in labor camps, but we're seeing more as the Einsatzgruppens do their work."

Eric turned away. He could not believe what he was hearing. This man who looked like a family doctor was discussing the extermination of people as though he was talking about harvesting tomatoes. "These vans," he said when he had his voice under control. "How many do you have?"

"Less than fifty. There is a great demand. I trust you will inform Obergruppenführer Heydrich that we are proceeding as rapidly as possible."

Eric was suddenly gripped by an intense feeling of hate. He wanted to take this man's throat in his hands and squeeze the life out of him. Somehow he had to make the man suffer. "I will judge what I will tell the Obergruppenführer," he said icily. "And whose name I will give to him."

The effect on the man was pleasantly startling. His face paled and he put his hand to his chest and gasped for breath. If he had not been burning with anger, Eric might have felt sorry for him.

Eric turned to Krischer. He had to clear the suspicion he saw in the man's eyes. "As the Führer suspected, your work here is totally inadequate. Unless there is immediate improvement, you will be replaced."

To Eric's relief, the suspicion in Krischer's eyes was replaced by a look of worry. "But, Herr Standartenführer, I am not responsible for this."

"You know the Führer—and the Reichsführer. Everyone will be held responsible."

"There are other methods underway, even now," Krischer said hastily. He turned to the doctor. "Show him the shower rooms."

"Oh. Of course." Dr. Prosner made a swift, nervous smile. "You will appreciate this, Excellency." He began walking toward the old prison and Eric swung in beside him.

Inside, Eric stayed close behind the doctor as they descended cement steps into a basement. A wide, long corridor ran through the entire length of the building with doors opening into rooms that had once been prison cells. The cement walls had been covered with gleaming white tile giving Eric the impression they actually were in a hospital.

Near the opposite end of the corridor, Dr. Prosner entered a large room that was tiled in light blue. There were benches against the walls and hooks for hanging clothes. In one side wall was a door with a small glass window safetied with imbedded wire mesh. "The subjects are first brought in here."

"Subjects?"

"For the experiments. They are told they are going to be given a shower and deloused. They take off their clothes and go into the shower room." The doctor pushed open the side door, which Eric saw could be secured with a heavy bolt on the outside.

The walls, floor and ceiling of the shower room were covered with white tile. On each side of the room there were four showers with handles for hot and cold water. The floor sloped to a central drain.

Dr. Prosner looked around with a smile of satisfaction. "Excellent. Even the showers work when we want them to."

Eric was silent, wondering if he was supposed to know what this man was talking about.

Krischer pointed to holes in the ceiling. "The gas comes in through those holes. Special fans have been constructed to provide a forced draft."

Gas? So that was it. This was a death chamber just as the vans were death chambers. For Gypsies. Eric's desire to smash his fists into the two men was so strong that it required all of his concentration to maintain his role. He stared at the holes in the ceiling with feigned appreciation. "I see. The subjects think they are coming in for a shower. You bolt the door and turn on the gas blowers."

"The bodies are removed through that large door in the back. It leads directly to the crematorium."

"You've tested these?"

"Oh, yes. Every day."

Every day! That explained the mystery. People went in but never came out. Eric controlled a desire to vomit by rubbing his hand hard across his dry mouth. "Very ingenious."

"I cannot take all the credit," Dr. Prosner said. "The idea was proposed by Herr Bouhler."

Eric searched his memory. The SOE had given him a crash course in German bureaucracy and the name popped into his mind. "Philipp Bouhler, of the Führer's personal chancellery?"

"Yes. In this room—and others like it at Brandenburg and other experimental stations—we have proven that the system is much more efficient than the vans. The technology can easily be transferred to larger rooms."

"How large?"

"Oh, large enough to hold a hundred people or more." Dr. Prosner continued talking as he led the way back out into the corridor. "They already have chambers in operation at two camps in Poland. And others are under construction."

"And how are they doing?"

"Very well. However, we are trying to speed up the operation. Carbon monoxide is effective and cheap. But it is slow and difficult to control. If it's administered too fast, there is considerable pain with the resultant excretions. This slows down the flow-through. And with the volume we expect, we're looking at other types of gas. At the moment a rat killer called Zyklon-B is the most promising."

As they left the building, Eric felt as though he were leaving hell. Could the basement of Gestapo headquarters be worse than this? And how many other basements through this vaunted Reichsland were execution grounds? He doubted he would ever be able to enter the basement of a government building again without experiencing a compulsion to vomit. And there was the fear. It seeped into the walls, the floor, into the brick and mortar. And not just from the victims. Fear also exuded from the guards, the soldiers and the officers. There was fear in the streets, in the shops, everywhere. Germany had become a nation of fear. Who would be next? Who would be awakened in the night by the Gestapo pounding at the door to become one of the nacht-und-nebel, those who vanish into the night and the fog?

Could a nation survive fueled by suspicion and fear? Apparently it could as long as power remained in the hands of men such as these.

During lunch in General Pohl's private dining room with Major Krischer, Eric caught himself slipping in and out of character as his mind refused to give up the pictures that kept entering. Pictures of hundreds of men, women and children being tricked into believing they were going to be given showers only to find themselves fighting for their lives in a cloud of gas. Rat poison, for God's sake. Could such a fate be in store for Anna? Could it have already happened? The next part of his mission was not going to be for the British; it was going to be for Anna and for all of Dr. Prosner's 'patients' and 'subjects.'

"You have personnel files here of Schutzstaffel officers?"

Krischer looked up from his plate. "Jawohl, Herr Standartenführer."

"Excellent. I have a cousin I have lost track of. Colonel von Liebermann. Perhaps we can locate him."

Krischer dabbed at his lips with his napkin. "Perhaps. Those files are being moved to our new headquarters at Oranienburg."

"When?"

"As a matter of fact, this very afternoon, if it hasn't been done already."

Eric could feel Anna slipping away again. If he had to make a trip to Oranienburg, it would increase his chances of being found out as an impostor. He pushed back his chair and stood up. "Then we had better go see."

Krischer hesitated. He was only half finished with his meal. Then he looked up at Eric's grim face and put down his napkin. "Jawohl, Herr Standartenführer."

Eric followed him past offices and storage rooms where prisoners packed and moved the contents of the rooms. Krischer stopped outside a room where prisoners were preparing to remove a bank of four-drawer file cabinets. Stenciled in gold letters on the door were the words 'Wirtschaft und Verwaltung-shauptamt, Arbeitskraft Abteilung-D Klasse-I, Klasse-II, Klasse-III.'

Eric studied the sign, his heart pounding. "Labor force records?"

"Yes, sir. We keep excellent records."

This was the room that might lead him to Ravanna. Eric recalled what Sir Malcolm had said about the camps: Class One camps conduct work essential to the Reich and receive the maximum in food and health care. Class Two camps are not as essential and their conditions were primitive. Prisoners in Class Three camps were not expected to survive.

Perhaps it would be prudent to wait, to go slow, but he had to know about Anna. Was she in a camp one? Or a camp three? "Interesting," he said. "You should certainly be able to locate von Liebermann.

"Yes. I believe so." Krischer glanced into the room, then looked at Eric and shook his head. "We are too late, I'm afraid. They have already begun the preparations to move."

"Tell them to stop."

"I'm sorry, Excellency. General Pohl himself ordered—"

"I am not interested in your orders. You will order them to stop until we locate that file."

Krischer's face paled, but he shook his head. "I do not have the authority to countermand the General's orders." He looked directly at Eric as though he had won a victory. "And neither do you, Herr Standartenführer."

Inside the room the prisoners and their supervising guard had stopped to watch. Eric was at a momentary loss. Should he attempt to force the issue? It might spell disaster for his mission. But if he did not, it could end his chance of finding Anna. He had to insist. How would von Liebermann or that SS bastard who had shot the mare handle this display of insubordination?

Eric flipped back the cover on the holster of his pistol and took out the Luger and pressed the muzzle against Krischer's temple. "This is my authority, Herr Krischer," he said softly. "Do you wish to argue?"

Krischer's eyes rolled to look at the gun and he croaked, "No, Herr Standartenführer. It will be as you say."

"Good. I will have Reichsführer Himmler explain to General Pohl. Now do it!"

"Jawohl, Excellency!" Krischer stepped into the room and said loudly, "Halt! Everyone stay where you are."

As Eric and the others watched, Krischer began reading the labels on the front of the cabinets. Eric stood holding the gun, marveling at its weight and the smooth feel of the handle. But more than that he marveled at the power it harbored. He had never felt this power at Arbor House when they had taught him to shoot. There, weapons were only mechanical devices designed to hurl projectiles. On the firing range there was no feeling that the projectiles were meant to kill. But now, here, the gun was not a mechanical device; it was naked power. And the black uniform gave him the authority to use that power. As he slowly slid the weapon back into its holster, his hand lingered on the smooth metal.

He turned his attention to Krischer who was checking the letters on the front of the filing cabinets. Eric watched his slow, meticulous perusal with mounting impatience. He wanted to shove the man aside and rip the files from the cabinets.

Krischer turned from the last filing cabinet and looked up at Eric with something in his eyes that Eric suspected was triumph. "I'm sorry, Excellency. It appears that we are too late. That file is already gone."

Gone! Oh God. To be this close. "When?" Eric turned to the guard. "When was that file removed?"

The guard's eyes were huge with fear. "Only moments ago, Herr Standartenführer."

"Then it could still be in the building. Or on the truck."

"On the truck, Jawohl, Herr Standartenführer."

"Show me."

The guard's eyes swung toward the prisoners. "But, Herr Standartenführer—"

Eric slapped the man across the face with his gloves, the sound like a pistol shot in the small room. "Show me!"

"Jawohl, Herr Standartenführer.

The man almost ran out of the room. Eric followed with long strides as the guard plunged down a flight of stairs and out through large double doors into the courtyard. Groups of prisoners were loading three large Mercedes-Benz trucks with the material being brought out of the building by other prisoners.

The guard stopped at the rear of one of the trucks where two sweating prisoners were struggling with a large file cabinet on a dolly, attempting to roll it up a ramp into the truck.

"Here it is, Herr Standartenführer," he said, relief clear in his voice.

Eric said to the prisoners. "Halt! Bring that down."

The prisoners stopped, straining to hold the heavy file cabinet, staring at him in confusion. There was a vague familiarity about the two men. A year ago they might have been prosperous merchants or farmers ordering Eric and other Gypsies to move off their land. Now he was giving the orders. Eric's hand dropped to the holster of his gun. "Bring it down!"

The guard reinforced Eric's words with a blow of his truncheon on the prisoners legs. "Down," he shouted. "Bring it down."

The prisoners hastened to comply. As they struggled to turn, a wheel of the dolly slipped from the ramp and the file cabinet toppled to the ground with a crash, dragging the prisoners with it and spilling its contents.

Eric growled in sudden fury. "Dummkopfs!"

The guard saw his opportunity to impresses an SS Colonel and began smashing the fallen men with his truncheon, screaming invectives. Another guard came running and joined in with his truncheon. The prisoners tried to use their arms to ward off the blows, but the guards smashed their arms aside giving them access to the men's vulnerable faces.

Eric stood, hypnotized. It was as though the guards were punishing all the wealthy, powerful men who had ever taken advantage of him. He could almost feel the heavy truncheons in his own hands. He wished that—

"Are you going to shoot them?"

Krischer was standing next to him, a sneer on his handsome face, and Eric became aware that his pistol was out of its holster and in his hand.

He stared at the weapon stupidly for a second, wondering how it had gotten into his hand. With a sudden fear that was more powerful than any he had ever known, he jammed the gun back into its holster. He opened his mouth to order the guards to stop. But they had already stopped because the men were unconscious, blood staining their clothing.

"The files," Eric said. "Don't get blood on the files. Move them."

The guards quickly dragged the inert bodies aside and Eric turned to Krischer. "See if you can find the file."

Krischer knelt on one knee and carefully examined the scattered papers. Eric watched him coldly, not glancing at the two unconscious men. His entire attention was concentrated on Krischer. The unconscious men held no meaning for him. They were objects. They would be replaced by others.

Krischer stood, a file folder in his hand. "Here it is.

Krischer opened the folder and, looking over his shoulder, Eric saw a copy of an official SS indoctrination certificate. Clipped to it was a series of pictures of von Liebermann in his uniform, but without a hat, similar to the pictures in a police file: left and right profile, full front. Krischer withdrew von Liebermann's personal record and studied it.

"Interesting man, your cousin. Heidelberg, Nuremberg. An Accountant until 1933. Then a schoolmaster." He looked up at Eric with a smile. "Accountant? You're sure he isn't a Jew." At the look on Eric's face, his smile dissolved. "I see. Yes."

"Forget all that," Eric snarled. "Just tell me where he is now."

"Let me see. He was in charge of the work camp at Arnschwang . . ."

"Is that the one near the Bohmer Wald on the Czech border?"

"The former Czech border, yes."

"And now?"

Krischer studied the document carefully. "Unbelievable. He must have very good connections."

Eric felt as though a giant fist was gripping his chest. What had happened to von Liebermann? "What? What is it?"

"Theresienstadt. They put him in charge of Theresienstadt. But he has no experience."

"Theresienstadt? What is that? Not a class three?"

"No, no. Better even than class one." Krischer gave Eric an odd look. "You don't know about Theresienstadt?"

The fist that had relaxed its grip for an instant was squeezing his chest again, harder than ever. He had almost forgotten the role he was playing. "You are not here to ask questions," he gritted. "You are here to answer them. Now tell me about this place Theresienstadt."

Krischer's face was pink when he straightened. He glanced toward the door to see if any of the soldiers had witnessed his humiliation. "Jawohl, Herr Standartenführer. Theresienstadt is a special ghetto that has been created for Jews. It is an ideal place to live and work. Better than a class one work camp."

Some of the tension drained out of Eric. "Where is it located?"

Krischer was on the edge of another question, but he caught himself and said, "Sudatenland. Near Prague."

Eric then understood the reason for Krischer's suspicions. Prague was a part of Heydrich's Einsatzgruppe-D. As a member of the Obergruppenführer's staff he should have known that. He covered his faux pax by saying, "Good. Thank you, major. I have little interest in such matters as Jewish ghettos, as you may imagine." He fixed Krischer with a pointed stare. "The concern of the Ahnenerbe is more for the dead than the living."

Krischer's hands trembled as he closed the file. "Is that the information you required, sir?"

"Yes. Theresienstadt. I will remember that name. And yours."

Krischer gently placed the file on the ground with the others, unsure whether Eric's memory of his name was going to result in a promotion or a trip to the basement. He chose to believe the former. "Thank you, sir." He looked at the two guards. "Have this cleaned up. Make sure the files are in order."

"Jawohl, Herr Sturmbannführer," they answered.

Krischer glanced at his watch. "It is early, Herr Standartenführer. Do you wish to inspect the facility?"

But Eric was not listening. He was staring at the spots of blood staining the concrete. Could he have saved those men? If he had the power to order punishment, he certainly had the power to stop it. So why hadn't he?

"Sir!"

He became aware that Krischer was addressing him and he jerked his head around. "Yes?"

"What would you like to inspect now?"

Eric flicked his gloves. "I will leave that to you."

Krischer looked from Eric's white face to the drops of blood and his lips pulled into a faint disdainful smile. "I don't believe you would be interested in the, ah, activities in our basement. Perhaps we should examine our communications section."

Communications? The major's words reminded Eric that he had to send the fateful Teletype to Reinhard Heydrich. This might be his chance. "Excellent," he said. "Communications are the essence of warfare."

As he walked back into the building, Eric reviewed the Teletype message that would start Heydrich on his journey to the Prague railway station. . . and his rendezvous with death.

But he had trouble concentrating on the text of the message. The name Theresienstadt kept sounding in his head. An ideal camp, Krischer had said. And von Liebermann was there. But was Anna still with him? Was she alive? It had been more than four months since von Liebermann and Anna had left the Arnschwang labor camp. He was tempted to leave Berlin immediately and find this Theresienstadt ghetto. With his new identity, he should have no trouble getting inside. However, getting out with Anna might be a problem. Von Liebermann would never allow her to leave willingly. Even so, he would find a way, of that he was certain.

But he would not have the chance if he gave away his disguise by acting improperly now. It was best that he continue his deception here in Berlin until time to leave. Fortunately, Theresienstadt was near Prague where the assassination was to take place. When it did, he would be there. If it occurred as planned, the confusion might work to his advantage. He would have to be patient until the time was right. Tomorrow. Tomorrow he would go for Anna.

Chapter 26

To Anna, a visit to the city of Prague was like stepping back into life. The city, one of the oldest and most beautiful in Europe, had escaped the destruction of war. The shops and stores were open; the movie houses and theaters were presenting their usual fare; the ancient buildings and beautiful tree-bordered streets continued to mellow, untouched by bombs or bullets. To be sure, German soldiers were everywhere. And the streets were often congested by military trucks and occasionally tanks and armored personnel carriers. At night the lights were dimmed, but the night life was wild, with the clubs and bistros engaging in the kind of desperate revelry generated by the fear of a tomorrow dying.

Sitting at a table in a small basement club in Old Town with von Liebermann, Captain Dieter Voss and Katalin, Anna was both miserable and pleased. She could feel the piece of paper concealed inside her brassiere that Dr. Steiner had sent to her almost two weeks before but that she had been unable to deliver.

This was the third time she had been able to talk Dieter Voss into bringing her to the city. But each time Katalin had insisted in joining them. Anna could not refuse. Katalin knew she was engaging in some mysterious pursuit and watched her with a cat-like intensity. She had made it clear she would say nothing about discovering Anna in the hotel basement if Anna helped insure her status with von Liebermann. She had learned enough German so she could inform on Anna if she wished. As a result, Anna had been unable to make contact with any of the Jews, even though Prague had one of the largest and best educated Jewish populations in Europe. Thousands had been taken from the city, but many had, thus far, remained untouched.

Now on the third trip, both Voss and Katalin seemed to have relaxed their vigilance. Unfortunately, this time von Liebermann had decided to come with them. But in a way, that might be helpful. Her previous trips had been one day affairs for shopping. This time they would be spending the night so she might be able to slip away to make delivery of Dr. Steiner's note. And if Katalin was entertaining von Liebermann she could not very well follow.

The curfew, however, was a problem. After eleven o'clock, anyone on the street was immediately arrested. Which was the reason Anna had chosen the Crozac Club for dinner. During her shopping tour of the city she had made it a point to frequent the shops in the Old Town's Josefev section that contained the Jewish ghetto. She had noted that the Crozac Club, on the north side of the Old Town Square, was less than a five-minute walk from the Old-New Synagogue and the old Jewish Cemetery. If she could slip away for a few minutes she could make her delivery and be back before she was missed.

Anna glanced across the table at Katalin who was laughing at something Voss had said. Von Liebermann had purchased a silk gown for the Gypsy girl as well as a new supply of makeup, which she had used skillfully. Anna had to admit that Katalin was strikingly beautiful. Her blue-black hair cascaded over her shoulders and down her back in a mass of curls. Huge loop earrings were partially concealed by her hair. Her dark eyebrows, carefully contoured with eyebrow pencil, highlighted her almond-shaped eyes. Her lips, now cherry red, were naturally cast in a sexual pout. The bodice of the dress, held up by spaghetti straps of rhinestones, was cut low, revealing the golden-ivory of her shoulders and the slopes of her breasts. The dress was short in the newest fashion, so Katalin was able to display her long, tapering legs and her new silk stockings and red high-heeled shoes.

In contrast, Anna wore a dark dirndl skirt with a tight, traditionally embroidered bodice over a long-sleeved blouse and she felt like a moth sitting next to a butterfly.

The small orchestra began playing the Vienna waltz and Voss raised an eyebrow at von Liebermann, who nodded and Voss asked Katalin if she would like to dance. Katalin smiled and drained her glass of wine and stood up. Anna wondered if Katalin had ever danced a waltz in her life, or for that matter, if she had ever worn high-heeled shoes. When Voss held out his arms she glanced at the other dancers for a clue as to her role, then slipped into place. She was a natural dancer with feline grace and after the first misdirected steps, she caught on quickly and was soon gliding across the floor on her toes, not trusting the support of the high heels.

Anna glanced at von Liebermann who was sipping his wine and watching the dancers. Did she detect a trace of jealousy? When she cast his next horoscope, she would explore his feelings toward Katalin. If she could cause a split in their relationship, she might be able to get Katalin out of her hair. But then what would happen to Katalin? Would von Liebermann send her back to the labor camp? Anna did not want that on her conscience.

Von Liebermann had turned his attention to the table top where he was pressing patterns in the white table cloth with the handle of his spoon. Something was troubling him and Anna decided to exploit the opportunity.

Anna put down her glass of wine. "What is it? Isn't this what you wanted?"

Von Liebermann looked toward the orchestra and the dancers with a curt smile. "Oh, no. I enjoy this. I need a change. It's just that . . ." He stopped.

Anna decided to rely on her instincts. "Your last chart said that you would be given added responsibilities. But I saw no promotion, no travel. It has started, hasn't it?"

"It will. They are sending five thousand more Jews."

"Five thousand. Where will you put them?"

"Precisely. Our resources are already strained to the limit. I will have to send at least three thousand to Auschwitz."

"Auschwitz? Another ghetto?"

"No. A terrible place." Suddenly he leaned across the table and looked into her eyes. "Anna. Don't ever let them send you to Auschwitz." He held her eyes for an instant before the intensity left his face and he leaned back in his chair. He took an Akita from his cigarette case and lit it, nervously blowing smoke toward the ceiling as though he had told Anna more than he wanted.

The song ended and Voss and Katalin came back to the table. Voss kept his arm around Katalin's trim waist as he said, "You're quite a dancer."

Katalin brushed damp curls away from her face. "I was always a good dancer. The best of the Gypsies."

Voss caught his lower lip with his teeth. "A Gypsy dancer? I will ask the orchestra to play a Gypsy song. You can show us how well you dance. What songs do you know?"

"All of them. If they can play, I can dance."

Voss laughed and said to von Liebermann. "What do you think, Herr Kommandant? Would you like to see a Gypsy dance?"

Von Liebermann smiled. "Yes, I would."

"Good."

Voss strode to the musicians who were preparing for the next song. He said something to the leader and handed him some money. As Voss walked back, the first violinist began playing a spirited *esárdá* and the other musicians joined in.

Voss made a small bow to Katalin. "Do us the honor."

Anna was watching with a small smile, wondering how Katalin was going to match the fierce rhythm of the music while wearing the red shoes. Katalin solved the problem by kicking off her shoes with a laugh and whirling out onto the deserted dance floor. Suddenly she stopped and came back to the table.

"You are Gypsy," she said to Anna in Romani. "You dance, too."

Anna stared at her. Katalin was a superb dancer, and although Anna had always thought she was as good a dancer as any of the other Gypsy children, she probably was not in a class with Katalin. Which meant that Katalin's reason for asking was to demonstrate to Voss and von Liebermann that there were some things she could do better than Anna.

She shook her head. "No, thank you."

Katalin put her fists on her hips which she swayed to the beat of the music. "Afraid?"

Anna felt the blood rising in her face. "I have no desire to dance."

"No desire? Maybe you are not Romani at all."

Voss had been watching the exchange and he could guess what Katalin was saying. "Go on," he said to Anna with a grin. "Two Gypsies are better than one."

Again Anna shook her head. "No. I'm not in the mood."

Voss kept his broad smile, but his eyes narrowed. "You don't understand, my dear. We want you to dance."

Anna wanted so much to slap the insolent smile from his face that she had to clinch her fist. It was not a request; it was a command. Perhaps she could get away with defying him, but people were watching. Besides, there were a thousand ways he could make her suffer later.

She smiled prettily. "I would be honored."

She kicked off her shoes and whirled out onto the dance floor, her arms raised and her hips swaying. She began clapping her hands above her head and launched into a flashing *gopak*.

Across from her Katalin was whirling and leaping as though in the grip of a Spanish *Tarantula*. Voss began clapping his hands in time with the beat of the music and the people in the cafe joined in, augmenting the beat so it pulsed like the blood of the Gypsies.

Anna forgot Katalin. She was again a wild urchin with her feet and her body caught in the spell of Gypsy violins. As the violinist embellished his music with trills, runs and glissandos, Anna did the same with her flying feet and swaying body. Only when the music lifted to a last arpeggio and ended with a crash was she transported back to reality.

Amid loud applause, she walked to the table and put on her shoes. She was breathing heavily and her body was filmed with perspiration. She glanced at Katalin who was having trouble getting her feet into her shoes. Katalin smiled at her, her eyes bright. "You are Romani, all right," she said. "Only a Gypsy could dance like that."

The compliment touched Anna deeply. This was the first time in her life she had ever felt truly accepted as a member of the tribe. She smiled at Katalin. "Yes. I am Gypsy."

But as she sat sipping her wine, she looked at Voss and von Liebermann and realized she could never be totally like Katalin. She could not conceive of the Gypsy girl putting her life in jeopardy for anyone. And that was exactly what she had to do—and quickly. It was getting late and her chance of delivering the note was diminishing with every minute. She had to find a means of slipping away for a few minutes.

She stood and said, "Would you please excuse me." She smiled with a small shrug. "The wine and the dancing . . ."

Von Liebermann and Voss stood up with murmured, "Of courses," and she threaded her way past the other tables to the door of the lady's room near the kitchen entrance.

The room was small, scarcely large enough for a table and a boudoir bench in front of a mirror and a single toilet and bidet in a closet,. But there was a narrow window high up in the wall that was already open a crack. She moved the boudoir bench below the window and climbed atop it. It took all her strength, but she was able to push the window almost fully open. Since the club was in the building's basement, the window was level with the ground of a scrupulously clean, brick-paved alley.

She reached to secure the catch on the door. It was broken, hanging by a single screw. Damn. She would have to take a chance that no one would see her. She was half out the window when the door opened and Katalin entered.

Katalin put her back against the door and smiled at Anna. "Going for a walk?"

As Anna eased back into the room, the note slipped from her brassiere and fluttered to the floor. Katalin picked it up and stared at the writing. "What is this?"

Anna snatched it from her hand. "Nothing. For the horoscope." She quickly put the note back in her pocket wondering how much she could trust the Gypsy girl who was staring at her suspiciously. If Katalin told Voss or von Liebermann what she had seen, she could deny it. But if they searched her they would find Dr. Steiner's note and that would be the end of it. She had no choice but to trust her. "I need your help. I've got to get away, just for a few minutes."

"Why? Where would you go?"

Anna hesitated. How much should she tell her? How much did she have to tell her to insure her cooperation. An idea flashed into her mind. "I found out something from the Kommandant. About the Gypsies. They're going to start rounding them up here. I've got to warn them."

"Gypsies. There are Gypsies here? In Prague?"

"Today I saw a *vardo* in a vacant park. Only a block from here. I could be there and back in minutes."

"If they catch you, you'll be punished."

"They won't catch me. Not if you help."

Katalin tilted her head and looked at Anna from beneath lowered lashes. She could have been a cat watching a bird. "Why should I get into trouble for you?"

"Not for me. For the Romanies. For all of us."

"I don't care about them. They are not my tribe."

"All right. What is it you want?"

Katalin smiled as though she had caught the bird. "When this is over—this war—I want your house."

"The Zorka house? I can't give you that."

"Then I will have to tell them."

She made a move to turn toward the door and Anna said, "Wait." She had to make a quick decision about her priorities. She could dismiss Katalin, tear up Dr. Steiner's note and rejoin von Liebermann and that would be the end of it. She could also lie to Katalin, tell her she could have the house. There were no witnesses. She could deny ever having made such a ridiculous bargain. Oh God. What was there inside her that made her reject both options?

"All right. You can have the house."

"You promise? A blood promise?"

"Yes, I promise."

"All right. I will keep them happy until you return." Katalin turned to the door. "But do not be long. They are suspicious people."

Katalin went out and the door clicked shut. Anna quickly wriggled out the window. The alley was very narrow and dark, the tops of the apartment buildings so close together they cut off all but the faintest moonlight. Running along the meandering medieval alley she had a moment when she thought she was lost. Then she was in the Square opposite the statue of Jan Hus and the five hundred year old 'Old Town Hall'. On her left she could see the Gothic spires of the Church of Our Lady of Tyn and the Golz-Kinsky Palace. They were to the south. She had to go north; the first corner to the right.

It was more than an hour before curfew and there were many people on the street and they looked at her curiously as she hurried past. They were bundled against the spring chill, but she wore no coat nor hat, and while her skirt and blouse were adequate inside the club, they were woefully inadequate for the night streets and she was soon shivering.

But one short block from the Square she passed into the silent, somber Jewish ghetto. The Jews remaining in the ghetto did not leave their homes at night and no one else had any reason to enter the ghetto . . . unless they were the dreaded soldiers of Heydrich's Einsatzgruppe-D.

After a few steps Anna recognized the wooden spire and cupola cap of the 16th Century Jewish Town Hall as they had been described by Dr. Steiner. There was no mistaking the tower clock with its Hebrew letters and hands that seemed to go backwards. Next to it was the Old New-Synagogue, the oldest in Europe, and behind the synagogue was the old Jewish Cemetery. She stared aghast at the vast field of tombstones, crypts and grave markers, most leaning at odd angles, the moss-tinted stones gleaming eerily in the dim moonlight. Chaim Weisner had given her directions to reach the grave where she was to leave the note, but he had not told her there were so many. Then she remembered that the Prague ghetto was hundreds of years old, one of the oldest in Europe, so that the Cemetery, with its finite boundary, had people buried up to twelve deep. If all the graves had markers, there had to be thousands—and time was short.

She tried to clear her mind of everything except the directions told to her by Chaim as she threaded her way past the jumble of grave markers, acutely conscious of the clock in her head ticking away.

When she finally located the designated grave, she checked the name on the stone: Rabbi Yehuda Low ben Bezalel. The name had been easy to remember because the legend of Rabbi Low and his Golem was known throughout Europe. The Golem was supposedly a giant figure made of clay but brought to life by the insertion of cabalistic formulae in its mouth, rather like the Frankenstein monster. Rabbi Low had been dead more than three hundred years, but pious Jews still placed small stones on his grave.

Anna removed the note from her pocket. She was about to place it beneath one of the stones as Chaim had directed, when a heavy voice behind her said, "Who are you? What are you doing here?"

She straightened and turned and her eyes widened in horror. It was Rabbi Low's Golem come to life! The figure was huge, wearing a long black cape and a broad-brimmed black hat. The face was concealed behind a full beard and where the eyes should have been moonlight glinted off small rimless glasses like lidless eyes.

He certainly was not SS. And she doubted that he was Gestapo. Even the most intrepid German agent would not enter the ghetto alone at night. "Are you a rabbi?"

His glasses flashed like miniature lightning as he turned his head to glance around the deserted graveyard. "Why do you ask?"

"Because Dr. Steiner sent me."

"Steiner?" The man took a step forward, his shoulders hunched and Anna felt herself cringing. "What do you know of Dr. Steiner? Where is he? Is he all right?"

Anna held out the note. "He asked me to leave this under one of the stones on this grave. He said some one would find it."

The man took the note and unfolded it carefully. He held it up to the faint moonlight. "Have you read it?"

"I can't read Hebrew."

"You're not a Jew?"

"No. I am Gypsy."

"And Dr. Steiner gave you this?" Suspicion was as heavy in his voice as its deep rumble.

"I work at Theresienstadt. I met Dr. Steiner. He trusted me enough to give me that note."

The man glanced at the note again. "It is in his handwriting. One moment." He reached in a pocket of his cape and took out a small two-cell flashlight. Then he crouched, and using the thick folds of the cape to conceal the light, he quickly skimmed the note.

When he had finished he snapped off the light and stood up. "Thank you for doing this."

She was aware that he was weeping. "When I saw Dr. Steiner, he was fine."

"I know. But he does not believe he has long to live. He does not believe that any of them have long to live."

"That can't be true. I know that conditions are terrible, but it is still their own ghetto."

"A sham. A horrible sham. They are dying. And those who do not die are being shipped to the death camps."

"Death camps?" What was he talking about? Then she knew. "Auschwitz."

"Auschwitz, Ravensbruck, Buchenwald, Dachau, Sachsenhausen, Mauthausen, Flossenburg that we know of. And now they're building more."

"To kill Jews?"

"Jews, Gypsies, anyone considered undesirable."

"Oh God. How can we stop them?"

"We cannot." The man sighed. "We thought we were safe here. But now. . ." He held up the note that was crumpled in his palm as though he wanted to absorb its contents through his pores. "If we can bring this to the world., they can do something."

"Halt!"

The voice rang through the darkness accompanied by the blinding light of powerful flashlights. With surprising agility the big man whirled, but was smashed to the ground by a rifle butt. He fell across the grave and Anna's wide eyes saw him quickly press the note under one of the stones before he rolled on top of it with a groan.

He was jerked to his feet by two German soldiers. Another grabbed Anna by the arm. In the glow of the flashlights, she saw that one of the lights was being held by Dieter Voss. Standing beside him was Colonel von Liebermann. On his other side, smiling at Anna, was Katalin.

Chapter 27

The ride back from Prague has been both physical and mental torture for Anna. With her hands manacled behind her, she had been forced into the back of a canvas-covered truck where she sat on a hard bench guarded by three wooden-faced Waffen-SS soldiers. On a bench across from her the Jewish man who looked like a rabbi, also with his hands manacled behind him, sat stoically. There was dried blood on his face and on the front of his shirt, from a cut on his forehead. Von Liebermann had allowed Anna to put on her coat, but it was almost midnight when they drove through the gates into the deserted streets of Theresienstadt and she was numb with cold.

The long ride had given her ample time to think about what a fool she was. She should never have allowed her conscience to drive her into involvement with the Jews. Now she would surely be punished in some way. She couldn't stop her mind from ranging through the possibilities. At the work camp she had seen men beaten and shot. Men like Wirtz and the other block leaders had been only too delighted to use their whips. She shuddered when she though of Wirtz. Would she be turned over to a beast like Wirtz?

How strong was her hold on von Liebermann? Could he continue to function without her psychic guidance? Did he believe he could? And if so, for how long? If her punishment was only a beating, she would be able to continue her work for him. She would probably be confined to her room. Certainly she would never be allowed any more trips outside the walls of the old fortress.

The truck seemed to be taking an unusually long time to get to the hotel, although she could tell by the sound of the tires they were on the brick pavement of Theresienstadt streets. Then the tone of the tires changed and she had the impression they were crossing a bridge. But the only bridge was the one over the river that led to the Small Fortress.

Oh, dear God! She was not being taken back to the hotel; she was being taken to the Small Fortress. What was it Chaim Weisner had said when she had asked him about it? 'You don't want to know.'

Now she was going to find out.

The truck stopped and the soldiers threw aside the canvas covering the tailgate and motioned for the prisoners to jump down. The Jew jumped down with surprising agility for a man his size. When Anna hesitated, unsure of her balance with her hands manacled, one of the guards reached up and grabbed her by the arm and pulled her so that she had to jump. She landed heavily but was able to keep her balance.

She was in the flagstone-paved courtyard of the Small Fortress. Electric floodlights had been affixed to the high stone walls of the old fort and they bathed the courtyard in light. The architect of the fortress had had no interest in beauty and the high, turreted walls gave the appearance of a Draconian castle. One of its massive double doors was pierced by a smaller door and the soldiers shoved Anna toward it.

Stumbling across the flagstones toward the waiting door was like being marched into hell. Anna had the impression that once that door closed behind her, she would never leave the monstrosity of a building alive.

But there was no way to avoid whatever horror was waiting on the other side, and she walked through the doorway with her heart pounding. The soldiers did not enter. As soon as Anna and the Jew were inside, they slammed the door shut as though they were happy they did not have to follow and she heard the truck drive away.

They were in a large, round vestibule with a high, domed ceiling, lighted by a suspended chandelier. The floor was constructed of marble, the walls of large stone blocks. The only decoration was a huge, blood-red Nazi flag with a swastika in a round, white circle that hung from ceiling to floor behind a steel desk. The Unterscharführer who had opened the door was short and heavy, dressed in the gray-green uniform of the Waffen-SS. An SS officer wearing a black uniform was pacing the marble floor, impatiently popping his gloves in the palm of his hand. He turned when Anna came through the door. It was von Liebermann.

When she saw him, Anna first experienced a flood of relief. She was about to speak when she saw his face was white with rage.

"Name?"

The SS sergeant had taken a seat behind the desk with a registration ledger in front of him and he looked at Anna expectantly.

"Zorka," she said. The sound of her own voice gave her courage and she repeated. "Zorka. Ravanna Zorka."

"Age?"

"Twenty-two."

He entered the information, then glanced questioningly at von Liebermann.

"Interrogation," the Kommandant said.

Interrogation. It sounded as though von Liebermann was intimately familiar with the grim building. But what was there to interrogate her about? There was nothing she could tell them except that she had been a complete fool.

The sergeant looked at the Jew. "Name?"

"Jakub Zlateho."

It took a moment for the sergeant to get the spelling correct and the man's age and address. Then he glanced at von Liebermann who said, "Interrogation."

When he finished writing, the sergeant closed the ledger and stood up. "Come," he said.

They followed as he led the way to a rear door that opened into a long hallway. Behind them Anna heard von Liebermann's boot heels striking echoes from the marble floor. She slowed and turned her head to say, "This is not necessary, Herr Kommandant. If there is anything you wish to know—"

"No talking!" Her words were cut off as the sergeant yanked her back.

They had arrived at a broad staircase. One flight spiraled upward and another downward. Keeping his grip on her arm the sergeant steered her toward the stairs leading downward, and all the awful stories she had ever heard of dungeons and torture chambers flashed through her mind. As though to confirm her worst fears, a faint sound from the darkness below raised the hairs on the back of her neck. It was a harsh cry that trailed off into any ugly moan as though the pain was too great to articulate with even the most primal sound of agony.

Anna was shocked into stopping, and the sergeant yanked her forward and she stumbled down the steps. The stairs ended in a small anti-chamber where two Waffen-SS soldiers sat behind steel desks guarding a corridor lined on either side by steel doors, each with a Judas window. Then she was jerked down another narrow flight of steps where the stone walls gave way to chiseled rock as though they were entering the bowels of the earth. It was so cold her breath was visible, and she was distressed to see she was breathing with the rapid gasps of fear.

The anti-room where the stairs terminated also held two steel desks, but their chairs were deserted. The corridor, carved out of the stone, was narrow and, like the one above, lined with steel doors. As they proceeded along the passage, one of the doors opened and two guards came out. One had blood on the front of his uniform that he brushed at angrily. The guards looked up at the sound of the approaching group, and when they saw von Liebermann, they snapped to attention. As they passed the open door, Anna heard low moans and she saw a naked figure huddled in a fetal position on the cement floor of a large, brightly lit room. She couldn't tell if it was a man or a woman.

They paused at one of the doors and the sergeant opened it with a large key and jerked his head for Zlateho to enter. When he passed Anna, he muttered, "Be brave. Tell them nothing."

The sergeant gave him a violent shove into the room, then slammed and locked the door.

Farther along the corridor a similar door was pulled open by the guard and she was shoved inside so hard she almost fell. It was a large room, similar to the one she had just seen. Light came from a powerful bulb in the ceiling enclosed in a clear glass protector. The concrete floor and walls were blotched with dark spots as though only a half-hearted attempt had been made to remove perverse stains. In one corner was a water connection and a fire hose with a brass nozzle. The floor sloped to a drain in the center. Hanging from the ceiling were several large hooks whose purpose Anna tried to put from her mind. A metal pipe ran the length of the back wall like the barre in a ballet studio. The only furnishings in the room were a heavy wooden table with two straight-backed chairs and a steel storage cabinet. All were painted a dull gray.

The guard produced a key and removed the manacles and Anna rubbed her wrists. They were raw where the steel bands had bitten into the flesh.

Von Liebermann nodded toward one of the chairs. "Sit down."

Anna did as she was ordered and placed her hands flat on the top of the table. The painted wood was icy cold, and with the turmoil in her mind, she was astounded that the fact even registered.

The guard took up a post near the door while von Liebermann began to pace the floor, drawing heavily on a cigarette. The echo of his steps beat against Anna's ears like the relentless drops of water in a Chinese torture. "You have placed me in a difficult position," von Liebermann said at last. "But we may be able to resolve it if you will answer a few questions."

Anna's throat was so dry she had to try twice before she could say, "I'll try."

"Good. First, why did you go to that cemetery?"

Anna had been expecting the question from the moment she had been caught and she had concocted a multitude of fictitious answers, but none of them sounded plausible even to her, even though she was certain that von Liebermann was hoping desperately that she would have a logical reason. How could one explain slipping away at night to make a secret visit to a Jewish cemetery? The only answer that made any sense at all was the truth.

"I wanted to visit the grave of Rabbi Low. I've been reading about him and his Golem since I was a little girl—"

"At night? Why didn't you go during the day? And why the secrecy? Who was that man? Where is the note?" The questions were shot at her with the rage of desperation. Von Liebermann could see the source of his mental security slipping away and his rage was the rage of fear.

"I couldn't go during the day." Anna kept her voice low and soothing, the way she would have talked to an upset child. "You know that Captain Voss would never have allowed that. I had to go at night and in secret."

"The man. You went there to meet him.'

For once she could tell the truth. "I did not. He must have seen me putting a stone on the grave. That's what you're supposed to do. I don't know who he is."

"The note. You had a note."

Damn Katalin to hell. The only way von Liebermann could know about the note was for her to tell him. "It's tradition to leave a message for the Rabbi. That's all it was."

"Tradition. You're not a Jew. I made sure of that."

"No, but I know some of their traditions. I would not violate them."

"Why? Why leave a note to a dead man?"

"It is supposed to bring good luck."

"You believe that nonsense?"

Anna shrugged. "I am Romani. We're very superstitious."

"It was written in Hebrew. It was a message."

"It was written in Romani. Katalin can't read. She wouldn't know one language from another."

"Then where is it?"

Anna hesitated. A mistake. One could only afford to hesitate if one was telling the truth. "I have no idea," she said quickly. "It must have fallen when your soldiers attack us."

Von Liebermann stopped pacing and stared at her, despair in his eyes. "You have been seen consorting with the Jews. I want to know who was your contact here. How you made this contact. I want to know what was in that note and where it is now."

"None of that is true." Anna tried to project innocence. And she was innocent. What harm was there in what she had done? "I wrote the note myself. I took it to the grave because I knew I would not be allowed to do it if I asked. I have no idea what happened to the note."

Von Liebermann drew deeply on his cigarette, then turned to the guard. "See what you can get out of the Jew.

The guard straightened. "Jawohl, Herr Kommandant. When should we begin?"

"Tonight."

"Jawohl, Herr Kommandant."

Von Liebermann went to the door, which the guard pushed open. He turned back to look at Anna. "Tomorrow you will be asked those questions again. I suggest you prepare better answers."

The two men went out and the door was shut and Anna heard a key turn in the lock. Then their footsteps receded down the corridor and she was alone. She sat at the table, suddenly more weary than she had ever been in her life. Oh God. How was she going to get out of this? If she told the truth, Dr. Steiner and the others would be punished, perhaps killed. She might be killed herself. Of course, she had known the dangers when she had agreed to help. But at the time the dangers seemed nebulous. If she was careful, she could not be caught. Except that she had been caught. And sitting in the frigid torture chamber made her gallantry seem more like incredible stupidity.

But what was done, was done. Now she had to find a way out. If they tortured her, could she keep silent? Should she? Were the lives of Dr. Steiner and the others of more value than her own? If what they had told her was true, they would probably die anyway. And perhaps she could save herself if she told the truth. Von Liebermann would like nothing better than to forgive her. Or give her some form of punishment that would not preclude the daily casting of his horoscope.

What was she thinking? Maybe she could not hold out against the torture, but she could not, she would not give up Dr. Steiner and the others voluntarily.

The cold that seeped in through the concrete of the walls also seeped through her coat and into her bones. She got up and paced the floor, thinking of the naked person in the nearby cell. If she was shivering while wearing a heavy coat, that person must be freezing. If he—or she—wasn't already dead.

She thought she heard footsteps approaching and went to the door were she could hear better, her throat dry with apprehension. They couldn't be coming for her. Not this soon. Von Liebermann had said tomorrow.

She heard a door open and seconds later slam shut. The Jew. It had to be the guards going into the cell of the Jew. Oh, dear God. They were going to torture him. What would he tell them? Would he tell them anything? And if he did, he could not possibly conceal her role in delivering the note. He would probably be made to tell what message it had contained. God. If it was anything very bad—sabotage plans, maybe—she could be painted with the same brush. Then, even the truth would not save her.

She was still pacing the floor a few minutes later, her mind churning with worry, when she was brought to a halt by the sound of a muffled cry of anguish. The Jew. Oh, no, no, no! Was he totally innocent? Am I responsible for this?

Even though she put her hands over her ears, for minutes that seemed like an eternity the cries rang in her ears.

When they stopped, she was sitting in the farthest corner from the door with her coat pulled up over her head and pressed against her ears. The cries had stopped, but in her head, they went on and on, piercing her brain like spikes driven by the hammer of guilt.

In the icy cell, huddled in her coat, her mind numb with despair, she had no idea whether it was morning or night when the door was unlocked and someone entered. She looked up and saw two SS guards. They were followed by Captain Dieter Voss, his black uniform looking like the raiment of a hangman.

He stood over her and offered his hand with a smile. "Well, my dear," he said. "It looks as though we are going to be lovers after all."

Anna's body was so stiff and cold she was not sure she could stand without falling and she walked stiffly to the table where she braced herself with one hand while feeling came back into her feet and legs. Then she realized what Voss had said and she looked at him.

"Lovers? What do you mean?"

"Oh, not right away. We have discovered that sexual intercourse—rape, if you will—while it might be distasteful, perhaps even painful, has never been known to make a woman tell anything. We have given it up as a means of interrogation. Pity." He smiled at Anna and she realized his smile, which she had considered boyish and charming, almost matched the grimace of the Death's Head on his hat. "No," he continued. "That will have to wait until we have induced the truth. Then we will have all the time in the world for our little dalliances."

The cheer in his voice was infinitely more menacing than the rage in von Liebermann's, and Anna found herself trembling, unable to articulate an answer.

Voss had kept his gloves on to protect his fingers from the cold and he suddenly slapped his hands together with a pop that made Anna flinch. "Now," he said, and his smile broadened. "I trust you have had ample time to consider your situation. Tell me, my love, what have you decided? The truth? Or more lies?"

"I have told the truth," Anna said. "I only went to the cemetery to visit the grave of Rabbi Low."

"Oh, excellent. Excellent." Voss rubbed his gloved hands together as though he had achieved a great victory. "I was afraid you would volunteer the truth. So now we can begin our little game."

"Game? Is this a game to you?"

"A contest then. My will against yours. My wit against yours. You will try to lie. I will try to find the truth. One of us will win. Of course, the odds are on my side. We shall begin by having you take off your clothes."

Anna backed away from the table, trying to put as much distance as possible between herself and Voss. "That's ridiculous. It's freezing in here."

"Oh, this isn't bad. You should be here in January. Actually, the nudity is helpful. Psychologically. We have found that it is more difficult to lie when one is naked. Nothing personal. Not yet."

Anna had backed against the wall and she stood staring at him, unable to believe this was the same man she had considered an exception to the other SS bastards. He had seemed so friendly, so open and cheerful, exhibiting none of the dark menace of the SS officers she had met.

"Come, come," Voss said. "Off with the clothes or my colleagues will have to take them off for you."

The same feeling came over Anna as she had experienced when Sergeant Wirtz had made her disrobe. She would not give him the satisfaction of cringing. But looking at Voss' impish, smiling face was worse than looking at Wirtz' heavy brutality. This evil was concealed, hidden behind a false charm, while Wirtz' evil was plain for all to see. The results, however, were the same.

She began taking off her clothes, letting the garments drop to the floor, her numb fingers fumbling with buttons and snaps. "You're sick," she said. "You're all sick. Evil. You're brains are filled with maggots. You think your kind is going to win? Never. God won't let that happen. You know that. You've got to know that, just like you know what's going to happen to you when you die. All these things you've done to people. They'll be returned to you ten times over. A hundred times."

The two guards shifted uneasily, their stony faces showing lines of worry. But Deiter Voss sat in one of the chairs backward and rested his chin on his hands on the back of the chair while he smiled at her.

"And you'll all be dead soon." She stood naked in front of them and pointed to each one. "You. You. You. You have the curse of blood on you, the curse of every Gypsy. Not just my tribe. Not just the living. You are cursed by the dead. They will be waiting for you. Gypsies and Jews. You are going to wish you could burn in hell!"

The guards stared at her dumbly, their faces white. But Voss slowly applauded with his gloved hands. "Bravo. I can hardly wait to see what it will be like in hell. But"—he stood—"I'm afraid yours is going to be here." Voss motioned to the guards. "I think we'll begin with the water."

Anna watched with the fascination of a mouse watching a hungry snake as one of the men went to the cabinet and took out a set of manacles that were affixed to a length of chain. After he manacled her hands in front of her, he led her into position under one of the hooks. He looped the chain over the hook and pulled until her hands were stretched over her head and she was forced to support her weight on her toes. He secured the other end of the chain to the iron pipe.

The other man picked up her clothes and put them on the table. He uncoiled the fire hose and turned on the water so that a powerful blast shot from the nozzle. Oh God, Anna thought. I'm already freezing. I'll never be able to stand this.

Voss moved a chair to a distance where he would not be splattered. "Are you certain you wouldn't like to change your mind?"

Dear God, she wanted to. She had vivid images of how the powerful stream of water would tear at her body, and she wanted to scream that, yes, she would tell him anything he wanted to know. But for some reason she could not fathom, she was unable to say it. She felt a curious detachment as some burning core deep inside her said, "I've told you the truth, you son-of-a-bitch."

Voss kept his smile, but his eyes went frosty, and he nodded to the man with the hose. As he turned the hose on Anna, the man's face did not change expression, retaining an impersonal woodeness that was as frightening as Voss' smile, as though he was simply doing a job like a carpenter or a farmer.

The first blast hit her in the stomach, the powerful force of the stream driving the breath from her. Her mouth flew open in an agonizing gasp and stayed that way as the man slowly directed the force of the blast over her body, keeping it away from her face, seeming to concentrate on her breasts. Anna thought she was going to die. She could not get her breath. Each racking gasp was driven from her lungs by a new shock as the man expertly painted her with the water, all the while keeping his face and eyes as devoid of expression as that of a painted doll. Then his eyes widened and he moved in so that the nozzle was only inches from her skin and she thought she was being flayed alive. She tried to scream, but the sound of agony came out as a rasping groan.

Anna was not sure whether she fainted or whether time cased to have meaning. She was dimly aware that the water had stopped, and Voss was standing in front of her, holding her by the chin and saying, "The note. Who gave you the note? What did it say? Are the Jews planning an uprising? Where is the note?"

She couldn't make her eyes focus and Voss' voice began to fade as she seemed to be slipping in and out of a thick, black fog. As blackness closed in, she clearly heard him say, "All right. Take her down. Give her time to think about it. Maybe we can get something out of that big Jew."

She found herself laying on the cold floor shivering violently. Her coat. Where was her coat? She forced herself to her hands and knees and crawled to the table. Clutching its edge, she hauled herself to her feet and reached for her clothes. Her eyes opened wide in the shock of a new pain. Her clothes were gone. She slipped to the wet concrete floor and huddled in a ball. Tomorrow when they came back she would tell them. She would tell them everything. Wouldn't she?

Chapter 28

Eric walked out of the Prague-Tesnov Railway Station carrying his black-leather briefcase, trailed by a porter carrying his valise. The only taxi in sight, an old Czech Aero limousine, was about to be entered by a heavy man with gray hair with his topcoat over his arm. An elderly woman was already in the rear seat. Eric tapped the man on the shoulder. "Out," he said. "You'll have to take another taxi."

The man straightened and turned, a protest on his lips. But when he saw the black SS officer's uniform with the Death's Head on the cap, he muttered something in Czech and gestured to his wife who got out reluctantly, her lips thin with anger.

The taxi driver got out of his seat and hurried to hold the door for Eric. Then he opened the trunk so the porter could deposit Eric's valise. Eric did not pay the porter. When they drove away the porter was talking to the Czech couple and waving his arms angrily. Good. The more hatred of the Nazis he spread, the better.

The driver looked around for instructions and Eric said, "Do you speak German?"

"A little."

"I can speak a little Czech. We'll get along if you do as you're told."

The driver's voice was wintery as he said, "Yes, sir."

"I am going to headquarters of Obergruppenführer Heydrich's Einsatzgruppe. You know where it is?"

"Yes, sir. At Hradcany Castle."

"Good. Take me there."

The driver made a face of exasperation as he accelerated. He probably did not expect to be paid for the long ride, but he knew better than to decline the fare. They took the Hlavka Bridge north over the Vltava. Eric settled back in the seat and tried to think of his next move. Heydrich would be taking this same route in the reverse direction to get to the railway station where he was supposed to meet von Sievers. The Operation Anthropoid plan was for the two Czech partisans to ambush him at some point on the highway. But where? The people at M.I.6 had not considered it necessary for him to know. It was likely that the two Czechs had the option of picking the place they liked best. The only thing he could do was intercept Heydrich before they did.

Eric touched the holstered Luger on his hip. In fulfilling his blood promise, he would also accomplish the Czechs' mission for them.

They crossed the peninsula-like Holesovice district formed by the long loop of the Vltava River and passed over the bridge leading to the Troja district. Shortly beyond the bridge the taxi slowed to negotiate a sharp bend in the road where it merged with the main Dresden-Prague Highway. Eric sat up straighter and made a quick observation out the window. This had to be the ambush location. A car had to almost stop to make the hairpin turn. The brick-paved street was wide, but not too wide because the tracks of an electric-powered streetcar ran down the center. That would keep Heydrich's car close to the curb.

Eric leaned forward and tapped the driver on the shoulder. "Driver, are there any more turns like this between here and the Einsatzgruppe headquarters?"

The driver shook his head. "No, sir."

"All right. Turn around. Go back to the beginning of the turn and stop. Pull well off the road."

The driver half turned his head as though to protest. Then he sighed and swung the Aero around, its small two-cylinder engine roaring in protest as he shifted through the gears.

Following Eric's directions, the taxi stopped near other cars close to the entrance of the hairpin turn. "Lie down in the seat," Eric told the driver.

The man turned his head, his mouth open. His eye grew big when he saw the Luger pointed at his head. As he lay down he said, "If you want my taxi, you can have it. But it is old and—"

"I don't want your taxi. Just stay out of sight. You won't be hurt."

Eric leaned across the back of the front seat and took the key out of the car's ignition and put it in his pocket. If he had to leave the car, he wanted to make sure it would be waiting. Then he slumped back in the seat and settled down to wait. There were only two possibilities: if the Czechs picked this place for their ambush, he would help them. If they did not, he would take care of Heydrich himself. Either way, the death of Reinhard Heydrich would cause a lot of heads to roll. He opened his briefcase and extracted a slip of paper. On it, he had written a list of names. These were the men he wanted to make pay for their crimes against his people: von Liebermann, Sergeant Blumdorf, Kommandant Muller, Major Krischer, Dr. Prosner. So they would not seem to be non-sequiturs, he had added the names of several of Heydrich's officers. Chances were that after today they would all be shot—if they were lucky. If they were not lucky, they would be interrogated before they were shot.

A thought occurred to Eric and he used his fountain pen to add one more name to the list, Albrecht Grantz. He wished he could be there to see the look on the bastard's face when the Gestapo knocked on his door in the dead of night. Grantz would never know why he was being arrested, even when they were standing him against a wall. As soon as he saw Anna, he would tell her that the Zorka name was avenged.

Thinking of Anna, Eric's euphoria vanished. Was she still at that place: Theresienstadt? He had to get there and find von Liebermann before the Gestapo did. As soon as they found the list of names, they would assume that von Liebermann was involved in Heydrich's death. The problem was that they might arrest anyone remotely associated with him, and that would include Anna. So he had to find her first.

"There is a place called Theresienstadt," he said. "Where is it?"

"Theresienstadt?" the driver said. "I have not heard of it."

Was the man lying? There was one way to find out. Eric took off his hat so he would not be so easily identified as an SS officer by anyone passing by and leaned over the seat. He put the muzzle of his pistol between the man's eyes. "Theresienstadt. Where is it?"

The driver's eyes blurred with sudden tears and his lips beneath his mustache began to tremble. "I don't know. Please. I am only a taxi driver. I know Prague only. Prague only."

Eric stared at the man, fascinated. How easy it would be to kill him. And if he was lying, he deserved to be killed. He had to be lying. Krischer's directions had been explicit: Theresienstadt was near Prague. His finger caressed the trigger. A slight tug and the man would be dead. Gone. Forever.

It was almost as though he was God, holding the man's life in his hand.

And the man knew it. A trickle of spittle was running from his mouth and his hands worked convulsively. "Please, please," he said over and over. "Please, please, please."

"A ghetto," Eric said, remembering. "The place used to be called Terezin."

The driver's hands came up as though he had seen a vision of The Virgin. "Terezin. Yes, yes. I know Terezin. It is to the north. Fifty kilometers."

"On what highway?"

"This one. To Dresden."

"Good."

Eric withdrew the pistol and the man drew a gasping breath and began to sob. Eric leaned back in the seat. He held the gun in his lap, acutely conscious of the pounding of his heart. It occurred to him that the power he had over the driver could be used against anyone. If he wanted something from a shop, he had only to take it. If he wanted money, he had only to take it. If he wanted a woman—any woman—he could take her. Who would dare protest? And if they did, he could call upon the power of the German army to teach them the folly of opposing an officer wearing the black uniform of the Schutzstaffel. It was a heady feeling, one that no Gypsy in history had ever experienced.

But it would soon be over. Once Reinhard Heydrich was dead and after he had found Anna, he would no longer have a need for the uniform, or the power.

He started to slip the Luger back into its holster, then stopped. The gun felt so natural in his hand. Would it really be necessary to relinquish its power after he had rescued Anna? He could not continue impersonating von Sievers, but he could assume a different name, a different identity. German soldiers rarely questioned an SS colonel. By traveling constantly, he could probably continue the deception for months.

And then . . .

Then at some point, someone would ask a question for which he would not have an answer and his house of cards would come crashing down. He would be stood against a wall and shot. Or, worse, turned over to the Gestapo. He would probably end up in the basement of the building on Prinz-AlbrechtStrasse. What a price for a few weeks of paradise.

But at the moment, power was everything.

Eric checked his wrist watch. Nine twenty-five. Where was Heydrich? If he planned to be on time for his expected meeting with von Sievers at the railway station, he should be passing at any moment. And where were the Czech agents?

He was thinking he might be wrong about the location, when a small two-cylinder Aero pulled up across the street and a man got out of the passenger side. The man carried a raincoat and Eric saw him drape it over a short automatic weapon that looked like a British Sten gun. A second man drove the car away, and the Czech agent took up a position where it appeared that he was waiting for a streetcar. His head swiveled as he carefully examined the area and Eric slid lower in the seat. Allowing the Czech agents to kill Heydrich would not be as satisfying as doing to job himself, but by participating, he was fulfilling his blood promise to his father.

He was wondering what the Czech's plan was and where the second man had gone, when he saw a flicker of light from the direction of the main highway. A signal. From the second man. It had to mean he had spotted Heydrich's car.

Eric gripped the pistol in his right hand. His palm was sweaty from anxiety. If something went wrong, if the Czechs failed to carry out their mission, he would do it himself. From his pocket, he took the list of names and wadded it up in his left hand. He was ready.

With a muffled roar, a large, dark green Daimler-Benz limousine with banners fluttering from the front fenders swept off the Dresden-Prague highway and the driver shifted down for the hairpin turn. In the middle of the turn, when the car was moving very slowly, the Czech stepped into the street and dropped the raincoat. He lifted the Sten gun and began firing at the limousine at point-blank range. But the Sten gun jammed!

The Czech stood in the center of the street, futilely pounding at the gun's ejector lever. Heydrich was going to get away! Eric growled in disgust and flung open the taxi door, snarling at the driver, "Don't move!"

He expected Heydrich's driver to speed away, but for some reason the man stopped the limousine and leaped out, a pistol in his hand. The Czech dropped the useless Sten gun and fled, and Heydrich's driver raised his pistol to shoot the Czech in the back. Eric snapped two quick shots at the man, firing from the hip as he had been taught by the British commandos. He was almost surprised when Heydrich's driver dropped his pistol and toppled to the ground. Now Heydrich was his!

Eric covered the short distance to the limousine on the run and leaned in through the driver's open door, his pistol pointed at the man in the rear seat. Eric recognized him instantly. Heydrich! The man who had murdered his father.

Heydrich was struggling to pull his own pistol from its holster and Eric snapped, "No. Leave it."

Heydrich let his hand drop and he stared at Eric. There was no fear in his eyes, only a look of disgust as though he was angry at himself for being in this situation.

Eric started to pull the trigger, but the expression in Heydrich's eyes angered him. He wanted this butcher to know why he was going to die. "Remember a Gypsy camp in Hungary?"

Heydrich continued to stare at him, his hands relaxed in his lap. "There have been many Gypsy camps."

"On the Zorka estate." When Heydrich's pale eyes showed no recognition, Eric added. "You shot a man. With a pistol like this."

Then recognition appeared in Heydrich's eyes. "Ah yes. An older man. Fat."

"Fat? My father, you son of a bitch."

Heydrich's gaze dropped to the black, dead eye of the gun. His hands clinched, and the beginning of fear was reflected in the way his eyes focused on Eric's finger on the gun's trigger. But his high pitched voice was calm as he said. "You are a Gypsy?"

"That is right."

"You speak excellent German." His eyes shifted to take in the insignia on Eric's uniform. "I see. You are the von Sievers who sent the Teletype." Eric was silent, and Heydrich continued. "Very good. Brilliant, in fact. You are to be congratulated. You must come to work for me."

Eric was startled by the remark, and the muzzle of the gun wavered for a second. "Work for you? I'm going to kill you."

"Why should you? You are an agent for the British, of course. They would not have to know. You can continue the role you are playing. Only it will be for the winning side."

Continue the role? Eric's mind raced through the implications. He would continue to have the power to control lives. Continue to give commands instead of receive them. He had proven he was suited for the task. It would be so easy to keep on with the role, only now without the danger of discovery. He would have the full weight of the German war machine behind him. He would be as close to a God on earth as any man could become short of the Führer himself. If he wanted to, he could take over the Zorka estates from Albrecht Grantz. Kill him if he protested. Anna would appreciate the justice.

Anna! He realized instantly he would have to give up Anna. She would never change. She would never love a Nazi. But as an SS Colonel, he could have any woman he wanted. He could command Anna to do anything he wanted. And if she refused . . .

He heard a sound beside him and he jerked his head around. The second Czech partisan was attempting to pull open the rear door of the car. He clutched a grenade in his hand with the pin pulled. But the door was locked and he yanked at it again and again, his face contorted with effort and anger.

Eric swung the gun until it was pointed at the Czech's head. The man froze, staring at the gun like it was the head of a cobra.

"Shoot him," Heydrich commanded. "Shoot!"

It was there in front of him, all the power, the wealth, the social acceptance he had wanted all his life. All he had to do was pull the trigger—forget his blood promise—forget Anna—save the life of Reinhard Heydrich and it would all be his.

"Go to hell," he said and he reached in and hit Heydrich on the side of the head with the pistol. Eric found the interior door handle and used it to open the door, and the Czech tossed in the grenade and slammed the door. Eric dropped the paper with the list of names on the front seat of the car where it would be protected from the blast and leaped away. As he turned to run, he saw Heydrich's eyes. The Nazi was staring at the grenade, and at last, his eyes were rigid with fear.

Chapter 29

Anna had no way of knowing whether it was morning or night; no way of knowing if she had been locked in the freezing cell for two hours or ten. Time was a curse that was filled with agony. She lived from minute to minute, breathing in short shallow breaths to ease the pain that came with the slightest movement. She wondered if there was internal bleeding. She might be dying. It would not surprise her.

She lay huddled on the cement floor, attempting to find a place, a position where she could escape the cold and the pain. Oh God. Why had she allowed her stupid sense of compassion to get her into this? All she had had to do was mind her own business, to look out for her own interests, and she could have survived the war in relative comfort and safety. Helping the Jews. No one else was lifting a finger to help them, nor to help the Gypsies. Why had she done so?

But even as she was berating herself, she knew the answer. She had not helped them because they were Jews; she had helped them because they were suffering people and there was no one else. And perhaps it was because her own people had suffered for so many years, hundreds of years, and virtually no one had helped them. Not even the Jews. They had treated the Gypsies as badly as anyone; They had thought no more about Gypsy slavery than anyone else. The Gypsies had been the undesirables of Europe for a thousand years. Like the untouchables of Japan, they were treated with contempt by any one higher on the social order. And that was everyone, even a Jew.

What a fool she was. All she had to do was signal the guard, pound on the door until he came and tell him she was ready to confess and all this misery would end. They would give her warm clothes, a warm bed, hot food.

So why didn't she do it? What the God damned hell was it inside of her that was preventing her from telling them what they wanted to know? Why couldn't she lie? Make up a story. Any story. Oh God. She had tried that and they hadn't believed her. That poor rabbi. They might be killing him right now. Locked in these cells, no one would know what kind of atrocities were being committed.

Well, they wouldn't get away with it. She was an American citizen and they would pay for it. All of them.

She chuckled at the absurdity and stopped when pain shot through her ribs. No one was going to help her. No one but herself. And what could she possibly do? She was alone, naked, half frozen, every movement agony. And there was no weapon, nothing she could possibly use as a weapon. The chairs and the table were too strong, too massive for her to even consider breaking. The metal cabinet was secured with a padlock. And the only other thing in the room was the hose with its horrible brass nozzle.

She stared at the hose as a faint idea tugged at her mind. The nozzle. It was big and heavy. If she could get it loose from the hose, she could use it as a weapon. She could pound on the door with it and when the guard came to investigate, she could hit him in the head and take his gun and—

Oh God. What fantasies. He was ten times stronger than she. She was not even sure she could lift her arms above her head, let alone use the nozzle as a club.

But still. . . It was all she had. There had to be a way to use it. What else was in the room? Damn! Damn! Nothing. Nothing except the light whose unrelenting glare was almost as painful as the cold. The light? Perhaps if she broke the bulb she could use the glass. Ridiculous. She had to disable the guard instantly or she would not have a chance. Electricity. Electricity could stun, even kill if the circumstances were right. Where did the light get its electricity? It couldn't have been part of the original castle. The wiring had to have been installed recently. There it was, a pipe-like conduit running up the back wall and across the ceiling, painted the same color as the wall. If she could rip the conduit down she could. . . Could what? Touch him with it? All that would do was give him a shock. With the wet floor and her bare feet she was more likely to electrocute herself.

She drew in a sudden breath, ignoring the pain. The wet floor! That was how she could do it. If she could induce the guard to take off his leather boots. She groaned. He would never do that. Her own feet were freezing from the water. Water? She bit her lip in sudden joy. Maybe. Maybe there was a way.

It was the desperation of hope that got her to her hands and knees and she crawled to the hose. The nozzle was screwed onto the coupling on the end of the hose and even using all her strength, ignoring the awful pain in her ribs and arms, she could not twist it loose. God. How could everything be against her? The hose was too short to reach the conduit so she could not pound it loose with the nozzle while it was still attached. She had to get it loose. Again she ignored the pain and twisted with all her strength. But her hands slipped on the wet metal. Useless! Totally Useless!

Her head dropped and she slumped to a sitting position against the wall, her lips blue with cold, her teeth chattering. She noted with a detachment that was like looking at someone else, that her bruised skin had turned a mottled blue. She had so many huge goose pimples that she looked like a hedgehog. She probably would catch a miserable cold.

She shook her head. What did it matter? She would probably be dead in a few hours unless she got that damned nozzle loose. Oh hell. Why didn't she just take the hose loose from the other end?

Stupid! Stupid! The coupling on the other end of the hose, where it was attached to the water faucet, had flanges sticking out so it could be knocked loose with a hammer if it was stuck. Using the heavy nozzle, it only took her seconds to pound the coupling loose and unscrew it from the faucet.

She started to drag the hose toward the conduit, then stopped. The moment the conduit was severed, the lights would go out. She had better make her other preparations first.

The first thing to do was block the drain so the water would not run out. Block it with what? There was nothing. Nothing except the concrete of the walls.

She searched until the found two places where the concrete had squished from the wooden forms and hardened when the room was constructed. Using the brass nozzle as a hammer, she pounded chips from the spill of concrete. Then she pried up the metal grating over the drain hole and smashed it into a shapeless mass that she hammered deep into the hole. She then filled the hole with the concrete chips and pounded them with the nozzle until the drain was packed and sealed.

Then she used the nozzle to smash the conduit free of the wall, taking care not to sever it.

Shoving the heavy table beneath the light fixture was one of the most painful, difficult struggles of her life. Painfully she pulled herself to a standing position atop the table and used the brass nozzle to pound at the conduit's ceiling attachments until the entire length of the conduit was hanging free, supported only by the light fixture. Clinching her teeth, she stretched to tie the end of the hose to the dangling conduit where it attached to the light fixture. The pain in her battered muscles was so agonizing she was afraid she was going to faint. Her numb fingers fumbled at the stiff canvas. She could not endure the pain another second! One more second! One more. One more! Done! She'd done it. The knot was far from tight. But she knew she could not do better. It had to hold when she yanked on the dangling hose. It just had to!

It was almost as painful to climb down from the table as it had been to climb up. Could she possible drag it back? She was tempted to leave it. No. She could not take the chance. The room would be dark when the light went out, but there might be enough light spilling through the door for the guard to see that the table had been moved. If so, he might not enter. And he had to enter. He had to.

An inch at a time, she managed to shove the table back to the side of the room.

She then placed one of the wooden chairs near the door where it would be available for her to stand on.

At the water faucet, she wrenched at the handle until water gushed out. She breathed a prayer as the water began forming a pool over the plugged drain. Would the plug hold? Was the material packed tight enough to keep the water from seeping away? Ten minutes. That's all she needed. Oh God. Make it hold for ten minutes.

As she prayed, the pool grew, slowly spreading across the floor. When the pool reached the bottom of the door, she turned the water off. She waited for a moment, studying the pool to see if it was holding. A few bubbles rose from the drain, but the pool did not shrink. It was holding!

She had to grit her teeth before she could bring herself to walk through the icy water. In its center, the pool was up to her ankles. She retrieved the nozzle end of the hose that dangled from the light fixture. Holding the nozzle, she gingerly made her way to the chair next to the door. If the fixture came loose now and fell into the water, it would be the end of her.

Clutching the nozzle end of the hose, she climbed on the wooden chair and expelled her breath in relief. Now then. Would it work? Would the knot hold? Was she strong enough to pull the fixture loose? When the conduit fell in the water, suppose all it did was blow a fuse somewhere? Had they build the old electrical system with fuses? Would the wooden chair insulate her from electrocution?

Well, what the hell did she have to lose?

She held the hose in her right hand and took the nozzle in her left and banged on the door with the heavy brass as hard as she could. The sound thundered through the room like strokes of doom. She listened. No sound. Would the guard hear? Would she hear his footsteps?

She pounded again, longer this time. And she heard them. Approaching steps. Oh my God. It was working. He was coming. She pounded again so he would find the right door. His approaching steps echoed like shots until they stopped in front of the door. A key fumbled at the lock. The key turned. The door started to open. Now! She sucked in her breath and yanked on the hose as hard as she could. The fixture shuttered, held. Oh my God no! Pull! Harder! Pull!

With a screech the fixture tore loose, plunging the room into instant darkness and she heard the cable splash into the water just as the door burst open. A shaft of light thrust into the room, partially blocked by the figure of the guard framed in the doorway.

"Vas?" he growled. "Vas ist das?"

Oh no! He wasn't coming in. He was standing, not moving. She would be caught. In desperation, she reached out and grabbed the front of the man's shirt and yanked. He spun, agile as a cat. But he was off balance, forced to step inside! The splash of his boots in the water was drowned by his shriek of agony. Anna stared as the man stood in the water, shaking as though gripped by a powerful hand. Then his legs buckled and he crashed face down into the death pool.

Anna stood on the chair, her hands over her face, on the edge of shock. It was not the shock of killing a man. The death of such a person had no meaning for her at all. She would have felt something had she been forced to kill a cat or a dog, even a rat. But now there was nothing. The shock was in the sudden release of fear. It was as though she had been surviving on the adrenaline of fright and now her body was drained.

But she had to go on. There were other guards. This one would be missed soon. She had to get away, to hide where she would not be found.

Holding the jamb of the door, she was able to swing her feet to the dry floor in the hall. She looked for the guards' keys but could not find them. He probably still had them in his hand. She would like to have found the Jewish man and released him, but that was out of the question now. Maybe she could do something about it later. If she got away herself.

She ran down the hall to the stairs and cautiously began climbing to the next floor where the guard had his desk. If there was another guard on duty, she did not know what she would do.

But the small chamber was deserted. Apparently, the dead guard had been alone when he had heard her banging on the cell door. There was a steam heater near the desk and Anna was drawn to it like a moth to flame. The man's greatcoat, hat and gloves were hanging on a hook and she put them on. It took all her will to move away from the heater, but she had to keep moving. What she needed more than heat, was a weapon.

She searched the desk and found two things that brought a breath of thanks. One of them was a pair of thick wool sox that she gratefully slipped over her feet. They were too large, but they felt like bliss.

Her other find was a key that fit a large cupboard. When she opened the door, she saw it was a gun closet containing several German army carbines. She selected a bolt action Mauser that reminded her of her father's old hunting rifle. She worked the bolt and a cartridge flipped out. Good. It was loaded. In a drawer of the cabinet, she found boxes of similar cartridges and she put several in the pocket of the greatcoat.

In the other pocket she slipped a Belgian Walther PPK automatic pistol.

Taking a deep breath, she began silently climbing the stairs where she would find freedom or death.

Chapter 30

Eric was not concerned about von Liebermann recognizing him. His disguise was more in his bearing, more in his attitude than in his physical appearance. Even if the Nazi might think he had seen him somewhere in the past, the chances of him guessing that an arrogant, clean-shaven SS colonel was actually the dirty, bearded Gypsy, Eric Imri, was highly improbable.

In fact, there was a high probability that von Liebermann would be too frightened to recognize his own mother. When a big Horch limousine bearing the staff emblem of Obergruppenführer Heydrich arrived on your doorsteps carrying an SS colonel wearing the RFSS cuff title of Himmler's special staff and followed by a truck with a squad of Waffen-SS troops, one seldom thought coolly and logically.

After the grenade had exploded in Heydrich's car, Eric had forced the taxi driver to return him to the Prague-Tesnov Railway Station. He had paid the driver generously and told him he was now implicated in the death of the Obergruppenführer, and if he was as intelligent as he looked, he would pretend he had remained in bed that morning. The man had been extremely happy to comply. Then Eric had simply waited. Heydrich's staff knew the general had been on his way to meet Colonel von Sievers at the station.

As soon as they received the news of the assassination attempt, a car had been sent for the man they assumed to be von Sievers and who, naturally, was furious at having been kept waiting until he learned Heydrich had been riddled with shrapnel from a grenade and was now in a coma. Heydrich was not expected to live more than a few hours.

Keeping to his role as von Sievers, Eric had insisted on being taken to the site of the assassination where he examined Heydrich's bomb-blasted car. Fortunately, the paper with the list of names had not burned. Eric grimly put forth the assumption that the paper had accidentally been dropped by the assassins and the names were some of their accomplices. He had volunteered to personally lead a squad of soldiers to Theresienstadt to arrest the traitorous von Liebermann, whose name was on the list.

Now his entourage charged through the gate of Theresienstadt and pulled to a stop in front of the hotel where the SS Kommandant made his headquarters. Leading his squad of soldiers, Eric marched into the hotel lobby. There were several SS soldiers in the lobby and they came to attention when they saw Eric's black uniform.

"Who is in charge here?" Eric snapped.

An Unterscharführer stepped forward and whipped his arm up in a Nazi salute. "I am, Herr Standartenführer. Heil Hitler."

"Standartenführer von Liebermann is to be placed under arrest. From now on you will take orders from me only. Is that clear?"

The sergeant's eyes betrayed a rising panic. If the Kommandant was in trouble, it might somehow implicate him. "But, Herr Standartenführer—"

"Is—that—clear?" Eric interrupted.

The sergeant's eyes darted to Eric's squad of soldiers who stood with their Schmeisser's ready. "Zu befehl, Standartenführer."

"Good." Eric turned to the other SS soldiers. "If you know what is best for you, you will not make trouble." He turned back to the sergeant. "Take me to the Kommandant."

"Jawohl, Standartenführer."

The sergeant started for the elevator and Eric said to the technical sergeant who was in charge of his squad. "Oberscharführer. Stay here. Make sure the traitor does not try to escape."

"Yes, sir. But. . . you may need us."

Eric hesitated. If he had read von Liebermann's character correctly, he was too much of a coward to put up a fight. Provided he was alone. But if he was not alone, it could get what the British called 'sticky.'

The real danger, however, would come if von Liebermann recognized him. He was only able to control the situation because everyone assumed that he was the real von Sievers. If he took the soldiers with him and von Liebermann convinced them he was an impostor, they would quickly turn on him.

It would be safer to confront von Liebermann alone accompanied only by the Unterscharführer.

"No," he told the squad leader. "The sergeant and I can handle this."

When they left the elevator and approached the door of von Liebermann's suite, Eric experienced a momentary apprehension. Anna could be here, in this very building. In minutes he would see her. Had she changed? Would she feel the same about him? Was she even alive? He would soon know.

At the door the Unterscharführer paused and looked at him. Eric took his pistol from its holster and motioned to the sergeant to knock. He did so and von Liebermann's voice said, "Kommen."

The sergeant opened the door and stepped inside and came to attention. Eric pulled the visor of his cap low over his eyes and stalked into the room. Von Liebermann was seated behind his desk, a telephone in his hand. His face was red with anger as he listened to someone on the line. He was so agitated that Eric's presence did not register and he shouted into the telephone, "Find her, you *arschloch*. Immediately!"

Then he saw Eric's pistol pointed at his head and his face changed from red to gray. His eyes came up to look into Eric's cold stare and the telephone slipped from his hand. Keeping the gun pointed at von Liebermann's head, Eric reached across the desk and placed the telephone back on its receptacle.

"Stand up," he said, emphasizing the command with a wave of his pistol.

Slowly von Liebermann rose to his feet, his eyes riveted on the pistol. "What is this?"

"I am Colonel Wolfram von Sievers, Reichsführer Himmler's personal staff. You are under arrest."

"Von Sievers. I've heard of you." Von Liebermann's eyes went back to the pistol. "But why . . . Arrest? Under arrest?"

"For the attempt to kill Reich Protector, Obergruppenführer Reinhard Heydrich."

"Heydrich? What attempt?"

"Do not claim ignorance to me. Your name was found."

"My name? Impossible. I don't understand. What attempt?" His hand reached for the telephone.

Eric gestured with the muzzle of the pistol and von Liebermann jerked his hand back. "The assassination attempt this morning. Your accomplices are already under arrest, or soon will be."

To Eric's surprise, von Liebermann had the courage to straighten and his head lifted. "I know nothing about an assassination. You are making a mistake."

"You can explain that at your trial. Come."

Von Liebermann began to move around the desk, then he paused and studied Eric's face. "Von Sievers? I have never met you."

Von Liebermann's statement was more like a question and Eric quickly said, "No. Never."

Von Liebermann continued to study Eric as he came from behind the desk. It was not the best time to ask the question that was pounding at Eric's brain—it might jog von Liebermann's memory—but he could not wait. "There is a woman also implicated. A Gypsy girl. Where is she?"

A puzzled looked appeared in von Liebermann's eyes. "The next suite. But she could not be implicated any more than I am."

Eric scarcely heard von Liebermann. Anna was alive. As close as the next suite. Suddenly, seeing her was the most important thing in his life. "Let's go," he snarled. "You lead."

Von Liebermann walked out the door, still with his forehead wrinkled in a puzzled frown. As he followed von Liebermann, Eric motioned to the Unterscharführer to come with them.

They walked along the carpeted hall to the next suite, and without knocking, von Liebermann opened the door and walked in. Eric crowded in close behind him, his gun pressed against von Liebermann's back so that if it was a trap, he could use the man's body as a shield.

But the room was deserted, and Eric looked around almost in a panic. "Well?" he gritted. "Where is she?"

"The bedroom," von Liebermann said. "She likes the bed."

Eric came close to striking the Nazi with the pistol. If this bastard had touched Anna, had used her like a Hamburg whore, he would beat him to a pulp before he put a bullet in his head. Without waiting for von Liebermann, he took three quick strides to the bedroom door and yanked it open. The room was strewn with discarded women's clothing and reeked of face powder and perfume. But she was there. Sitting up in bed. Pulling satin sheets up to her chin. Her eyes wide and her dark hair tousled.

"Katalin!"

The word slipped out on an exploding breath of relief, and he knew instantly it was a deadly mistake because Katalin's eyes narrowed and she said, "Eric? Eric!"

Von Liebermann stood in the doorway, staring at Eric. "Eric?" he said. "You're the Gypsy!"

Moving faster than Eric thought possible, von Liebermann shoved Eric so hard he fell, skidding across the carpet. At the same time von Liebermann shouted at the sergeant, "He's an impostor. Kill him."

The sergeant stood frozen, uncertain who to believe. Von Liebermann was bringing his own pistol from its holster when Eric twisted onto his back and fired. Blam! The sound was unbelievably loud in the small room. The 9mm bullet struck von Liebermann just above his left eye and he crumbled, his pistol dropping from his nerveless hand with a heavy thud.

The sound galvanized the sergeant and he swung his pistol toward Eric, firing without aiming. Eric's shot was like an echo of the first and his bullet struck the sergeant in the chest. The sergeant stood looking down at the small hole in the center of his necktie. Then his eyes glazed and he fell forward, his hands hanging limply at his sides.

Katalin stared at the two bodies, her eyes wide in fright, her mouth opened in a soundless scream.

"Anna!" Eric shouted. "Where is Anna?"

Katalin's eyes focused on him and she snapped back into reality with the speed of a born survivor. "The Small Fortress. They took her there last night."

Took her there? The words sounded terribly ominous. "Where is it?"

"Over there." She waved vaguely toward the north-west. "Not far."

"Can you show me?"

A strange look flickered in the Gypsy girl's eyes as she quickly nodded. "Yes. I know where it is."

"All right. Get dressed. Quickly."

The floor was already trembling from the thud of boots as the squad of soldiers raced up the stairs in response to the sound of the shots. Eric hurried to the hall door and waited for them. When his sergeant saw him standing with the pistol in his hand, he motioned for the men behind him to halt.

Eric slipped the pistol back in its holster. "It's all right. The Kommandant did not relish being interrogated. He tried to escape."

The Waffen-SS Oberscharführer nodded in understanding. He would have chosen death himself to being questioned by the SS or Gestapo investigating the assassination of Obergruppenführer Heydrich.

"Go downstairs," Eric commanded. "We are going to a place called the Small Fortress. I will be there in a moment."

The sergeant glanced toward the open bedroom door where the edge of the satin covered bed was visible. His face was impassive, but there was a sneer in his voice as he said, "Jawohl, Standartenführer. We will wait."

Eric caught the implication and it disgusted him. Were all these SS men animals? This pig of a sergeant expected him to do what he would have done in his place: rape the colonel's mistress, then either kill her or appropriate her for himself. Behind him, Eric could see the German soldiers hiding smiles.

"Get the men in the truck," he growled. "We will be there in two minutes."

The sergeant realized he had misjudged the situation and his cheek twitched as he said hastily, "Jawohl!" He spun around and trotted toward the stairs, followed by the sober-faced troopers.

Eric went back into the bedroom. Katalin had dressed in a skirt, blouse and sweater and was pulling on boots. She ran her fingers through her hair and smiled at him. "I am ready."

"Good."

She did not so much as glance at the body of her former lover as she followed Eric into the hall.

Walking toward the elevator, Eric suppressed a grudging admiration for Katalin. She had not only escaped the work camp but had found an easy life. His voice was warmer as he asked, "Anna. How is she?"

"She was fine the last time I saw her."

"This Small Fortress. What is it?"

"Kind of a prison."

"Prison! Why is she there?"

"They found out that she was helping the Jews. They wanted to ask her some questions."

Questions! Mother of Christ! At this very moment she might be undergoing torture at the hands of some sadistic SS madman. Damn the elevator. Where was it? He grabbed Katalin's arm and headed for the stairs, dragging her down two steps at a time.

He strode through the lobby with Katalin trotting beside him. Without breaking stride he snatched a Schmeisser rifle from the hands of a young Schutze who was standing at attention with a stunned look on his face. "You! Notify Einsatzgruppe headquarters that von Liebermann was killed attempting to escape."

"Jawohl, Herr Standartenführer."

Eric pushed Katalin into the Horch limousine. "Which way?"

She pointed. "There."

Eric said to the driver. "You hear that? Go! Schnell!"

The big Horch leaped forward and behind them the truck carrying the soldiers slowly began to move. Eric checked the Schmeisser to make sure it was fully loaded and levered a cartridge into the chamber. "Faster," he told the driver. "Faster, damn it, faster!"

"But, sir. We are losing the truck."

"Never mind the truck. Get moving."

In answer, the driver jammed the accelerator down and the car leaped forward. There were few people in the street and fewer vehicles, but the driver kept one hand working on the klaxon as the limousine roared through the streets. Katalin pointed out the bridge leading to the courtyard of the medieval fortress. Without slowing, the Horch raced over the bridge and into the courtyard where it slewed to a squealing stop.

There was a Kubelwagen parked near the fortress entrance and an armored personnel carrier near the wall. Two SS-soldiers were standing near the entrance armed with Mauser carbines. Although the limousine's klaxon had warned them of its approach, they did not move from their positions.

Eric leaped from the still moving car and ran toward them carrying the Schmeisser. The soldiers came to attention and one of them said, "Careful, Standartenführer. She has a rifle."

She? Did he mean Anna? With a rifle? That was the reason for von Liebermann's telephone call. Anna had escaped. But for how long? The place had to be swarming with soldiers. "Who? Which prisoner is it?"

"I don't know. Only that it's a woman."

Eric started through the door and almost ran into Deiter Voss who was striding out, a pistol in his hand. He saw Eric and stopped in surprise, his eyes taking in the Horch and the flags of the Einsatzgruppe headquarters on its fender mounts. He snapped to attention. "Sorry, Standartenführer. I thought you were Colonel von Liebermann."

Your name?"

"Voss, Standartenführer. Deiter Voss." Voss clicked his heels. "At - your—"

"Enough! Von Liebermann has been relieved of command. I am now in command. Who is in there?"

Instead of answering directly, Voss swept Eric with a glanced that lingered on his RFSS cuff. "And you are?"

The man's arrogance made Eric want to shoot him. But he needed him alive. "Standartenführer Wolfram von Sievers." He noted that Voss stiffened slightly at the name.

From behind him Katalin said, "No, he isn't. He's a Gypsy. His name is Eric Imri."

Voss' pistol snapped up, pointed at Eric's chest. "Sorry, sir. I'll have to check this with the colonel."

"You can't," Katalin said. "He killed von Liebermann."

Voss took the news with icy detachment. "I see." He reached for the Schmeisser. "I'll take that until we straighten this out."

Eric cursed to himself. Damn Katalin. She was making herself a hero to what she was sure was going to be the winning side. He might be able to overcome this arrogant bastard's suspicions if he had time, but time was not on his side. Anna needed him! Now!

From deep inside the fortress there was the sound of a shot. For an instant Voss' eyes flickered and Eric swung the butt of the rifle up, smashing the pistol from Voss' hand.

Voss reacted instantly, grabbing at the rifle and screaming to the two stunned guards, "Shoot! Shoot!"

One of the guards snapped a hasty shot and Eric heard the bullet smack into flesh, and Katalin's breath came out in an ugly gasp. Then he wrenched the Schmeisser loose and smashed Voss across the temple with the barrel. He whirled and shot both guards and ran into the fortress.

There was a guard standing next to a reception desk, a pistol slack in his hand, staring at him with big eyes.

Which way? The stairs went both up and down. Eric pointed the Schmeisser at the man. "Which way?" When the man did not answer instantly, he fired past the man's head. "Where are they?"

The man pointed with his pistol toward the stairs leading downward. Eric smashed him in the side of the head with the rifle butt and the man crumpled. Eric raced to the stairs just as a shot sounded and a bullet plucked at his sleeve. He twisted, ready to shoot. Voss! He was leveling one of the Mausers for a second shot. Caught in the open, Eric was an easy target and he leaped down the wide stairwell.

At the first landing he saw four SS-guards. They were using any available cover as they trained their weapons on a narrow flight of stairs leading to a lower level. He saw with horror that one man had released the safety on a grenade and was preparing to toss it down the stairs. They looked up, startled, when Eric burst into the anti-room.

At the moment, Eric had the advantage as they stared at him in surprise. But he could already hear Voss behind him, and he knew a command from the captain would start them firing. And if the man threw the grenade down the stairs, it would surely kill Anna.

With one quick motion, he aimed the Schmeisser and shot the man through the head and the grenade tumbled to the floor. Then he leaped for the lower stairs, shouting. "Anna! Anna! Don't shoot!"

He dropped the Schmeisser and dived, less afraid of breaking bones than being blown to pieces. He landed on the concrete steps in a rolling dive, his head tucked under the way he had been taught by the British commandos, just as behind him the grenade exploded with a thunderous roar. The blast slammed him the remainder of the way to the base of the stairs where his head smashed into a wall and he lay stunned. When he could focus his eyes, he saw a rifle pointed at his face. It was held by a wild-eyed woman whose white face was framed by dark hair that dampness had turned into a disheveled mass of ringlets. She used the muzzle of the Mauser to warily push his hat up away from his face.

"Eric?" Anna said. "Oh God. Eric!"

Then the carbine clattered on the floor as she gathered him in her arms and the numb fear that she had felt for her own life was replaced by a new and worse fear: Eric was wounded, perhaps dying.

"Oh no. God no," she murmured as she used the rough cloth of her sleeve to wipe away blood oozing from a raw scrape on his cheekbone.

Eric squinted at her. "Ow, dammit. Do you have to be so rough? What kind of a nurse are you?"

"Oh, Eric." She was laughing and crying at the same time. "I was afraid you were killed."

"Killed?" Eric's face hardened as he remembered where he was, and he scrambled to his feet, wincing at the pain of strained muscles and bruises. "Stay against the wall." He picked up the Schmeisser.

"Is there another way out of here?"

She shook her head. "No. Only the stairs."

He scooped up her carbine and handed it to her. "You obviously know how to use this. Stay behind me."

For some strange reason when she had thought she was going to die, Anna had felt little fear. She was prepared to die. But she was not prepared to see Eric die. "Oh God, Eric," she said. "Can't we stay here?"

"No. We'd be trapped. We've got to get out before they get reinforcements. Stay behind me."

He gave her no time to protest that she would rather die in his arms than be killed while separated from him. He moved up the stairs, hugging the wall. She followed close behind, her carbine ready to protect his life.

When they skirted the guard's body on the stairs and entered the anti-chamber, Anna stopped in horror. Grenade shrapnel had riddled the three soldiers and the floor was slippery with blood. She felt it seeping into the wool of the heavy sox with sickening distaste and she hurried to the last flight of stairs. There was another body on the stairs, a body wearing the black uniform of an SS officer. Deiter Voss. The grenade had exploded just as he had reached the base of the stairs and shrapnel had smashed through his legs, chest and stomach. His face had not been touched and his lips were frozen in a sardonic smile as though it was their natural bent. Anna felt no sorrow. How could she have been so wrong about a person? A day earlier she might have mourned the death of someone who was almost a friend. But his familiarity with the torture room had revealed the soul of a sadist. After she stepped over him, his dead eyes stared at her bloody footprints as though in morbid fascination.

Eric was beginning to climb the wide stairs when he stopped and turned back. "Watch the stairs," he said. He crossed to the steel desk and began yanking open drawers. From one of them he extracted a ring of keys and he ran down the corridor to the first door and used one of the keys to open it. He vanished inside for a moment and came back into view leading an emaciated man with an unkempt beard and matted hair who blinked at the harsh light. Eric thrust the keys into the man's hands. "Here. Use these. Let the others out."

The man stared at the keys as though unsure of what they were and Eric added, "Can you do that?"

The man looked toward the anti-chamber and the dead guards and his body straightened. "Ja," he said. "Ja, ja."

The man started down the corridor and Eric hurried back to Anna. "Stay close. If we run into any more soldiers, follow my lead. Don't shoot unless you have to."

"But they'll kill you."

"They don't know who I am. They'll do as I tell them."

"Let's hope so."

Taking the stairs two at a time, they hurried to the vestibule and past the bodies of the guards into the courtyard. Only minutes had passed since Eric had dashed into the fortress and the truck carrying the squad of troops was just arriving.

When Anna saw Katalin crumpled on the cold flagstones with blood on the front of her blouse, she dropped to her knees beside her, forgetting her hatred for the Gypsy girl. She put her fingers on Katalin's neck to feel for a pulse, but the Gypsy girl's staring eyes told her it was useless. Gently Anna closed the dead girl's eyes, wondering as she did so what Katalin's life could have been if there had been no war. Marriage, children, music. A vagabond existence of living from hand to mouth. Growing old at thirty. Dying young. A life that most *Gorgios* despised but which a pure Gypsy thought of as paradise. Well, perhaps Katalin's soul had found its own kind of paradise.

Eric stepped into the path of the truck. He held up his hand and the truck bucked to a stop. He strode to the truck cab and said to the Oberscharführer sitting beside the driver. "Things are under control here. Return to headquarters. Wait there."

The sergeant glanced toward Anna with a puzzled expression, but he was too disciplined to question the orders of a colonel and he said, "Jawohl, Standartenführer." The driver put the truck in gear and began a turn toward the gate.

Eric, still carrying the Schmeisser, took Anna's arm and began walking toward the Horch. Suddenly, the driver of the limousine opened its door and stepped out in front of the truck, waving his arms. "Halt," he shouted. "He is not von Sievers. He's an impostor. He—"

In his haste, the man had misjudged the truck's speed and the fender of the big truck struck him, hurling him into the side of the Horch with a sickening thud.

By the time its driver was able to bring the truck to a stop, Eric had shouted to Anna, "Stay back," and was kneeling beside the unconscious Horch driver, feeling for a pulse. The truck driver and the Oberscharführer jumped out of the truck and ran to peer over his shoulder.

"He ran in front of me," the driver said, his face pinched with fright. "I could not stop."

"I saw that," Eric reassured him. "It was not your fault."

"Why did he do it?" the sergeant's eyes were wide with alarm. "What was he saying?"

"There may be more fighting here," Eric explained. "He didn't want to stay."

The sergeant's lip lifted in a sneer. "No stomach for fighting. I've seen plenty of them. They make good staff car drivers."

"I know." Eric patted the Schmeisser. "He was afraid of my friend here."

The sergeant chuckled. "Who isn't? You will need another driver. I will find a man."

"No," Eric said quickly. "I have work to do here. They will find a driver."

The sergeant nodded toward the body of the driver. "I think he is dead. Shall I take him?"

Eric could see the man was right. The driver had stopped breathing and his eyes had rolled back in the blank stare of death. "They will pick him up with the others. You go on."

"Jawohl." The sergeant looked at the cold gray stones of the fortress with distaste. He jerked his head toward the truck driver. "Come. We have no part in this." He stood and saluted Eric without the usual 'Heil Hitler', then climbed into the cab of the truck.

As the truck rolled out the gate, Eric said to Anna. "Hurry. Help me get his clothes off." And he began disrobing the dead driver.

"His clothes? Why?"

"I'll need a driver. You're him. You can drive this beast, can't you?"

"Yes, but . . . Can we get away with it?"

Eric tossed the man's cap to Anna. "See if you can tuck your hair under this. If you can't, we'll have to cut it off."

Given such a choice, Anna piled her hair on top of her head and pulled the cap over it. Fortunately, the cap was large and she was able to jam it into place. Then she sat on the running board of the Horch and gingerly stripped off the blood-soaked sox. Before she took off the heavy overcoat, she hesitated and looked around. "I don't have anything on under this."

"Good God. We might be dead in a minute. Get out of it."

Anna shrugged off the coat and, for a second, stood shivering while she stared at the fortress, wondering if anyone could be watching. Even though the driver's injuries had been internal, so that there was no blood, she donned his clothing with distaste. The uniform was several sizes too large, especially the shoes and Anna felt like a clown when she had finished.

"If we have to stop," Eric said as he helped her tie her necktie, "just stay in the car. Nobody pays much attention to an officer's driver."

"Where are we going?"

"Greece. It's the only place where they're not picking up Gypsies."

"But that has to be a thousand kilometers. We'll never make it."

"We'll make it. Who's going to stop an Einsatzgruppe staff car? Besides, we might not have to go that far."

"Why not?"

"The minute we see a Gypsy *vardo* or hear a Gypsy violin, we stop."

"Then what?"

"Then we go back to our people. They'll never take us. Not again."

Anna nodded. It was the only answer. By blending with a group of Gypsies, they could work their way south where the long arm of the Nazi Einsatzgruppe did not reach. "All right. But when this is over, we're going back to Eger. I've got to make sure that Albrecht Grantz gets what he has coming to him."

Eric thought of the list of names he had deliberately left at the site of Heydrich's assassination. "Don't worry," he said with a grim smile. "He will be punished long before then. I guarantee it."

As she took her place in the big car and started the engine, she turned to Eric who was getting into the rear seat. "Aren't you going to sit up here with me?"

He grinned at her, his eyes sparkling, something she had thought she would never see again, and she was overcome with such a feeling of thankfulness that she felt faint. "How would that look?" he chuckled. "An SS officer who kept trying to kiss his driver."

"Well, all right," she answered reluctantly. "But we can stop along the way, can't we?"

"Many stops," Eric said. "Many, many stops."

Anna put the big car in gear and drove away from the old fortress, leaving behind its horrors. It was over. It was a horrible past that could only come into her life again as a nightmare. But as she drove through the streets of Theresienstadt, she promised herself that this was one part of her life that was not over. She carried the message of Dr. Steiner and the Jews of Theresienstadt in her heart just as she carried a message of the Nazi treatment of the Gypsies. She would make sure the message was given to the world. That was her blood promise.

The end

Epilogue

The Nazi treatment of the Gypsies and other people during World War II is a matter of fact. Although mention is made of certain events and political and military leaders within the historical context of the period, this is a work of fiction and no reference is intended to living persons.

Reich Protector of Bohemia and Moravia, Obergruppenführer (Lieutenant General) Reinhard Tristan Eugen Heydrich, one of the most heinous figures of Nazi Germany, died one week after the assassination attack of 27 May, 1942. In revenge of his death, Hitler ordered the execution of 10,000 Czechs. And, while the actual number of persons who paid with their lives for the death of Reinhard Heydrich is unknown, it is known that within five days 1,500 Czechs were murdered and a number of Nazi suspects were executed.

The two Czech partisans, Joseph Gabcik and Jan Kubis, were located by the Nazis after other partisans were tortured into revealing their hiding places in a Prague church. Both men died in the battle to capture them.

When the SS discovered that some villages were harboring members of the Czech resistance, for punishment they singled out the village of Lidice, population 492. On the 10th of June, all the men of Lidice were marched outside the village and shot. Jewish prisoners from Theresienstadt were brought in and forced to strip the bodies of valuables. The bodies were then buried in a mass grave.

The women of Lidice were sent to concentration camps. Of the 98 children, all were separated from their mothers and most sent to concentration camps in Poland. Less than ten were adopted by German families.

As a further retaliation, the entire village of Lidice was razed by bulldozers. The site was leveled and planted with grain, effectively wiping the village from the face of the earth, but leaving a monument in memory that will live forever.

From the Nazi concentration camp of Theresienstadt, thousands of Jews were deported to Auschwitz and other death camps. Near the end of the war, during the month of September, 1944 alone, 16,902 persons were shipped to Auschwitz.

Today Theresienstadt is once again the village of Terezin. And the infamous concentration camp is a garrison for the Czechoslovakian Army and a museum where tourists come to visit the Big Fortress and the Small Fortress. A national cemetery has been built in front of the Small Fortress as a symbol of the estimated 120,000 Jews who perished in Theresienstadt.

The treatment of the Jews and the numbers imprisoned and exterminated as a result of the Nazi Holocaust. is well documented, but little has been recorded regarding the fate of Gypsy captives.

It is estimated, however, that 500,000 Gypsies were exterminated by the Nazis, amounting to 75 per cent of the world's Gypsy population!

It is also not generally known that for centuries Gypsies were used as slaves in many parts of Balkan Europe. It was not until 1856 that the last Gypsy slaves in Rumania were freed by proclamation.

But the Gypsies continue to survive, often unwanted, finding it difficult to assimilate, often persecuted, but asking no quarter, desiring only to be allowed to live their lives in peace.

Robert L. Hecker

Robert L. Hecker

ROBERT L. HECKER was born in Provo, Utah but grew up in Long Beach, CA. Graduating from high school just as the US entered WWII. Enlisting in the Army Air Corps, he flew B-17s in thirty missions over Europe, earning five Air Medals and the Distinguished Flying Cross. After the war he began writing radio and TV dramas, then moved on to writing and producing more than 500 documentary, educational and marketing films on subjects ranging from military and astronaut training, nuclear physics, aeronautics, the education of Eskimos and Native Americans, psychology, lasers, radars, satellites and submarines. His short stories and articles have been published in numerous magazines, and he is currently working on several movie screenplays as well as other novels. A graduate of the Pasadena Playhouse School of Theater and the Westlake College of Music, recently Robert has begun song writing and has songs in country, gospel and big-band albums. His wife, the former Frances Kavanaugh, a legendary screenwriter of westerns, has a permanent exhibit in the Autry Museum of Western Heritage. They have two children and four grandchildren. And he still is a pretty fair tennis player.

Double Dragon Publishing

Other books by Robert L. Hecker

Whispers in the Night
Rush to Glory - EPPIE AWARD WINNER

All titles available in Trade Paper Back format
or multi-format eBook

http://www.double-dragon-ebooks.com

Printed in the United States
838600003B